The
Tiger Pit

ADRIAN HILL

WHYDOWN

FIRST PUBLISHED IN GREAT BRITAIN 1992
BY WHYDOWN BOOKS, SUSSEX
COPYRIGHT © ADRIAN HILL 1992

ISBN 1-874262-01-2

DESIGNED BY SIMON HUNT
TYPESET BY ROBINCLAY LTD BEXHILL-ON-SEA, SUSSEX
PRINTED IN GREAT BRITAIN
BY BIDDLES LTD, GUILDFORD, SURREY

AUTHOR'S NOTE

A man is as good as his friends. I would like to thank Moy Gammell, Ronnie Bloom, Frances Lumley and Freddie Hodgson for their editorial reading. Sarah and Gill for suffering my learning curve on their computers. Robin, Phil and Brenda for therapy. And very special thanks to a very special Penny who turned scruffy typing into something humans might read.

Simon Hunt for his cover and map and the story layout. My son for his talent as a photographer. Brian, John, Trevor, and kind friends in the media, books - more dangerous trades - not only gave encouragement, but sound counsel and real support. I was amazed at times, how busy people with a thousand more pressing matters on their minds, spared time to show another climber a route up the rock face.

My American and Korean friends are owed thanks for the doors they opened, hidden treasures they revealed many months before the Olympic Games. I name only the late Colonel Leon Young, whose warm and all too short a friendship, remains treasured.

My family took the brunt. Months living with a sleep walker whose mind strayed thousand of miles during normal conversation. My deep thanks to Regine and our children. For keeping my feet on the ground when gravity failed, my daughter, Margot, deserves first prize : she still worries in case her English teacher passes a shop with that tiger in the window.

For
Regine, Julian and Margot.

FOREWORD

A story follows no rules. On these pages two real years are crammed into six months. I hope they convey my admiration for Korean - and American - friends, some in business and the media, many in the Army, National Security and the Police, who safely delivered two babes : democracy and the Olympics.

To my knowledge, there was no plot as described, revealed or otherwise, planned by anybody. The airship floats forlornly from a mast at Kimpo airport.

O'Brien, Kang and their agents have no counterparts in real life. I borrowed names from Korean friends because they were easy for a western reader. Americans need not fear that their senior military were moonlighting with a British secret agent. There never was a President Chung, nor a General Kim, though it would be impossible to deny that some were like them.

ADRIAN HILL
Jamaica, West Indies.

"A hundred questions are worth less
than seeing once."

AN OLD KOREAN PROVERB FROM CHINA.

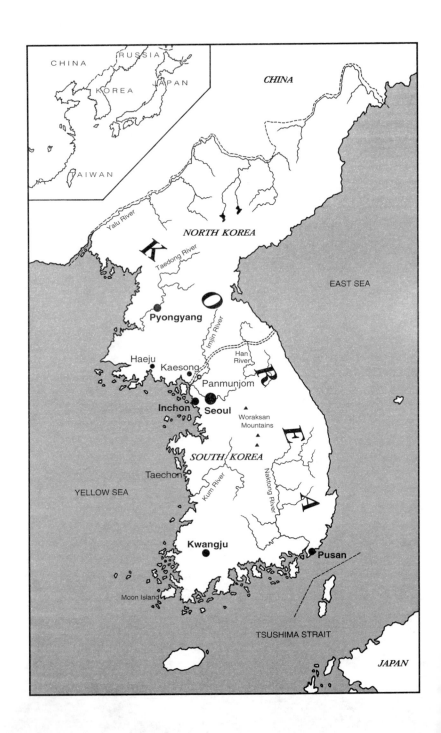

PART ONE

1

Clouds gathered among lunar mountains, creation's ramparts, scarred parchment rock and stunted firs powdered with spring snow, now growing sharper as rain scented a rising wind. The ridge of fortress peaks dwarfed sprawling royal palaces and beyond their winter gardens, from the lime dome crowning the national museum, along vast Sejong Street where brutal offices towered over the naked gingkyo trees, thousands of cars, trucks and buses pumped fumes into the stiff breeze. Whistles shrilled. Near the wooden gatehouse through a palace wall, a file of white capped police advanced into the grumbling traffic, dammed the road with steel barricades, emptied wide lanes, choking downtown Seoul.

O'Brien wedged himself painfully in the bullet proof black sedan, stretching his long legs over its back seat without crumpling his old blue suit, nor distracting his tense Korean driver. Marksmen stood on the Plaza Hotel's concrete sugar lump. Opposite, mounted on the granite bunker of City Hall, an illuminated clock showed barely two hundred days before the Olympic flame arrived in South Korea.

Checking rearwards in the mirror, ready for trouble, O'Brien met his own reflection, confronted a lean face with alert lines stretching from a disciplined mouth, clever blue eyes that held secrets, thick waves of copper hair.

Cramped, he grumbled at his old chauffeur." Sammy.... even the North Koreans couldn't smash through this snarl-up."

Song's silver head turned slightly as his small shoulders shrugged off the nightmare of two thousand hostile tanks across the Imjin River only forty minutes north. But his white gloved fingers tapped the steering wheel.

Less than an hour before a flash message from Hong Kong warned that North Korea, capable of anything, with two trained thugs hidden among Seoul's human lava, proposed to kill President Chung on the city streets, and bury the Seoul Olympic Games. They had raced downtown and loitered in a small street before slipping into Seoul's central plaza at the last second.

Rain from the circle of mountains found the stalled traffic, O'Brien stared morosely as tiny drops spread like mist over the windscreen.

"Chung should travel by chopper instead of throttling the whole 'blody town."

Song quietly reminded, "Somebody might blow our beloved president from the sky."

General Kim of National Security worried each time the President sortied from the *Blue House*. O'Brien imagined grubby film shows at the presidential palace and watched telepathy crease the driver's teak face into a disrespectful smile.

The President raced along cleared streets in a car that weighed four tons .... escorted by a dozen more packed with crack shots ... even that might not work today. Look for something heavy, a parked truck. Their own car was an easy target, more exposed with each second - pressing a central button, he opened all its windows, despite Sammy's protests and damp air attacking old wounds in his legs, enjoying fresh rain as he searched every neighbouring black limousine manned by a frustrated Korean chauffeur.

Ahead, the Koreana Hotel rose like a giant concrete block. Saturday crowds hurried under its sheltered portals, briefly escaping the steady drizzle. O'Brien grimaced: Seoul, asia's ugly duckling, trapped by fate and gambling on a future, the capital of plots in a land of riddles.

He urged, "Keep sharp, Sammy. Not long now."

"Mun che opsimnida," Song confirmed: no problem.

He scanned the pavements for somebody wearing a bulky coat or anorak among hundreds of office workers spilling from wet side streets, knowing his task was almost impossible, comforted by the hard metal of a large gun hidden under his jacket.

Song, worrying, asked flatly, "We forget visit to river site where General Kim say National Security Agency build hangar for airship?"

"We'd probably find an empty paddy field."

Several months among these ruthless, blinkered hermits, taught O'Brien that nothing in Korea was certain, not even when over. A British airship patrolling the Olympic Games in September, looked impossible, short of a miracle, a magic wand, or dirty tricks.

A smile strayed across his weathered face. How would Mason, his chief in London, react to far eastern gutter violence on breakfast TV news? Britain still slept during the early Korean afternoon.

Leaning out, he stared along a line of silent cars stretching from the South Gate's oriental stone ark, past the Samsung tower, past the Toksu Palace and the British Embassy gatehouse, for nearly a mile towards the museum that once served as parliament and which Japan piled there to hide the royal palaces and smother a culture. Forty years after the Japanese left, still few on the pavements dared openly watch as groups of olive clad riot police surveyed the stream of clerks and secretaries forming long lines at bus stops and taxi stands, crowding around each subway staircase.

O'Brien, restless, patted the black uniformed shoulder in front. What would he do without Sammy who drove all day, waited throughout night, no questions asked, nothing expected. Thirty years before Sammy Song guided an infantry brigade when another British generation blasted a Chinese army off mountains fifty miles east.

O'Brien twisted round and began searching the first floor windows. Nothing odd, nobody looking through the downpour, yet trouble lurked in the long sombre street.

Song warned, "Many plain clothes police among the crowds."

"Most wearing the same blue jean creation."

O'Brien's strong fingers strayed to a dark silk tie that matched his lightweight suit as he stared at the crowded wet pavement: too many oriental eyes squinted through the rain for a slick withdrawal. Beyond the police line, among empty streets, sirens wailed.

"Ruling party gorillas watching the national police." Song pointed out a tall squad wearing uniform blue ski jackets, forming on the steps of Bright Party headquarters, the dark side of Korea's economic miracle. Rain spattered the windscreen and Song started the wipers. The traffic stood. Drivers sat stiffly, while in the backseats, lone Koreans in dark suits stared blankly forward. Song switched off the whispering engine.

"Keep it running, Sam."

Song flicked the ignition key instantly.

"Stay inside the car when trouble starts, Sammy, this time Chung is the target for a ground attack."

Song stayed silent. Koreans learned early to hide their ears, eyes and mouths from politics. Those who did not, soon found themselves in trouble with jealous factions or the national police.

Through sudden driving rain, glaring yellow discs closed fast : motor cycle outriders. O'Brien felt under his jacket, touched cold metal, patted the spare magazines strapped under his right armpit. He checked the battery pack securely stowed in his right trouser pocket, examined his left wrist, tugged the aerial wire hooked into the child's Swatch that hid a long range radio. Already, fragile unreality crept over physical objects, the car no longer metal and glass, his mind tricked by cruel signals as he reached that strange mortal threshold where our surroundings become a dream and heard his voice switch onto a faster speed.

"Here comes the second most unpopular head of state on the Korean peninsular."

For an instant his mind roved back twenty years, saw a small dry colonel, new in Vietnam, seeming out of place with his bald head and glasses, sipping beer in the Saigon airborne club, before the little man flew north, and took command of Korea's airborne regiment. O'Brien glanced at the resigned traffic. Not a bad return for months in those jungled mountains fighting the North Vietnamese Army, spinning a web of loyal lieutenants, who returned to Korea, waited ten years before they struck down a government and installed themselves as warrior kings. Now a whole city stood still for a small oriental Ceasar.

He breathed out, released some tension, observing the mass of traffic washed by sudden rain squalls. Kim's National Security Agency knew there was an imminent threat; Mason had taken parallel action through their man in London. Chung would understand that signal : O'Brien was somewhere on the Seoul streets.

"Where's he been?" asked Song, frowning.

"Media lunch hosted by Doctor Francis Moon," replied O'Brien. His fingers hovered over the door handle as the irony struck. "The Doctor and his fellow publishers wanted to confront Chung, warn that widespread violent riots may cost Korea the Olympic Games, unless there is some real democracy."

Song remarked tersely, "President wears dark glasses."

"Then his press secretary should show him the headlines each morning, on cardboard sheets, written in big characters." O'Brien swung open the left hand door.

"Where I wait?" called a bewildered Song.

"Go home, Sammy," he ordered gently, narrowing his eyes against wind and rain. "Don't risk your brains washed in a basement bath."

Sirens howled, trapped between drab office blocks and the Plaza Hotel. Two lights burned through the murk; another pair of motorcyclists approached fast, swung right, roaring into a narrow lane behind the palace garden wall. O'Brien blinked into the storm, wrestling with the ambush options, his eyes checking round the square, mind ticking off empty windows on each floor of the white hotel. The angles were too difficult and he counted several police marksmen on watching roofs : from among the nervously creeping cars, slipped two young Koreans, cheap coats black with rain.

Suit rapidly soaked, his right hand slid under his jacket, cool fingers closing round the butt of a machine pistol .... a personal job, lightweight, silent, thirty rounds magazine, a brutal rate of fire. His eyes followed both men weaving through the impatient crawling cars, ready for that slight movement, the bulk of a weapon, the mistake that gave away lethal motive. His heart thumped and his shirt grew cold.

Both drenched Koreans ran for the far pavement, dodging through opposing lines of cars and buses, heading for the palace gate, before they pushed into confused afternoon crowds plodding under the heavy downpour. Clearing Sejong only to turn the motorcade into a sidestreet was a clever trick, but the ruse failed: he started running.

Many lemon lights cut through the gloom as a fleet of sleek black cars, shielded by more outriders, took the corner with grace and speed. One sprinting young Korean turned, anxiously glanced back.

Something stirred in O'Brien's memory. Both faces were hidden by coat collars pulled high. Yet there was a familiarity about the taller...... or was he wrong, imagining, plain tired even as he ran faster. Photographs and descriptions stored in his mind flooded from terror's portrait gallery......take no chances, ordered his racing brain as he charged from the blinding storm.

Along the street hurried many moon shaped faces; some turned in his direction, stared. O'Brien gripped the hard metal under his jacket, instinctively swerved, breathing faster, hair plastered over his face, horribly conscious that his cover was stripped away.

On the pavement by the old wooden gateway, the tall youth darted forward, threw off a sodden raincoat, ignoring its flight into the flooded gutter. Slung around his body was a web belt heavy with fat cartridges and he cradled the familiar short barrel of a grenade launcher.

O'Brien's hand inside the jacket drew the machine pistol, kept the weapon low and level, gambling on a last shred of brute shock. A huge cadillac with drawn curtains swept towards the street corner....... escort cars like fighters jockeying behind.... he saw the fat grey barrel and varnished butt, the youth lean forward, lock onto the large black car : he felt his moist fingers round the pistol grip, tighten, flick off the safety catch: nobody else in his line of fire, the second youth turned, gaping. O'Brien squeezed.

Wind cut rain. Splinters exploded along the granite palace wall. Too high. He fired as the boy dived onto the slimy pavement.

A crimson flash leapt off an office wall. Diamonds fountained. Grey smoke thickened, a dull thump punched into his eardrums: glass shattered.

Tyres screaming, the big car almost rolled, snaking violently into the side street, leaving a throaty roar among the crammed houses. O'Brien saw the youths rise and dash past the palace gateway. Acrid fumes stung his nostrils. The gun scorched through his sodden shirt. Shots cracked behind. Women started screaming.

O'Brien reached grimy wet pavement. He lunged for the leader who dived among shocked faces, swaying, an impossible target, covered by his bodyguard, weaving through the stunned crowds, pushing people aside, racing for the nearest subway staircase. Rain and acrid smoke blinded. O'Brien barged into the dazed mass, ignoring horrified office girls, businessmen frozen with confusion. Two Ruling Party thugs in anoraks converged on him at the subway steps and relying on speed he shoved both aside, tumbled down the concrete stairs, scrambled onto his feet and clutching the gun under his coat, swerved past a bewildered beggar woman, knocked over her bowl, showering coins : he found himself in an underground shopping mall, dazzled by cold strip lights, sucking in breaths that tasted of bitter garlic.

Another, much darker tunnel, curved back towards the Plaza Hotel through which swarmed an army of cheap suited clerks and smart young girls exploring a labyrinth of shops and kiosks. Dim roof lights revealed neither quarry. Fuming, he pressed onwards, knowing the pair were still near, hiding among young Koreans scurrying in all directions down in this oriental ant nest : both were gone.

Covering the gun, he ran down the dim tunnel past boutiques and cafes but nobody hid in any shop and he slowed, recovered breath, strolled towards a packed staircase. At the top, in gloomy twilight, he squeezed through huddled, wet and worried people, braving the storm, nervously chattering while they stared across the square at a hideous traffic jam and watched the afternoon streets drown.

Silver raindrops, plump as marbles, spilled from a heavy black cloud. Frantic police ran amongst crawling cars and buses, whistles signalled conflicting orders as cars pressed forward, bullied by huge buses pushing into the metal tangle, filling the air with stinking fumes, showering dirty spray onto the trapped black cars.

O'Brien slipped under the Plaza Hotel porch where a line of large taxis waited before the row of glass doors. Rain streamed down his face from saturated hair, his suit clung heavily, stiff cold trousers hindered walking. He supressed frustration, the nagging message that somebody played human marrionettes because nothing else made sense : traffic blocked the lanes towards City Hall ... but the road leading back up the short hill past a street fountain between Myong Dong post office and the Bank of Korea, towards the tunnel through Namsan Mountain, stretched empty. He called the front taxi.

A young Korean, his broad face shining with sweat, peered from the open driver's window, reached behind and swung open the passenger door. The driver brushed back a thick shock of hair, revealing an intelligent forehead.

He asked cheerfully, "Where?"

"Dong Bingyo Dong, uroo ka chusayo," snapped O'Brien, falling across the back seat and keeping the gun out of sight, shivering, slammed the door. He was too old for far eastern wars.

2

The Korean slipped his taxi into gear and shot from the hotel front, pleased when the engine surged with power. They chased frenetic traffic streaming for the poorly lit tunnel through Namsan Mountain as the needle tower on its summit was lost in swirling mist. O'Brien sneezed twice. They barely slowed for the toll gates where his driver flung a coin into a metal basket. O'Brien, still frozen, breathed slower when the taxi emerged into the dark afternoon and sped along a wide rain swept street. His driver jerked round and smiled broadly.

"For an old guy, that was pretty fast....Mike."

O'Brien shook his head slowly from side to side and slipped the warm gun back in its holster. "I could have done without this afternoon, J.P."

"You did shoot?" Kang passed back the carphone before touching a button and humming announced a six-foot roof antenna extending.

"Two bursts. Enough to land us all in the dole queue."

Kang sucked air through his teeth. "Where's Sammy?"

"Going straight home - I sincerely pray. What a shambles! An own goal which tore off our last shreds of decent cover."

"Nobody on our side of the square heard shots....only when the M79 launcher fired."

"Wishful thinking." O'Brien felt adrenalin start to burn in his stomach and fingers. What a stupid way for a man with a medical discharge from the SAS to earn his civilian living.

"Not at all," insisted Kang, relishing some excitement. "You were seen but our police were shooting wildly. Confusion ruled. No Korean dare admit a foreign barbarian was faster. Enormous lost face!"

"I hope to God you're right." O'Brien punched the code for Hong Kong, listening to static, chewing his lower lip. There was a high-pitched bleep and then a girl's voice burst from the telephone.

"Penny it's Mike."

"Where are you?" Her voice spluttered with interference from the gusting storm.

"We've run into a spot of excitement... like to switch over." O'Brien pushed the scramble button, waited while static roared. Suddenly the girl's voice was back, cool, diamond sharp.

"Listen, Penny," O'Brien crouched forward, his face drawn. "Tell Genesis that Noah's news was on the nail."

"Are you alright?"

"For the moment." His wrists throbbed. "Linebacker had to open Pandora's Box." Doubtless a blistering signal would wing its way from the hot-line desk in London during that night. Mason would be furious, or delighted, nobody ever forecast.

"Do you want that to go Solar?" The girl sounded reluctant.

He dreaded the Prime Minister's reaction. She was tidy. This afternoon was a mess on a valuable oriental carpet. She might shut down the whole Linebacker Operation. Delay served nobody.

"Solar."

The girl pressed, "Was anybody hurt?"

"Goldfish remains intact." O'Brien granted himself a weary scowl.

"I don't think Noah would want you exposed," the girl worried, "but he's water-skiing all afternoon. Ought you to parachute?"

O'Brien's eyebrows lifted: so much for twenty-four hour service.....water skiing! But he responded kindly. "Nothing to fear, Penny, we'll signal a full report. Tell Genesis that we *must* work from Legacy. This afternoon is proof enough."

"Alright," she answered doubtfully.

"Nothing else?"

"We have some traffic for you." She sounded amused.

"Helpful?"

"Don't be silly."

O'Brien grunted farewell and replaced the telephone. Kang shortened the aerial, dropped out of the heavy traffic, climbed a steep hill, then drove into a quiet lane where walled gardens hid large houses. Ahead, trees over hung a high wall and the wind had blown open varnished teak doors under a traditional gatehouse.

Kang drove inside and parked by a large lawn crammed with bare fruit trees and rose bushes still wrapped in straw bandages for winter. Beyond, on a bleached grassy bank, stood a brick mansion, sheltering under a curved roof of peacock tiles. O'Brien clambered from the car, listened as the heavy gates groaned against a fierce wind. Rain drummed on the tiled roofs, splashed down chains which served as drain-pipes. He dashed for broad front steps.

"Any other messages this morning?" He shivered while Kang opened the thick glass door. Saturday afternoon was *Agima's* time for shopping. She would return soon to cook dinner.

"Solar expected from Genesis via Noah in Hong Kong," replied Kang, moving aside for him to pass ahead.

London *was* nervous. By tomorrow they might calm down. If he emerged unscathed after a street fight, the operation would survive disaster. O'Brien asked, "How's your knee?"

"Mending fast," shouted Kang, running back to shut the wooden gates, shirt grey with splashes.

O'Brien smiled thankfully. The young man was tall, wide shouldered, agile, a fourth dan black belt in Tae Kwon Do, Korea's answer to lesser martial arts. Kang trained daily. The previous morning, he slightly injured a knee while splitting a two-inch thick plank with a lightning upward kick. Fully fit, Kang was a superb bodyguard, lethal, taught to release the power and strength of his whole body through each fist or foot.

"Jae Pil." The young Korean turned round.

"I know - listen to the radio."

"We might need to leave town in a hurry." O'Brien allowed the corners of his mouth to crease before running into the hall, climbing thickly carpeted stairs that muffled sounds; Kang was on his heels within seconds.

"Any news on our electronics package, Jae Pil?"

Kang delivered a broad smile that worried O'Brien. "Munche op siminda! The equipment leaves Britain tomorrow. General Kim ordered our letter of credit extended by the bank in New York."

O'Brien stopped on the wide stairs. "You pulled that off!"

London provided their operational cover by taking over a company in Kent that built small airships for commercial and military tasks. The management were 'keen' on the far east. By a variety of criminal skills, O'Brien and Kang, working their cover as sales representatives for the British firm, secured a contract with the Korean Government to supply and build an airship to patrol the Seoul skies during the forthcoming Olympic Games. There were delays, this time over the airborne electronics and television package.

O'Brien glanced severely at Kang. An annoying Chinese custom survived on the Korean peninsular: tell only pleasant news. He waited for the missing detail.

"I have made some tea," announced Kang.

O'Brien sighed, threw his damp jacket over a chair and advanced towards the study windows, resembling a Chicago gangster, for on him the machine-pistol was a toy and the spare magazine almost hidden under his powerful left arm. He stared westwards, desperately playing back the last hour in his racing brain.

Huddled roofs marched down towards an immense grey river and from an island rose Asia's first skyscraper, an insurance company's golden tower. Thick clouds swallowed its radio masts. One day, O'Brien knew, that island would become the eastern Manhattan.

For the present, it was a cleverly disguised stronghold, enclosing the National Assembly, the main radio and television stations, even an old airport survived as a vast parade plaza: all of which could be sealed off ..... should a day come when the generals in suits who governed Korea, decided to don their uniforms, bring back discipline and social order; which gave a whole country nightmares.

"We shall hold one engine in Kent." Kang beamed. "And General Kim remains ignorant that the airship needs two."

"You've repaired my day, JP."

From long french windows that ran the length of the warm, pine-walled study, O'Brien watched rain thrash the garden and narrow street. His hands and wrists trembled, he needed a strong drink. North Korea searched tirelessly for any means of spoiling the Seoul Olympics... God willing ... perhaps short of open warfare. This afternoon was the most dangerous gambit for weeks. Korea was a pressure cooker, brimming with opposing dreams, ready to explode: most western countries barely heard the rising hiss.

He stared morosely through the rain-spattered window. About a mile down the hill, straight in front, stretched Itaewon, its broad avenue of shops and bars deserted. Nearer the river, on the American army golf course, few players braved the heavy storm. He tried calculating the value of eighteen holes in a city of ten millions. America, he concluded gloomily, invested so much more in this lost finger of Chinese mountains where this afternoon arctic winds reached southern seas.

Kang joined him at the windows, large deceptively smooth hands bearing mugs of steaming tea. O'Brien politely took one and his nose filled with ginseng's earthy scent. He looked at his young helper, at the elegant balcony which was awash, at the flooded garden where swaying trees waited for spring to dress their stark branches, then sipped scalding tea : they were lucky: otherwise security heavies would have smashed down the front door while the kettle boiled. He craved for a hot bath. Water trickled down his back and legs to form damp patches on the carpet. He leaned on his desk and thought before scribbling down a report in his clipped prose.

"Can you read that weasle-worded history of a gunfight?" He passed the message to Kang and confessed, "Thank God everybody missed!"

"Now I'll give you the bad news." Kang pulled a soggy computer message from his shirt pocket. A television aerial on the roof doubled as a satellite dish. O'Brien could signal anywhere in the world equipped to unscramble his personal codes. Kang handed over the sheet then sat silent in an armchair near the long windows.

O'Brien began reading a row of small capitals:

PERSONAL AND SOLAR: FOR DANIEL FROM GENESIS
LINEBACKER: CIA has withdrawn its front company bid for the surveillance contract. Unable to supply fully certified airship and electronics package within South Korean's time - frame.

He wondered if this was another fickle smile from fortune. Only one American company threatened their grip on the airship contract. Their rival failed its American certificate of air-worthiness? The Americans could assemble an electronics package..... easily ..... for he had passed all the specifications to CIA through his own American contact in Korea. CIA wanted the Brits' flying over the Seoul Games. Much less political risk. He read further.

1045Z26288 : report from Soviet Government source indicates three attacks planned within LINEBACKER operational zone. Soviet Government believes Eastern Bloc teams potential targets for South Korean terror group acting on behalf of North Korea. Eastern Bloc have no diplomatic missions inside South Korea and Soviet Government insists they have no - repeat no -

operations running inside LINEBACKER operational zone.

1105Z26288 : report from sensitive and reliable source within Chinese Government reports that command of North Korean military and security effectively in the hands of 'Dear Leader' Kim Jong Il, son and heir to the 'Great Leader' Kim Il Sung now aged seventy-seven years. Recent operations were mass assassination of South Korean cabinet ministers praying at a temple outside Bangkok and destruction of a Korean Air jumbo over Bay of Bengal through a bomb planted by two North Korean agents . . . one female captured alive in Bahrain and now held by General Kim's National Security for public trial in Seoul.
Comment: neither source claimed to know specific targets. Grateful urgent report.

FLASH 1225HK27288: most sensitive and reliable source reports that an attack will take place today on President Chung of South Korea. Source believes that Chung's motorcade is the target.
Comment: South Korean source in London confirmed that Chung will drive to and from a lunch with Doctor Francis Moon and other newspaper owners, today, but could not provide exact times. Source will alert his head office that you may also take spoiling action with a request for urgent briefing on the motorcade route.

He frowned at this oblique order now obeyed. How did Mason imagine he spent each day struggling towards the heart of this living Chinese puzzle. There was the usual dismissive paragraph from the research staff.

AMERICAN LIASON : from bitter experience, our CIA link regards General Kim and South Korean Security as difficult, corrupt, penetrated, cavalier at meeting dead-lines, shrewdly mean over support facilities, breaking promises far more often than keeping any. Withdrawal from the airship contract seems a political choice .... we know of no technical grounds for their airship to fail its air-worthiness test .... CIA link welcomes our forward role.
Given the volatile political conditions caused by the selection of Seoul for an Olympic Games, we are not in direct conflict with Eastern Bloc intelligence agencies. There might be profit in pursuit of parallel objectives. We told CIA link that, for sound political reasons, we would never support any

plan which risked exposing our existence to any other intelligence service. CIA link concurred. Same arguments rehearsed over China with identical mutual conclusion. But the suprising similarity of content and timing of Soviet and Chinese reports may indicate parallel action by their intelligence services.

O'Brien swore.

There may be an opening for a more aggressive tactical plan. No hostile or friendly operations are known which might confuse backcloth. We realise that you will consult MUSIC-MAKER (his very senior and sole American contact in country) *before taking decision. Next move is at your discretion.*

Bastards, thought O'Brien, digesting clearance to fight every terror expert and dirty trick that North Korea could deploy in the South..... on behalf of Britain, America, Russia, the Eastern Bloc and China... because London appeared to have consulted the three super-powers and none raised objection to a lone Briton fighting their proxy battles in South Korea with crime and deception. London, he suspected, saw the Olympic Games as a chance to make Tom Thumb seem a bungling amateur.... Mason persuaded the Americans to hoodwink Russia and China that the West deployed a small army on the Seoul streets, then forward sold the electronic intelligence which the airship would gather over Korea - to the National Security Agency in Washington.

Mason stalked a vast leap in the power and scope of British ultra secret operations and for scant risk. The man believed the Cold War almost over, nuclear chaos the approaching horror, and wanted to create the first intelligence super-power. And he could, for trivial stakes, because their few Korean agents were patriotic, silent, cheap. Should they succeed, the resulting surge of influence would lift Mason and his tiny service onto a level with CIA and KBG whose resources were measured in billions. Failure merely risked the exposure of a low key intelligence operation whose cost was covered the moment Korea's Government paid in full for their clever airship. Deals with the USA were clear profit.

O'Brien sat down at his tidy desk. "Let's pray nobody else reads this gambler's charter."

Kang watched closely as his leader's expression changed from disbelief to wry amusement. The Korean remarked, "Sounds as though we should request more salary."

"I'd rather have heavy tanks...." O'Brien suddenly picked up the message sheet and examined the top left corner. "We're copper-bottomed!"

"I don't understand," said Kang.

"You received this message at 1325 local time.... I resorted to street violence at 1407."

"Then we *were* obeying orders?"

"God knows what that did for our cover in Korea.... after Mason's blown it in three capitals... same effect as an Exocet." O'Brien stared at the message sheet again, feeling a headache start.

A plump Korean woman wearing a floral apron over her loose trousers and claret sweater peered round the doorway. She welcomed the men back with a nervous smile then asked Kang in Korean if the patron wanted his clothes dried. Kang told her urgent business needed finishing. Reluctantly, she accepted, though not without a sharp stare of disapproval in Kang's direction before she waddled downstairs to the basement and her ironing board. She was a good soul, not imposing, knowing enough, sent to care for the house by Doctor Moon, ally and mentor in all things. O'Brien prayed that she would not leave a faint whiff of garlic all over his comfortable home.

How could Mason be so reckless? Never mind training, experience, plain instinct warned, first look after your friends: Mason's hand was stamped all over those final comments, their frightening logic. The South Koreans must realise that he enjoyed intelligence links. How else could he obtain sophisticated electronics. There was evidence that Kim's Security Agency was penetrated by the communist North. The Russians and Chinese might not know of his small operation, but Mason, sensibly, must allow that they obtained reports on the airship project, probably could calculate its technical frontiers. Better, decided Mason, tell the Russians and Chinese enough to slow their probing and confuse the North Koreans, gain precious time for an aggressive campaign which might yet flush out the threats timed to destroy the Olympic Games.

Today was a shave from disaster. No more dramas. What fate could his agent network expect? Kang was tough, born a survivor. The father retired following the coup eight years earlier, a three-star general, Chief of Security for the previous regime, given a 'battlefield' promotion among the smashed crystal and bloody linen when the first lady was shot dead by the former Chief of Intelligence... who aimed, with shaky hand, at the President across the dining-table: he missed and was gunned down within seconds by Kang senior.

The son could have followed an army career to general's stars, but next time the President did not escape the marked bullets, his regime toppled by the little colonel from Vietnam. Though father Kang owned many powerful friends, his son was warned, stay away from the army and politics.

O'Brien wondered whether he should release the young Korean. There was still time. He stared bleakly at the stormy afternoon. "Listen JP," he announced, if we're blown, Chung is not famed for a warm heart."

"I know," the young man replied with disarming confidence.

O'Brien answered sourly, "No you don't.... we're now deniable in four countries, including South Korea." He waved the message sheet. "My people can be very clever.... and utter shits."

Kang merely shrugged. "Koreans cannot turn back the clock on City Hall."

He faced the young man for he wanted to be sure that Kang understood the full danger. "There are now two hostile and highly professional intelligence services, both of which have close and long ties with their North Korean allies, briefed by London and Langley, not on our existence, not even on our cover, but our mission. You are free to leave with my utmost respect."

"Young people in my country want changes," replied Kang firmly from the chair. "Few know how. All Koreans wish to favour their own house.... I am no different, but you teach many tricks which are useful in business..... for myself later." He seemed suddenly older.

"Well," sighed O'Brien thankfully, "that's a new approach." And his leathery face began to show defeat. "At least," he finally laughed, "the Queen is a more distinguished overseas patron than the American dollar or Japanese Yen."

A huge boom shook the french windows. "She's late," complained O'Brien, glaring towards the sombre sky as rain delivered the punch from an American spy-plane sweeping over Korea at three times the speed of sound, sixteen miles above the murk, photographing trucks on North Korean roads, a half-hour drive from where they talked.

"Time we tried something stronger." O'Brien loosened his shoulder holster, slipped off the machine-pistol and magazine, laying the weapon and harness ready for cleaning near a letter to his married sister, still not finished on his writing desk. He switched on the reading lamp, bathing the gun in soothing light while he searched in a mahogany cupboard built under shelves crammed with books on Korea, Asia and oriental birds. He pulled out a bottle of single malt and two glasses. "May I tempt you, just once?"

Normally, Kang never touched alcohol, but on this blustery evening, he accepted without protest. O'Brien poured a small tot then filled his own glass. "Hangun masul, JP." he said, "Korean magic", waving the glass in his assistant's direction before he sat on the chair arm, enjoying the Scotch burn a path down into his empty stomach, watching darkness fall, hoping that Sammy Song would call soon. Streetlamps and house windows winked through the dusk, car headlamps flowed endlessly across the river bridges.

His right leg ached from the weather and he needed diversion. "Tell me something cheerful, JP."

"One million dollars downpayment, safely in our bank's Manhattan office," Kang sipped cautiously, "apart from the letter of credit?"

All the money was put up by a Korean finance house with the airship as collateral. Nobody in the Korean Government owned a chequebook. "You faxed Detmold?"

Kang nodded.

Despite neat whisky and no visit from the Korean police, O'Brien felt his neck muscles stiffen. He removed his damp neck-tie, folded it neatly, laid it on his desk with the gun and holster. "When does the container ship sail?" he asked, peeling off his wet shirt, employing it like a towel and rubbing his tanned chest and stomach muscles, at last feeling warm.

"First of March."

Six weeks to reach Pusan. He stretched out his sore leg, ignoring sudden rainshowers beating on the french windows, slowly relaxing. Customs clearance would take weeks unless several officials were persuaded otherwise, through hefty donations towards their personal pension plans. "We may have to pass over some green bags."

Kang smiled. "Our main problem is that Kim's HQ still have no idea where to find a hangar big enough for building the airship."

"That's to our advantage." O'Brien paused, watching the silent telephone. "Providing one is found or built somewhere.... and in time."

Kang looked amused. "Kim was inspecting a floating dock on the east coast this morning. How long will our crew need for construction?"

The idea of General Kim crawling over a floating dock, with all the warning signals of a Korean last minute rush, set O'Brien's neck into rigid tension. He drank more scotch. "Thirty days is all we need, JP... from wrapping paper to first test flight."

This brought content to Kang's face - though not his own.

The Korean said, "Then the airship will fly long before the opening ceremony."

"With a green police pilot?" O'Brien shuddered: "Not if all works out as forecast."

"By the way, today I managed to photocopy the contract between the sponsors and Magnolia Trading for advertising with the airship during the Olympic Games." Kang indulged in a modest yet knowing smile. "One million-and-a-half dollars every twenty-four hours."

"We should take over this blimp..... when the operation closes down." O'Brien was serious.

Plenty of companies offered Kang jobs because of his Princeton degree and family connections. The mother's strong influence steered Kang towards a more elusive trade. She had two mountains promised for her son. When he reached thirty, early maturity in Korean custom, she would build a luxury resort for skiers and golfers. The lady merely wanted her son to learn about navigation on the inside track: O'Brien enjoyed the back-handed compliment.

Darkness fell. O'Brien turned on the radio and a Mozart piano concerto in velvet stereo soothed his tired mind. Gusts shook the windows as the storm raged. "I don't like that part where the message refers to three attacks" he thought aloud, "I was working on a pair".

"Who, save the President, would the North Koreans want to kill," Kang exclaimed, genuinely surprised. "Not foreign athletes."

"A foreign VIP guest..... plenty of them in the Royal Box," O'Brien replied absently, glancing at the obstinate telephone, though suspecting the target might be grateful for once in his scheming life. Suddenly its ring shattered their nervous tension.

O'Brien reached out, listened, then smiled. "Thank Christ for that", he said, slamming it down, "Sam's O.K." Now they could solve 'world' disasters.

Noah went into North Korea almost weekly. He knew that some two hundred kilometers north in the deceptively empty city of Pyongyang, shrewd minds worked round-the-clock, seeking the cheapest means for their strange dynasty to stop the Olympic Games. Logic played no role in these calculations: Kim Il Sung and his odd son were pressing on with their vast and beautiful Azalea stadium on the wooded banks of the Taedong River close to their silent capital. Face alone counted. And fear. Despite their military might and numbers compared to the softer South, money talks : their brother nation could grow so rich that even the communist bloc would ignore Pyongyang, for all its air and naval bases to threaten Japan or China, allow the North to sink deeper into debt and poverty, stagnate then wither, become northern Asia's lone region of famine.

There was calculation in Kang's eyes when he leaned forward in the armchair, obviously preparing himself to ask an awkward question, or seek a special favour. O'Brien swiftly anticipated the problem for it bothered him as much. "We are pushed, Jae Pil, and somebody should watch our tails. We could use a good girl with a smart head on her shoulders." Only an innocent could be talked into shoving her head into the tiger's gaping jaws. "And that's useless for this operation."

"They offered."

"London have a young lady waiting with suitcases packed."

"You refused."

O'Brien shrugged, enjoying the Mozart, right leg hooked over the chair arm. "She's on hold."

Kang took a long slow breath. "There's no more time for lessons... we're in the fast lane." Another boom kicked the house, rattling every window, as America's spyplane flew home.

3

During a long night the storm blew over the Yellow Sea. Daybreak revealed a circle of shere peaks and the Han River sliding like an old serpent through a busy city. O'Brien had rewarded Sammy Song with a day off, and by seven-thirty he drove through teeming traffic, crossed the river by the top span of Panpo Bridge, then headed along the new Olympic freeway on its southern bank, towards the stadiums, enjoying a fresh morning.

Fifteen minutes past the bridge, dwarfing a backcloth of offices and apartment blocks, Chamsil Sports complex drifted into view, the huge concrete coracle of the main stadium beached on the riverside. Leaving the river bank and a skeleton Olympic bridge, O'Brien headed south, towards a white office tower which surveyed half-built gymnasiums and swimming pools that rose from a park full of hideous sculptures and the gentle mound of an ancient hill fortress. O'Brien had been set three tasks by his moderate chief in London: send reliable intelligence about stability on the Korean peninsular, destroy all covert threats to the games, don't start a war over Korea.

On this bright morning he prepared for yet another mental chess match with General Kim Dung Chi, overall commander of the one-hundred-thousand troops, police and national security personnel guarding the Olympic Games. General Kim - since nothing escaped the Korean craze for abbreviations - lived on the top floor of SLOOC, otherwise the Seoul Olympic Organising Committee. With luck, O'Brien would pull off a last, but crucial detail, grant himself ultimate command of the airship - in a moment of 'national importance'. During hours haggling, over several weeks, so far, General Kim remained oblivious that the world 'national' in the contract might have more than a single interpretation. Kang put this attitude down to his ancestors, who evolved a language where lateral explanation - and therefore thought - was difficult and rare. Convinced that O'Brien's firm was petrified of legal action by the Korean

Government if, during some crucial moment, there was a system failure, General Kim saw no danger.

Drab blocks of apartments flanked a wide boulevard lined with gaunt trees that let heavy traffic escape southwards from the Han bank. O'Brien was reminded of a Warsaw with money. When he arrived at the steel mesh fence surrounding SLOOC centre, he slowed the car and stopped by a concrete pedestal on which a policeman sheltered under a gaily painted metal parasol. The policeman cradled his M16 rifle with one arm while O'Brien slid down his window and passed out an identity card. The policeman checked on a hand-held radio if O'Brien's car was on the visitor's list that morning, while three other armed police covered him from behind a sandbagged guardpost. Static then conversation burst from the radio: back though the window came his ID card. O'Brien drove to the next check-point. He glanced at his watch: four minutes before eight. He parked in a row where every car faced the other way, only to hear a whistle, and see a guard run after him, calling out, waving his hand in a circle. SLOOC itself was run by another former general with fixed ideas about keeping his base tidy. Visitors must feel that efficiency lurked in the very air near this white concrete and glass tower. Further controls, discreet yet thorough, passed O'Brien from the front doors to pretty lift girls and the topmost floor. When the lift doors slid open, General Kim, the security chief himself, towered in the lobby, brow heavy with accusation, distracted.

Kim bowed slightly, the harsh mouth shaping a curt greeting while his ruthless eyes checked the wall clock: eight precisely. Beckoning his visitor to hurry, Kim charged along a bare corridor, scattering secretaries and messengers; his dark suit cleverly hid powerful shoulders, muscular arms, and almost concealed the bulge from a pistol holster. O'Brien was not armed for this call: nobody would kill him instead of General Kim when facing both at short range in a small room. Kim spun round but O'Brien kept pace. The easy movement betrayed Kim's lasting fitness and agility; a slight thickening at the belt, a certain swelling around the watchful eyes told O'Brien that, sometimes, General Kim tasted softer living.

"Where is Mister Kang this morning?' Kim asked sharply as he strode into an outer office where a number of serious young Koreans in dark suits worked silently apart from one older man, who sat alone, hissing into a telephone.

"Taken a day off, general, to preserve the relationship with his fiancée," replied O'Brien, hoping that Kang was not followed, for at that moment the boy was breaking and entering a company downtown.

The general's office was protected by that of his secretary, Miss Kim, a porcelain beauty in a green Olympic blazer whose delicate profile and shining hair, discrete figure and lovely hands reminded that Korean princesses were much sought after in the court of Imperial China. Miss Kim bowed deeply and as the general hurried past, dark provocative eyes allowed O'Brien a lingering glance.

Kim led him into a vast room furnished according to confucian ritual. A wide desk and high leather chair stood near long windows beyond which miniature pines climbed a ridge of ochre mountains to meet the crisp sky. Tiny houses flowed down the distant hillsides towards a Han River full and muddy from the night rains. Kim briskly waved him towards one of the seats around a low table near the windows. A master chair at one end was armed with the mandatory battery of telephones: Kim sat, hostile, stiff, examining his view.

"We must pray for rain like last night in early September". Kim approved the bright northern sky." Our pollution will sail over the mountains towards Pyongyang."

"Before their games." O'Brien settled into a sofa-sized chair and waited for the inevitable loaded question.

"You have been rather busy", observed Kim while his eyes swept his visitor's respectful face, watching for a false reaction. Mind-sharpened by yesterday, memory refreshed that morning by reading the file on O'Brien and Kang, the general would record every muscle twitch.

News is never given directly in Korea: O'Brien played modest. "Remarkably public spirited?"

Kim allowed his mouth a slight stretch then pressed a buzzer under the table-top. "Coffee or tea?"

"Ginseng tea, please, general."

Kim pressed again: two buzzes signalled tea: how many times would the general press after a cup of poison from Miss Kim? This diversion gave O'Brien an opening for business since, he, as guest, must make the first move.

"Our company sent some good news yesterday." He watched faint puzzlement descend over Kim while the general wondered if his command missed any intercepts from O'Brien's telephone and fax. "We are ready with the avionics package for the airship. We propose to ship the whole construction kit by a container vessel next week. When the airship arrives in seven weeks time, our build team will need a hangar, at least sixty meters long, thirty meters high, and doors twenty meters wide. Provide that and painless customs clearance and your airship will be test flown by early June." O'Brien paused and reached into his suit pocket for a white envelope which he lowered into Kim's waiting palm. "I've set everything down so that both costs and deadlines are easier on the eyes."

Kim almost smiled. The general's thick fingers reached for an elegant paper knife; he neatly slit open the envelope, read the single sheet, then looked towards the door. "Miss Kim." He was rewarded with a seductive, "Nae?"

"Please ask Mr. Yoon to join us - at once."

While Miss Kim purred into the telephone, summoning Yoon, the general went over the letter and O'Brien began to understand that Kang was right - nobody would raise yesterday afternoon - until they cornered him, on something else. Giving nothing away, Kim poured over its contents, a signal that the price was likely to suffer further savage bargaining: all quotations in Korea are challenged, for every price bid opens at criminal height. London wanted Kim and his security service hooked on the British airship and its avionics: no other route gave O'Brien instant television surveillance over the Olympic sites: yet the deal must look genuine, its price tough, otherwise Kim would smell trickery.

"Just a matter of timing," soothed O'Brien, "so long as we agree this package covers your requirement . . . . . . and our price. We spent a lot of British brain cells on that silver bubble."

Kim sat back, smoothed greying hair, strong impatient fingers tapping the chair arm while he waited for Yoon.

The door opened. Miss Kim rested her engaging smile on O'Brien for a significant second before ushering in a tall Korean with a sharp face and hunted eyes whose smart suit failed to hide a man who kills for his living.

Yoon bowed deeply, as though greeting an opponent, then slid into the arm-chair on his chief's left. After a brief search of his pockets, he produced a small leather wallet, from which emerged a business card. Offering it with the right hand, he gave time to read, before crushing O'Brien's waiting fingers.

"I see . . . . . our pilot," winced O'Brien studying a card covered in Yoon's degrees and qualifications. Miss Kim returned with three cups of ginseng tea on a small tray. Again an engaging smile found O'Brien: a gentle brush of her hand against his thigh as she set down his cup was a surprise pleasure. He turned round in time to observe the general fighting for control of his furious face; perhaps Miss Kim had overdone her duty to distract an awkward visitor.

"Mostly choppers," replied Yoon innocently.

"He has four thousand hours," added Kim when diplomacy returned.

"You won't find our little ship boring," O'Brien promised. All along Kim had displayed a sublime ignorance toward the demanding art of flying airships: one flight in a gentle wind usually shook the boldest rotor pilot. "But the airship must be built for your first lesson."

Kim suffered this reminder with a sharp intake of breath which hissed past his teeth. The general held three-star rank, trained in America as an electronics engineer, survived two combat tours in Vietnam and emerged a personal crony of the President; his pastimes included martial arts, spying, gambling, drinking and women. Kim normally gave orders, plainly hated O'Brien's insolence, yet moved on with suspiciously obvious haste. "I want you to call a friend of mine, Mr. O'Brien, who will handle the import and its advertising business. He provides *our* cover."

"Do you have his card?" requested O'Brien, trying to sound stupid, though Kim's morals lay naked. The advertising potential was a licence to print several currencies in large denomination notes. Only that prize, dangled in front of Kim, enabled O'Brien to advance deep into Chung's spider's web. Money first. The safety of some twelve thousand of the world's finest athletes, some nine-thousand media, perhaps two-hundred thousand visitors, trailed behind.

"We were at high-school together." Kim handed over the card of a Mr. Park Jae Bol, President of Magnolia Trading Company.

"Does Mr. Park have a full security clearance?" O'Brien asked cheerfully.

A muscle twitched under Kim's cheekbone while Yoon plainly wished he was deaf. Kim recovered and threatened silkily, "Our national president tasked - *me* - with security and *calm* for the Olympic Games."

"Our company only wishes to serve that ambition." O'Brien suppressed a strong urge to plant his fist in Kim's cruel plastic face. "And the security of - *our* - technology is vital for that success." He watched Yoon, who seemed much too comfortable with Kim for the most able police pilot, display that cool detachment of a man privy to the blackest national secrets and guessed that Yoon was from the Blue House - Chon Hwa Dae - the presidential palace: he also guessed what was coming next.

"My good friend Yoon is a pilot and electronics engineer." The general raised the cup hidden by his fingers and invited both men to drink their ginseng tea. "From this morning, he is directly responsible - to me- for the airship project, which we codename Operation Mole."

O'Brien showed respectful surprise, relaxing only when Kim appeared satisfied that his visitor was suitably grateful for such privileged information.

"Yoon must coordinate with several agencies. You, Mr. O'Brien, must assist with this operation in every way. Training is central," Kim lowered the tea cup, let his eyes impatiently burn.

O'Brien took a sip of warm tea. Kim had just confirmed that he kept virtual control of the airship. Only his 'training pilot' could judge the 'progress' of Yoon or any other pilot and groundcrew. A few small yet vital details held back and O'Brien, with Kang, could monitor each flight, which met London's first requirement. Time to set a faster pace. Modestly, O'Brien proposed, "Our best training captain is ready to catch a plane to Seoul."

Kim ignored him and studied the letter on his table for some moments. "You say the technical package is ready," he remarked coldly.

O'Brien had been waiting for a question about engines or street gunfights. Thankful that Kim's staff did not follow the news or check paperwork thoroughly, he confirmed the contents of his letter, which lay like an accusation on the varnished table.

"We have a package designed by the best British experts. Your electronics are linked to a satellite zoom lens mounted on a revolving nodule under the gondola. Your pictures can be monitored from the airship, remotely controlled from your command centre on this floor, or across the Olympic Park at your alternate HQ. We can install lines for feeding visual data to your computer bank."

Kim suppressed fascination. "Range?"

"Best results from five-thousand feet."

Kim looked over at Yoon, neither raised an eye-brow. The general probed further. "Definition?"

"Single faces at fifty miles slant range."

Kim was seduced. "Eighty kilometres!"

O'Brien decided to risk an unwelcome question. "Was construction of our hangar authorised by the Blue House?"

"We want their encouragement," Kim deflected brusquely, "not control ... there will be hangar ready."

O'Brien stared north at the mountain wall, now turning salmon under morning sunshine. An infinite blue sky slowly gathered thin white haze. For as the wind died, already smog spread among riverside suburbs. Something was cleverly obscured. London needed the airship, but not quite so desperately. He decided the moment had arrived to put General Kim in his place. With a faint smile he revealed, "Our airship . . . frankly . . . . . can fly perfectly steady more than four miles above the ground. Even with your Korean hills and mountains, on a lovely morning such as this, we'll let you watch Kim Il Sung drive to work."

"Remind me . . .how much?" Kim studiously dismissed the open letter.

"With the training package," he faked mental arithmetic, "seven million dollars."

Yoon coughed.

4

Magnolia Trading Company: O'Brien blinked through harsh sunlight at a small brass plate lost among others set in the wall alongside double glass doors into a dreary stone office block. The narrow street lay quiet. Few people hurried past, not a car in sight; just a tangle of old houses, most worn down, some with charm, a forgotten quarter. Only the steady rumble of traffic told that he stood barely a hundred yards from City Hall. Bull-dozers soon would batter and crush this quaint sanctuary into rubble and dust. The lane curved behind the monstrous Sejong art centre which soared above the humble roofs like a Thebes temple carved from living concrete. Clever Mr. Park, muttered O'Brien, pushing open the heavy glass doors; this crumbling office slum was a building site worth millions.

He pulled a fat brown envelope from an inside pocket and felt his gun firmly in its holster, walked into the building. Clutching the envelope, which contained a bogus contract, he nodded politely at a guard drowsing behind a metal desk, crossed the clean though dank foyer: stale Kimchi attacked his nostrils. He reached the lift before the guard straightened in his uncomfortable chair; four o'clock on Saturday afternoon was an excellent time for breaking into most Korean offices. The guard drooped over his bare desk.

Distant carhorns, restless traffic, sudden brittle footsteps and girls' chatter spilt through the glass doors. Several dozen yards distant, the working population of Seoul poured into warm streets, another week over, heading for buses, taxis, the smart new subway imported from Britain. O'Brien waited until the guard's eyelids firmly closed then rode the lift to the fifth floor. Korea preserves China's fables . . . the word death and number four sound identical and both rarely enjoy display. He stepped briskly from the lift, waited, went down a flight of stairs, found a pair of firedoors marked F, which he warily opened.

A deserted corridor. Cunning Mr. Park. What foresight . . . . only one office suite traded from the unlucky floor. He loosened his jacket, freeing the machine-pistol, before listening at the thick frosted glass door: no sound. He watched the lift warning button: no lights displayed. From his coat, he took a pair of white cotton driver's gloves, pulled them on, took out a ring with a dozen keys cellotaped together for silence. Facing the window at the far end, keeping the lift doors in sight, silently removing the cellotape, he worked with his key set.

London discovered a Birmingham locksmith in bitter strife with a Korean partner over stolen technology for intricate security locks. O'Brien collected a set of keys in Hong Kong . . . which could open any British original . . . . and take care of all Korean copies, providing the piracy was perfect.

At least the lock was the right fake brand: Kang had passed along the numberless floor that morning. After testing five keys, O'Brien resigned himself to a long job when the next slid smoothly into the lock, proving masterly reproduction. He turned it, heard the baffles click, let the door open gently. From the corridor he checked the lock, doorframe, then threshold: there were two alarm systems. Confident he took a long stride into the room, avoided a pressure alarm badly concealed under the drab carpet, quietly closed the door.

A net-curtained room stored two desks, both bare, save for new telephones and the usual biro sets mounted in grotesque marble. Two cherrywood cabinets were crammed with files and ledgers. He started reading. None held a paper concerned with advertising. All records covered defunct companies owned by the industrious Mr. Park, mail-shots from American cosmetic firms seeking a Korean agent; few replies had left Magnolia Trading. What caught his attention most was the absence of the mandatory low conference table, flanking sofas, overseen by the presidential chair and its telephone battery. Meetings were rare with anybody in this company.

Neither desk was locked. The drawers of both were neatly filled with headed-paper, empty folders, boxes of staples and enough pencils and rubbers to open a small school. He looked towards an ornate wall clock: three minutes already: a framed certificate hung behind the larger desk and proclaimed that Mr. Park mastered in business studies from Stanford. O'Brien wondered if the document was fake. No other Stanford graduate in Seoul worked from such a humble base for amazingly meagre results. He moved nearer the windows.

Another low office block stood opposite and an apartment house next door. Beyond thin ginkyos, along the warm skyline, marched the golden rock and clinging firs of Pogwang Mountain.

O'Brien carefully studied the whole room. Almost hidden, a fat folder caught his eye, tucked in a pile of newspapers stacked under the window. Avoiding the electronic strip of carpet, making no noise, he crouched by the newspapers and silently pulled at the large envelope.

Opening its flap, inside he found several of his own glossy booklets on the wonders of modern airships . . . . one pamphlet written by himself.

Whatever Mr. Park's role in the project, front company for the actual contracts, advertising, operating, banking, graft, it required no knowledge of airships.

O'Brien left the folder on the nearest desk. He started with the shelves and searched every folder and file, repeated this task with each desk drawer, but not one scrap of paper anywhere in the room recorded a payment or receipt. He picked up a telephone and heard the dialling tone. A fax machine stood in a corner, green lights glowing, connected. There was no sign of any bills from the Korea Telecoms Authority.

He wiped the telephone with gloved hands. Magnolia Trading employed one person, possibly two judging by the desks, sent no letters, rarely answered mail, earned no money, paid no money, yet could afford a rented office, fax and telephone. Next step was turn over Park's house but that was a job for Kang or an experienced burglar . . . not a large Celt.

No wonder Kim was determined their airship would patrol above the Olympics Games, so wary of involving more than a handful of his corrupt cabal: Operation Mole was worth millions for certain privileged pockets.

He picked up the folder intending to slip it back among the piled newspapers when something fell to the worn green carpet: a crinkled photograph landed face down. He flicked it over . . . . . a young Korean; slightly arrogant eyes ruled an otherwise intelligent face, long hair, perhaps a student, but oddly familiar. The traffic jam, blinding rain, two young men dashing among the snarled traffic . . . sudden violence . . . why leave a picture waiting in such an obvious place? The whole idea was too clever by half, too stupid for a professional, unless a third intruder called at Magnolia Trading.

He twisted his watch, aimed the camera lens, steadied his left wrist above the photograph, switched on the flash, took three pictures of the Korean youth, slid the camera round, shut off the flash and covered the lens, checked that it resembled a watch once more.

He replaced the file among the old newspapers, took a final look at the small office. Stepping into the corridor he locked and cleaned the door handle, then climbed upstairs to the fifth floor. Empty. He pressed the lift button and the doors slid apart. In the foyer, the guard sat bolt upright with chin lowered and lids shut. O'Brien strolled into a sunny street, turned the corner, joined bustling crowds hurrying home along Sejong.

5

Ragged clouds towed fat shadows along low mountains with purple splashes on their parched flanks, wild azaleas caught by noon sun. The road north ran like a causeway across empty paddys in a wide valley. On either side, footpaths meandered along dikes towards tiny farmhouses, humble islands among resting fields, where black and white cattle grazed by flimsy shacks. Nearer the roadside, a russet buffalo ambled deliberately, leading an old man wearing a grey jacket and felt trilby. Driving fast, O'Brien waved and a greeting returned from the dusty embankment.

Within weeks rain would flood these fields, young rice shoots turn the valley fresh green. O'Brien savoured his visits into the hills watching the Imjin River and where Doctor Moon controlled Asia's widest spynet from among brooding mountains. Once clear of the great anti-tank walls guarding Seoul, leaving behind granite blocks and military check-points, that subtle opium began: a dangerous frontier. The road climbed into a deep valley, and mountains towered on either side. He passed a battery of 155m howitzers, self propelled, dug deep into a rocky slope, camouflage nets slung over sandbags for protection, young soldiers chasing chickens off a vegetable garden near their tin huts.

Scrub trees clung onto the rocky flanks of a verticle mountain and below it nestled a small park. He slowed, leaned out of the window, observed neat shrubs, gravel weeded, a short flag-pole. Teenage girls from a local commercial high school tended this garden which cradled the Gloucester's memorial carved into the foot of the mountain on which a thousand Britons fought off thirty-thousand Chinese during four days and nights. Their stand saved Seoul, yet, he reflected, speeding onwards, only the little girls of remote Choksong city *always* remembered.

From the valley mouth, he turned east, where lower hills led into gentle mountains. Hot sun burned away morning clouds. Between O'Brien and North Korea snaked the yellow Imjin River. A man could wade through that sleepy water at most seasons. Only people with permits - or barbarian soldiers - were allowed over the rare bridges. Beyond the river, on bare hills, watch-towers and sandbag forts faced across four kilometers of deserted open country, scarred by a wide endless furrow of red earth, the military demarkation line, bull-dozed clean for thirty years to rupture a people.

This noon, lilac mountains climbed from spring haze, innocently close, beyond reach for more than a generation, a moonscape wilderness behind which hid Asia's most remote society.

The first communist dynasty never ceased to fascinate O'Brien: for Stalin, the northern half of Korea was a little extra booty in the final hours of World War Two, Captain Kim Il Sung of the Red Army chosen as its vassal prince. The aging tyrant, embattled in Pyongyang, proposed to hand over on his deathbed to his weird and impatient son, promising a country more brain-washed than before. And then O'Brien thought of that other eighty year old, who still watched from these mountains like a wily hawk after four decades of vigil, teaching his eldest son how to fight a secret war. Moon was right. The gravest danger - both sides of that thin red scar wandering over the dry hills - was a Korean talent for seeing only straight in front, never looking either side, let alone behind.

O'Brien drove through a massive gateway carved through the hill side, giant concrete fascines lashed on either cliff, ready for dropping, charged with explosives for instantly blocking the pass against North Korea's tanks and tracked artillery. He stopped the car as his throat tightened with forgotten emotion and let the wind soothe.

On the left, a lone steep hill rose like a castle, overgrown with short scrub trees. Once his father watched from that hill, guarding the Imjin fords, until the first waves of Chinese plunged across the river for a massive night attack. O'Brien drove on sadly, leaving behind a small Bhuddist temple, the little shacks of a ginseng field, part of himself. Soon, he swung off the tarmac road, onto a track, bumping over red earth, climbing eastwards and higher into endless mountains.

The track followed a stream which trickled from a ridge, leaving its sandy bed littered with smooth stones, debris of a million springs and summers when rain soaked the hills for weeks. O'Brien changed into four-wheel drive as the track led over a shoulder, misty emerald with young pines. Soon he saw a lake, smooth, dark even in strong sunlight, an overgrown bank of earth and stones that kept it full all year. Across the lake, concealed among more firs, sloped the grey pine tiles of a traditional Korean roof, its wide eaves supported by heavy painted beams to carry winter snows. Shutters stood open the length of a veranda where a small elderly man sat cross-legged on a bamboo mat, smoking a thin pipe, admiring the peaceful lake that reflected azaleas blossoming on quiet mountains.

When he saw car trailing dust, the old man rose swiftly, his walnut face broke into a humble smile.

O'Brien switched off the engine and climbed out, feeling stiff after two hours of driving, tasting cool mountain wind. He seized the old man's dry hands. "Francis, you look younger each week........ while I feel older each day."

"Live up here," rasped the old man, his chest shaking from silent laughter.

"Not enough camouflage for my species," reminded O'Brien, admiring the mountains, knowing that for a few hours, he could escape the capital's relentless pressure. Nowhere in Korea matched this remote and cleverly guarded valley for timeless peace. He needed a chance for finding bearings. How perfect the irony: four miles distant lay a frontier which boasted more tanks, guns and men per mile than any other. Yet this calm was real, at weekends small children played and picnicked among these friendly mountains. No such gentle world existed any longer around General Kim's closely guarded Olympic sites.... not even a child could climb over the mesh fences without suspicion. Thank God for this tiny man basking in the noon warmth, born a leader, stalking freedom with a most determined human spirit.

The little doctor was a month short of eighty yet his vigour and cunning seemed stronger. O'Brien gazed down at his fragile host, "Any news?"

"Not yet."

Doctor Francis Moon, clad as a village elder, aware that his pipe-bowl grew cold, pulled a leather pouch from his baggy silk trousers, took out some dark strands of local tobacco, pressed the pipe-bowl with his small soft thumb and searched for matches. O'Brien obliged with a box picked up from a Seoul restaurant. Thin smoke drifted towards the lake as afternoon wind hurried through the pines and southwards.

"When did you come up?" asked O'Brien, listening to the swishing fir trees.

"Three days before."

"You let your son run the newspaper and magazines!" teased O'Brien, thrusting his hands into his pockets, laughing aloud, wise blue eyes, contemplating the old man.

The Moons were a dynasty of writers and despite occupation, war, coups, military rule followed by political oppression, managed to create a vast empire on honest though prudent words. Now the old Doctor owned the largest and most influential paper - only the Buk A Ilbo dared criticise the present government - plus a library of magazines. Ten years earlier his several radio stations had been 'suspended for merger', purged of their brightest reporters and swallowed by the state broadcaster to drone mindless propaganda all day for the central news service. Moon firmly believed, eventually, those radio stations would return to their founder, regarding the money as lost, trivial.

The old man's cheeks puffed like a fish, while his brain groped for the proper English words - his sixth language. Small shrewd eyes peered from under thick brows. "Here at Yongpyong, all has been .... uncannily silent ... not as you in Seoul. Was Chung grateful?"

O'Brien tilted his head, thinking it over. "No strangers on my doorstep at four in the morning, no footprints round my garden at dawn, no peculiar telephone calls at all hours and several days already passed."

"Then you are still welcome," Doctor Moon declared breezily though in his narrow eyes a hard glint lingered.

"Nothing beats confidence," returned O'Brien, far from convinced that the Sejong shooting was remembered though buried by a grateful president.

"Kim himself signed the 'guidance' for our nation's media : not a word allowed my friend, not a word, or face closure." Moon took him by the wrist and laughed until his chest shuddered then exploded a hacking cough. "They want something!"

"More gambling," despaired O'Brien.

"Plenty of time yet: my dear Michael, we have more than one hundred and seventy days. Plenty of time for the world to spin faster." Moon cleared his throat like an old car starting on a damp morning. "Poker *is* Chung's favoured relaxation."

"No strangers among these mountains?" O'Brien worried about the old man's safety. Moon was 'uncle' to the local villages but they could not watch every mountain path.

The Doctor shrugged his small shoulders, jerking his pipe at a fine wire mast firmly fixed to the stone chimney. "Nor airwaves."

"Silence from Hodori."

"Two days late," admitted Moon, no longer at ease.

"We've suffered that frustration before." O'Brien looked towards the silent house. "Somebody up here?"

"Only Paul .... Hodori is usually prompt .... a northern crisis is my guess." The doctor sucked his thin pipe. "Our friend is rather senior."

"They can't change plans more often in Pyongyang than Seoul!"

A warm glitter returned to Moon's eyes and he gave O'Brien a sharp stare. "You forget my birthplace, old friend, which lies far beyond the northern bank of that Imjin River flowing round the bottom of this mountain."

O'Brien rubbed his jaw: forty-eight hours late: that was long. "I'll ask Hong Kong to assess the risk involved with a contact. Noah could run a businessman into Pyongyang next week. Let's pray Hodori comes through."

Suddenly, breaking into a boyish smile, the doctor cried in apology, "But what am I doing, my good friend, what a *disgraceful* host. You saw how your father's memorial is kept well." He stumbled over the English consonents, exaggerating slightly and brushing aside O'Brien's sudden shyness, held him firmly by the arm, ordered him to park the car under sheltering pines, took his guest's small bag. The car safely screened among the firs, O'Brien climbed the wide steps, kicked off his shoes at the open french windows, stepped into waiting slippers, greeted the doctor's eldest son.

Paul Moon, already the publishing group controller in his early forties, waited serious and sad behind thick spectacles, devoted to his father and democracy, still not wed though a golden catch for any Korean girl. Paul made summer a time of escape from the predatory matrons of Seoul who, each year, tried luring him into marriage with a favoured relative. Mountain dragons were less perilous than a hunting urban tigress.

They followed Paul's slight figure over the threshold into a long room. From both sides, rows of french windows poured light onto richly embroidered chinese carpets. Huge pine beams braced a panelled timber roof. At each end of the long room, rose a wall of books with doors cut through shelves loaded with leather volumes and fading papers. O'Brien wandered to the windows, admired the greatest secret of this cleverly sited haven. Pines stood sentinel along the lakeshore but eastward, beyond small firs growing on the mountain shoulder, a wandering snake of gold water, the Imjin, escaped from the North

Korean mountains.

"Come on through," Paul called from the far archway under the books.

O'Brien entered a small sitting room with Korean cushions and a low table. Beyond them, in the teak floor, a trap-door lay open revealing a ladder into a dimly lit cellar carved from the granite mountainside. Paul clambered below, waited, holding the ladder, watching his father come slowly down. O'Brien followed.

"My dear Michael," the old man regained his breath, "now we must open the wizard's box."

With a nod of approval from his father, Paul Moon's slippered feet shuffled across the stone. He opened a big wooden cupboard and pulled out a large, old, dusty radio which he stood on a sturdy scratched work-bench. O'Brien observed the extreme care that Paul took to avoid finger marks on its grimy controls. Gently, he pressed the power button, looking at his watch as the big set warmed, waiting, now and then cradling his fingers, concentration filling his sombre eyes. Thin wire ran from the back of the radio and inside the tall cupboard to an aerial, not the one fastened to the stone chimney, but something bigger, more sophisticated, hidden behind the house among the taller pines.

O'Brien teased Moon senior, "What's your range?"

"Northern Manchuria," the old man replied with a modest smile, "but the Yalu River is far enough for my generation."

Paul Moon raised his head, glanced at his father, then sighed. "My dear Papa still believes that we Koreans are descended from Tangun the son of a mythical Manchurian bear."

O'Brien laughed. Many Koreans, including Doctor Moon, wished to regain Manchuria, ancient birthplace of the Korean race where legend claimed a bear mated with a woman who bore the first Korean, five-thousand years past. Three-million Koreans still farmed the remote region in modern China.

"Who first wades the Imjin River?" grumbled Paul and resumed twisting his fingers together, when the radio started hissing. Silently, they waited, the cavern chill as night drew close. Only the crackle and hiss of empty wavebands came from the radio speaker. After ten minutes, Doctor Moon shrugged his narrow shoulders, looked at Paul.

"Stay patient. Leave the main power supply hooked and keep listening while we eat. Our northern relative, doubtless, risks equal nervousness and suspicion from *authority* in the other half of this discontented land."

"Not impressed with the army's style of democratic government?" O'Brien waited with mischief for the doctor's answer.

"My dear friend," Moon puffed his cheeks in sly mirth before he declared acidly, "few mortals are so pig-headed as our generals in business suits who govern South Korea."

"Save for their rivals in North Korea," O'Brien countered.

The old man's hooded eyes almost closed. "Nobody ever accused Koreans of wisdom."

Dusk swallowed the facing mountain, next the valley, finally smothering the quiet lake and whispering pines. Still no message came from across the silent Imjin, yet the old doctor kept calm, busied himself taking command of supper, giving an order, sometimes encouragement, while Paul heated charcoal in a brazier that stood on the sloping lawn. Within minutes the coals glowed marmalade. O'Brien watched from the veranda steps, sipping rice wine, savouring every new mood of the doctor's animated face, somehow enhanced by the burning coals. Paul went into the house and he returned carrying a large tray loaded with countless spicy side-dishes and plates piled with thinly sliced beef steak rolled around the chopped bones. He placed a grill over the fierce coals, waited while it grew hot, then, with a pair of chopsticks, began rolling the meat, spreading it sizzling onto the grill, choking the night with pungent smoke. Weilding the chopsticks with intense care, Paul flicked over the strips of meat, his face pink from sudden tiny flames. Again, he hurried into the house, only to emerge, moments later with another tray on which were a dish of large lettuce leaves and six covered bowls, each filled with steaming rice or savoury soup. Paul lent over the brazier, poking with the chopsticks, skillfully turning the meat strips. He straightened, cocking his head towards the open veranda doors, dropped the chopsticks and ran headlong, vaulted the steps, swerved into the dimly lit house, dashing past the french windows, O'Brien close behind.

Paul grabbed the ladder with both hands, steadied himself for an instant, dropped onto the stone floor. O'Brien caught up, swung his legs through the trap-door, let his feet catch one rung to break the fall, before dropping heavily. A red light glowed on the radio-set. Paul's anxious face bent over the tape recorder as cheek muscles taut, he pressed the stop button, took out a cassette. "We'll play this on the other machine," he remarked hoarsely, turning to face O'Brien and a shy smile spread over his serious face.

Paul opened the wooden cupboard and lifted out a new Japanese tape-recorder. There was nothing cheap or simple about this machine. It could handle almost any tape, size or speed, invented. Paul fitted the cassette and checked the speed control. "We slow it down a hundred times," he remarked without looking round, devoted to his immediate task. Satisfied, he pushed the button for play. They heard only a faint hiss before a thin sweet voice, a small girl, sang in haunting Korean about a jilted woman whose lover flees from their village under a mythical mountain in North Korea named Arrirang. From where he crouched, O'Brien watched Paul's struggling face and realised that he, also, did not understand.

Paul pursed his lips, then remarked hopelessly, "What father finds simple is often too complicated for anybody normal."

O'Brien searched his brain for a plain though delicately screened message: logic, not immediately obvious, save to Doctor Moon himself, conveyed not in the words but the song's very nature. He debated aloud. "Arrirang does not exist though it's Korea's best known mountain: Hodori is telling us something hidden yet obvious?"

Paul pocketed the tape. "Also, that song is rarely sung in the north.... unless requested by a Swedish television crew!"

"Let's pray that Hodori sent the burst signal."

They found Doctor Moon patiently turning over the Kalbi steaks, pausing every few moments, standing back from the heat and smoke, despite the cold night. "Not long now," called the doctor, perhaps reading the blank stares on their faces.

Paul folded his arms, rubbing the backs of his hands to keep warm, confronted his father with the taped message, reported its contents. "I simply do not understand," he finished.

Moon showed no surprise. "My dear friend who sent that message is a very senior general today in Kim Il Sung's State Political Security Department, who takes no chances, and believes in simple orders. I have known Hodori all my life. Before the Second World War we were very close, waging common struggles against Japanese colonists. In those days, I was like a father, now, we're both fifty years older." Moon admired the night as mist rose under the still pines. The old man whispered hoarsely, "Arrirang.... an important and secret order has been given by the second highest authority, not Kim Il Sung, the Great Leader, but by his peculiar son. Arrirang is a mythical mountain, not a real peak: if you follow our private logic?" He smiled kindly.

"Your private logic implies a part of the northern regime is reckless, maverick, and probably out of control." Paul gave his father a questioning stare. "And dismisses recent Russian efforts to buy Olympic calm with the latest MIGS and long range rockets."

"An order for what?" pursued O'Brien.

Was Hodori warning of the next terror attack? London expected three and oblique messages were worthless, unless, somehow, the target was spotlighted. Forty two million people lived in South Korea. All were potential targets for North Korean terror squads. "We could be looking for one person in millions," he added.

"Less!" replied a confident Moon.

Paul frowned. "Arrirang is sung by a woman, who mocks her fickle lover, scoffing that he cannot reach the next town without blistered feet."

"A woman under threat?" O'Brien was sceptical. None were in public life. Korean women still struggled for civilised treatment from their rigid conservative men. He scratched his rough chin and a doubtful smile creased his tired face. "Skirts might hint towards Heaven, an important priest, somebody we know? But that would be a deliberate attempt at mass chaos."

Paul was horrified. "Chung could declare martial law within hours."

"I'm half serious," calmed O'Brien, "your father probably knows their target."

"Providing he remembers," despaired Paul, in a rare protest.

Doctor Moon, lost in concentration, paced round and round the grilling meat, sometimes prodding with his chopsticks, almost unaware of his physical actions: perhaps his mind sifted through years of operations for the crucial key which would open his memory, reveal the message wrapped in a child's song.

"May we help?" Paul began lifting off the sizzling steaks onto warm plates.

But his father merely ruled, "I must reflect."

* * * * * * * * *

O'Brien spread out his light ondol mattress and thin quilt, piled a couple of pillows, sat on the warm floor. Earlier, Paul had crammed logs into the kitchen stove, from which long pipes ran under the house, eventually becoming a chimney at its far end: Koreans had kept themselves snug this way for two-thousand years. O'Brien yawned, pondering these tenacious people, enjoying the pure night air after a day of wind and sun, an evening of frustration, talk,

Korean barbecue and rice wine. He slid into the bed and tried reading a book on the beautiful Manchurian white crane, which the Doctor had chosen personally for his guest's education and relaxation, knowing O'Brien's love of the natural world; but his eyes kept closing. Checking his pistol was close at hand, tucked under a large cushion, O'Brien turned off the low lamp, slept soundly for about three hours; he awoke to find Paul peering down.

"Your spell," Paul apologised quietly.

O'Brien sat up in the darkness, drugged with sleep. "Nothing".

"Nothing," confirmed Paul.

Throughout the remaining hours of a night, O'Brien stood watch, ignoring the cold discomfort of a stone cellar. But the old radio stayed obstinately silent. Misty dawn brought chilled bones and an exhaused mind. When they took breakfast with the Doctor, who needed little sleep at eighty, both younger men were worn, slowing. Moon forgave their failing stamina with a jovial mood.

"My dear boys," consoled Moon, "I am no nearer solving Hodori's message after a night of sleep than you two after a night of almost none."

"Thank you father," replied Paul with terse filial respect.

O'Brien yawned and drank some scalding ginseng tea while sitting cross-legged on an embroidered floor cushion. Sweet scent rose from the large tureen of hot pine porridge. Though hungry, he wanted to test Dr. Moon's opinion. "Direct involvement by the Northern leadership makes our task easier - in one sense - we can watch a single window."

"The threat," answered Moon, "remains North Korea but their targets will be here, in the South, closely concerned with the Olympic Games."

"I have a hunch that song is warning about something sooner," argued O'Brien, trying the sweet gruel.

Moon, arms folded across his narrow chest, cautioned, "When we have no collateral."

O'Brien set down his soupbowl. "The marathon is final event in the Olympic stadium?"

The Doctor shook his head vigorously, "Not so. The Closing Ceremony follows at dusk."

"And ends long after dark at that time of year." O'Brien stared at them both. The morning was passing, he knew, but the signal remained a mystery. He asked Paul, "How often has Hodori sent a signal this year?"

"Three times."

"Those are routine," intervened his father, "a different song."

"Which says what?" O'Brien asked reluctantly. He prefered to know nothing about Moon's operational procedures. Should the old man die, suffer arrest, London had decreed long ago that Hong Kong would take control and every agent in South Korea declared compromised.

Moon hesitated. Perhaps the same warning passed through the old man's mind, before he disclosed, "We listen for Amazing Grace. This confirms Hodori is safe, all reports which reach Hong Kong are reliable, we can act upon the *in..for...mation.*"

"Your man in Hong Kong passes all material to Noah."

"Of course," said Moon senior.

"A new song is rather significant," admitted Paul.

Neither Moon wished to know anything about Hong Kong's operations in North Korea. Both realised that certain British businessmen who visited that closed country brought back more than cheap slippers made from rice straw and bottled snakes. Moon sat silent for some time.

"Alright," he conceded, "a contact with the north must be risked. That may take a few days. Meanwhile, even a second message, one that positively enhances our first signal, may not reveal the unfortunate victim."

"Assuming one exists," reminded Paul.

"I think Paul is right," answered Moon, sounding short of breath, "it is too extra-ordinary."

"Without the key," said O'Brien frankly, "a thousand songs mean nothing."

"Who sets up this contact?" asked Paul.

"I do," his father decreed, "minutes may be diamonds."

"Shall I keep watch for another night?" asked Paul.

"Of course," answered his father.

O'Brien did not envy Paul, that cellar was cold. He rose from the floor cushion and bowed gratefully, "Stay in touch."

"How do we find you?" Moon rasped, stiff on his cushion from morning damp.

"I carry my telephone everywhere," smiled O'Brien and added without rancour. "Helps General Kim trail me around Korea."

"Where should he listen tomorrow night?" enquired Paul.

"Myong Dong Cathedral." O'Brien's tired eyes shone from dry humour. "The students plan a *peaceful* demonstration."

Moon grunted disapproval. "Cardinal Min does not enjoy his church serving as a battleground for mobs of rival pagans.

"Min is abroad this week." O'Brien glanced down. "The Archbishop is taking a service tomorrow."

Moon bluntly dismissed this fresh potential victim. "Not popular enough. A timid shepherd. Few enemies, less friends. No harm will befall our Archbishop."

"And the Cardinal?" O'Brien watched closely as the old man reached for his tea.

Moon stared over the small bowl at his guest. "Min *is* vulnerable".

"Though not in the same league as Chung, Cha, and your Olympic Committee President."

"Chung abhors all critics." Moon sipped a little tea, swilled it round his mouth, then cheeks bulging, noisily swallowed. "Kim Il Sung fears all southern leaders who fight for personal liberty."

"You be careful, Francis."

O'Brien wearily climbed into his dirty car. There was no hurry, only riots and more haggling over customs duty and prices waited for him in Seoul. His personal life was bare, on hold, apart from the precious times when he could relax among friends in Hong Kong. He was losing touch with normal people, slowly, but for certain. He had lost his career and command of the SAS to an ambush among the hedgerows of South Armagh which put an armalite bullet through his right leg; he shot down the ambush party when they ran for a waiting car. But for months it was the end of life for O'Brien, a time which he wanted to wipe from his wounded memory and scars only fade with years. Now loneliness remained.

The one person with whom he could share ordinary troubles was his married sister, and she had a family to worry over. Their mother was frail, their father killed at the Imjin River Battle almost forty years past. For all the fables about its women, Korea already had cost him one romance.

He drove back slowly, stopping on the mountain shoulder, taking a final look at the lost valley which baked in brilliant morning sun; azalea blossomed like mauve brush strokes all over the mountains, streams sparkled down smooth rock faces and fresh green dusted the fir branches.

6

Above old flat roofs, Namsan's white television tower stabbed a brittle sky. Distant car horns blared, reminding of the evening rush a few blocks west. Kang dodged into a doorway, shadowed by O'Brien: they had reached almost the heart of Myong Dong, *bright village*, a quarter which combined Bond Street with Soho, where Seoul's young sauntered, shopped, drank and talked after a frantic day. Along the narrow street, small groups of olive clad riot police sat, backs resting against shop walls, chopsticks flashing, evening rice bowls balanced in their laps, darth vader helmets and gas-masks ready at their sides, soft chatter their only surrender towards fear: violence would start before nightfall.

Far down the busy lane rose the gaunt brick spire of the Catholic Cathedral, lantern for democracy and rallying point for student riots. Late afternoon crowds already jostled, endless footsteps hurrying past, while along the little street, above shop windows filled with modish clothes, strips of oriental writing flashed and glowed as fairy land climbed towards a fading sky.

O'Brien felt the pistol snug in its holster, the small camera firmly strapped on his left wrist. He pulled the ski-jacket hood lower over his forehead and concealed his orange hair.

"What's the news?" he asked Kang.

Pungent dried fish covered a barrow stall owned by a plump agima wrapped against the spring evening with a fake burberry headscarfe and a cheap quilt coat. Piled newspapers dwindled at her side, replaced by silver coins thrown by people hurrying for bus and subway. Kang took a copy of the Buk A Ilbo, flicked a coin into the waiting bowl, glanced sideways, face hidden by the collar of a thick leather coat. There was no trouble yet along the crowded lane.

Holding the paper beyond the shop door for better light, Kang translated verticle and sometimes horizontal lines of Korean written in Chinese characters, growing amazed. "All Seoul assumes Paul Moon is a serious fellow who listens to nothing save grand opera," he shrugged in disbelief, "now he writes an opinion - quite amusing too - on the Olympic theme song. Pirated?"

"But does he praise or condemn." O'Brien was impatient. He recognised that Kang's indoctrination to the Moon network drew close yet more safety remained for the young Korean by staying ignorant of the deepest truth. He glanced at Namsan mountain: Seoul television tower flicked on yellow floodlights.

Kang read more. "Neither ... simply advises people to listen, contemplate its message."

O'Brien wished he understood more Korean. "Anything else?".

Surprised at O'Brien's nagging, Kang offered, "Just the words. 'See the fire in the sky'. You enjoy pop' music, Mike?"

"Sometimes, JP, sometimes," he answered vaguely. At that instant his respect for Paul know no boundary: it was simple, daring, foolproof. Paul confirmed Hodori's second message by a story in the same Seoul newspaper which Hodori would read within a few hours, when North Korean sympathisers in Japan faxed the entire paper to Pyongyang, for North Korea's Security Ministry. All three legs of their secret tripod now stood firmly, on a restless peninsular, but for a while they could move forward in harness. His next words amazed Kang, "Can we buy a tape around here, JP." They set off towards the cathedral tower.

Even as Kang found a tiny shop crammed with the latest pirated cassettes, taughtness charged the evening air, the street seemed emptier, shouting started somewhere near the dimly lit cathedral. O'Brien felt conspicuous, but nobody noticed him or Kang, for at that moment the riot police started clearing away their supper, some standing, others still squatting, though all preparing to move quickly. There was a methodical rhythm about their chores; first the meal tins were cleared and stored, next equipment checks, then the gas-grenade launchers readied, helmets on tight. An officer appeared and with a flick of his swagger cane, marched the squad of around sixty men towards the cathedral between twin rows of curious faces, for a crowd gathered. That was unusual. Keeping a safe distance, merging among the growing mob, O'Brien and Kang also advanced.

Instinct brought O'Brien to this narrow street. Now gut feeling drove him towards brutal shouting from a loudspeaker, convinced that a key , perhaps a person, would be found tonight somewhere near the gloomy cathedral. Were two familiar faces involved on this chill evening? Who was their target, when and why?

"Keep close," he called to Kang. The first molotov cocktail smashed and exploded in apricot flame. More burst. Petrol bombs swiftly left a no-man's land with the students massed in the cathedral gateway and riot police spread across the lane, cordoning off any escape from the cathedral yard, patiently waiting for an order to advance. O'Brien grew aware that in the shadows a crowd grew. Office workers watched from doorways and side-alleys for the inevitable crushing of young spirits. Fire bombs blossomed. Students charged from the cathedral courtyard, masks over their faces, clad in jeans and sweaters, rushing the stoic olive green wall which blocked the narrow street. Orders snapped: tear gas canisters flew through the cold air. Stiff white puffs spread. Choking silver mist filled the whole street. Shop signs vanished. Office girls ran, wiping their eyes, still a few hardy clerks loitered and stood their ground as self-conscious cheers rippled from shop doorways. Somebody started singing. People leaned from windows and began clapping while dusk became acid fog.

O'Brien called, "That's new, J P."

Kang wiped his eyes in confirmation. "I've never known it happen before, never. Our people are growing angry."

Another squad of riot police arrived. Facing the cathedral courtyard, they formed up, grenade launchers ready: one man accidentally fired. The whole squad panicked.

Tear gas canisters exploded among students and by-standers near the cathedral yard. Dozens scattered as milky fog spread. O'Brien lost his vision as his eyes stung and water flowed down his raw cheeks. A priest staggered past leading to safety a dozen old ladies who had abandoned their evening prayers. More grenades burst within the courtyard. Students, now numbering hundreds, screamed slogans, hurled back petrol bombs. A riot policeman caught fire, whirling in agony while his comrades smothered the golden flames with grey spray. The whole evening turned nastier. Student riots were rituals: most riot police were students only a few months earlier. But tonight was different, reminded O'Brien of Northern Ireland where the streets were filled with that unspoken urge to kill. More riot police arrived. Glass smashed. Huge stones fell among the horrified crowd. A battle started.

"Watch out," called Kang. Another molotov cocktail burst in the road:

cruel flames scorched O'Brien's legs before choking black smoke mingled with the stinging gas.

"Keep *your* eyes sharp J P!" cried O'Brien, "somebody may break for cover . . . and I can't see a bloody thing."

Two tall figures in ski jackets, faces covered by thick scarves, slipped through the tightening cordon, but not fast enough to avoid O'Brien's painful stare. He raised his left wrist to activate the tiny flat camera. Eyes burning, tears streaming down his face, he took picture after picture, mouth tight when he realised a third youth was dragged between the tall pair; somebody hurt, a prisoner. O'Brien swung his camera arm lower for a series of close shots. One of the youths realised, turned, grabbed for his arm, shocked by the moment of recognition, trying to snatch the camera. Kang spun. The small youth seemed to struggle: Kang was airborne, his right leg driving upwards, smashing the nearest mouth, hurling a body across the shallow gutter. O'Brien swerved for a clean punch, when the second student jerked his captive clear, lunged at the camera, swinging for O'Brien's neck.

Kang leapt, span, legs cutting a lightning scissors, left foot shooting deep into the stomach, forcing out wind, dropping its victim onto the hard street. O'Brien grabbed the small youth as the boy sank to his knees, taking him firmly under the shoulder. Both thugs lay in the gutter: one out cold and the second rolling on his side, clutching his stomach, vomit gushing from mouth and nostrils as O'Brien kicked his crotch, hard, then reached down, ripped off the scarf, memorised a small scar low on the neck.

"Run", screamed Kang.

He needed no second invitation. Gripping the boy firmly, he charged after Kang, brushing aside stalls and shoppers, dragging the boy until they were lost among crowds of office-workers outside the huge Lotte store. His eyes stung, his lungs burned. Chest exploding, he coughed, "Let's split, J P. . . meet you back in the Dong."

"What about him?" Kang sucked breath, pointed at O'Brien's sagging charge.

O'Brien spat into the clean gutter. "I'll throw him over the back seat."

"A live clue?" Kang grinned then vanished among evening crowds.

The youth was surprisingly light, his face cocooned under a wool helmet, his breathing anguished sobs. O'Brien pulled the boy, sometimes near carried him, down side alleys, towards his car parked on a building site: Kang would find some friends in a bar, learn more about the evening's violence before collecting the anonymous black taxi.

O'Brien reached his car and debated whether to abandon the limp body. Not once had the hidden face looked from the ground and, hearing a few words of English, probably would presume his rescuers were American. Or should J P first interrogate him, somewhere else and thoroughly. Tempted to tie the boy's ankles and wrists then lock him inside the car trunk, O'Brien recognised he might suffocate. Instead, he loosened his grip, opened the car door while the boy slid face down on the dusty concrete.

Cursing, he lifted the helpless body, with one foot flicked open the rear door, threw the unconscious bundle across the back seat. He frisked the boy's armpits for weapons: clean: nothing showing through his gloves or poking from his trainers. O'Brien slammed the door, glanced towards the broken gates. Nobody in sight. He jumped into the car, drove fast along small lanes, reached the heavy traffic and garish neon symbols along the main shopping streets, headed for the quiet western suburbs before swinging eastwards along the dark river bank and reaching his own Dong.

Night long had fallen when the car roared up the steep hill. He glanced at the mirror once more as a low moan came from the prostrate body. Perhaps the boy struck his head when he passed out in that downtown building site. He hoped J P would return soon. The faster they lost this pathetic thug, the less threatened their fraying cover.

The car headlights swept high walls along the narrow lane where few lamps burned in the gateways of big houses that hid in complete darkness: he stopped outside his own front gates and leaned round in time to see the silent bundle move slightly, before groaning. O'Brien cursed then climbed out of the idling car. What a bloody fool, he gloomily concluded, what an idiot, stuck with some communist midget he could have dumped in a gutter . . . . . the little bastard probably knows nothing; he swore aloud, pushing open the gates, surprised at the freezing wind.

His next problem was to drag his instant captive up the steps and into the house. There was only one quick method. He reached inside the car and pulled the boy out by his ankles, sliding him over the car seat, then turning, heaved the boy over his shoulder, felt the head bump on his lower back and the hands brush his thighs. He kicked the car door closed, mounted the wide steps.

Once through the thick glass door, he strode along the hall and into the warm lounge, switching on a table lamp with his free hand, revealing oil and water colour originals hanging from teak panelled walls. Reaching a long sofa, he lowered his burden face down, relieved when he saw no blood on the woolly helmet. He crossed over to the wide french windows and closed heavy silk curtains, switched on another low lamp before staring at a slight figure in jeans, trainers, cheap anorak, This boy even wore ski gloves. O'Brien jerked them free, surprised by little hands. Either the boy felt cold or left no skin exposed to the searing heat and pain of petrol burns: perhaps the most professional rioter sometimes wounded his own side, mused O'Brien, wondering how much longer J P needed downtown. The body breathed, plainly alive. He checked the old brass ship's chronometer set on the teak wall near the kitchen door: two minutes before nine. Why not start. Some doting family might miss this scruffy dwarf.

"Time for questions, my little man!" O'Brien's fingers closed over the woolly hat.

7

Masses of black silk hair tumbled over slim shoulders. Sable brows arched and veiled by thick lashes, warm brandy eyes pleaded from a lovely face, the wide mouth invited even as she gasped, and child's hands clutched the satin cushions.

"A 'blody toddler", breathed O'Brien, recoiling. The stocking hat fell onto the thick grey carpet.

Tugging the zipper on his jacket, unaware the machine pistol showed in its long flat holster, he silently swore; she tricked him for almost two hours.

He frisked her fawn anorak, long white sweater and worn blue jeans for weapons while she stared meekly, shocked, a cornered animal. Finally, from beneath her long lashes, the dark eyes flashed in tearful protest.

"Please don't hurt me more, sir," she whispered.

"So you speak English my bloody girl." O'Brien felt cold sweat forming on his forehead: she could have driven a knife through his ribcage.

He moved his right hand away from the machine pistol, watching her closely, still furious with himself. This girl was either very clever or thoroughly trained, but no political infant. Whatever her motives, his Irish temper, smouldering from the street fight, growled into her dazed face, "I ought to thrash you."

She fought tears. "Sir, let me go, please."

"Then why allow me to cart you over my shoulder and drive half way round this city tonight?"

"I *must* go home, please, help me stand." Her eyes suddenly grew confused, her cheeks pale.

He leaned down, firmly took small cold hands, amazed by her lightness yet strength, made her bend slightly to stop the faint before propping the girl upright with another fat cushion, silent on the wide sofa, her anorak and sweater like a tent falling over slender thighs. O'Brien, decided they *both* needed some strong drink.

"Let's start with your name," he instructed, reaching into a tall glass case, taking down a crystal decanter of amber whisky and two tumblers, heading into the kitchen for ice. Still no answer. He considered diluting her drink with Soksu fizzy water then decided neat single malt would loosen her tongue much faster.

He returned with two full glasses and gave the girl time to sip gingerly. She coughed and sagged towards the fawn carpet. For a moment, he feared that she would vomit. O'Brien gazed down at her luxurious hair, amazed by the drained face with trembling lips, enchanting, despite choking from his best scotch. Who ordered this beautiful waif dragged from the Catholic Cathedral? Why this girl snatched by a North Korean terror squad.

"Drink it slowly," groaned O'Brien, watching twenty year old whisky treated as suspected poison.

"Who are you?" she asked in a voice so quiet that he lent forward.

O'Brien sat on a chair-arm between the girl and the doors leading into his kitchen and hall. He suspected they saved her from a severe beating. "Where did they hit you?" he began gently, hoping to steady her shaken nerves.

"Kicked .... my stomach." She was still near tears.

"Bad?"

She hesitated then mumbled, "Sore."

"Low or high?"

She lightly rested a hand over her lower crotch and in a weak voice, explained, "I think they wanted me winded.... so I couldn't run off."

He scolded kindly, "You *were* dressed as a boy."

A rueful frown passed over her ivory face then the liquid eyes caught him off guard and for a moment he became their prisoner. "Why were you taking photographs?"

He decided to sound merely puzzled. "I wanted the flash to dazzle them both."

He watched her desperately trying to make sense of the situation, groping for reasons, some advantage. She was tough: truth might not come easily, he must listen for those little inconsistencies which reveal each layer of falsehood. He suspected the girl was playing the same game.

She croaked from bewilderment, "Are you American?"

O'Brien nodded. "Could you identify that pair?"

She tensed.

"We can leave them for the National Police."

Tears began rolling down her cheeks. She begged, "Not the Police."

O'Brien leaned back, absently gripping the chair-arm, watching the girl grow desperate, about to start talking.

"How can I trust you?" Her face was in turmoil.

"Try your name."

She rested her elbows on the dusty knees of her jeans : she must have fought hard : then buried her face in nervous hands. "You won't understand," she forecast miserably.

"Why you?"

She pulled a handkerchief from the pocket of her anorak, clumsily wiped her nose and brittle eyes, glanced at him hopefully. "They're not students.... not from our action group."

He pretended ignorance. "Sorry, my girl, whatever is an action group?"

"Similar to the pair you were photographing," she returned with sudden boldness.

"Less violent.... I hope," evaded O'Brien nearly caught off guard.

Recovery, he was learning, with this girl, took place at breathtaking pace. Though tears lingered, fear had fled those worried eyes and confidence returned, there was a hint of honey on her cheeks. And that was the inconsistency which nagged: she seemed too ardent for the greenest recruit in a carefully directed and communist student group. He began to conclude that she might actually believe most people spoke as they thought. A foolish move or thoughtless word would drive this timid bird scurrying back into her fragile shell.

"What's your group?" he asked mildly though alert for her next smokescreen.

"Women struggling for peaceful democracy." She risked a slight though defensive smile, "I suppose you think we're naive."

"Nonsense," soothed O'Brien, sipping his drink, appalled at how increasingly foolish young people seemed each year, depressed by a relentless warning of middle-age. He saw from the girl's wounded expression that she was not convinced.

There was an obvious flaw. "How does a girl from a group which supports peaceful action.... find herself dragged from a rioting mob by two thugs?"

A rich wave of hair fell over her brow, she pushed it back, sat despondently, explained in a quiet voice. "Those two came to our meetings at Ewha Women's University. They claimed to be from Yonsei University which is very active. We were flattered... and stupid. Most militant students only believe in petrol bombs for television cameras."

"They're probably right," muttered O'Brien, "but carry on, child."

"I wish you would stop calling me a child."

He ignored this further symptom, youth's obsession with themselves, horror that few cared, least of all burnt and torn adults. He persisted, "Why were you there tonight?"

She volunteered a helpless shrug. "We wanted to show that girls were equal to men."

"By throwing molotov cocktails at riot police."

No response. She hovered on a cliff edge. O'Brien knew he must slowly draw her into a subtle cage. She hid something important behind this naive facade, possibly the identities of her captors, but he began to suspect that her own identity was the one she dared not reveal.

"I feel foolish." She glanced towards the curtained windows. "And I'm frightened. Taken prisoner twice, now by a man with no name, yet a badly hidden gun." She stared at him in furtive reproach.

O'Brien quickly apologised. "No harm intended."

The girl wavered. She looked down and the lustrous hair framed her nervous face yet she said softly, "I am Diana Park."

He was through the last barrier in her struggling mind. He could open fresh cracks, probe for truth, strip away her camouflage, until her story gave no more defence than the woolly hat which lay forgotten on the thick carpet. Plaintive sceptical eyes gave the first warning that the price was protection. O'Brien placed his glass on the carpet by her discarded hat, loosened his ski jacket, snapped open the quick release hooks, slid off his shoulder holster and threw the heavy gun onto the sofa beside her: she flinched but he ignored this, lowered himself onto the carpet, rested his back on the chair and stretched out his legs with a tired sigh. "We have all night if you want, Diana."

She released a long breath. Without raising her chin, hesitantly, she began talking. "They weren't expected at the rally... tonight... we're trying to free Cha Se Dong from house arrest.... when I saw them both, well, I followed. Then the tear-gas started, one spotted me, next moment they were dragging me from our group inside the cathedral yard... " her voice trailed off.

O'Brien calculated that he could relax a little and folded his arms loosely across his chest. "Why you?"

She leaned forward, suddenly alarmed, her face questioning. "Are you Catholic?"

"With my name!"

Her brow clouded so swiftly that he feared she would reveal nothing more. Little purpose was served by hiding a simple fact now probably recorded on files in Moscow and Peking, when, for the girl, this question appeared significant. Bemused, revealing a glimpse of Irish charm, O'Brien confessed, "I should be really... born in Kerry.... but my father married a protestant English girl! I'm a little of both." He wondered what was coming next.

"They wanted to kill the Cardinal." The girl stared, defiant, challenging him to prove her mistaken. "I heard them."

"You're sure?"

The Cardinal was revered, by Catholics, protestants, Buddhists : only Doctor Moon consistently spoke out with the same simple clarity through which ordinary people recognised their own emotions : whether he condemned student riots or their brutal suppression, Cardinal Min championed freedom of the mind, tolerance of the human spirit. Chung had many reasons for wanting the powerful priest silenced. But proxy-murder? O'Brien dismissed the very suggestion.... not on Chung's orders, at least, not direct. The communists' motives were more subtle. Utter chaos would sweep South Korea if the masses most beloved hero was savagely cut down. And, in the popular mind, only one man could be so ruthless : Chung.

He studied the girl with new curiosity. Perhaps she had stumbled onto a murder plot, innocently saved Cardinal Min from assassination.... brought herself within minutes of violent death. Yet that did not explain Min's absence from Myong Dong on a trip abroad. Nor the girl's presence. Not at all convinced, he obeyed the ground rules of his trade, further insisting, "What did you hear ... that made you so scared?"

She avoided his level eyes and twisted her small fingers, glancing at her cheap trainers, before lifting an accusing face and startling emotion thickened her soft voice. "Would you care?"

"Diana, I can't help... unless I know *exactly* what you heard tonight." There was resistance. "What is your name?"

"Mike O'Brien." He tried to disarm her swiftly with his cover operation.

"I sell airships."

For the first time her eyes shone with hope and complete disbelief when she blurted, "You're crazy!"

"Irish," he solemnly replied.

"Mr. O'Bean...."

"O'Brien," he winced.

Yet her drained face told that the barriers had slid apart in that exhausted mind. She did believe him, at least a little, perhaps enough to trust this mad foreigner who was probably more sane than most of her recent companions and certainly less violent.

She declared with a helpless sigh, "Maybe I'm foolish... I believe people's faces tell their lives."

"Saints preserve mine," he reached for his whisky glass. "I've more lines than a Buddha carved onto a mountainside."

"Yes.... and that makes me feel rather safe," she replied with devastating candour.

Lost for words he watched the girl cautiously relax. A heavy burden seemed to fly from her slight determined shoulders, leaving behind on the sofa a new person, and, for an instant, he caught a tantalising glimpse of a free spirit whose dreams were not concerned with rioting students and corrupt generals.

8

A car echoed up the narrow street. Its sounds faded. His attention returned to the girl, who sat watchful, no longer afraid, though shy and pale.

"When did you eat last?" he asked.

"Lunchtime.. ramyon, noodle soup."

"Do you eat bread and cheese?"

She looked doubtful, but her mouth softened.

He rose and went into the large kitchen, dubious that she knew how to fire an automatic weapon. "I'm listening," he called, opening the refrigerator, pulling out a precious lump of mature stilton, before he gambled, "You studied abroad..... but not stateside'."

"Cambridge... I read your social history during the eighteenth century."

Which explains your British accent," remarked O'Brien, closing the huge white door before commencing to saw fat slices off a rye loaf. He placed the butter dish on a tray as strong aroma filled the tidy kitchen. There was slight sound at his side and he glanced round. She must have silently crossed the room. Now she stood at the door, hovering, expectant, making no secret that she was extremely hungry although wary of the cheese lump.

"Then you probably drink wine?" he enquired not certain of her answer.

"Sometimes." A first coy smile gave away nothing.

A bottle of claret stood open on the kitchen table. He removed the cork and sniffed while the girl watched intently.

He explained, "It's from a good year and a night breathing sometimes makes for a smoother drink!" He turned and smiled down at her, amazed, for her head barely reached his shoulders. "If you look under the glass doors in that sideboard, Diana, you'll find plates, glasses and cutlery."

She went so humbly that he almost felt remorse when she knelt down and opened the teak doors, finding plates and glasses, before pulling open a drawer of jingling silver, plastering fingerprints on all she touched without restraint.

"We can eat on that small round table by the sofa," he proposed and carried on sawing bread, observed her take out the plates and silver then return to the sideboard, kneel and persist with her search until she found a neat stack of linen napkins. She leaned round, resting a hand on the carpet, "May I?"

"Please." He was intrigued. She responded instantly to western surroundings as though switching to another language. She also seemed in no particular hurry to leave newly discovered safety.

"Are you living with your parents?"

The thick hair spilled down her back when she straightened and replied, "My cousin... she's more like an aunt... I stay with her, across the river, near New Giant Department Store."

He recalled the suburb, tidy rows of huge apartment blocks within vast walled compounds, affordable havens for the new middle class. She would be safe in there but he speculated that the girl still must suffer culture shock.

He asked wryly, "How do you find Seoul ... after sleepy Cambridge?"

She ignored his question but her cheeks turned soft peach.

O'Brien raised his eyebrows, granted himself a wicked smile, then strolled across the living room carrying the food and drink which he placed carefully on the low table. She began setting out their places. Rewarding her with an approving nod, he slipped off his ski jacket, picked up the large gun, laid both on a bed in the neighbouring room. The girl seemed a little nervous, despite her growing faith. Sensing her alarm, he offered, "Why not take off that rioter's coat?"

She shed it without a murmur and revealed that the huge white sweater and worn jeans hid boyish hips and shapely legs. He took the jacket to the next door room and returned to find her kneeling once more, placing the food and wine on the low table. "Won't your aunt worry... indeed your parents?"

"My aunt won't... not yet... nor my parents," she insisted, as though wanting his opinion. "They don't live in Seoul. We are from the south west. Many families that we trust have suffered much during the last years."

He poured two glasses of crimson wine and passed the least full to the suddenly worried girl. "It's not lethal."

She raised it to her lips, cautiously sniffed, but after a taste, she relaxed and went on talking. "Papa has a silk factory with several hundred workers. It's the biggest company in our small town. Have you heard about the Kwangju uprising eight years past? We're further South."

When Chung declared martial law and made himself KCIA chief as a prelude to sacking the whole Government and snatching power, the southern city resisted.

O'Brien pulled an armchair towards the cluttered table and sat down, slipping off his shoes, brushing his fingers over a sensitive electronic pad under the table rim which started a tape recorder. "I am told that a thousand people were killed."

She became melancholy. "Chung sent his Special Forces at first. After two days of bullying and beating and bayonet stabbings, our citizens threw out Chung's black berets. Kwangju was sealed from the outside world for ten days while Chung sent south a whole division of twenty thousand men. Some of the students were armed by this time... they broke into the civil defence stores."

O'Brien knew: Chung decided to make an example of the rebellious provincial capital. His troops drove armoured vehicles into the city and turned automatic cannon fire onto a student mob defending the Province Office behind a barricade of smashed buses and burnt taxis.

"I've seen videos."

"I can't watch."

"You saw that?"

"Mama sent me into the city that Sunday with our driver. We had telephoned David, who told that all was calm and the soldiers withdrawing. My brother was always too clever *and* too hopeful."

"Your brother... "

"Leading the students."

Now he understood. She was a live witness to the massacre which Chung and his powerful circle preferred forgotten. Her brother stood openly against the military coup. Small wonder she was still frightened. "Didn't your mother risk your life!"

"Not that Sunday," she defended sadly, "Mama had no reason for fear. Our Bishop spoke to the army general.... within hours, we sincerely believed, the soldiers would go away. Mama wanted David home by noon. She thought he would listen to little sister." The girl slowly revolved her glass with both hands. "I could make him do almost anything. We were close."

"An old Korean family."

She lowered her eyes and huskily retorted, "By tradition Korean women govern more than foreigners understand."

"Your Brother refused."

"I never found him. David was gone ... too clever ... I was constantly watched."

O'Brien felt his right leg ache and flexed his foot several times on the thick carpet until the circulation returned.

She frowned. "That foot hurts."

His mind saw again neat hedgerows winding into a wet Irish dusk, lived that animal instinct which made him slam the brakes, before the car windscreen exploded in his face while something numbed his lower legs. Two shadowy figures in combat gear sprinting towards a muddy Landrover; snatching his Uzi from the dash as his car rolled, blasting a long burst over the cart-wheeling bonnet. Both gunmen fell. A second and third burst finding the landrover's tank. White flame scorching through the hedge as his own car, engine surging, ploughed leftwards into a wide ditch. Then his chase car pulled alongside and his bodyguards peered through the open windscreen as a third trooper wearing a business suit fired brisk bursts into the bodies and burning wreck. He recalled concluding this was the *last* way to complete a tour of your most exposed squadron on secret duties in Northern Ireland. O'Brien smiled within himself. Those cheerful words floated through his brain as he remembered when Staff Sergeant Rose: Abdul to his friends: shot him full of morphine, grinning that only the IRA could wipe themselves out trying to kill an Irishman.

"Why do you smile?"

He had forgotten Diana, sitting there, patiently starving. He invited her to start at once: it was pointless explaining. "I was thinking of a joke... long time ago."

Swiftly, the girl piled her plate with cheese and bread slices thick with salty butter. O'Brien took some himself before following his original thread. He was careful. Although her manner implied otherwise, the story seemed familiar, and perhaps her brother died during the street battles. "What happened after you lost your brother?"

"I didn't lose him," she countered hotly, "there was no means of reaching David."

O'Brien knew that a hard core of armed students fortified the South Cholla Government headquarters for a last defiant stand. Most were killed. "Inside the Province Office?"

"Yes... when the shooting started my driver forced me into the car, drove through back alleys, then over the big mountain. We were blessed with divine protection. They shot girls my own age... some were friends.... when they walked from the hospital after giving blood. At three that night the soldiers returned to the city streets. Small tanks opened fire on the province building. We thought everybody inside was killed." She took a deep breath. "We couldn't enter the city for several days. Helicopters shot at anybody trying to cross the town river. One night our city police chief called on my father."

"Your brother was still alive."

"Father *didn't* know." She seemed to picture the scene. "The police chief was a relation, also a broken man. A thug from Chung's security committee came with him...... who told my father to bring in his son or the silk factory would burn down." Revenge smouldered in her sad eyes as she confronted ugly memories. "We endured a horrible fortnight. Somehow the students sent word to my brother at a mountain village where he was hiding. Early one morning, David stood at our door, tired, drawn, proud. He told father they must go to the military police compound on the city outskirts. We never heard from him for five months."

"Was he tortured?"

This time she flared. "David swears the girls were treated worst.... electric shocks on their breasts and genitals or nearly drowned, chained near-naked in a filthy cellar, while they forced fake confessions about Cha Se Dong."

He listened further, let disgust hide resignation. Nothing she described came as a surprise about the law enforcement skills of the Chung Republic. What impressed him deeply was the layered penetration by the Moon clan of national security and the ruling party for 'Freedom with Justice'. No government secret was safe from the old publisher : before setting off for Korea the previous summer, on a rainy afternoon in London, Mason tossed across his vast desk, translation after translation of interrogation reports. Beating fingers with wooden rods was merely one of many proven means for purifying the female body and mind. Mason had recounted how after Kwangju the military leadership desperately tried to smear their most feared critic with the blame for all the violence, claiming that Cha Se Dong, a native of the most southern province, secretly orchestrated the street protests from his Seoul prison. With a little 'information', western television crews soon ridiculed this malicious nonsense: bus and taxi drivers witnessed a week of rising brutality on their own city streets and for twenty-four hours they blocked the central roads, several days before the first shootings. Where was her brother now, brooded

O'Brien, convinced that Moon's private library held a fat dossier on David Park, likely thicker than its twin at National Security Headquarters.

He tackled the girl more gently. "I hope your brother was cured of political ambition?"

"Working with father," she replied without much conviction and placed more cheese on a bread slice.

"Where?"

O'Brien served himself a fat sandwich.

"Chinju Man on Tal Sum; we're a big island, almost the southern tip of Korea. Our silk factory is just north of the town. We live further along the coast facing towards the mainland."

Silently, O'Brien translated the Korean names, she brought back his Irish childhood with those alone; Pearl Bay on Moon Island. He bit into the bread and cheese, washed it down with velvet wine. She seemed oddly protective towards the brother and he suspected silk was not David Park's only business.

"Are there other children?" he enquired casually.

"Two more girls."

"Also spinning silk?"

"Not exactly," she reproached with shy humour. "My sisters are still at high school!"

They heard a motor idling, the gates swing open. A car roared into the courtyard and the wooden gates slammed closed. Footsteps sounded on the garden path. Startled, she sat rigid, bewildered eyes imploring protection.

Disturbed by fear's easy mastery over the girl, he leaned round and smiled conspiracy, faced the open hall doorway. He called out, "Is that you Jae Pil?"

A key turned and Kang let himself inside the house then locked the front door. "Sorry I was so long time", returned his cheerful voice, "but I learnt a few secrets tonight."

O'Brien winked at the scared girl as he invited, "Meet our surprise guest."

Kang towered in the doorway, his shoulders almost blocking its entire width. At first he delivered a bothered stare before his face switched on a smile which could have melted a safe door. Kang, highly amused, let his gaze shift from the woolly hat abandoned on the carpet to the speechless elf frozen onto the large sofa. Recovering, he bowed a fraction, greeted her with a Korean pleasantry.

The girl thawed enough to bow her head and murmer her name. O'Brien intervened: "Allow me to introduce Miss Park.... who has been teaching me quite a lot about the south west and Chung's Government." He paused to make certain Kang understood his warning signal. "And also about tonight. She overheard them plotting a murder."

Kang pulled a magnificent shocked expression.

O'Brien glared: stop flirting with melodrama, he wanted the girl to feel safe, not mocked: even the modern Kang was a conservative Korean male when dealing with Korean women. The girl once more was entwining her fingers. "Trust us Diana... you nearly died."

She struggled within herself. "I want to... really I do.... I'm so frightened."

"We can protect you, Diana, *once* we know their names."

He needed a short cut which would convince her this was no empty promise, no hidden threat, merely a straight forward offer to end daily terror.

"Look," he suggested, glancing at Kang who at once stood looser. "When we rescued you tonight.... can you remember anything at all following that big flash?"

She sighed helpless.

Kang sprang clean over the table, launched a whirling kick at the chandelier, missed the dangling glass droplets by a wind breath, before landing smoothly, ready like a panther for his next attack. O'Brien shook his head: God knew what a replacement chandelier cost, but open lips proved the girl's awed conversion.

He reached over and took her cool hands. "Tell J P everything you can remember about them with the exact times and places. We will do the rest; Diana, you can stop worrying over Chung *and* the Communists." He released her hands and asked Kang, "Have you eaten?"

"Plenty," the young Korean smiled.

"I don't know how you can leap around with a quart of noodles splashing round your stomach." O'Brien rose and brought Kang a glass of fresh orange juice, reflecting that the mixture would make a normal person sick. Kang lowered himself into an armchair.

"I'll listen," said O'Brien, wanting to concentrate on her words without the distraction of designing each new question.

Kang took over, his charm masterly. Removing his leather jacket gave an opening air of calm relaxation, leaving no doubt in the girl's mind that Kang was more than a simple interpreter, his duties free ranging, dangerous and probably illegal.

She stared at both men with a mixture of respect and alarm. "I'll do my best," she promised. Out came a torrent of Korean, which Kang sometimes interrupted, keeping O'Brien fully alongside, while the details poured from her lips. She had joined the movement after high school during her first weeks at university. She never dared tell her parents who suffered troubles enough with their only son. She opposed violence. Otherwise, she and her friends, tried to avoid politics. At first their meetings were simply excuses for dreaming, chattering around a coffee house table, sometimes meeting boys. After their first year the group became larger, met on campus about once a week, though an inner circle of founder members still made their way to coffee houses. She recalled that towards the last months of her university studies, when most of the original members were concentrating on their final examinations, somehow, at the coffee house, two young men often sat nearby; she never discovered who gave the original invitation.

O'Brien stopped her excited flow. "Did they talk with you, Diana?"

"They asked us......"

"No," he repeated the question, "I meant to you alone."

Her brow showed faint furrows. "Never about politics." She paused until his meaning was clear and her forehead became smoother than a babe's. "Yes... only our families... where we lived, who we were and our parents wealth, but once Kwon.... he seemed leader..... asked whether I needed help with money."

"We're getting warm." He glanced from the girl's troubled face to Kang's vague smile.

"Did you suffer any problems?" asked Kang. Poverty was normal for Korean students.

"No... and I never told him a thing about my family," she insisted, anticipating their drift.

Kang paused for a drink from his orange glass and returned it to the table with an approving flourish. He placed his clasped hands round the glass. "The other is named Nam Jong Woo."

Her pretty mouth fell open. She stared at her questioners with growing wonder. When her curiosity returned, her voice quavered as the strain departed. She protested gratefully. "Then why ask all these questions?"

"Because," replied Kang with a used-car-dealer's smile, "his real name is Han Che Song."

O'Brien sympathised as her eyes opened wider and her thick brows arched higher. Poor girl, he thought, suffering so many shocks in a single evening. But she lived.

"Why the Cardinal?" asked Kang in case she had forgotten.

O'Brien raised his hands in the mode of prayer, held them before his mouth, waited for her answer.

"I am not sure why," she said respectfully, "but they were definite. Kwon and Han.... stood in a corner of the cathedral courtyard. Kwon asked which door Cardinal Min used mostly."

"Was the Cardinal there tonight?" tested O'Brien.

"No... and they knew... we all knew. The demonstration was held tonight for that reason." She was still shaken for her hands trembled.

"Don't worry," smiled O'Brien, regretting the fresh fear they were causing, though determined to extract this last nugget. "Tell us their exact words."

She twisted her hair in her lap while remembering. "Kwon paced the distance from the cathedral door to a shop beyond the courtyard gates. He looked pleased. Called it a clear pistol shot over eighty meters?" Her eyes shone from angry frustration, "Han urged that they watch the riot from the shop doorway.... to see if they could fire over the crowd at Easter. And then I gasped... because that's when the Cardinal blesses a crowd... which could turn into a bloody riot."

Kang suggested smoothly, "You were close."

She missed, or ignored the hidden question, and nodded. "Too near. Han spun round. I tried to run away. They were fast."

O'Brien leaned back in his armchair. She was in danger but those two would not risk more exposure, not tonight, not for several weeks. An attack on the Cardinal was probably an extinct option. Three people knew. They would assume that National Security would alert the highly experienced police close protection division. Should he tell General Kim? Perhaps. Kang was pulling faces and obviously knew something more which he would not discuss in front of this young girl. Was she a gift, a potential source of hard news about the student movements, an innocent who had dropped into their laps and wanted twenty four hours protection, or a beautiful poisonous snake.

9

Once Kang's taxi with the girl nervously chatting had safely rolled down the narrow lane, O'Brien closed the steel gates. Few stars managed to burn through a frozen fog overhead, he hurried back into the warm house.

First he removed the tape and slipped it into a trouser pocket. Next he took the girl's plate upstairs and into the dark study where he closed the curtains and switched on his reading lamp. From a drawer in the writing desk he removed a small jar of white powder. Carefully, he dusted the plate, until her finger prints showed.

Across the study, near the full-length curtains, a small room served as a wardrobe. Along a shelf, from among large boxes, he lifted down a leather briefcase, opened it with care. Removing tissue paper and padding material, he checked a personal computer.

Back at his desk, he opened its tough plastic lid, switched on the display screen, and watched until a tiny red light blinked on the keyboard. Soon the red pinprick faded. An accessory resembling a torch fitted into a bracket on the left side.

He moved the plate until the powdered fingerprints were directly beneath the torch lens, a microscopic video camera, and began typing. The screen flickered.

A series of grey smudges spread outwards, widening fuzzy lines. He started tuning with three control knobs set beneath the display screen. After making several fine improvements, the screen suddenly cleared, leaving sharp grey and white lines like contours on a map; the girl's thumbprint magnified over two hundred times.

O'Brien studied where the circling lines branched, occasionally pressing a button to employ the zoom lens. He typed an instruction and the screen split into four; three blank squares, one with the thumb print image now shown smaller in the top right square. Further typing ordered a systematic search. O'Brien rubbed his eyes, waited.

An optical disc sifted through a two-gigabyte memory that held four hundred thousand fingerprints. Thirty seconds later three more images filled the vacant squares. He pushed another button for the graphics mode. Yet no zones of similarity were marked with tiny yellow rings. The candidate prints did not match any North Koreans living in Japan, whose prints were on the soft disc, pirated from the Tokyo Police Headquarters where one official was ready to share secrets with the barbarians in exchange for a bank account in Lichtenstien.

London had constructed a vast library of espionage and terror which could be carried on three and a half inch plastic discs. Another small disc brought new candidates onto the vacant square for browsing. O'Brien typed instructions which automatically would generate match reports. He waited a few minutes: three squares remained blank. He repeated the search request, suprised, and waited, but only for the same result.

O'Brien switched discs. The next stored prints of South Koreans known by their Government as student dissidents linked with North Korea. Only the FBI held a larger library of its fellow citizens' finger prints; even the KGB owned a smaller collection. Japan began the creeping advance of this policeman's ideal society, nearly eighty years back, distrustful of her unruly colony.

Over forty million finger prints were stored in the Korean National Police archives, none filed electronically. But, privately, Moon collected thousands over several years through a student medical insurance scheme in a land where, before, none existed, passing the applications weekly to Mason's paperkeepers in a Pall Mall garrett. The medical insurance scheme was highly successful among the worried cash hungry parents of South Korea. Membership became universal.

Bright grey flickering commenced in the top left hand square. He watched, fascinated, while a fingerprint gradually emerged, focussed: a latent hit. Now he wanted a confirmed name, he tapped in a request for full data on the candidate. Almost at once yellow capitals ran across the lower screen with the personal dates and detail of a young man aged thirty-three. One of his four aliases was David Park.

"Then we're not dealing with a liar but somebody who, in the land of face might be refreshingly open." And he told himself, hope rising, that the girl was hidden gold, a reliable source, providing she consented to recruitment.

He read the lines of glowing yellow print. Every life profile detail matched. Variations were subtle. To the entry "Has candidate ever been found guilty in a Court?" was an observation, "Not a Law Court". O'Brien smiled at these cool perceptive words. Tonight he would call Hong Kong and file the data into their main image retrieval store for the Far East theatre. He hoped the evening's photographs were clear enough results for entering in the memory bank. He had earned a second glass of red wine before heading for the dark room.

Walking through the kitchen, he collected the bottle and filled his glass, before descending into a cellar which spread below the complete ground floor. Along its main passage were several doors, one blocked the far end. His thumb touched the sensor pad, opened this door, switched on a low red lamp before snapping open his wrist camera and removing its tiny disc film. He heard a voice and stood silent.

"Back," shouted Kang from the kitchen staircase.

O'Brien relaxed "Bring the tape-recorder, J P; you can listen to the girl while we talk."

Down in the cellar room they worked under crimson light, listening to the earlier conversations. Within minutes Kang passed him the first set of coloured negatives.

"What do you make of our girl?" He examined the brown and red celluloid and passed them back for Kang to decide which would blow up into large prints.

Kang grunted over his shoulder as he worked, "David Park must be her brother."

"Finger prints match."

"Famous.... around Kwangju.... hated at the Blue House."

"They worked him over enough to cool any political ambitions."

Kang handed him the first print. "David Park took out a wise insurance policy: an interview on CBS News during which he described the torturing of girls at that military compound."

"Suprised he's alive." O'Brien studied the sharp picture. Kang was becoming professional.

"They've tried to kill Park a couple of times. Both bungled."

"Jackpot," mouthed O'Brien.

"Good pictures?" enquired Kang.

"My jungle instincts are still sharp."

"You've seen *both* before... on Sejong in the rain."

"Where does that leave our lady friend?" O'Brien reached across and switched off the tape recorder.

Kang reasoned cheerfully, "We check her out, Mike, but she really was scared tonight."

"I only hope she was scared of these two characters, rather than *exposure* by you and me!" He perused the next print.

He pictured rain sweeping over jammed cars, a pair of young Koreans slipping among the standing traffic, recalled that sudden tautness which made him reach for the machine pistol. Was their dash before the grenade attack a risky pass for flushing out himself, filing his face, until a more favourable moment came for killing, then clean escape? Terror was no job for heroes; victory went to the swift and silent. Was there already a leak at that time? After a shooting and the street fight in Myong Dong, twice thwarting this busy pair, their controller would be searching for a tidy ambush, determined that nobody would block his next operation. Stealing the girl was insult piled onto injury. He stopped speculating. Build from facts, identify the bastards.

"I've blown up six good shots," announced Kang, pushing open the dark room door.

They hurried upstairs to the computer. "This is the best," Kang passed a sharp photograph of the taller Han.

"Let's enter some details from the girl's memory banks!" O'Brien sat before the screen and began typing in the two alias names, height, weight, turning to Kang each time for his opinion. "What have we missed, J P?" he wondered, finally stretching and easing his stiff back.

Kang lit a cigarette and watched its smoke float. "Specialise in women? They were pretty regular supporters of a women's group."

"We'll have to make that digestable for a floppy disc," replied O'Brien thoughtfully and typed, "Weakness for younger girl students."

"Shouldn't we put in training with heavy weapons!"

O'Brien smiled. "I'm not assuming it's sex driven..... rather more general, J P, but here goes."

He placed the photograph under the video torch, switched the discs, then accessed a programme which sifted through a hundred thousand colour photographs of Japanese and Korean dissidents known to have attended political meetings held by student groups that sympathised with North Korea.

"This will take a while," he said and drank more wine, then rummaged in the desk for a pack of cigars. Soon the room filled with grey fug. The computer screen blanked then returned with six squares. Every few minutes a face would fill in each square and they would peer at the screen hoping to spot familiar features.

None matched. They repeated the process with the second candidate. Still no success. "We're doing something wrong," decided O'Brien.

"That kit is incredible," said Kang, disappointed.

"No better than the data which humans file on these tiny discs." He drew on his cigar and blew smoke across the room, when the obvious registered.

"Where are your archives?"

"In the cellar. On my way".

No wonder they were struggling. Months of work were on the little disc but not all Kang's superb recent material.

Throughout the night he and Kang toiled in cigar smoke and whisky fumes. They pulled out every file Kang kept in the house strongroom, scanning for the faces photographed that night in the streets of Myong Dong. By four o'clock the study stank of alcohol and stale smoke as he drank while Kang smoked. Cigarette ends piled in the ashtray like a small rubbish tip until O'Brien began to question the very purpose for this night turmoil. Find answers, destroy all threats. Easy to say in Hong Kong or London, impossible orders for a man groping inside Seoul. Both faces almost matched three sets of pictures. The first candidates were activists in favour of Cha Se Dong, the brightest opposition star now held under house arrest in a Seoul suburb, directing a student campaign for his own freedom. A second pair were agents of North Korea, working within the student movement, attacking the American presence and secretly fighting against democratic government in the turbulant south. The third deck of photographs were two of General Kim's younger South Korean agents on the bleak Seoul streets; more a service industry than patriotic chore, but that didn't make sense. They were stalled.

Or were they? O'Brien pushed aside the portraits, except the pair of South Koreans.

"Nearly there?" Kang smiled with endless patience.

"Gut feeling." He drank more scotch. Rough skin reminded that he had not shaved since the previous day. "If they *are* North Koreans then we had better find *their* prime target."

He did not need to spell out the probable secondary targets. They're after

Cha Se Dong, thought O'Brien. Nobody else matched the opposition leader in popularity. The man once escaped assassination in Jakarta only to meet arrest on return. Now he enjoyed comparative safety locked in his own home. That could vanish if he regained freedom.

"Think about it." O'Brien yawned, "Cha is the reigning Olympic Games fan among all the opposition candidates. He is the only one with any real knowledge of what's involved, internationally known and respected, revered at home, the single alternative national president. Shoot him..... and you have revolution on the streets." Despondent light spread through the curtains and advanced over the lounge carpet.

"We don't want to blunder into one of General Kim's penetration jobs," said Kang, "Hong Kong have every record from all our sources."

O'Brien hated asking Hong Kong for help with his own operational tasks. "Let's run them through our flash records one last time."

Positive identity would take the Hong Kong experts a whole day. They were down to six portraits. There was a core of around five-hundred Trotskyist students in the Seoul universities and most campus agitation started from their brain work. But thousands of other students had been involved over the last ten years. His mind kept returning to that narrow gas choked street. Petrol bombs were an expression of impatience with military culture. Nobody told the little crowd to applaud nor somebody else to sing with all the emotion which these earthy people could switch on without warning.

He went down to the kitchen and made a pot of coffee. Summer would be long, hot and dangerous. No wonder Kim was so keen on their clever airship.

He found Kang sitting cross legged on the study carpet, thumbing through a folder of photographs. Each picture was accompanied by a page with personal details. All were known North Korean sympathisers, suspected agents, dissident leaders, that Kang, personally, snapped over the last months. Some were on the fringes, others deeply involved, trained and indoctrinated. A rare few operated through the Japanese Red Army, but, O'Brien reflected, nowadays that was a gang of aging delinquents. Younger communist agents were committed, lethal, and the women more deadly because they carried out orders with oriental female obedience.

"I've got one," said Kang cautiously.

"Show me." O'Brien took a sip of coffee, put the cup on his desk, kneeled where Kang placed two photographs side by side.

Not a shadow of doubt: one feature matched. A small scar on the youth's neck showed clearly in the photograph taken outside a restaurant in Sinsa Dong, a quarter where students gathered, sometimes running a street show of music and poetry at weekends. O'Brien felt confident. "Congratulations J.P., nobody could have done better. Nailed. The little thug has taken a facelift. See how his skin looks tight. Rare for them to forget a small detail. Sure, we'll send his photo to Hong Kong, but now we won't have to eat humble pie."

Kang offered a contented smile, slightly amazed that his own photograph was clear, accurate, better than pictures supplied from Langley. He read the caption. This subject uses the alias *Kim Che Song* and has been a North Korean sympathiser for at least ten years. Records suggest that he is heavily involved with all student demonstrations, suspected of blackmailing class leaders to bring their fellow students onto the campus or streets, known criminal record in Japan.

"Shoplifting," presumed O'Brien.

"Han!" replied Kang, amused by the warped logic, for student agitators were always broke.

"And our second man?"

"Not so far," apologised Kang.

"Don't worry, J P, we've found Han."

Now it was simply a matter of computer time. He placed the photograph under the video torch and began typing. After a few moments the top three squares filled out with two similar faces and their first candidate.

"Easy when you know how!" grimaced O'Brien, rising wearily, back sore.

The candidate was photographed several times, all taken over the last few months, for this gave the researchers in London and Hong Kong a more distinct feel for an individual identity. Kang took pictures of Han Che Song walking along a crowded street, drinking with students in a bar, talking urgently to a girl outside an apartment block during a winter afternoon, watching a student riot at Yonsei Campus gates.

Kang found pictures which showed students demonstrating then slid the set towards O'Brien. He pointed at a shy face almost hidden among the other students. "That's our second man."

O'Brien reached across for Kang's printed notes and began reading. Aged twenty-seven, student of economics at Seoul National University for the last eight years: avoiding military service: father a junior manager with one of the Chaibols, those vast conglomerates that ran Korea's economy. He glanced at the most recent photograph: there was a slight familiarity about the mild thin face with its tight mouth and lowered eye-lids. More surgery? He read on: presently employing the alias Kwon Jae Hong, but real name confirmed as Shin Ock Jin. A detailed history listed links with radical students while at high school, one of whom was Park otherwise Han Che Song, followed by recruitment to the Troskyst Group which led Shin into the active leadership. O'Brien sucked his teeth.

"Greedy little man," he exclaimed quietly and passed the papers back to Kang.

"Two salaries?"

"Recruited by a close personal aide of our good friend General Kim, that's my hunch. Since 1985, when National Security ran an offensive campaign against the student movement because they feared disruption of the Asian Games in September 1986. He's an expert..... try your next pictures. My guess is that Shin plans, directs that bomb at Kimpo eighteen months back when the Chinese Team arrived, yet keeps National Security up to speed throughout the entire operation."

Anger showed on Kang's normally calm face, "What a bastard."

"You mean what bastards," corrected O'Brien.

"Kim monitored the whole incident? But two cleaners were blown to bits." Kang sat appalled. "Where's their purpose?"

"If you were planning an attack on the Summer Olympics," O'Brien studied the next photograph as he talked, "who would you recruit to carry out your terror mission?"

"A cell with local knowledge who can blend into the masses".

"And can prove, if possible, a recent, similar success."

"Kim is clever..... but not mad."

"An Olympics is worth more than any regional Games. Korea is spending three-billion dollars to advertise a country. That was five-per-cent of GNP when Chung first bid for the Summer Games . . . a lot of money by any standard . . . but this country still has no system of pensions, social security, or public health for the mass population. I'm not suprised that many intellectual Koreans call it Chung's replay of 1936 and Hitler's pagan rite at Munich. Kim probably controlled the whole incident. Better lose two cleaners than China's Team. Remember; nobody was arrested afterwards, officially, the case was never solved." O'Brien finished his thought line. "All a calculated gamble.... and knowing Kim, who wisely works on the solid foundation that Shin has no loyalty to the Chung Government, Kim bought him, for cash, or threats. We ought to find out which and quickly."

Kang still leaned over the desk, he flicked through Shin's pictures, until he reached another recent photograph. He slid it towards the twin history of Han and studied the picture of both drinking in a student bar. Satisfaction spread across his concentrating face. "I know that bar," he ventured guardedly, "it's near Myong Dong Cathedral."

"Be careful," instructed O'Brien, "Han is now an extremely nervous person."

Kang smiled both obedience and dismissal. "May I give our airship a little media exposure?"

"Clever boy. Sometimes it pays handsomely to let people know you buy information with a hard currency. I'll give you a steer... place a story in the Buk A Ilbo monthly magazine.......... we may learn more than we bargained".

Kang slipped on his jacket. "Thousands of dollars involved in the airship's advertising contract, handled by a small company."

"Millions," instructed O'Brien and reached sideways, pulled open a desk drawer and took out a large envelope. His face relented with tired pride. "Didn't want your mind cluttered by early judgements. Be my guest."

Kang slid three photographs from the envelope, blow-ups of the same head and shoulders. "Where did you take these?" His broad face bent over the pictures as he searched and found familiar features. Kang's relief proved that an elementary mistake by O'Brien would have astonished him more than the three photographs. "Definitely a neck scar....Shin.... so where?"

O'Brien folded his arms and leaned back from the wide desk. "Tucked in a folder among piled newspapers."

"That's crazy!" frowned Kang.

"Not in our business," yawned O'Brien. "See what you can find out, J.P. there's a reason."

"You think Han is running Shin?"

"Worse."

"Kim won't admit that," said Kang with absolute conviction. "Just the rumour would bring most of Seoul's students into the central streets."

O'Brien looked at his watch. "Which is an excellent reason for making certain that he knows it might leak."

10

Kang replaced the telephone, lit a cigarette and breathed out smoke that floated through the open french windows into an early spring morning. Green buds sprouted on the small trees and in the next door garden, cream magnolias and snowy cherries blossomed under a flawless sky.

A gentle breeze moved the curtains. Kang swung round in his chair, waiting until O'Brien finished reading fax messages, spread over the low table. "That was Yoon".

O'Brien pushed aside a long message from Detfold. "I hope Yoon is near panic. Abdul sent these faxes for Kim's intercept staff."

"Kim is impatient?"

"He wants our airship for crowd suppression long before the Olympic Games".

O'Brien passed the fax messages. All tools and handling equipment, which included a mast-truck for tethering the airship, waited in a pair of containers at the company hangar on Detfold airfield. Their chief engineer, a zealot called Grubb, built airships for the company long before the secret fund became its major share-holder : an event which passed beyond Grubb whose mind prowled the endless sky or the soil that nursed his vegetables and fruit trees in East Sussex. Although signed 'Grubb', the author of these dire warnings was Rose.

Each fax reminded that a clock ticked remorselessly towards the summer games...deadlines for building, checking, test-flying, all approached at frightening speed. Rose sniped from ten-thousand miles away. A container ship carrying the airship envelope, its motors, the gondola and other kit, steadily crossed the Indian Ocean, while Kang was locked in a bitter struggle with Yoon over finding a hangar where the dirigible could be built . . . in time for training competent Korean pilots. Neither was hopeful. There were days when relentless mental skirmishing ground down Kang. This was such a moment.

"We're not winning," he despaired.

"Yes, we are, JP." O'Brien suffered few qualms about employing his talent for making something move fast at the last moment. "We can have that airship flying, but, frankly, Yoon can't conjure qualified pilots out of the police force in less than three months . . . . Abdul will patrol the Olympic Stadium."

"Then we only have a single pilot for the whole games."

"Rose eats half-trained enthusiasts," laughed O'Brien.

"Yoon has a pool of good pilots from the police helicopter wing."

"They won't be anywhere near competent. We can narrow our airborne suspects to one person."

"Yoon a terrorist!"

O'Brien did not repent. "I wouldn't trust Kim further than I can throw the Olympic Stadium with one hand. They'll have open season on the local population from five grand."

"Who flies shot-gun?" worried Kang.

"Yoon works for Kim. Neither can fly that airship let alone master its unique electronics package." O'Brien let his words settle in Kang's mind before reminding," Somebody from our company must fly with Yoon and somebody else must interpret to train the police camera operators . . . . that's you and Abdul."

Kang stared at the garden basking under spring sunshine while he contemplated this startling new duty. "I promised to call back."

"Tell Yoon we need that hangar built yesterday. No hangar, no airship, no full security at the Olympic Games. Who fends off the American media once they smell a hot story?"

"That's not the Korean way." Kang looked troubled.

O'Brien's face was sympathetic though firm. "It's not British . . . but we'll call a spade a shovel and start snapping at Olympic Centre."

O'Brien felt almost sorry for the Police pilot. Koreans surpassed the British habit of switching direction at the final second. Neither Korean Air nor the American Air Force possessed a structure large enough for building and floating the airship, anywhere in the country. A hangar must be built, fast, somewhere: Yoon had four weeks left before eighty packing cases full of bits landed at Pusan docks.

O'Brien flicked through the remaining fax messages, stopping abruptly when he read one from Hong Kong. *'Quality control testing your latest consignment. Might require a further three days. All parts returned this week.'* Good, he noted, a thorough check of those photographs.

"Anyhow," Kang remarked brightly, "Kim won't have our airship by Sunday morning. The opposition claim around a million people will head for the huge plaza on Yoido Island."

Concern showed briefly in O'Brien's thoughtful eyes when he faced Kang.

"My information is that Chung will block off every bridge, subway station, bus-stop, university gate with a hundred-thousand riot police and street security thugs."

He omitted mentioning that Todd, who commanded the American and Korean Armies, gave orders the previous afternoon that confined all American troops and families to their own bases on Sunday morning. Todd and his staff were convinced the morning could not pass without injury or death. Cha, locked in his suburban prison, Chung trapped in his Presidential Blue House, chose Sunday morning for the opening battle Seoul's Olympic summer.

"We must go early," insisted Kang, "before roads on to the island are sealed."

"Take a day off, J P.," O'Brien offered. "Nobody will tear-gas a long - nosed barbarian driving his own car. I'll masquerade as a reporter."

"Sam and I wish to be present," answered Kang with surprising stubbornness and O'Brien smiled defeat.

Privately he was glad that Kang and Song wanted to spend their Sunday morning dodging gas grenades, flirting with street fights. He gave no odds for the opposition leaders. Chung would crush them with numbers. Cha Se Dong already needed a magic carpet to pass from his small front garden into which, the previous day, Kim crowded more than a hundred policemen, themselves penned in by twice as many photographers and television crews. A ritual opening of the front door followed by some token shoving from the leader's aides would satisfy the world press. Yet instinct warned him that tomorrow was the last time the game would be played within these rules.

"Your country," he declared amiably," your right to witness still-born revolution."

"Sam enjoys overtime."

O'Brien could not resist, "Her Majesty won't pay that well." But he supposed that if Sam drove, they might just be mistaken for an American businessman touring Seoul's main entertainment.

* * * * * * *

Song drove fast. Small groups of riot police stood every few yards along deserted pavements. Across the gaunt span of Panpo Bridge, sparse traffic flowed, even for a Sunday morning. The Han River mourned winter and its steel surface reflected fresh sorrow as morning brought thick cloud. Within minutes Song turned right, sped onto the new Olympic Highway, racing for the golden tower that soared above Yoido Island. No families walked among the river gardens. For a day when one million people were rallying on a single vast square, a whole city was either in bed late, or hiding.

When they reached Yoido, large squads of riot police, olive combat suits and black helmets blending with dull office blocks and apartment buildings, clustered like insects along all routes onto the deserted island. And there were others. Solid men, huddled against the cool wind, wrapped in thick quilted anoraks, no expressions on brutal faces. The previous night, following Chung's orders, hundreds of buses lifted the party bully boys into the capital, a ruthless show of strength, threatening alike the friends and foes of social discipline and moral order.

O'Brien wore no gun: this morning arrest was very possible. He told Song to drive around. Near a subway station they watched a family emerge from an apartment building, three generations heading for an outing, a birthday party, judging by the little girls with black velvet dresses. White gas puffs exploded round them on the pavement. The grandfather grabbed the smallest children as his screaming flock rushed back into their drab block. The street, once more, looked empty.

"Time we stop," said O'Brien.

"Where though?" asked Song, voice terse, plainly wondering what else they needed to see; for Chung, whatever his short-comings, never made any secret of his highly efficient forces for political suppression.

"Near the Plaza."

"Go careful, Sam," urged Kang, leaning forward.

"Obsimnida," replied the driver. Song gave up a night fishing in the Imjin River for this escapade.

"Drop us here, Sam . . . . circle around . . . . .then come back in five minutes," instructed O'Brien.

Song refused. "I wait here."

"We're tough, Sam, don't worry." He eased himself from the car and followed Kang onto the huge parade plaza.

A small party of thugs watched from a distance, hostile stares trailed Kang across the vast windswept tarmac where on brighter days children hired cheap bicycles. Not a riot policeman stood within five-hundred yards. O'Brien glanced back. He could not see the car but Song was completely reliable. For a moment, he listened: no phuts of gas-grenades broke the heavy silence.

He stared over acres of tarmac at Goldstar's twin electronically heated glass towers, dwarfed by the golden windows on Building 63 climbing into a morose sky. A mile distant the green copula on the concrete National Assembly watched like a giant pill-box. Nothing moved. O'Brien turned, seeking Kang's reaction, saw his young assistant running back towards small gingkyo trees lining the river road. He called after Kang in vain.

Worried there was trouble with the riot police, hoping nothing would wreck their cover, reluctantly he hurried back, concluding the tour was a little rash.

He saw the car still parked near the trees and Kang leaning through its open front door; his wide back bent lower.

O'Brien reached the car and stared inside. Song sat peacefully, black eyes aimed at the mirror, slight surprise shaping his mouth. A small bruise spread along the side of his neck. The pulse was fluttering. "Bastards," mouthed O'Brien while cold fury spread through him.

"He breaths," Kang announced bleakly.

"Not much else." O'Brien felt the neck with caution. "Thank God . . . no obvious fracture."

He checked underneath the car before they gingerly lifted Song clear of the steering wheel then stretched him over the back seat. They placed their ski-jackets around the silent body. O'Brien studied the road and plaza before scanning the closest buildings: nobody, of course. Yet those thugs were watching and from somewhere close. "Get in, J P," he snapped and Kang leapt into the front passenger seat.

Small budding gingkyo trees divided the plaza from a road that led onto the huge Mapo bridge, these screened their departure though a few riot police ran across the empty acres in their direction. He slipped the car into forward, rammed down his foot, drove towards the charging olive line. Kang reached for the wheel, hardly believing his eyes, when the car swerved, scattering green bodies.

O'Brien seemed distracted, studying the mirror and a blue Bongo minibus chasing over the plaza, before throwing the car into a drifting turn. Screeching tyres held the tilting car on bumpy tarmac. He pulled the turn tighter, spinning the wheel, suddenly on a collision course for the minibus. "Gotcha", he breathed then warned casually," hold tight."

A blue shape flashed past, Kang clutched the dashboard. O'Brien roared off the plaza towards the steep bridge ramp, checking his mirror as the minibus made a wide unstable turn, then followed. Somebody wanted to give him a blunt warning.

"How's your knee?"

"No problem." Kang released the dashboard, growing a taste for this mad sport.

"I'll lose them on the bridge." O'Brien set the car straight at the steep ramp, climbing fast, watching his mirror.

"They're coming also," yelled Kang, staring behind.

"Perfect," muttered O'Brien, baring his teeth as the minibus closed over the long concrete bridge. At its far end, a small group of demonstrators braved a drifting salvo of white teargas, waving placards, standing their ground, even advancing towards a lonely squad of riot police, themselves closely watched by Chung's thugs in quilted jackets. He calculated his velocity with cold patience. The minibus drew alongside and its driver stared through sunglasses while several men in the back wiped steamy windows and revealed faces masked by thick scarfs.

The first screeching nudge was a warning to pull over. Next a solid bang propelled the car straight at the blurred concrete balustrade. He recovered control without trouble. Kang braced himself for impact with rushing cement.

O'Brien nudged his shoulder hard," They're about to become a pleasure cruiser."

Metal screamed and the bus started pushing. O'Brien held his speed steady and gripped the wheel till his knuckles whitened. With no warning he kicked the gas pedal, shot left across the wide bridge, stood on the brakes, swept behind the bus and bored forwards. He took a split second to find a line, caught its rear fender at the critical angle, smiled thinly when the minibus ploughed into solid masonry. Lumps flew, dust exploded, while the bus smashed down the bridge wall.

"My God," croaked Kang.

"Shallow water," dismissed O'Brien, accelerating over the bridge, past gaping riot police, ignoring the shocked faces of demonstrators, foot hard down for lost suburban streets. Kim might have given orders to scare them off but he was sceptical : no, this was Chung's message, a warning to keep out of his political war.

Face was at stake . . . . with luck Sam might recover in peace . . . but he and Kang would enjoy no more calm. Sail well, you bastards, wished O'Brien, barely slowing for traffic lights. Nobody would follow. Nobody would question. Korea had no laws, save the wishes of President Chung.

Today the big spider had lost a minor skirmish. The price for O'Brien was high. He openly fought his corner, lined up with those rare individuals who defied Chung, a serious crime, which gave hope to the little people in ten million simple homes who wanted freedom without the North Koreans. What a country, thought O'Brien, pulling away from the lights. That serpent Kim, who always hedged his bets, might have more respect after this morning's carnage than from weeks of business meetings, and O'Brien grimly recited, "Peng-mun-Ee, puryo-il-gun."

Kang shook his head slowly. "You proved that."

"So did Chung: let's take Sam to his local hospital," replied O'Brien sadly, blaming himself; nobody would question Song for several weeks.

11

Rush-hour traffic hurried over Chongno Bridge. Endless headlamps blinded, rain spat onto the windscreen, and night cloaked a black Han. Beyond the bridge, over gloomy apartment blocks, bold lights burned on the Hyundai Department store and following Kim's instructions, O'Brien turned along a street of humble shops that ran westwards near the riverbank. He spotted a garage, ahead on the left, entered its forecourt, drove past the pumps, down a short lane, found a small square lit by cheerful Korean restaurants.

O'Brien parked and was climbing from the car when a shadowy watchman appeared, clutching a weak torch. Resigned to fate, he slid back into the driver's seat, switched on the engine, then moved the car a few pointless yards further. When he enquired the whereabouts of the Chogga-chip Restaurant, his insistent warden became a grovelling serf, muttering the name Kim for fifty yards until they stopped at a low house which stood in near darkness.

One small push opened its front door. He advanced along a narrow passage towards another heavy varnished door. Tiny remote-television cameras watched him from the pine ceiling. There was a bell which he pressed though heard no answering sound.

When the door eventually opened, he was greeted by a shy girl wearing a traditional long-skirted Hanbok gathered at her breasts with a large ribbon tied in a bow, warm red silk setting off the girl's delicate skin and excited eyes, her long black braid decorated with plastic flowers. Chewing gum, she bowed, led the way into a courtyard garden where a rustic wooden water wheel driven by a monotonous electric motor, filled a small pond. Around the garden was a path of giant stepping stones, and every few yards, small causeways branched towards wide steps into private dining rooms where paper walls and sliding doors glowed yellow beneath the low tiled roof. He stood, listening as male voices were followed by girls' laughter, for a moment reminded of a shadow puppet show.

His guide called softly and a paper door slid open. Kim's massive shape trapped the mellow light. O'Brien kicked off his shoes, found a pair of waiting slippers, climbed into the simple room. Kim took his jacket for the girl to hang and probably search, then, waving him onto the vacant crimson cushion, enquired, "No problem finding this place," before rolling up his sleeves to expose smooth strong forearms.

"Is it a national secret?" probed O'Brien.

"Personal while prices soar as the Olympic Games approach."

Kim's eyes were red from tiredness, his large face thinner and his stomach bulged less under his shirt when he sat, cross legged, facing his alert guest.

O'Brien thought back over the last week and his mind always returned to the same conclusion: Kim was not completely in Chung's pocket, otherwise he and Kang would have 'disappeared' several days past for 'questioning' in a police station cellar. Kim wanted something which only they could deliver and tonight, he suspected, airships were not on the general's shopping list.

"What did you make of the weekend, Mr. O'Brien?" Kim asked darkly while two more pretty girls knelt and set out a dozen side-dishes, two large glasses and a fourty-ounce bottle of VIP whisky.

"Chung can *only* do that once." O'Brien said it firmly, blue eyes neutral, leaving an unspoken threat hanging in the cool room.

Kim's face showed not a flicker and he carefully poured out whisky until both glasses were brim-full. He passed O'Brien one without spilling a drop then raised his own.

"Tusayo,..... O'Brien."

"Peace to you, General."

They touched glasses. O'Brien resigned himself to a long evening on blended, instead of single malt; at least Kim drank scotch and not bottled chemistry from the Happy Liquor Company. He drained the glass, feeling his throat scorch, his cheeks burn, while observing Kim's temples glow faint claret. Another lethal toast was exchanged before rescue came and the girls lowered a brazier full of red hot coals into a hole in the low table, began to barbecue thin strips of fillet steak. Seaford arrived later as a digestive. Neither man had eaten all day. The level in the whisky bottle sank faster. Japanese oyster with egg soup accompanied the rice and pine seed tea. O'Brien stretched his legs, moving to clear his head, saw a cigar pack in his own shirt pocket and rose awkwardly. The floor rocked gently like a ship in harbour. When he sat cross-legged once more, he offered Kim a cigar, which the general examined sternly.

From his trouser pocket, Kim slowly pulled an old zippo lighter, held it across the table, flicked it into life, holding the flame absolutely steady while O'Brien drew on the fat cigar. After the girls had taken away the clutter, Kim lit his own. There was a mellowness about Kim which surprised O'Brien: small wonder that women found the General attractive and not merely power's erotic gravity.

O'Brien sipped the sweet tea and chewed sobering seeds floating on its surface. "I have a zippo lighter at home." He gave Kim a moment to absorb this sudden opening into his past, then watched for the considered reaction. But Kim filled both glasses, a polite sign that he wished to kill the bottle and massacre a second, before he was ready for serious bargaining.

"Vietnam." murmured Kim.

"Several times..... from 'sixty-five through 'seventy-two."

"Three tours," replied Kim with new respect, "my last in 'seventy-one."

"I knew a few Koreans."

Kim laughed softly. "One did well."

"For how long." O'Brien steered towards their present troubles.

Kim blew smoke towards the high ceiling and glanced across the littered table. "Chogga-chip. We say Mother's house. No Korean husband ever lies when he comes home late. He knows we are here."

"I doubt that an invitation to the Blue House would serve your reputation.... nor mine."

Kim roared with laughter. "Chung sent his compliments as an old friend."

"In other words," smiled O'Brien, "we're even."

Silence fell in the tiny room while Kim puffed smoke.

O'Brien understood. The President was discarding his thugs who brutally beat one of O'Brien's 'circle'.... so Chung still followed Buddha with his own warped brand of devotion. Kim had orders to buy something else tonight; London's support?

O'Brien set down his tea-bowl. "Send my compliments back to the President. . . as an old friend.. . tell him please that my orders are only to help bring the world to Seoul...... and send them away again safely."

Details were out of place in this exchange. Presidents and their Security Chiefs were not concerned with trivial matters. O'Brien knew he must stake out all important ground over this oriental feast : afterthoughts were a symbol of weakness unless you were their author and Korean. Among these cultured bandits, favours cost favours, and no Korean gave without the anticipation of a reasonable return. O'Brien smoked his cigar, contemplating the patient Kim, whose silence about a shooting and grenade attack downtown (which saved the President's skin), a recent scuffle in a Myong Dong alley, a burnt mini-bus and seven lightly injured though angry political thugs, offered more evidence that 'Student Shin' was controlled directly from the general's desk. Yet the general sat like a smiling Buddha, warning that O'Brien must show his hand first.

O'Brien remarked as casually as possible for such a mouthful, "President Chung's personal support for our mutual project would make our lives less hectic and more fruitful," hoping Kim understood that he was capable of leap-frogging the general and seeking his 'old friend's' intervention.

"I will convey your message, O'Brien."

"You haven't answered my question."

"I took it as a challenge." Kim raised the glass to his lips and stared smugly over the little table.

"Not at all," O'Brien smiled back. "We want the same result."

Kim reached over for O'Brien's glass, emptied the whisky bottle, called for another. Though his head slowly resembled a huge plum with drooping eyelids and neat grey hair, his mind and speech became sharper. Both the real gamblers on this conversation were elsewhere: one was dining in sumptuous isolation in his palace at the foot of a mountain across the Han River, the other was about to stroll across St. James's Park for a quick lunch at his club. And O'Brien sensed that Kim agreed, perhaps all along, that the first absent face had far more to lose than the second.

Kim laid his cigar to smoulder in an ash-tray. "We don't need the president," he purred, "for a mere technical task."

O'Brien felt his pulse quicken, not only from too much whisky. Was Kim merely saving face, preserving authority? Had the general already made promises to his officials working on the airship, bought their loyalty, and silence, when he divided the advertising fees into private windfalls? Or was there something more, still too sensitive for this first effort at 'Kibun', that Korean essential ingredient for all worthwhile business deals, mutual comfort between partners.

Kim peered through sore eyes which focussed less cautiously as a long day and the second bottle wore him down. "The President makes his own political judgements, O'Brien, nor does he often heed advice."

"Wise man........ providing you're riding success."

"I entirely agree."

O'Brien became more than alert. Watching the smoke spread, he gazed at Kim, then gambled. "Nobody can rely on the new middle classes for silence, not anymore. They're embarrassed by a modern economy chained to fifteenth century politics. Change won't stop."

Kim glowered but nodded thoughtfully. "There will be trouble long before this summer. We could lose the Games even at a late stage."

"Are you worried about Seoul," pushed O'Brien, becoming astonished by Kim's openness.

"Not only," said Kim quietly, mouth suddenly tighter, "but I must speak prudently tonight. Remember, however, that its streets are home for more than a quarter of our people."

"As you say" deferred O'Brien, holding out his near empty glass, taking the hint. Conversations were taped.

"We should understand each other better, Mr O'Brien" With his little finger and thumb, Kim twisted the cap off the fresh bottle. "You must feel lonely sometimes," he probed with disarming charm.

"You're giving me a warm welcome General," protested O'Brien, failing to prevent a slight curl at the corners of his mouth, wondering what took Kim so long when he fulfilled all the basic case ingredients: male, fit, single, ten thousand miles from home base. Who could be easier to buy with a warm sweet body.

"I meant *pleasure*," said Kim persuasively. He drank slower. Perhaps some girls waited in another room.

Kim was persistent which tonight seemed mighty odd. A visible line existed between making that first approach; always roulette, no matter how experienced, how wily the secret poacher; and a clumsy bribe, unless Kim was hinting at somebody else, whom O'Brien already knew. He must break the silence before the monitor noticed his wariness.

O'Brien laughed. "No time for playing, General, not with my company Chairman."

Kim responded warmly. "He works hard."

"Works his people!" shot back O'Brien.

It crossed his mind that prisoners dragged from riots were usually questioned in the back of riot police buses, only very special cases volunteered more thorough confessions at National Security Headquarters. Were Shin and Han trying to act such a scene. Nobody would have blocked their escape path. The real police were busy fighting. Only five people were involved that night. Either Shin reported almost daily to Kim, or, *he* and Kang were watched extremely closely. O'Brien thought back. That night he followed all the ground rules to slip a tail. He remained certain there was none. But supposing there had been no need to follow his car because Kim knew precisely where the captive was heading, controlling the entire incident, masterly theatre, drawing them into a sophisticated trap. Was the girl prisoner a pot of cultured honey? Moving towards the riot had been a maverick gambit. And kill Cardinal Min? Never unless his agents were playing on both sides behind his back. Kim had faults but the general was not stupid.

Raising his glass, O'Brien offered, "To our friendship, General, may we prosper."

"Mutual success," modified Kim, holding out his massive paw.

"Mutual success," consented O'Brien, reaching across the table and fingers gentle as a strangler's crushed his own.

****

Soft rain fell and headlamps flickered morbidly in a million filthy puddles, night granted O'Brien a cloak that lost his car among the Seoul late-evening rush when businessmen drove from drunken stag dinner to dark saloon bar graced with expensive lifeless girls. Later would come the pornographic floorshow and finally home to the marital bed in one of the concrete apartment blocks which spread like fungus overnight. What a bloody awful existence, reflected O'Brien, keeping his speed low, steadfastly heading against glaring headlamps for a quiet back gate into Eighth Army Headquarters. He slowed and turned into a narrow street of darkened shops and let the car crawl towards tall gates through a chicken mesh fence. A young American military policeman stepped from the night and shone a torch into O'Brien's face; satisfied, he saluted, fingers flicking to wet helmet, camouflage suit black with rain. O'Brien slid a green pass back in his ski-jacket pocket then drove into America.

Dim street lamps, order, dark avenues of bare maples bordered by tidy lawns before small ranch-style houses. Wood smoke drifting like scent in the sad night. O'Brien reached the house within minutes. There was nobody around and no other cars but he parked some distance away outside a colonel's quarter, walked back through the rain and along the path under short maple trees towards a lantern hanging over the white front door of a brick colonial house. A few lights downstairs were enough to confirm that a professional warrior had returned to lick his wounds after a gruelling day with the world's most awkward ally.

A shaft of light fell across the pathway as the door swung open to reveal a tall spare American with thick sandy hair set off by ice blue eyes from some long-past Scots ancestor. Harry Todd blinked when he found O'Brien in his porch, glanced down at his own stale green army vest, camouflage trousers, muddy combat boots, then apologised under his breath after three cans of beer. Todd assured O'Brien that, only minutes before, he walked back into his quarters; his wife had fallen asleep reading in bed, tired of waiting and wondering if, for once, her man would escape from Korea early.

Todd was a friend, their lives joined by savage years, painful memories which would never quit, brutal pictures that always surfaced, harrowing voices which still cried out from the murdered lands of Indo-China. Both men had abandoned faithful friends though only after ruthless orders from weak governments which they mutually despised. Todd fought his own war from Korea, bludgeoning the American Embassy on behalf of his soldiers, ensuring that messages sent to Korean politicians and generals sounded as though they came from the same country.

"The British are coming," whispered O'Brien, exaggerating his Irish brogue, knowing Mrs Todd's need for slumber.

"Your mouth stinks like a petrol bomb," replied the United Nations Commander in Chief, a grin breaking on his austere face, closing the door gently, leading O'Brien into his lounge where a log fire smouldered. Without asking, Todd found a tall glass in the drinks cabinet and filled it with Scotch, ice and water. "Somethin' must be horribly fuckin' wrong for this honour, Mike."

O'Brien took his drink and advanced more steadily towards the fire, enjoying its warmth, a magic touch called home, that strange comfort which came from suddenly finding himself among old friends. No questions. Years rolled past: his mind saw himself, younger, fitter, clad in combat greens like Todd tonight, the 'seconded' expert on counter-insurgency, fighting Vietnamese Communists, when Camelot was fresh in American minds and success still assured, so long ago.

"Honour!" sighed O'Brien, enjoying whisky fire mingling with ice in his vandalised stomach. "I've just been a dinner guest of General Kim."

Todd laughed quietly, delighted to find this British pirate at last beached on his doorstep; knowing the risk involved with the operation O'Brien now chased, the general's mind moved forward. "Want me to set my counter-intelligence staff working."

"Hole-in-one," smiled O'Brien, pacing the room, pulling the set of pictures from his suit pocket, handing them over for Todd to study while he admired the fire's flickering crimson.

"Names?" said Todd.

"We know one. Han Che Song." O'Brien paused while his mind groped for a clear pattern, "Possibly a second, Kwon. I'm not sure what I'm hunting. On face value I've tripped over a pair of North Korean activists. Summer will bring riots, maybe changes. While President Chung rules, others, including his Security Chief, wait in the wings, yet the only real popular hero is Cha Se Dong."

"Cha could be President before summer is autumn." Todd pulled the cap off another beer with a loud fizz.

O'Brien had two arguments. The extreme right wing factions in the Army enjoyed tremendous power. And one other. "Chung has been stashing billions of dollars overseas. He's well placed. The country can fire him but that spider already owns a return ticket."

Todd took a slow pull on his beer can. Fire-glow made his face swarthy. "Sounds another Korean charade. Who's gonna' bring the sonofabitch back home?"

O'Brien stared at the fire. "Suppose they knock off Cha Se Dong. Parties here are factions built around one man. People come onto the streets demanding a headless government resigns. No Cha ... no point in any elections. The present Assembly offers to work longer with Chung."

Todd winced. "Our friends in the National Police claim they worry more about somebody knocking off Cha than the President."

"That's my problem, Harry, so far........ no money, no bets, no answers."

"It would be a repeat of the coup that put Chung in power," agreed Todd. "Last time Cha was gang raped. Chung stole his job, stripped all his property, then parked him in gaol for this past five years."

The American general paced the room: soft lights revealed countless photographs from years overseas; three presidents, O'Brien's Queen, all carefully framed, signed, a gentle reminder that Todd found power an easy burden. There had been failures, but none laid at his door. Now he commanded a force far from home, forty-thousand disciplined young Americans, ready to prove their valour, sitting over an oriental army of more than half-a-million. The fuse was short and Todd kept the match in his trouser pocket. Korea, one day, could trigger American revenge on Asia's communists.

"So far, Mike, you haven't mentioned the crazy Kims in Pyongyang," remarked Todd, leaning on the mantelpiece, warming his back, staring straight across the room at O'Brien who stood near the bookshelves, curious about which classic writers Todd had bought for the Korean winter.

"We had a tip this week that our two candidates targetted Cardinal Min." O'Brien slowly turned and saw Todd's brows shoot upwards. "What have we and your people learnt, Harry? That the lunatic Kims are totally off balance, capable of anything from bombing planes to flooding Seoul by bursting a huge dam while we're still waiting for the Russians to buy them off with long range missiles and the latest Migs."

Todd threw another log on the slow fire, watched sparks fly, waited for those first flames. "We have assets, some ready, some preparing. By summer, I'll have three carrier groups off this peninsular, effectively doubling the air assets tasked for defending South Korea. But its more than numbers, Mike, those navy jets are flown by Americans from our own sovereign territory. Half the airpower around this peninsular is mine from July."

O'Brien laughed as a mad idea occurred. "Can I fix you a hot-line into our airship?"

Holding the can of Budweiser, his eyes warming with interest, Todd lowered himself into the sofa, carelessly throwing a long leg over its arm, before sipping more cold beer. "I thought you'd never ask."

"You should know me better, Harry."

"My counter-intelligence guy will wet himself."

"We can fit a channel direct into your crisis centre."

"More private, Mike, gotta' hide that kind of *money*."

"No introduction fee," stressed O'Brien.

"Gift from Her Majesty!" Todd smiled like a hawk.

"Something like that."

"Who pays?" Todd stared, serious.

"Our good friend General Kim."

Todd was sceptical.

"Built into the overall price.... operational training."

Todd liked that. "How much space?"

O'Brien thought for a few seconds. "A small office with room for all the phones and a couple of computer terminals from your counter-intelligence and you'll have the means to check portraits. We'll supply the television terminal. And, by that stage, since things will become dangerous, even a young Korean, my assistant, who took most of our photograph gallery..... as your link with our operation."

The idea came as he spoke. There was no point throwing Kang into the perils of an operation where several people would be dead by the Closing Ceremony. He was too valuable. O'Brien would never forgive himself if he lost the young Korean, who could be of incredible worth to Todd and the American Forces, safely on Yongsan Base, sitting next door to the Commander in Chief: speaking both languages, monitoring everything that was passed over the radio and television cameras, following all the bugged conversations on board and in Kim's command centre. Kang, by that time, would fully comprehend exactly what the airship could, or could not tell those on the confined ground.

"Which brings me to the reason for this midnight visit."

"I'm sure it's a new brand," said Todd with relish. "How you guys stumble on so much stuff amazes my staff..... thank God they know not how I keep ahead of the snarling pack."

"Stumble is the right word, Harry." He explained about the riot. "We rescued a struggling youth who turned into a girl!" He paused and his mouth changed expression, "I suppose you expected a frog."

Todd laughed, remembering not to wake his sleeping wife.

O'Brien described the girl's background, all the technical checks he carried out so far.... which he sent Hong Kong for expert screening. At length, he concluded, suddenly feeling sleepy, "J P extracted some more material from her on the taxi-ride. It's almost as though she knows that her brother is planning another confrontation. She doesn't dare or can't decide where to turn for help."

"Who to trust."

"Absolutely, Harry, and, at present, she's our safest route to the dissident brother."

"Who sounds like a mad monk."

O'Brien was becoming heavy-lidded yet glad Kim's blended whisky was smothered by Todd's single malt even if the water was a philistine crime. He said blankly, "We know nothing more, Harry."

Todd pursed his lips and shrugged. "Nobody's raised that at my morning briefings. My staff tend to look north; we're not scanning for something that would happen further south."

"I think that's risky," said O'Brien, rubbing his sore eyes, concerned that the Americans had no intelligence on possible violent demonstrations in the more southern provinces: most American material came through agents with links to the National Security and the National Police. O'Brien started yawning.

"Is she pretty?" Todd enquired from his comfortable bed on the sofa.

O'Brien hesitated then surprised himself. "Frankly, Harry, she's the most beautiful rioter I ever snatched, a little film star."

"Should my counter-intelligence people take her for a private chat?"

He weighed opportunity against risk. It might cut a corner although she was very frightened. She might not see any difference between an interrogation from the Americans and one by a Korean Government that she loathed and feared.

"She could run out of sight. We can't risk losing contact, Harry, and we can't ask the Koreans to bring her back. Diana's scared."

"Show her a lolly pop," stirred Todd with a lecherous glint and then stared curiously at his tired friend.

12

For several days a warm wind gusted, filling the sky with a sandy haze from the Gobi Desert, leaving yellow dust over the city and circling mountains. Tired magnolias and infant cherry blossom hung on the garden trees: spring courted Seoul, and though winter retreated, the dirt stayed.

O'Brien paced his waking garden, finding with approval that Sammy Song, now back on light duties, had stripped the trees of their winter bandages, checked these were burnt, killing off the hiding grubs. Saturday morning was O'Brien's time for contemplation, when the dong browsed peacefully since most residents were at their company offices.

Three weeks had passed since Hong Kong reported the girl benign and her brother as possibly malignant. Kang was adamant. They must wait for voluntary contact, she must *need* their help. O'Brien recognised this as common sense although with increasing frustration. He watched agima dusting the lounge furniture then set off across the lawn, still parched from a long winter, quietly fuming: despite further massaging, his 'kibun' with General Kim showed all the warning signs of a Korean business arrangement - while his partner kept hoping next time all would change, the general broke every promise.

"Four weeks in Pusan Customs," muttered O'Brien. Maybe it *was* time for Kim to learn that this airship needed *two* engines. He strode the rest of his lawn, spun round, jerked his chin towards a delicate sky, watched the lime flash as a golden auriole swooped over the garden wall and vanished behind a tall fir.

There was an airship still in boxes at Pusan and Rose on stand-by at Detfold. Yesterday a signal arrived from London with the worst possible news: Mason was restless. This meant, that unless there were sudden results, wheeling and dealing would commence from London and utter chaos would become their normal daily life in Korea. Enough time had been wasted.

He went indoors and telephoned Kim's office. Miss Secretary Kim's bedroom voice apologised for the general's absence at a meeting - O'Brien declared equal sorrow for brow beating the general on a busy day but he worried about the airship cooking on a Pusan quayside.

"One moment," she requested seductively. The answer came back so fast that he wondered if she was sitting on Kim's lap. She breathed, "General Kim could see you at four o'clock on *twelve* floor of National Police HQ."

"I look forward to our meeting," O'Brien lied politely.

He rang Kang. "Do you want to meet there or here, J.P.?"

Kang laughed knowingly. "I prefer to drive your car, Mike."

"Why?"

There was silence until Kang's surprised voice asked, "Have you forgotten? There's a huge demonstration scheduled for five o'clock. We'll be out on the central streets just on time for gas and fire."

"I had forgotten," groaned O'Brien.

The main opposition party suffered a bitter lesson on Yoido Island but would not yield. Rumours were rife of plans for a crowd so vast that even Chung's police force would be swallowed alive. Moon seemed barely interested. Despite three secret meetings O'Brien could not persuade the old man of its importance: Moon simply rocked with silent laughter, pausing only for a coughing fit, dismissing the whole affair as children's games. When O'Brien asked what he would do instead, with a charming smile, the old man suggested that leaking a few of the opinion polls which the papers were forbidden to publish, might inflict more lasting damage. Forget mass rallies. And O'Brien recalled the old man confiding with a vague smile that ten thousand demonstrations by a few people would scatter all the police in Korea to the fours corners of Seoul City.

* * * *

Olive green cohorts stood behind black shield walls, their gladiators' helmets reflecting harsh sunshine, two stoic medieval armies holding the pavements along both sides of Sejong, waiting under the leafy gingkyo trees. The clock on City Hall shone weakly into the hot afternoon, recording just over a hundred days before the Olympic torch would burn in the square below, with luck and appropriate social discipline.

Light traffic flowed in both directions as sensible people quit the city's epicentre for its baking suburbs. The old assembly's pale dome seemed dwarfed by a mountain wall withdrawing into grey haze as heat lifted exhaust fumes into the choked sky.

Kang drove faster, glanced cynically at the green bronze admiral who had beaten the Japanese with his turtle ships three centuries before Korea was colonised by its Eastern neighbour. He kept looking warily to either side, turned slightly, grimaced at O'Brien. The white stones and green roof tiles of Seoul's North Gate barred the road ahead.

"You can smell the tear gas . . . before they start." Kang learnt much, in exchange for rides from student fares.

O'Brien's forbording was swopped briefly for dry humour." Let's hope our meeting is very short or lasts all night. By five o'clock down town will be a battlefield."

"American Forces Radio claims they will try mass tactics."

Kang made a screeching u-turn before the ancient gate, swerved into the outside lane, raced back towards the Koreana Hotel, pointing out marksmen on every tall building, save the Buk A Ilbo. He observed with grudging respect, "Doctor Moon stands aloof from the streets, too strong even for Chung."

"Moon is patient . . . his cards concealed," said O'Brien, knowing that Kang must eventually learn of his link with the old doctor, but not yet. No purpose would be served by making Kang a fertile target for the interrogation experts at Yongsan police station, where a student had died the day before and his memorial riot now gathered on the tense streets. He awaited their afternoon conference with growing curiosity. There was no better address for measuring the government's future.

* * * *

A granite and glass palace served as police headquarters. Rifle carrying policemen at the gates directed Kang into a reserved parking space. Inside the bullet-proof glass doors, issued with passes, cooler, they were escorted across a spacious marble hall, delivered to remarkably attractive lift girls. Controlled calm filled the bright modern building. A few uniformed police in short-sleeves waited at the lift, a party wearing identical cheap suits swarmed out, chattering, heading for the splendid glass doors and a troubled world.

O'Brien and Kang were sucked a dozen floors skyward then ushered into a large office. Kim, huge and smooth in an expensive dark suit, rose from the master chair and welcomed them like newly discovered relations.

The weasel faced Yoon hovered at his general's shoulder while four police generals and a pair of suited security officials presented themselves by sliding rank; last, a small civilian with a rabbit's smile and dyed hair was introduced and bowed deeply, holding out his business card with both hands for O'Brien's perusal.

"Mr. Park of Magnolia Trading," Kim intervened swiftly, "who takes care of publicity matters."

They sank into long sofas that faced each other across a low table and O'Brien was reminded of two football teams with Kim playing the corrupt referee. Kang whispered, "They all have the same press cuttings and . . . I do believe . . . draft questions for the National Assembly."

"Can't imagine what about," said O'Brien, dropping his voice when Kim looked up from his own papers.

"The Buk A ran a story this morning . . .," hissed Kang, then fell silent, suddenly comprehending. A disgruntled Seoul businessman had claimed that he paid the Blue House a large sum of money for an exclusive licence to fly airships over Korea.

"Let's ask right away," O'Brien urged blandly, keeping a serious face while Kang enquired in Korean, and threw the room into disarray.

Kim tapped his fist on the table and halted the anxious conversation. "There is a licence in my office at SLOOC which bears the Interior Minister's chop and signature. I would not believe scribbling in our press, Mr. O'Brien, who are idle, corrupt, and easily swayed."

"I never do," he assured Kim, making a note in his mind that tomorrow a token of thanks should reach Paul Moon. He suspected the luckless journalist was under close watch until the furious businessman was bought off with his own cash. He teased Kim, "Who are the letters from?"

"Government National Assembly Members," said Kim sourly. Yoon watched the tense faces of the four generals sitting in a row. Both security men seemed in a trance. Park displayed his buck teeth in a foolish smile and was punished with a scowl from Kim.

"Tell us your problem, my dear O'Brien," soothed Kim, glaring down either side of the long table, reducing seven senior officers to cringing silence; even Park closed his mouth. Kim pushed a bell and called for refreshments though nobody would have been shocked if a firing squad had stormed through the door.

O'Brien displayed open palms. "Time."

"May I, Mike?" Kang pleaded rather than waste an hour interpreting into Korean.

O'Brien encouraged, "I can follow but ask when you want help."

Kang went over all the dead-lines involved at each phase of construction, testing and training. Already a month was lost, the airship stood in Pusan Customs, boxes gathering dust, the envelope suffering from heat and humidity. Why not release the parts and start building: their engineer was ready to fly out from Britain. A crisis approached. The British Company might withdraw from the project. That risked a public scandal over Olympic security. Kang drew breath. A row of blank faces looked at Kim, who launched into a sad monologue, listing all the attempts to find a hangar that was large enough: ship yards, floating docks, strip mills, American airbases, Korean Air, even the police academy parade ground. O'Brien wondered what else the police had time for; but questions were better saved for another day. Instead he contented himself picturing a posse of police generals clambering over the rust and grease of a strip mill.

"We Koreans," Kim finished grandly, "always solve difficulties at the last moment."

"Educate him, J.P." requested O'Brien, voice held low. "I think this is just the right time." Two policewomen wearing tight blouses entered and began serving orange peel tea.

Kang was about to deliver their best card when the telephone bleeped at Kim's side. The general answered with instant courtesy and passed the receiver to his neighbour, a senior police general, who began to sweat, sitting stiffly, listening to a distorted voice barking into his tormented ear. Kim glanced at O'Brien. "Our National President has just fired the Interior Minister. The General is next . . . . after this public disorder stops."

"I thought nothing was likely until five," prompted O'Brien.

"So did the Interior Minister," scoffed Kim, cold eyes delivering a withering rebuke at the luckless general. "Small riots are breaking out all over the city, thousands are on the streets, office workers have been arrested near the main railway station."

"An airship," O'Brien throttled a smile," would multiply the value of your ground force. What a pity."

"No games O'Brien," warned Kim, ignoring the shaken general as the room filled with senior policemen and telephones in the outer office began frantic ringing.

"My company President," began O'Brien, who thought Mason would approve that gloss at such a moment of rising stress, " kept back one engine in Britain until he was more confident of Korean Government intentions."

Kim placed his large fingers over the telephone mouth, shoved his furious face towards the sweating general, then spat, "Did you know it had *two* engines?"

"We can fly it here within seventy-two hours," rescued O'Brien.

Kim leapt to his feet. Glittering eyes awarded them a split second of bitter respect. "This is chaos," he fumed, looking at the struggling general and then snapped, "O'Brien . . . and you Kang . . . we're going on the roof."

Kim bounded for the outer office and a path opened through the shouting mob of senior policemen. "Send me a radio-phone," he threatened, "with somebody competent. Yoon!"

Kim's tight mouth fired bursts of orders while Yoon's thin face turned plastic from concentration, before he jerked his head forward and slithered through the door as new arrivals found no places to sit, milled round, talking nervously, reminding O'Brien of children who feared that they swotted the wrong facts for a crucial examination. Then Kim spotted Mr. Park, silently finishing his tea, without the slightest hurry; the general span and snarled at the little man who scurried after Yoon.

From the scorching roof they stared over the central streets. Namsan's woods and its white needle basked in brilliant sun from a powder blue sky. O'Brien and Kang followed Kim who stepped past a huge radio mast and gazed down from the safety railings. Below on almost deserted streets, buses raced each other and a few trucks grumbled towards shimmering sidings beyond Seoul station. Rare cars sped through the burning heat. Kim pointed a thick accusing finger at Sejong where twin armies of olive ants stood passively, flanking a mile of empty avenue that mocked the inflexible brain who ruled Korea. The message was not lost on Kim and his knuckles went white from temper.

"Where's that radio-phone," he growled, leaning over the steel mesh barrier, studying the streets. A policeman arrived, shirt soaked, struggling with a fat black attaché case.

O'Brien stood back, giving the man some space, taking a close look when the case was unlocked and laid open on the sweltering roof. Squatting on his heels, the policeman pulled out the aerial, listened on the telephone receiver as he checked the secure links to Kim's control centre across the river near the Olympic Park, then inserted a thin card with the daily code, before switching on the scrambler. Although a Korean name was printed on the radio, after a few seconds, O'Brien spotted a number of American components: that night he would set the engineers in Hong Kong onto breaking into Kim's portable command network; it might be their only real time source if Yoon damaged the airship and that risk was gaining a certain inevitability, assuming the monster flew at all during the Summer Games.

Kim took the telephone and leaned on the steel rail, spat an instruction, never taking half-closed eyes from the glare over small streets beyond Seoul Station. A mile east, from the fake Norman tower of the Anglican Cathedral, over a loud speaker a woman started screaming slogans: Kim sent for field-glasses.

Kang interpreted for O'Brien. "General Kim is re-deploying most of the riot police but keeping some hidden behind City Hall."

Even as Kang spoke, two columns of armoured buses entered Sejong from opposite directions, raced along each side of the vast street, before halting like toy trains. Thousands of green ants swarmed around them, soon vanishing on board. The buses hurried away, despatched to a hundred parts of the city, leaving Sejong shocked and silent.

Kim waited impatiently for the field-glasses, his massive shoulders hunched, testing his weight on the steel rail. "O'Brien," conceded the general with a hint of envy, "I'm sending Yoon to Pusan tonight. He's not to come back without your airship. Park will deal with the Customs."

"Judging from this afternoon," sympathised O'Brien as a huge roar from angry voices floated through the stifling air from somewhere near the Lotte Hotel's butterscotch tower, "you could use some sophisticated wizardry."

Another sweating policeman arrived with the field-glasses through which Kim scowled towards the hotel and a giant crane that swung over its skeletal twin extension for Olympic tourists.

"Those fools," exploded Kim, "they failed to close your new British subway. That mob has just ridden a train downtown."

The first splutters of tear-gas launchers reached the roof and the shouting rose whilst the woman began chanting more slogans. Kim looked at his fat gold Rolex: "Two minutes before five." White mist spread and smothered City Hall. Tear-gas popped in the surrounding streets. A voice crackled on the secure-phone. Kim listened with the telephone pressed to his ear then said, "Another group are trying to march over Panpo Bridge while a mob rampages through the East Gate market."

He gave more orders in stacato Korean.

Brittle chimes drifted from the cathedral tower. Five o'clock. All over the city motor-horns blared, churchbells rang from far directions, drowning the worn strings and droning sermon on the evening public broadcast of the national anthem. O'Brien stared down at the car park. Policeman scampered randomly, spreading confusion amongst themselves with about as much purpose as a disturbed sheep flock: two cars reversed into each other and Kang shook his head. On Sejong, buses and trucks blasted their horns, while some dodged tear-gas grenades fired by forlorn groups of riot police standing defeated near Toksu Palace : nobody could arrest the city traffic. White mist rose above the buildings in a thickening cloud as more whistles blew, shouts rose, volleys of grenades coughed and popped, while among the muddled office blocks somewhere a police siren moaned.

O'Brien folded his arms and surveyed widespread chaos, impressed by Moon's gift for grand tactics, enjoying the rare music of churchbells peeling across the empty sun-baked city. He became aware of Kang's face displaying utter amazement.

"Well, JP," he remarked towards the softening skyline, "that's the level of political debate in your country . . . . tear gas versus motor-horns."

"But we have a debate now," said Kim, peacefully lowering his field-glasses, watching the future.

13

Dusk fell and they stayed on the cooling roof. Ten thousand cold lights burned from office blocks, neon signs flickered through foul vapour over Myong Dong, a dark Namsan and its golden mast floated in a troubled night. Kim spoke rarely into his radio-telephone. Messengers reported frequently. A terse conversation took place with the President and judging from the courteous farewell, Kim was bringing the capital under control.

"You're letting the demonstrators come into the streets around City Hall," guessed O'Brien.

"Precisely." Kim relaxed.

"Before surrounding them with a ring of riot police," hinted O'Brien.

Kim, looming in the dark, an oriental warlord wearing an automatic under his conservative dark suit, approved. "You are smart,"

"Bitter experience," replied O'Brien.

"Where did you study?" Kim asked Kang.

"Princeton, General."

"Your major?"

"Business studies."

"No time for riots," presumed Kim.

"No interest," Kang smiled through the closing darkness.

Kim laughed softly at this bold truth from a young mouth then raised the telephone to his own compressed lips. "I have a hundred multiple gas launchers and forty-thousand riot police down there . . . let's see if our students enjoy a taste of my teaching methods." He spoke briefly into the telephone and for several minutes endless muffled explosions rippled around the city streets. Traffic sounds faded. Whistles shrieked. Grenade launchers echoed, screams and angry shouts drifted on the night wind, stinging mist attacked their eyes as white fog slowly swallowed Myong Dong until only the cathedral spires stood forlornly aloof. Multiple launchers thudded. Human ants fled along the central streets from angry police and gas grenades. Kim lifted his telephone and spoke a few sharp words. "We don't want to exhaust our gas supply," he explained with a cold smile.

* * * * * * * * * * *

They went below for a bowl of sticky noodle soup in the busy office and watched the general practice his personal brand of terrorism on the national police high command. There was no hope of reaching the house while thousands of police fought widespread riots. It was a hot night, the room humid, and the flock of generals sat with their blue trousers rolled above the knees like toddlers ready for paddling. Kim ignored this extraordinary dress style and telephoned the President.

At ten o'clock, Kim decided the streets were calm enough: they declined a police escort, not wishing to offend but with no ambition to offer brick-throwers a surprise target.

O'Brien drove while Kang kept watch from the back-seat. Burning smog tortured their eyes, the headlamps picked out small groups of youths lurking in side-alleys. Rubble lay scattered over desolate streets. They avoided City Hall and sped past the main station, solid beneath its granite dome. Firebombs licked the road ahead. Shadowy riot police appeared like raiders from another world, and waved red torches. O'Brien braked hard. A stone clanged over the bonnet, bouncing past the windscreen. A second smashed into his door. O'Brien saw a line of angry youths surge from the station, rush across the littered road, tear gas exploding in grey puffs among their sprinting feet. Then they were gone, lost among the alleys below Namsan, pursued by a sinister squad in trainers and track suits. Red torches called the car forward. A nervous sweaty face peered from under a grilled vizor; guttural Korean demanded identity cards.

Kang sat forward, coolly rested his arms on the seat-back, and mentioned his 'uncle', General Kim: hurried consultations took place with the patrol commander who moodily kicked the strewn rubble, sparing the car an occasional suspicious scowl. Torches beckoned; O'Brien slammed his foot onto the gas pedal, becoming aware of the warm steering wheel, slippery from his own moist fingers.

Minutes later, they drove between the small trees along Itaewon;

through young leaves, seductive neon messages burned and flashed, happy crowds pressed along the narrow pavements, taxis raced each other past the crawling traffic : no student was brave enough to attack this stronghold of pimps, fashion pirates and restaurant barons. O'Brien turned up an alley and drove over a hill into his tiny dong.

He climbed from the car and stood in the narrow street. His eyes stung. Gas must have blown right across the western suburbs from Yonsei University. Kang pushed the bell three times. Falsetto squawks escaped from the wall microphone and Kang calmed a worried agima. Loud buzzing announced open gates.

O'Brien squinted at his luminous Swatch: only ten-thirty? Musicmaker should be ready for something stronger than beer after this turbulent night. He kept a bottled of Tullymore Dew stored in the glove compartment. There would be tight security around the base but only American MPs within its wooded haven.

"Listen, J.P," he yawned, trying to sound convincing, "You go home. No more work. I fancy a drink on the base - suffering withdrawal symptoms from a night with Kim."

Kang probably thought he was destined for the Embassy Club where girls in long slit skirts served icy beer in a bar lit by crimson gloom. O'Brien added collateral. "I might eat an American steak."

Kang hovered in the street, an understanding smirk spreading on his tolerant face. "We can set the gate for your key." He examined his dusty shoes, "All I can face is my sleep."

The main gate onto the base was guarded by edgy Korean police: O'Brien slowed. Two giant black MPs treated their midget allies with tolerant contempt and waved him through. He coasted down a gentle hill past the officers' club tennis courts and the new chapel, turned up another short hill to the Embassy Club where he parked and waited five minutes. Nobody passed. O'Brien drove off, took a winding lane, followed a meagre necklace of small street lamps under bushy maples. Once headlights flashed in his mirror but soon vanished.

Todd, wearing combat fatigues, opened the door, and bowed in mock oriental welcome. "They say trouble always comes at night." He smiled approval when he saw the bottle tucked under O'Brien's arm.

"Telepathy," declared his visitor, bowing lower.

Todd straightened. A small path round his colonial house led towards the back yard. "Been sittin' around for damn' near a half-hour," he complained, turning the corner and strolling onto a neat lawn. "Thirsty work since you can't anticipate fine old whisky with cheap new beer."

"Twenty years old," promised O'Brien wearily, holding the label under a string of paper lanterns for Todd's inspection before setting the bottle on a picnic table with benches fixed either side. An ice-bucket and two crystal glasses stood waiting on the thickly varnished oak.

They sat either side, enjoying insects whispering in the cool night, while Todd filled the glasses with ice then pushed them across to O'Brien who opened the bottle and poured two good measures of golden liquor.

"We've spent the last five hours with Kim on the roof of NPHQ," explained O'Brien, tasting the first sip of peat and iced water.

"He pulled their shit together today." Todd raised his glass to admire its colour before drinking. Impressed, he declared with a grateful sigh, "And this stuff sure beats the shit out of Pyonyang viper wine!"

"It's not finished yet. Narrowly missed a stoning, half an hour back, right outside the Central Station." O'Brien held out his fingers, checking, but they were steady.

Todd's blue eyes sharpened. "Who's we?"

"Young Kang..... smart boy..... curiously, I believe he was taken by surprise when church bells and car horns entertained the forces of lawful suppression."

"Not the only Korean with that problem tonight." Todd scratched his sun browned forearms. "Chung will try and play this down tomorrow . . . but some of the stuff my people reported! Students joined on the streets by office clerks. Rich ladies in big cars hammerin' their horns in serenade with sweaty truck drivers. Bells tolled right across Seoul!"

O'Brien pictured that moment on the roof-top. "Harry, this evening, our friend Kim reminded me of the general who warned Louis Seize there was a difference between a great rebellion and a great revolution." He revolved his glass for a few seconds watching condensation form on its sides. "It's only a gut feeling, nothing more, but Kim will distance himself from Chung."

Todd offered a troubled smile. "Let me frame your picture."

"Restless troops?"

"Generals."

O'Brien stopped twisting the whisky glass. "Since how long?"

"My intelligence people report that some mighty scandal has been shelved for the last week." Todd shrugged and swung round on the bench so that he could admire the first roses on bushes flanking his wide lawn. "The Koreans, of course, are silent. We know Chung toured.... 'inspected'..... forward troops along the DMZ, two days back." Todd examined his jungle boots. "These staged visits are designed as set-pieces, a show briefing for the photographers, pictures of the mighty leader in full control, fending off the red hordes, striking terror into the evil Northern leaders." He paused and tasted more whisky. "This time, no pictures, no allied comrades as witnesses. Our private pals came back with reports of an angry slanging match with several young generals from which Chung came off worst."

"No wonder Chung was so polite to Kim over the telephone this afternoon."

"Loyalty is last month's flavour."

Todd became aware their glasses were already low and reached for the ice bucket. He began spooning little frozen hearts into each glass while he talked. "Chung needs the army and bought most senior officers with key jobs. Those who oppose him find themselves swiftly pigeon-holed with no troops and no intelligence access." Todd passed the glasses across for O'Brien to add more whisky. "But most generals are growing nervous..... so are we...... what happens when these demonstrations are beyond the control of riot police? Martial Law."

O'Brien poured carefully. "The Olympics would disintegrate. Have the IOC ever held a Games in a country under military rule?" Neither could remember.

Todd held the bottle both hands then slid it back towards his guest; he looked tired. "My information is that were Chung to order troops into Seoul.... or another city..... he would provoke a mutiny. You can guess what a temptation that presents for Kim Il Sung."

"Only Koreans or else the British could design such a mess at the worst possible moment for themselves." O'Brien was appalled.

Todd was confronted with an impossible task. The American general commanded the South Korean army with orders from Washington to stand aside from internal squabbles and even worse, politics. But how could his American friend ignore South Korean morale and combat readiness, when all the intricate plans for safeguarding the Summer Games against threats that stretched from sabotage through street chaos to massed invading tanks, depended on the South Korean Army and National Police.

"You must be furious."

"Madder than Hell."

"I'll try and cheer your evening, Harry."

And he briefed Todd on their progress with the three suspected threats timed for the Summer Games while Todd rested his chin in his cupped hands, and how an informant among the opposition reported steadily on demonstrations : he omitted... nor would Todd wish to know.... how Moon played for high stakes.

"Our most trusted informant in Korea," apologised O'Brien, wishing Moon had given better news, "still forecasts civil disorder, increasing towards the games, culminating with personal attacks on Chung or Cha Se Dong . . . by radical students who are North Korean agents. Our student sources, pass over nothing about any terrorist plan."

Todd reached in a pocket of his combat jacket and slid out a pack of cigars. He tore open the cellophane, delved in a trouser pocket, found an old Zippo lighter which he passed over the table. "Chung's gotten' one of these for visiting Congressmen." He smiled sarcastically.

O'Brien lit his cigar then handed back the shiny lighter. "So's Kim."

"Those bastards did well outa' Nam."

"They're not through either, Harry."

Todd watched the first thin smoke float across his lawn as though observing artillery fire. He was baffled. "You're the only guy who scored. Counter-intelligence insists they have nothin'. No indication exists of any terrorist threat, other than our general apprehensions that both northern Kims are probably insane. CIA and National Security are tripping over themselves on the Seoul streets trying to find a real live terrorist." Todd drew on his cigar until its tip glowed. "No matter how much General Kim goes on television showing off his black suited commandos, begging the World's terrorists to try an attack, maybe they won't come! After all," he concluded dryly, "they too can see the Games better at home by watching TV."

O'Brien laughed until he coughed. "Harry, my master remains adamant, so do the Russians and Chinese, three attacks." For nothing had been sent from London repealing Mason's message during February

"We're talking about three threats," said Todd, sucking the cigar, cheeks hollow, arms folded across his camouflaged chest, trying to form tidy options in his mind. "Students, North Koreans; well, they could hide more than a single threat. But we can't ignore Soviet and Chinese claims that Kim Jong Il has a private terror campaign running."

"Papasan has little control."

"Who knows," Todd mouthed through a smoke cloud while he filled their glasses with fresh ice-hearts. "Where does all this position our good general?"

"I could be reading the wrong signals or drawing false conclusions. Kim makes no secret of enjoying political power yet needs a Godfather. He lacks any power-base in the Government party. I regard him as our weather-vane. Kim will go with the winner, whoever holds the military card." O'Brien went further. "Since early winter, almost all our hard evidence of terror threats has come from communist sources - *nothing* has emerged from dissident student groups in South Korea, all of which Kim penetrated, monitors constantly: no money on them pulling off a spectacular atrocity."

"Unless Chung wants one," said Todd vaguely.

O'Brien was dubious. "He moves like a spider, stealthy kills. Reckless murder isn't his personal style."

"Chung sent the airborne regiment and a full infantry division into Kwangju City, Mike, and that ended with a couple of thousand dead and wounded civilians."

O'Brien could not argue; it was history, but grabbing power sanctioned harsher skills than avoiding it slipping away. Besides, O'Brien firmly believed that Chung deployed his most loyal followers to the opposition capital with the clear aim of teaching its population a lesson: Diana Park's story merely confirmed his own conclusions. He suggested, "That was a risky and savage first act to show all South Korea who was boss."

"You think North Korea might orchestrate another shocking incident in the south west?" Todd's sceptical jaw proved that he found this concept far-fetched.

" We can't cross our hearts and eliminate that scenario. Remember our girl and her brother. David Park may start an insurrection not realising it's a North Korean plan. Despite weeks of our chasing hares, vast dispersal of American manpower and electronic gadgets, neither you nor I can confirm . . . or deny . . . whether a specific terrorist threat exists. We can guess the most obvious potential targets. But without knowing who we're fighting ... even with close bodyguard protection for our VIPs..... we're still naked."

"We've one potential super-weapon!" Todd unfolded his arms and his large hands shaped a huge egg a foot above the whisky bottle. "Mike...... the sooner we have this blimp up and operational.... the more you and I will sleep."

"Today helped. Yoon is bullying Pusan Customs even as we savour these gentle night breezes.... Kim sent him two hours ago."

Todd's blue eyes warmed at this surprise news. "Something finally shook that collected sonofabitch."

O'Brien hoped silently that Kim was frightened enough to pay promptly. He said, "Tonight I shall ask Mason for his signature and authority before three million dollars worth of airship leaves a Pusan Customs shed and enters honest Kim's Korea. I shall also request his signature for four million dollars worth of satellite camera and electronics with authority for Detfold to hand the steel containers into Cathay Pacific's seasoned hands at Gatwick. My pilot has been at the Gatwick Hilton for three days and Her Majesty finds him hideously expensive." O'Brien feared a warning shot from finance when nothing developed. The airship must be built, tested and flying, for his 'company' to complete its contract, demand payment. Mason hated wasting money, even more, he hated the press finding out.

"A room is ready in my signals battalion on the base," said Todd.

"Not your headquarters?" worried O'Brien. A signals battalion numbered almost four-hundred intelligent and inquisitive professional soldiers.

"Too many Koreans." Todd elaborated sourly. "Kim is one of my regular callers these days. Everything we request, Kim delivers half. I'm threatening to provide half a carrier, half a jet-fighter, half a tank and half-rations."

"Good luck," consoled O'Brien realising that Todd was talking common sense, for the signals battalion roster was rich in technicians capable of servicing most faults on his monitoring package. He admitted concern. "We intended to keep the surveillance camera and electronics in Hong Kong until the airship makes its first flight."

"Why not educate my signals battalion commander who is an electronics engineer?" said Todd, persuasively adding, "I can spare him for a week. Would Hong Kong need longer?"

O'Brien recognised reality. "I shouldn't think so, Harry...... and then Kang need only swot up faces....... he can forget about how the technology works."

Todd leaned forward and his eyes challenged with savage mirth. "We'll arrange a ton of Kim Chi in an airtight fridge, but, I'll wager you another bottle of this fine brew.... your man won't find time for watching private TV."

"That's fully possible," dreaded O'Brien, remembering that Barry 'Abdul' Rose, natural civilian, brilliant pilot, energetic and thorough build crew chief, arrived at Kimpo Airport in less than ten hours. Rose could start another Korean War all on his own. He had won every secret fight that he started for British Governments.

14

An antique clock which he had bought years ago in Paris, chimed twice softly, when O'Brien slowly climbed the stairs, employing the bannister as a map, feeling his elastic legs grow heavy. Upon reaching the landing, his eyes gradually focused on a sheet of paper sticky taped to the spare bedroom door. He advanced, leaned on the door frame and read small neat writing: a message, from somebody, waited on his desk in the neighbouring study. With a solid push, near sleep, he launched himself off the door frame, turned clumsily, remembered how he drove back, then took the last few careful paces before swaying over his writing chair.

A scrap of paper admonished him from the blotting pad. Gripping the chairback, he leaned forward and read, mind clearing fast. The same tidy hand reported: *'Paul telephoned at five o'clock this afternoon. He was concerned that you know a meeting takes place in the library, tomorrow, where Paul will wait from noon onwards. He thought you could talk peacefully. He didn't want a reply but insisted I stay until your return: I had important news about my brother. Paul urged that I tell you tonight. He said you will understand why it is important. I wish you people were less crushing with your habitual mind reading. Sorry to be a pest. Diana Park.'*

He groped and flicked over the paper. There was no explanation when she came to the house nor what time she left: no telephone number scribbled either. Annoying. Kang could go to her relative's apartment in the morning. He began writing a note of instructions, only then did he realise what was carried in Paul's words.

"Library," he muttered absently, sitting down, turning over the word in his mind.

More than a library; a treasure house full of children's games, puzzles, magic tricks. He considered the wording of his most recent message to Mason and the helpful reply. Mason recognised that he felt un-sighted, promised that risks would be taken, and, if no other way presented itself within the time left, vigorous efforts made to put him right, including major assets: Hong Kong could call on the Royal Navy for clandestine support.

Why employ the girl as herald? Unless. Had there been a contact? The girl must have called round that afternoon, sent by Paul, who waited for his reply? Perhaps the relationship existed through Korea's network of wealthy families, those who supported earlier governments but now kept their heads down, guarded their wealth until better times. If there was a link, Paul must explain fully, before they raced along diverging paths.

He sat forward and read once more, feeling the scrap paper as though it might provide deeper meaning to those spruce little words. Had she misheard? There was no purpose ringing anybody at gone two in the morning: only General Kim's computer technicians would gain immediate advantage. Was it possible that Moon senior was pulling off a masterstroke? The risks were frightful. And how could he control such an adventure? Cover stories must be woven into a tapestry and that could not be done within hours of a live contact.

The curtains were not drawn and he studied the long pink halo of Itaewon; strings of tiny orange lights crossed an invisible river, the distant cold white windows of Building 63 stabbed a moonless night.

O'Brien loved covert geometry and this equation might hide a trail of brilliant mirrors stretching over fifty years. He lounged in the chair, laid the little message on his desk and quietly laughed, vaguely aware that excitement prowled through his drowsy body. Though God, he was tired.

Slumped in the chair, he snored for several minutes, then, leaving the note where it lay, pulled himself up, resolved to start early in the morning for the rendezvous was a full three hours drive over country roads. As he crossed the wide landing a reflex stopped him outside a spare bedroom used for visitors from Hong Kong or Detfold. It would house Rose, the airship king, while the craft was built and presently it sheltered a stock of liquor for this savage battle. O'Brien also kept the room as his nostalgia den, where he planned further surgery to his Sussex farmhouse on his sister's small estate, nestled close under the Downs, yet in a saddle where the sun found his garden all day winter and summer. There had been no time for a rush trip back to Britain at Christmas. Now he suffered a rare attack of homesickness.

Giving himself a brief sentimental moment, he opened the door, allowed a narrow shaft into the room that caught one corner of a photograph. He could just pick out a huge tiled roof, a vast lawn boasting a pair of fine cedar trees.

Gentle sighs came from the darkness. O'Brien froze. Long black hair cascaded over the white pillow, there was a bulge in the duvet, the rhythm of infant breathing, a little hand stretched open. The sleeping face lay towards him but the eyelids barely flickered, perhaps dreaming, perhaps disturbed by the narrow intruding beam. O'Brien blinked twice. He began to close the door, gently, shaken.

"Who's that?" called a drowsy worried voice.

He stood rigid, then peered through the darkness. "Yes?".

She pushed back tousled hair from her sleepy face. "Did you find my message"?

Warning signals poured into his waking brain. Feeling stupid, furious that Agima had allowed her inside the house then gone to bed herself, he also hoped the relatives were not searching Seoul for a lost girl. Agima was mad: she wore one of his own clean vests as a night shirt and might have scoured the whole house. Kang would have to sweep for electronic bugs in the morning. An instinct warned that now was the wrong time for hard questions. The girl behaved completely out of character with a comfortable family background. Perhaps she was under orders, lied with talent, certainly she was desperate or bold, but on whose orders? He masked surprise.

"Are you in trouble?"

"You must think me shocking. Korean virgins are not supposed to sleep under a stranger's roof." She rested an arm on the pillow and shielded her eyes from the landing light.

"When did you come?"

"Ten o'clock." She became flustered, suddenly horrified at her predicament. Her voice caught. "Paul Moon insisted that I must tell you in person : no telephone calls: I had to wait for your return."

"I bet agima was pleased," grumbled O'Brien.

"Furious." She placed a small hand over her mouth and yawned. "I'm sorry. But I know what David plans and he must be stopped . . . for everybody's sake. I feel disloyal. Was I wrong?" she asked miserably.

"No . . . . absolutely right." He advanced into the room, sat on the warm bed. She had slept, probably for some hours; and he relaxed. Paul sent her! It was possible, though bizarre. "Paul have any other messages?"

She shook her head. "Only that I was welcome tomorrow . . . he promised you would understand."

"I do." He did not. "Won't your family be worried."

"I feel safe."

O'Brien wearily patted her hand and recognised defeat. He was in no shape to drive a wheelbarrow. "Paul sent you."

"My father was at high school with Paul."

"Sleep well instant daughter from the Korean night."

He rose and started for the door when her soft voice called. "Mr. O'Bean you're very kind, God bless you."

He tilted his head in her direction and stared through the darkness, feeling sorry for poor Kang, who somehow, next day, must return from Pusan and scan the entire house for electronic listening devices. He could kill Agima sleeping soundly in her ground floor room.

At seven he woke to furtive spring sunshine probing the bedroom windows. He lifted a wounded, throbbing head, squinted at the new day. Haze concealed the far river bank and its rows of numbered concrete apartment blocks. Only the golden skyscraper poked through pale morning murk.

Whisky did not blend with tear gas. He reached grimly for the Soksu bottle by his bedside and poured a full glass of fizzing water. It helped enough to lift himself out of bed and make a cocktail of more Soksu, Aspirins and Alka Seltzers, which he drank slowly in the bathroom while studying the mirror, surprised that his hair stood in wavy tufts as though a gale had blown all night through the bedroom. He was about to pull off his pyjama jersey when busy, light footsteps sounded along the landing. When he heard nothing more, he guessed that she was listening at the bedroom door. The girl asked timidly, "Are you awake, Mr. O'Breen, hello."

"Coming," he croaked and pulled on a thin sweater. As he opened the door, she stood back, her petite nose withdrawing from high octane breath.

"You look exhausted." She abandoned sympathy, politely retreating a yard, smart in a cream summer skirt and white blouse, dark eyes lively, shining hair faintly scented.

O'Brien suspected that he reeked like a bar-room. His beard felt sore, his head ached, his pyjamas stuck to his body and he smelt the tang of whisky from his own mouth. "Take no notice of my morning shambles, Diana, but may I ask a favour?"

She shook her head with a knowing smile. "How many eggs Mr. O'Breen? Your coffee is already made, by Agima."

"Korean efficiency. Two please. My poor head," groaned O'Brien, weakly smiling, and resolving to shower and shave within the next minutes, watched the girl hurry away, enjoying her flat bottom shown off by the cleverly cut short skirt, those pretty legs skipping down the wide stairs: a surprise daughter had suddenly taken over as his domestic fairy. What had Agima made of the girl's presence at daybreak. There was no longer a curfew in Seoul. Fortunately, Sunday was her day off when she dashed for the central bus-station; otherwise severe looks, grumbling, perhaps dark hostility would be deployed to emphasise the old housekeeper's disappointment and lost face. Agima had no patience with business girls from neighbouring Itaewon. Though she had not thrown Diana back on to the street last night; which proved that the Moons' word carried remarkable weight in this confusing land.

Strong coffee and salty fumes met his nose when he finally arrived downstairs. She had laid breakfast on the kitchen table as though for final examination at a Swiss finishing school. Silver, linen knapkins, his best Wedgwood. He sat where instructed. She served him a fluffy cheese omelette with crisp bacon slices. "What about you?" he insisted before tasting a morsel.

"I normally fuel myself for the day with a cup of coffee and a fried egg. A real Korean breakfast takes all morning." She watched obediently, for him to start, long hair falling over her shoulders, framing her troubled face.

O'Brien took a fork of cheese omelette, drank some coffee, and leaned back in the old wooden chair. "Your forgiven for housebreaking."

"Really?"

She was content, and served her own omelette, began eating, rarely taking devoted eyes from his tired face. O'Brien holding his coffee cup so that he could enjoy its aroma, felt awake enough to retain whatever fresh disaster she wanted to report involving her elusive brother.

"Well," he began with a faint smile creasing his mouth at the corners, "You certainly took me by surprise last night."

"I'm sorry, though, I slept really deeply, it's so quiet in this house." She added seriously, "Don't punish Agima."

"I see she handed you my underwear," growled O'Brien sipping more coffee, wondering what they had discussed while he was drinking half the night with Harry Todd.

She blushed then filled her own coffee cup, and, perhaps hoping to change the subject, enquired, "Would you like it washed?"

O'Brien declined this invitation. "Tell me about your brother," he gently ordered, at last feeling food conquer his headache, otherwise it would be purgatory driving.

A frown left not a mark her smooth brow. "Now?"

"Perfect time, now, your superb breakfast pulled me wide awake."

Diana's intense expression showed that she wanted to share her burden with another person. Yet she gazed into her empty plate, her nervous face questioning: an unspoken message crossed the breakfast table.

"You can talk," he assured her, "this place is bugged only by J.P. and myself. Nobody can place a device in here without our knowing."

She watched him for the slightest warning of doubt then asked more confidently, "I trust you, Mr. O'Been, but you *are* certain?"

"It's technically impossible." He leaned back in his chair and stretched out his long legs. "We're a few light years ahead of Korea when it comes to electronic gadgets."

"I'm sorry." She stared harder at her empty plate.

"Forgiven."

She began talking, her soft voice almost a whisper. "David works with father and lives in our family home. There's only one big town on our island."

"Peaceful."

She looked up with in surprise. "You know already?"

"I know nothing," returned O'Brien.

"He wants the local people to declare autonomy from the mainland regime." She sighed helplessly. "I can't tell father . . . but, somehow, I must stop him, before he ruins our lovely island."

He felt a wave of sympathy for the long suffering parents and sisters of David Park. He might be clever but he sounded a reckless gambler. He warned, "Chung will send troops by helicopter. No government can allow a local revolution."

She made little attempt to hide bitter disappointment at betrayal by the brother she had admired since childhood, and her eyes blazed. "How could he think up such a stupid selfish plot, Mr. O'Been. He can only bring violence and misery to one of the few parts of Korea which always managed to avoid trouble. Nobody on our island minds him making heroic gestures on the mainland. They'll never forgive our family if David plays at God on their own doorsteps."

"And with their own children as his followers," he rubbed his hollow cheeks. "When did you learn all this?"

"Last week," she replied sadly, "I went home."

"Who told you?"

She fidgeted and furiously tossed back her long hair. "I found his diary and read some pages." She almost smiled. "I was hoping to find out his girl friends and tease him later. All I learned were times for meetings ... no names, no places. I know David."

"Any idea when?"

She brooded. "He can't wait long. Nobody will care a damn, once the Olympic teams arrive from Russian and China and America."

"We're talking about the next few weeks. Russia's National Olympic Secretary is making his final pre-Games visit this month."

"You must help, our island is so sweet., not oppressive, no grubby Seoul which seems like a boot camp in business suits."

He was impressed. "How many hours were you home?"

"Not enough."

"We'll do our best, Diana, meanwhile you mustn't fret." He contemplated the breakfast litter. She swallowed the bait easily and he left her clearing the dishes, went into the lounge and making certain she was out of earshot, yet within sight, telephoned Kang.

"You left your watch here last night."

"Should I pick it up before going to Pusan?" asked Kang in a flat voice.

"Might be sensible," agreed O'Brien and rang off.

Twenty minutes later, before they were across Panpo river bridge, she fell asleep. He glanced down at the black silk mane. She must have been exhausted from day after day of cruel tension. There seemed no half measures in the Park family from Moon Island. At least while she slept, he could relax; there were no awkward questions.

He checked Diana was breathing deeply then reached for the car telephone, dialled Hong Kong, listened to a ringing tone fifteen hundred miles south. Maybe Penny was long gone for a day sailing among the outer islands: Korea was an hour ahead. Somebody lifted the telephone and he heard a breathless voice. "Sorry . . . . in the shower . . . hello."

"My apologies, Penny, but I wanted to catch you."

"Mike . . . . did you have a message?"

"Yesterday?" Now it made sense. Paul was responding to a Hong Kong or London directed operation.

"From somebody local," said the clear English voice.

"I'm heading for the seaside now."

"Send us a post card."

"Tonight," promised O'Brien. "By the way," he said slowly to ensure that Penny heard the first time, "candidate three is on board. My friends gave the invitation. Three has relative trouble brewing at home. We may take prophylactic action."

"Your friend invited three for today?" Penny had that worried tone which meant that Mason had intervened. "Three is benign - no doubts whatsoever."

"Perhaps Genesis sees some potential."

"That rings alarms."

"Keep in touch."

"Nobody else along?" She wanted to know if Kang would alert them should something go severely wrong.

"No . . . I'll ring tonight."

He replaced the telephone and swung into the outside lane, overtaking trucks and buses, heavily loaded cars with families quitting the city smog for a few stolen hours of countryside. He glanced at the sleeping girl, debating her motives. Korean girls, at least respectable ones who claimed decent parentage, simply did not stray under a foreigner's roof, not even for one innocent night. Leaving that aside, she was sweet and full of surprises, he had enjoyed her fussing concern this morning; but there was a restless spirit inside that beautiful body.

Several miles south of the Han River, after passing Osan's high perimeter fences punctuated with floodlamps and watchtowers, its grey blastpens lurking among scattered fir and maple copses, he turned off the concrete highway to Pusan, losing deafening convoys of silver buses and smoking rusty trucks, an endless flow of cheap cars poisoning spring. A sullen roar from the glaring sky announced a pair of fighters, wheels lowered, trailing thin fumes over the paddies, sinking towards Osan runway. He drove westwards along winding country roads with flowers blooming on the verges under endless shading trees.

Only three towns served for landmarks through the gentle countryside: a resort spa which waited for night when its hot baths soothed shattered nerves and wounded pride from jungle business ethics; a small market town resembling a thousand others; finally a pretty little city with a shallow ochre river lured through its heart by a wide canal, along whose banks cheerful washer - women toiled beneath pale green clouds of mature ginkyos. Beyond the town, paddies basked and white cherry blossom covered the low rolling hills. Few people moved on tiny farms. Noon was the hour of noodle soup. Salt air blasted through the open windows and the heat rose.

"Not far now," said O'Brien to the drowsing girl, taking a narrow dirt road that wound among small paddies and fruit orchards towards a brilliant sky. A bend in the orange dust snake took the road over a hill thickly planted with short apple trees. Their young bushy foliage filtered the strong sun. Suddenly they were driving alongside a sparkling ocean throwing foam scrolls onto wet sand. She sat up and rubbed her eyes. O'Brien watched as she gazed out to sea; along the horizon, small islands resembled a school of grey whales.

Ten minutes later, he slowed for moss grown stone gateposts and drove over a dust track under tall pines disturbed by the afternoon breeze. Among scented firs by the seashore, wooden cottages sheltered and beyond, still dressed for spring, pink and white magnolia trees faced damp sands and a fast retreating sea.

"Where is Paul?" she worried sleepily.

"Waiting," he replied though curious about Moon's reason for wanting the girl present.

"What is this place?"

"Somewhere American missionaries escape from Koreans." He smiled without mercy.

Moon was standing on the steps of a crude cottage built from bleached pine planks and roofed with tin sheets. Cool wind gusted off the playful sea as breakers boomed onto the shallows. Tufts of grass were snatched, bowled onto the scrub, brief toys soon lost among pines defending the long empty shore.

O'Brien saw the old man jerk an arm skywards as he started towards them along the sandy track. Moon shouted into a fierce bluster, "We borrowed the children's library."

"Adult games?" asked O'Brien through the open car window.

"In a moment, in a moment," promised Moon, his expression welcoming, though strangely alert, for the eyes were impatient, concentrating somewhere else.

"How is Paul?" asked O'Brien.

"Walking." The old man's arm pointed at a small figure strolling away from the little houses among the shore pines.

"Will he be long?"

Moon held up his watch and studied it closely. "Fifteen minutes."

"You're up to something," accused O'Brien.

"Rather special," replied Moon, stumbling on the English consonants and moving around the bonnet to open the door for the girl. With his usual reserved courtesy, he shook her hand, but gave no immediate reaction, and promptly described the evening riots.

"Kim is right," murmured the old man, after hearing about the roof of police headquarters.

"He suspects that you orchestrated the whole show."

Moon smiled contempt. "Only Chung has that gift."

"But he *can't* recognise the times are changing fast."

"Kim is not foolish," agreed Moon, "just suffering from a severe case of tunnel vision."

The old man turned for the small wooden house, leaning into the wind, his eyelids near closed, leading the way, strong gusts flinging dust and grit at their faces while they struggled forwards. O'Brien drew alongside Moon and gave him a searching stare.

"No difficulty," the doctor smiled absently, "more than welcome. She can help."

O'Brien returned a stiff smile. "Kang is the one who ought to be aware that we are close . . . for all our sakes."

Moon nodded. "We are not inde . . scruct . . able."

Sand blew past in a stinging cloud. The girl bent low and caught up with the hurrying men. She tied a flapping silk scarf over her flying hair. "Is there anything I can do?" she asked breathlessly as the wind snatched at her skirt.

"I'm not in charge," shouted O'Brien and looked at Moon who shook his head firmly and suggested, "Take a walk by the seashore . . God's clear wind will blow away all your troubles, child."

"Do I look that harassed?" she protested though was still a little in awe of the old man.

Moon laughed, coughed, then his voice became firm. "Sadness wastes time. Off you go."

Later that afternoon the wind fell and the tide pulled the sea far back over wet sands. Small breakers whispered, while the mournful gulls screamed, searching the beach for stranded starfish and tiny crabs. A small white launch spluttered shorewards, crossing the shallows, trailing grey hazy smoke over an olive calm. Low in the water, the boat was packed with old women saved from the strong sun under their wide straw hats, clutching bundles and bags crammed with dried fish and fresh vegetables from the outer islands which now lurked along the sharp horizon.

Paul Moon, trousers rolled above his knees, waited on the wet sand, watching the launch approach, standing back from a small crowd, island village women loaded with shopping, ready to clamber aboard. When the launch slid onto the beach, rocking slightly at each small explosion of foam and sand, the old women began to clamber over her side, passing their cloth bundles to the pressing crowd in the gentle surf.

O'Brien saw a tern lazily swoop over the flat waves, watched it lift swiftly before circling. Then he became aware that Paul waded through the water, helping an old woman with a heavy basket, grasping her arm, bringing her steadily through the surf. Paul took the basket while she clung to a large straw hat with a brim wide enough to hide her features, escorted her up the long beach. She wore baggy trousers and a loose quilt jacket. Her steps were quick yet not hurried, oddly familiar, an aura of natural dignity.

He was not sure. But the resemblance was striking. He kept control, forced himself to turn away, following the diving tern, before wandering back towards the bushy pines.

He allowed Paul a few minutes to reach the wooden house then stood on a sandy rise and searched the whole beach. The white launch, weighed down with women and shopping, chugged seawards. A slight figure was paddling in the foam, moving away, sometimes bending to admire a seashell, taking all the time in the world.

Muffled Korean voices came from the wooden house as he climbed sand strewn, bleached steps and pushed open the library door. Sudden wind slammed it onto his shoulder, then he pulled the door shut behind, found himself in a children's world. Hundreds of books and boxes of games were neatly stacked on shelves which ran round the walls and divided the room. He advanced into the musty den. Strong sunlight invaded through a high window screened with fly mesh and defended from the buffeting wind by a wooden shutter held open at a slant by a thick bamboo pole. Behind the central row of shelves, stood a simple table. Around it, blinking through the sunshine, sat the old doctor, Paul and the elderly woman off the island ferry. An empty chair waited under the crude window.

Moon smiled in a way that O'Brien had never seen. The old woman's large hat hung from her chair and there was no doubt : she had the same shrewd eyes and wise mouth, that engaging, hesitant warmth, coupled with a hint of ruthless determination emphasised by cropped grey hair. She rose slowly and held out a small smooth hand.

"Your sister?"

"My twin . . . Mee Sook." confirmed Moon, revealing rare pride.

O'Brien stooped, took the dry gentle hand, searched for words, and instead emotion swelled in his parched throat. He confessed without a hint of flattery, "Your valour is a legend which only a small circle may ever know, but we few, treasure your friendship all the more."

She smiled with her mouth while penetrating eyes considered him before her hand squeezed with sudden strength. She chided in slow English without an accent, "You are full of Irish talk . . . blarney is the correct expression . . . so we learn."

O'Brien laughed but he was not deflected. "Was it dangerous?"

"Not even long," she replied, withdrawing her hand with such charm that he felt his own released from a polite duty.

Moon faced the open window and looked at the grey islands floating on a silver sea. "We are only a hundred miles south of Haeju port."

"Three hours by fast launch," said Paul.

"Less", she corrected.

O'Brien wondered how she actually reached the outer islands and suspected a Royal Navy nuclear submarine more than a North Korean speedboat. He hoped Mason also could send her safely home, then pulled the vacant chair nearer the table and sat down, keeping on his golf jacket, for a fresh salt breeze blustered through the mesh screen.

Paul arranged a thermos and five plastic cups on the dusty table; he poured green tea into four. "She'll be back, but not for an hour," he checked O'Brien's face for confirmation, then screwed on the thermos cap.

O'Brien and Sister Moon grew used to the proximity of each other. Both savoured a rare calm yet sensed the clock snatching its seconds from a unique moment, leaving their brains in sudden turmoil as years of pressing questions exploded from the memory cells and they laughed nervously like shy lovers.

O'Brien suddenly fumbled in his jacket pocket until he found a little tissue paper parcel. "My gastric juices warned me to bring a present."

15

She took the package and with tender care, peeled off layers of flimsy paper.

"Nothing fragile," he promised.

She held up a cheerful toy tiger wearing a Korean farmer's traditional hat from which curled a long silk tassle. Hugging the soft animal, she bowed towards him, and smiled with touching surprise." The real Hodori will need much luck and all your prayers." The small room electrified.

Resting his hands on the table, throat still a little dry, O'Brien told her frankly, "Our greatest worry is your personal safety."

"I never doubt," she answered yet fear seemed an extravagance.

"We shall do our utmost in this half of Korea. But it's poker. We almost lost President Chung in late February."

She knew. "I live close to the voice that gave those orders."

O'Brien displayed open palms though gently insisted, "We don't want you taking further suicidal risks.... let's just say this visit was beyond my authority."

She was not deterred by the polite message, and her expression confirmed they understood each other perfectly. Nobody could save her life should the operation falter.

"Mason enjoys wider vision from London," allowed O'Brien prudently, "but that means we have to shout louder when the sharks lurk close inshore."

Doctor Moon patted O'Brien's shoulder. With disarming charm the old man took over. "These Olympics can bring us closer together. Communists racing in Seoul! Why not capitalists in Pyongyang? Why not a single Korean team at the Peking Asian Games? Political walls crumble before they finally fall."

She intervened swiftly. "Unless blood is spilled this summer."

"My sister... is... right," stuttered Moon, seeming at home among leather bound volumes of Treasure Island, Kidnapped and a hundred other classics stacked on the shelves behind. "One futile death," he warned solemnly, "ensures our grandchildren hate each other across that bitter red scar ploughed our over empty hills. Great causes deserve great risks."

O'Brien sat back, impressed by piled boxes of Monopoly on the shelf at his elbow, while his mind sifted adult business. Moon employed simple diagrams; they were climbing the right mountain, the questions came down to which track.

All three Moons listened patiently to his own arguments, courteous enough to speak his language all the time: O'Brien, very aware of their forbearance, tried hard to avoid confusing, thankful that the Moon family devoted themselves to noble causes and charming trivia. Finally, he repeated Harry Todd's favourite dictum. "So long as Kim Il Sung takes breakfast noodles and American troops munch evening hamburgers, this peninsular remains stable. Take away one and we're in big trouble."

Her smile showed the years had been merciful to an honest face. "Our future leadership believes only in chaos and violence."

"Enough to invade?" O'Brien stared hard at her, knowing they must weigh every threat. No other choice lay open; the Games began on the seventeenth of September, this was their last chance for talking.

She placed the toy tiger on the table and her gentle fingers stroked its orange and black stomach. "Two military plans were delivered last month by our generals: rivalry brings results!"

"Can we forget massed tanks rolling across the Imjin River and into Seoul?" O'Brien waited.

She took a moment for reflection. "Yes.... because an artillery bombardment of a border city won favour. They are looking at Munsan. It's ten kilometers south of the DMZ. Our guns can hit the town by shooting over the Imjin River."

"That would start a panic," said Paul, raising his brows, distracted by tiny chinks of daylight that revealed rough repairs to the roof planks.

Concerned, though voice flat, O'Brien worked through his mental list. "Special forces landing from swarms of small planes?"

She granted herself an artful smile." Even our leadership recognises its madness!"

"We'll keep that scheme on our list."

For all her confident dismissal, the threat alone forced widespread dispersal of the US and South Korean forces, yet such an attack meant open warfare and he suspected North Korea's capacity to fight without allies.

Sister Moon suddenly ignored the tiger and asked her brother, "What truth lies behind Chung's great 'Peace Dam' near Kumgang Mountains?"

The old man's thin chest shuddered with hoarse laughter. "But that is to pro...tect us from yours!" She smiled defeat.

Oriental pantomimes with their casts of thousands no longer troubled O'Brien : North Korea was building a huge dam just over the border, capturing the head waters of the northern Han. Chung claimed a deliberate dam burst would flood Seoul, and started a rival dam. Immediately North Korea accused the South of stealing its precious watershed. Each wall was nowhere near complete, the twin threats a charade, serving both sides in the propaganda war. He asked like a doctor, "Any tunnels...germs, chemical, nuclear?"

"Discard the first three," she replied, then with a humble glance around the table, pleaded for more time on the last.

O'Brien absorbed this awesome news. A plutonium plant, weapons. Harry Todd stored the tactical nuclear bombs for his strike fighters safely locked under a mountain in south eastern Korea : Russia promised North Korea the latest Migs and long range rockets but none intended for nuclear strikes. He recalled a report filed by NOAH about the risk of North Korea head-hunting Soviet nuclear scientists for a secret plant near the Yalu River along China's frontier, and wondered whether the worst case was upon them already. "How much time?"

"The programme is experimental, run by a sealed cell."

Doctor Moon vigorously shook his head.

O'Brien fully supported him. "We have space photography for delicate technical tasks. And this sounds urgent."

"You're no physicist, Auntie," vetoed Paul, staring into the afternoon light, watching a rebellion fade in her determined eyes and those meek hands return to the tiger's stomach.

O'Brien restored peace. "You're too precious and besides, you can help more by identifying the banker, since North Korea itself has empty pockets."

"So we're back to the wretched students," grumbled Paul, speaking for them all.

She smiled. "They aren't your main headache."

O'Brien raised his soft irish voice above the wind. "Your Dear Leader pretends to meddle in southern protests. So long as there is plenty of western newsreel showing riots and strikes, he can claim credit, prove further victories, concentrate on real threats right under his nose."

"Quite right." She marked the next trap along a dangerous path. "Our Dear Leader wants an illusion that southern workers and students crave for his leadership. Proof for North Koreans that a charismatic hero, one day, could unite our torn country."

O'Brien frowned with quiet admiration. There was an expensive strategy: war - and another, which beckoned, paved with easy victories, cheap. Kill a moderate southern leader, kill a student, both instantly effective, then sit back, watch South Korea plunge into wild turmoil.

The Olympic Games collapsed, no rapprochement took place between the West and East, Russia and Eastern Europe turned their backs on reform. Forty years of isolation stood vindicated. North Korea kept her wavering allies and displayed frightening political power across the writhing Asian tapestry. He recognised, too, they only had to kill a handful of the right people for heady success. North Korea's throne stayed warm for the old King's son.

"Spotting his targets is comparatively simple." O'Brien desperately wanted a map and compass.

"Few lives are at risk," she agreed, "but each death target is highly sensitive."

O'Brien nodded. "Then we need a tighter warning system."

She asked her brother, "How did you receive the Chung threat?"

Moon shrugged his thin shoulders. "We didn't."

"From Hong Kong," explained O'Brien briskly, "Noah passed it direct. I can send a courier.... whatever you wish..... but that eats time. Three hours flying to Beijing, another four or five hours to reach Pyongyang."

Sister and brother sat silently, twin Buddhas consulting through meditation and gene telepathy until Paul cleared his throat and protested.

"The music works providing we solve the riddle. But what if something happens to you, father, and we can't fathom the real message. Isn't it time that you both review the logic hidden behind your tastes in music!"

O'Brien watched two pairs of old stubborn eyes switch their attention to him.

"Well?" Moon reluctantly asked his sister.

"We should have done this years ago."

"Be fair!" complained Moon.

She unzipped her quilt jacket and taunted kindly, "Were you thinking of my safety?"

"Even a politburo member can falter," said Moon with mild exasperation.

Watching this remarkable pair, O'Brien gradually absorbed that he sat with the finest brain and second most senior general in Kim Il Sung's Political Security Bureau. The most successful spies were those who heard most and spoke least. They reminded O'Brien of master astronomers whose brains served as great telescopes, probing the hidden shame of mankind, because they could peer into the most remote and lost realms of human experience. A sparrow could not fall, he thought, watching Sister Moon, but that she would soon find out why.

Paul was finding his father trying and aunt deceptively difficult. They appeared to have weeks at their disposal and Paul's frustrated weariness told that he thoroughly disagreed, yet all his background, years of cultivated breeding, held him back from speaking, openly criticising his old father and aunt. He could only suggest, plead, persuade.

"Can't we work from our current known threats," he argued, "just match them with individual trigger songs. I know your system is infinitely flexible, but only you two, with respect, father, auntie, only you both understand its messages."

She laughed at her brother's peturbed expression." Southern family society is almost more confucian than our northern dictatorship."

"List your situ.....ations," Doctor Moon chided his perplexed son.

"Auntie, *you* must give us a list." Paul appealed to her directly, much relieved when she nodded, and he, for once, prevailed. His father was not ready to change a lifetime doctrine but one small victory was better than nothing. And Paul would not hurry along blind pathways as the price. He reminded sharply, "We must work from Pyongyang's official plans.... not our theories."

Amused, his aunt cried, "He resembles father!"

"Very obstinate." Moon coughed a dignified surrender and noticed a book returned upside down. His chair scraped as he rose and set right 'Charlotte's Web' while his sister offered a description of life inside Pyongyang. The others listened intently as a wind rose off the seashore and Doctor Moon, seeming detached, studied the neighbouring shelves, eventually resuming his seat at the small table.

Moon paused for breath. "There is a Chinese corner in each Korean soul. Kim Il Sung is not immune, he represents the most conservative survivor in any communist society, Asia's Stalin."

Sudden wind beat on the flimsy walls, rattling and lifting the wooden shutters, and raising her voice just enough, she advised, "Learn the wisdom of Sun Tzu, philosopher before general, scholar before warrior of ancient China."

"I did in the British Army," remarked O'Brien, who, to his endless despair, had seen the Vietnamese Communists beat America by following a twenty-five-hundred years old strategy. He recited from memory." Attack an inferior force with a superior one where the enemy least expects. The worst generalship is to besiege walled cities."

"They won't," she cautioned mildly.

"Those leaks came from somebody brilliantly placed, who enjoyed access to raw intelligence from more than South Korean sources." O'Brien stared at the faces round the wooden table.

She spoke quietly but her words struck like a typhoon, "We *have* somebody inserted with the power to create national disorder and open the gates for our people's army."

"You forget American power," scoffed her brother.

She warned, "A clever strategy is followed by our high command. We have a time-table. We know the enemy's plans."

Paul said, "Chung's only plan is to stay in power."

"Chung's more ambitious," laughed his aunt. "These Olympics serve three gambles."

"I must agree," said O'Brien, though Paul was often right. "The Government stays popular because the games are a success, the economy improves, relations open with Communist countries thus isolating North Korea."

She reminded the three men, "We are building the beautiful Azelea Stadium by the Taedong River and with seating capacity twice the size of its rival on the Han River. We cannot afford a communist boycott in summer *next* year! North Korea must attack the Seoul Olympics stealthily,"

"But the plan hung on a destruction of the Seoul Games - by any means - which allowed Pyongyang to offer itself as emergency host city." Doctor Moon waited for his sister's answer.

"Providing it appeared the work of southern dissident students, even the attempt on Chung's life." She watched their faces. "The new plan is not so obvious."

"At least that means Kwon and Han are key instruments for a northern success."

O'Brien was both glad and horrified: nearly all their efforts, so far, went along one promising road. He knew North Korea would run more than one operation. What were the others and who was in control? Sister Moon was close to power, she did not rule, only the two Kims gave orders. If the new plan was an invitation for open warfare, South Korea might strike back.

As though reading his thoughts, she stressed, "We must not become distracted by communist agents. There are hundreds. Most dormant. We must concentrate on those with Olympic tasks."

"Is there an open opinion clash?" asked O'Brien, resisting an urge to touch a conjuring set within arm's reach near the window. He supposed such a situation possible even in a communist kingdom.

She replied confidently. "The leaders *are* forced to listen because they need the support of our security bureau *and* our military's backing. Danger starts when they play off one faction against another."

"By favouring an aggressive plan made behind your backs," realised O'Brien, still drawn to the child's game.

"Never forget," she warned with deliberate sharpness, "father and son are both extremely unpredictable. I cannot emphasise that too often. We generals are the last to hear about some new operations."

"Sounds like Mason," observed O'Brien, not entirely frivolous.

She stroked the tiger while she talked. "Our leader takes little daily interest in state business. We deal with a middle-aged bachelor who wears high-heeled shoes and is so self-conscious about his five feet few inches that he perms his hair to appear taller! He weighs nearly two-hundred pounds and avoids thick clothing. A heavy drinker and smoker yet obsessed with health, who sanitizes the house each day, keeps away anybody with a contagious disease, even brings his own food to social events."

"He also sounds a trifle insecure." O'Brien smiled vaguely.

She shrugged off personal responsibility. "How can I do his character justice? He's irrational, self-righteous, un-predictable. Hates losing, resents even a hint of personal criticism, easily insulted. Forgets most appointments but never a friend's birthday. Loves attention, often draws it through cruel pranks : he sent senior officials home naked from one of his wild receptions!"

O'Brien wondered how Kim treated his female cadre. "What's his attitude towards women?"

"Mixed. He shows almost a blind respect for his natural mother but is overcome with contempt towards his step-mother : he vandalises her photographs. He's never alone yet distrusts his closest followers. As a woman, of course, I don't count, not as a threat."

"I gather he enjoys comfort," said O'Brien

"Lives in luxury."

"No special girl."

"A mansion in Pyongyang is staffed by graduates of outstanding beauty who returned from nursing training overseas. He keeps a large library of pornographic films. Escalators avoid stairs! But that is also a Japanese taste. He has country houses in our resort regions which are similarly comfortable."

"He enjoys watching executions" sighed Paul before she listed more hobbies.

She didn't react . "His Achilles heel remains stalwart faith in the creed of self-help invented by his father : Juche: seek no help, survive alone. He sticks to whatever he fully controls....often reckless.... though watertight operations."

"We know the killer-squad is a live threat," said Paul, now displaying less impatience, reaching for the thermos. "Who are the other dangerous cases?"

His aunt postponed this question with a charming smile. She turned to her brother and her calm face warned that she bargained hard. She demanded sweetly, "Can you deliver?"

"We did, yesterday, in the national capital. Obviously we can reduce the power of the military in South Korean politics." Moon gave a tolerant flap of his wrinkled hand towards the open window but he made a condition. "As long as there are no fresh outrages. Then nobody will control our generals, least of all themselves, restraint will be un-fashionable."

"So will peace..... I do not trust some of our soldiers this summer." She glanced towards Paul. "That brings us to your concern, plans that exist, known threats." She paused, clearing her thoughts, choosing English words with painstaking concern.

"We are running an agent at senior level inside South Korea's national security. The agent is placed in the Olympic Command and Control Centre. I know only that his duties are extensive. Our Dear Leader controls this operation through his personal cabinet. This is dangerous."

"Only one agent," frowned O'Brien, watching those elderly, cunning faces. He was worried by her remark about North Korea's generals, and compared this news with the latest concerns of another general, Harry Todd.

"Only one to my knowledge," she confirmed with quiet authority before delivering her next blow. "This agent is deeply involved with your fascinating airship." She sat back, passed her cup to Paul, watched their faces, judging the shocked atmosphere while the room buffeted from afternoon breeze.

O'Brien whistled through his teeth, the news was timely and dreadful. "That narrows the field somewhat."

"It's a tightly controlled operation," she cautioned, "and there's a western code-name... Mole."

"A neat touch," conceded O'Brien enviously. "which certainly avoids any confusion."

She paid for this compliment with a brief smile. "Pyongyang runs by invitation only. I never see raw material from Mole. I know he reports rarely but is respected, sensitive, hides behind an important political cloak, one of great weight. Mole has a future, solid prospects; somebody worth adventures."

"Is Mole alarmed by the delay in our airship programme?" O'Brien did not expect a precise answer. He grew conscious that, probably, Mole was the most dangerous foe. On the windy beach, a seabird screamed.

"You may have solved a riddle." Sister Moon looked at him curiously. "There has been a flurry of Mole activity in the Dear Leader's cabinet for several weeks."

He contemplated her smooth old face and wondered if anything in Korea was too absurd for reality. Was the jig-saw at last coming together. He said, "Yesterday night General Kim sent his senior airship man, Yoon, down to Pusan with orders not to return empty handed from the harbour customs."

Doctor Moon rasped, "He will succeed. Pusan harbour is dirty and extremely deep."

"Let us wait," proposed his sister quietly. "If calm descends over the Dear Leader's staff..... within a few days..... that would imply a possible link."

"Why the airship," asked O'Brien, doubts lingering. General Kim had cordoned off the Olympic sites with a hundred thousand police and soldiers. They trained daily. A division of rangers would guard the Athletes' Village alone. He wanted proof. "Who can rate our airship as that potent?"

She sat with her wax smooth hands clasped on the table, that kind mouth amused, her narrow eyes deadly serious. "Perhaps your sales talk was rather effective.

Were the North Koreans frightened of the camera and its incredible range? Nobody could cross the border, day or night, without detection. An infra-red system for night vision was part of its technical architecture. Flying over the Games should be like taking a snakes and ladders board off one of the packed bookshelves. The whole Olympic Stadium and its neighbouring park, where gymnastics, swimming, tennis and other sports took place, would be seen at a glance. Was there a spectacular threat? Harry Todd swore that Kim Il Sung was capable of anything from terrorism to a full scale attack. Todd devoured raw intelligence yet refused each demand from the Pentagon for a final risk prediction. Todd, instead, devised a plan where aircraft flying in men and equipment, would lift out a quarter of a million people, including most of the Olympic Teams. The Russians were coming by cruise liner from Vladivostok. China was debating whether its team should fly to Seoul on specially escorted flights. Nobody was confident. For all General Kim's declarations on American television, South Korea still could not promise a safe Olympics.

She added ominously, "Within my hearing, last week, the Dear Leader expressed fears that your airship won't fly in time for the Seoul Games."

"What *is* he after?" Nothing made sense on this remote peninsular, until you turned a theory inside out, whereupon, all became hideously obvious.

No South Korean police pilot would be ready for solo flying by September. A British pilot would patrol over the Seoul Games. This situation was accepted by General Kim but to save face a title would be concocted: Rose was about to become a 'technical' flying adviser. What did the North Koreans want? The airship was filled with helium, there was no risk a small bomb could create a fireball over the main stadium. He supposed they could monitor its signal traffic, which would grant instant access to every television picture fed into Kim's command and control centre at the Olympic Park. O'Brien had always expected an attack on the airship operation but this news made him very uneasy for it implied that North Korea wanted to exploit the airship for some perverted role during the actual games.

He recognised that a floating spy was vulnerable, an obvious visible weapon, reminding the entire world how the host country daily kept order. Anything more lethal than space cameras would have to slip past Rose's suspicious tyranny and Rose distrusted slant-eyed people, nursed fond memories of shooting Indonesians at night in the Borneo jungle.

"We are bringing in our own man from Britain. No build crew. Our chief pilot is a professional bastard. The kit will be under his personal control all twenty four hours." O'Brien stayed sceptical.

"Maybe the damage has been done," said Paul.

"Those boxes spent too long in Pusan Customs but our pilot will check every part before it goes anywhere near the construction site."

"Where is that?" asked Sister Moon, finally allowing herself a distraction, taken with a sea shell collection nestling in a cardboard box placed on a table near the creaking door.

O'Brien also admired the shells. They were all shapes, colours, and sizes. Then he answered. "Near the Han River Regatta Course.... we hear rumours!"

"Not ready yet?" She smiled sympathy.

"Kim should have our hangar up within a fortnight," he maintained stoutly, while his mind relived the previous night's riots.

She spoke his own next thoughts, "Clear warning signals are essential... and closer liaison."

"I'll alert Noah in Hong Kong," said O'Brien.

"Makes one alarmed at what's not yet discovered." Paul remarked in a gloomy mood.

His aunt promptly stripped the camouflage from another communist penetration. "We have a live agent at lower level whose targets are connected with the airship operation."

O'Brien almost despaired. Not another policeman. And what operation? Providing Yoon was effective and Kim truly feared, at that moment, the airship lay in boxes on the back of a container truck, grinding north towards Seoul. Nobody yet knew where it should be built... or did they? Kang would meet Yoon in the morning to pin down the final choice. "Can you be more specific?" he urged, wrists already gently throbbing.

"I wish there was more detail on these persons who directly threaten your work," she apologised with her humble smile then lowered her voice for attention. "There is another important agent who operates at political level with orders to cause widespread riots before the Olympic Games."

"Name?" asked O'Brien, impressed, and drank some cold tea before his neck muscles tightened.

"That's my problem," she confessed, "younger Kim has the reins.... nobody else."

Paul was about to speak when, his father intervened. "As you can imagine, Michael, years back we had to choose a career path for my sister: on balance, we found it wiser, safer, that she could protect our network, rather than direct hostile operations. My sister became Chief of Counter-Intelligence."

O'Brien set down his tea cup and let his eyes rest for a second on Mark Twain occupying a shelf with Stevenson. While South Korean governments tried and often failed to penetrate the north, by blind-folding the communist regime, Sister Moon ensured their network flourished until they enjoyed a more balanced and detailed understanding of the Korean peninsular than either of its governments. The price was no direct knowledge and therefore no control over North Korean offensive plans. But it was a long war in a country where the leadership grew old together.

"Your political agent sounds horribly similar to Cha Se Dong," said O'Brien though Heaven knew what Cha would gain from taking North Korean money and setting about the collapse of South Korean society.

"Cha Se Dong is his own man," insisted the Doctor, chest shaking, cunning eyes near closed, cheeks inflating with humour. "Perhaps Kim Il Sung pays a little towards our love of democratic freedom? But not through Cha..... although our students have less scruples...... he may pay for their riots."

"Japanese banks pay," scorned his sister, "they fear sixty million Koreans toiling together in asia's Prussia."

"Who else knows?" persisted O'Brien. Now those original warnings from Moscow and Peking, which told Mason about three threats to the Seoul Games, matched the news brought by Sister Moon. Nothing was too devious for Mason : but was she the original source of Moscow and Peking's reports? What better way to feed the Soviet Union's and China's distrust of North Korea. He waited for the crucial answer; his strategy rode or fell on her next words.

"Younger Kim's personal cabinet know, I know... you all know." She settled sharp eyes on him, wanting a reaction, confirmation that her message was clear before adding, "There could have been leaks out of Pyongyang from other mouths and in other directions.... but only that an operation is live, that its purpose is political sabotage through instability, no details."

"Doubters exist even in his personal cabinet?" delved O'Brien, guessing that somebody talked, wishing nobody had.

She regarded the question as superfluous. "They're told nothing and quickly discarded. I'll spare you sordid details."

More than a few North Koreans would shy at orders to attack the Olympic teams of their Communist allies but he remarked calmly enough,

"We have identified three main threats.... now we must match faces."

Nobody disagreed : O'Brien felt his neck muscles rest. Sister Moon was not working in six directions at once but only four: Moscow and Peking ran at least one agent together in Pyongyang. Life was simpler. There were *only* three hostile operations and all run from Pyongyang.

Outside the wind died as the sun sank. O'Brien twisted his wrist and saw that it was nearly six o'clock. For a few more minutes they could speak freely. Paul still had not explained why he wanted the girl brought. Usually his father was behind these strange decisions, which proved, without exception, founded on brilliant simplicity. Just for an instant O'Brien tried calculating how they would deal with these threats, confident now, that the original three terrorist attacks were reduced by one failed attempt on Chung. There remained the Cardinal and a third target who might be Cha Se Dong though the Olympic Committee could not be ignored in this lethal equation.

"Last but not least, one mature student," said Doctor Moon, "who wishes to lead a second Kwangju uprising against Chung and his military party."

Was this why the Moon's had allowed the girl within a few yards of their most sensitive meeting in thirty years. O'Brien volunteered an envious shake of the head and scratched his wavy hair. "I suppose," he recognised wistfully, "long life brings surprising rewards. You take her warning seriously."

"Yes," said the Doctor firmly. "That boy is determined, clever, stubborn, and, providing he doesn't destroy himself through foolhardy gestures, might become presi...dent."

"You want him kept alive." O'Brien stared into the old man's misty eyes where he met only friendship. He understood now. "Francis, we'll lift him."

"There is no alternative," apologised Paul.

"Will the girl help?" Sister Moon glanced at their faces, her own questioned whether they were assuming rather too readily that a girl would react like a man.

"Paul's going to ask her in a few minutes," said the Doctor.

"Then stick to saving lives," she ordered Paul and shot a stern glance across the small table at his father. "Most young girls don't care for politicians and she may not regard an Olympic Games as anymore than bloodless war."

"Yes Mee-Sook," sighed her brother but Paul left no doubt the instructions were understood.

Silently O'Brien wished him luck. Diana was a riddle, her motives impossible to understand, yet, without Diana's help, the job was much harder, though not impossible. What would Paul do if she refused to fall into line? Though he guessed that the Moons knew most things about the girl, including some dark event or moment which placed her in their power or debt, which made refusal quite impossible, still he gave them an account of discovering a surprise visitor during the small hours.

"Am I paranoic," he asked blankly, directing his question at the only female in the little room, adding with some restraint," Surely well bred young Korean girls never shelter under a stranger's roof, never visit foreign houses without a close escort."

Paul vigorously scratched his head in an attempt to deflect the awkward question. O'Brien ignored him and waited for an opinion from his aunt who at least seemed equally lost.

She retreated behind a bemused expression which made plain that both age and address disqualified her opinions on manners for modern South Korean girls. "Paul....you have grown daughters...tell Michael whether he should fear for our network or his freedom!"

Paul lost control, almost laughing aloud, his eyes glistening from the absurd irony, yet realising the trouble caused by her strange behaviour. "My fault, Mike, though allow that time was racing past and you were missing for several hours. They're a very honest family. But direct to a fault, no nuances no subtleties. She interpreted my orders with Park iron discipline....almost North Korean!" Paul was rattled.

O'Brien had no wish to offend, there was no time for polite fencing. He remarked cheerfully, hoping to provoke, succeeding, "A salon communist."

Paul became adamant. "Communists hold no monopoly on democratic progress in South Korea. That is our constant message, Mike, why we're all here."

"You know the family well."

"Generations," declared Paul, smiling forgiveness, calmer. "Diana is smart, a little stubborn, but utterly loyal. Give her another chance, she will learn fast. Don't forget, Mike, we run great personal risks when working with these young people. So do they with our generations."

That argument made sense and O'Brien retreated. "Why don't we leave you alone, Paul, so you can talk......she won't be long now."

"Father?"

"Cap.....ital." The Doctor rose, scraping his chair on the wooden floor, shuffled to the open window and studied the beach for several seconds while evening's steadier wind lifted his thin white hair. "Ah..... I see her about to wan...der up the sands. We must take away our cups. Come," he turned towards his sister, "let us choose some revolutionary music for Paul's taste in the peace of our cottage."

"Whistle a sad love song." For once Paul grinned disrespectfully at his father then looked across the table at O'Brien. "She'll bite... just allow me one hour, then pick her up from here. We don't want her even noticing a lantern among the firs."

They stood quickly, tidied the chairs and table. O'Brien stared nostalgically around the little wooden house. A children's world surrounded their struggle, watched them from shelves crammed with books and games, silent, inquisitive, involved. Who played games the most, O'Brien asked himself. Was it children in summer time? Adults on this spring afternoon? Nobody could tell. Still far too many twists and bumps lay along the road for knowing whether they would win or lose. Yet, somehow, these children's dreams served as a sheet anchor, reminded one of a world where ideals counted. Or were they all four, merely in love with childhood, secrets and magic spells, thrills and adventures, wild moments, a little calculated mischief at which parental authority would smile, forget and forgive.

No longer certain of his own motives, leaving the flimsy door ajar, he smiled encouragement at a placid Paul who sat ready, those small hunched shoulders and artist's hands, that mild face touched by the golden light, an oriental Peter Pan waiting to spring a nursery trap. O'Brien hurried down the wooden steps into the late afternoon. The sun sank towards its silver path on the quiet sea. Small waves crept onto the flat sands and along the gentle beach an elfin figure stared resolutely seawards. O'Brien turned and followed the older Moons' voices through the bushy pines.

16

Among the pines a cottage made from white planks loomed ahead; its tin roof, steeply pitched against summer rains, blurred with sudden night. Magnolia's seductive perfume drifted on a cold seawind which brought waves breaking onto empty sands. For the first time since his journey into the Imjin mountains, O'Brien marvelled at a sky scattered with timid fires from countless stars. The senior Moons, engrossed, ambled in front, chattering softly, finding a bridge across lost years. He felt they deserved some time together and strolled among other little cottages tucked under the bushy pines. He wondered how Paul would deal with the girl: Moon senior would not want to reveal his sister to anybody, let alone a girl recruited an hour previously. Soon he wandered back towards the shadowy cottage.

"Michael?" called the Doctor's voice.

"Coming.... how is Diana?"

"Don't worry," said Moon gruffly, "Paul is expert."

"I meant afterwards.... even if she reacts positively."

He drew closer and saw their outlines on a rickety veranda. They were sitting on thin cushions, drinking rice wine from small porcelain cups. A fat jug stood on a tiny table. The Doctor coughed and spoke from the gathering darkness. "Paul expects you down at the library in ten minutes."

"I'm sorry this was so short," came his sister's voice.

"Longer next time." O'Brien's tone gave away his concern for her return without discovery. Sister Moon came from the bravest breed of agent: those who fought from spiritual belief. For over two hours they had carried on with an intensive de-briefing that covered every aspect of North Korea and its strange regime which could impact on the South and the Seoul Olympic Games. Music had been selected as emergency triggers, warnings of imminent danger like the falling barometer when a hurricane approaches. But O'Brien would urge Noah that something more sophisticated than a tape-recorder and radio was required in Pyongyang: Sister Moon desperately needed highly advanced miniaturised electronics, assuming they wanted her kept alive.

She came silently and took his right hand in both hers, warm smooth skin passing its messages: sincerity, friendship, mutual respect from shared dangers which tore down all barriers, cut through the tribal mists. "We will not see each other again this side of the Olympic Games, Michael, may God bring us all safely to peace and happier years."

"Yours will be the greatest burden," said O'Brien, holding his fingers steady as she examined them and approved the rough skin of hands worked often.

"And yours the worst," she smiled kindly while they memorised each other in the cool night.

When she released his fingers, O'Brien lowered his voice to a hoarse whisper, "God speed and I'll send you some modern kit."

What a world, he thought, taking a last look at the intelligent calm on her remarkably preserved face: she could have passed for fifty instead of more than seventy. Perhaps there was a slower pace in Pyongyang though the threatening atmosphere ground on relentlessly. He saw her arm raised, more a feminine salute than a matron's farewell; would they ever meet a second time? His mind turned over the last hours of conversation as he walked slowly through the dark, finding his way along the sandy path, not hurrying when night vision took command, vaguely aware of the pines swishing overhead as chill night wind brought a crash of surf from the invisible beach. There was a dim lamp hanging over the library door. He clambered up the steps and gently pushed the worn handle.

Two slight figures faced each other across the round table on which an oil lamp burned, steadily filling the library with a grey fug, throwing canary light over the book shelves. Paul, instructing the tense girl, wore a severe expression, distorting his mild face, perhaps annoyed by somebody interrupting. The girl seemed composed with her back to the door but he noticed how she sat ramrod straight. Both stared round. The girl began anxiously twisting her tiny fingers as he entered the drafty room. Paul had lowered the shutters, probably at night fall, keeping out the wind, safeguarding their privacy: few people wandered on the beach at night, only soldiers from a neighbouring ranger school patrolled. Nobody would take much notice of the outside security lantern which burned all year round. O'Brien closed the door carefully.

"May I join you?" he asked the seated pair.

"We're just finishing." Paul smiled encouragement at the pale girl.

O'Brien exchanged glances with a suddenly drained Paul, slid a chair from the table and sat down. "Can we help each other?"

Paul looked at the girl whose eyes flashed in the warm glow.

"I hope so," she whispered.

O'Brien watched her shadow on the books behind. Her crown was perfectly rounded and he wondered if the blood of another race flowed through her veins. He rested his forearms on the table. "We must leave."

"Keep us fully informed," chided Paul sternly, "no weakness, no second thoughts, Diana."

"I will." She brushed back her wealth of tangled hair with small nervous fingers.

O'Brien looked purposefully at Paul whose sad eyes granted permission to press the most delicate question and leave the girl one further option for her shocked conscience.

"Would money help persuade your brother that his scheme is mad and cruel on his own home and district?"

He saw her face stiffen with bitter pride. Blank eyes challenged his own while sooty brows arched in scorn, before, voice husky, she pounced, "My family never take bribes, Mr O'Bean; I am shamed that you even consider buying David as a serious choice."

He smoothed over the inept moment. "You're quite sure that David is not under any financial pressure..... from somebody wishing to make use of his name."

"Positive," she replied coldly although her eyes relented; perhaps she began to wonder whether her first reaction was too hasty.

"We had to know," said O'Brien, gently pushing further, but she lowered her long lashes to avoid his remorseless stare.

"You know where to find our family, Diana." Paul rose from the small table, allowing the girl and O'Brien to stand before lifting the oil lamp and holding it shoulder high. Their shadows danced on the rows of books and children's games, chased each other over the planks and beams of the crude ceiling.

She stood to attention before Paul and bowed abruptly. He responded with an awkward bend of his torso that made the lamp flicker more wildly.

"You have to go, Mike, I gather," he said as the lamp flame steadied and thick smoke rose and spread beneath the roof beams.

"My apologies, Paul," said O'Brien, keeping up theatre, feeling slight shame, for the girl looked worn out and doubtless was starving. "How I wish it were possible to stay tonight in this sea air."

"Another time soon," smiled Paul sincerely, "Taum pun pepshida." He gave the weary girl some final advice. "We *all* care. No Korean who loves our country wishes the Olympics ruined..... David swims into a flood tide."

"I am alright," she insisted.

O'Brien opened the door and stared into the starry night. Sharp wind tugged at the pines and a sea broke heavily along the empty beach.

"Coast is clear."

He shook Paul's free hand then quickly beckoned the girl to follow. "Sorry to rush you around, Diana." He felt sympathy as she trailed meekly down the wooden steps. "We'll buy some Ramyon on the road home."

They stood below while Paul locked the frail door and waved farewell. Sinking into the sand, they walked towards the car hidden under a large pine tree. Starlight marked their path, an ebbing tide exploded then sucked at the wet beach, sad wind rustled among pine branches fragrant with magnolia.

A phut echoed, then a second. Two orange flares soared above the wooded headland, hung in the night, trailed thick smoke, revealing every wave inside a dazzling circle, until they spluttered and slowly died.

One eye closed to save his night vision, he stumbled into the girl, reached down and gratefully squeezed her firm shoulder.

"Sorry.... I'm clumsy tonight," he breathed, recovering balance, wincing as the awkward movement shot pain into his old leg wound. She seemed not offended and drew close to support him better.

"What was that?" she whispered nervously.

"A parachute flare... fired from a mortar." He took the weight off his aching leg and listened for several seconds. There was silence from the small headland. He explained quietly, "The Rangers shoot out to sea in case somebody tries to come ashore at night."

"From North Korea?" She looked wide-eyed into his face. "Our island must be too far south. I've never seen that before."

"I expect you're right." He offered a silent prayer, glad that Sister Moon was safely chatting with her brother a few hundred yards inland. He felt the pain recede and loosened his grip on the girl's shoulder.

"I don't mind," she invited softly, "what happened to your leg?"

"Somebody shot it."

She stared at him with parted lips. The night made her face tender like a child suddenly confronted by a new and cruel reality. He smothered a smile. When they found the car, sprinkled with magnolia petals and pine needles, he held open the passenger door.

Keeping his voice low, he urged, "Don't be frightened, we'll cover the first mile without headlamps."

"I won't scream," she retorted and obediently slid into her seat, closed the door without a further word.

The engine warm, he slipped the car into first gear, let it roll slowly forward, crunching over the pine twigs. Starglow was enough. On their left lay the black sea sparsely decorated with faint lights. Soon the beach was left behind and they were driving north. She released a tense breath.

"Feeling better?" he asked.

She did not answer but concentrated on the road curving towards the headlamp beams, studied the way he drove, that special elastic judgement which sets aside the veteran parachutist. She enjoyed the sense of relaxed speed and her eyes widened in the darkness. O'Brien suggested, "Try the radio...... might be some good music on KBS."

She leaned forward then found the switch, illuminating her lovely face while she searched for a station, eventually filling the car with Vivaldi's joyful oboe concerto. She slid back and rested her head so that she could watch her chauffeur.

"Do you believe in fate Mr. O'Bean?"

There was a simple solution. "Why don't you try my first name."

She asked seriously, "Michael or Mike?"

"Either, but, please, never O'Bean."

"You're awfully patient," she complimented but he glimpsed her lips form a teasing smile.

"We can stop for soup soon," he assured her a few moments later, "just want us nearer the Seoul Pusan Highway."

"You haven't answered."

O'Brien's left hand strayed to his wavy copper hair and he scratched his scalp which itched from tiredness. He shrugged, for once, caught.

"Well?" she challenged.

"More than I care to think," he laughed.

"You mean that?"

He nodded and returned his hand to the wheel for a sharp climbing bend. "Don't worry about your brother. I'm not sure exactly what we'll do..... let alone how.... we'll take care of David's revolution."

"There's barely a month."

"When's the anniversary of Kwangju?"

"May twenty-eight. I dread this month." She added reverently, "If you stop him, you're a saint."

"Less a sinner."

She yawned twice then and fell fast asleep. He drove over hills and the headlamps probed orchards and paddies while the road snaked through haunted countryside. After an hour, not far off, he saw the low lanterns of a restaurant nestling under a ginkyo copse. He slowed and the girl woke. She rubbed her eyes and offered, "Stretch your legs......Mike.... I'll buy our soup."

"Let me give you some money." He dug his fingers into a pocket found a few crumpled thousand won notes and placed them in her lap.

She jumped smartly out of the car, proudly flicked her tumbling hair, leaving the money behind, ensuring no further discussion. He enjoyed her determined short strides towards the poorly lit old wooden house, then climbed out and paced back and forth under shadowy ginkyos. She must choose when to speak; frankly, he hoped she really understood Paul. He searched for a quiet place and relieved himself into an azalea bush. Comfortable, he walked back, found her already sitting with the car door open.

She held out a tray on which stood a large tin bowl full of steaming soup, a cup of boiled rice, wooden chopsticks wrapped in thin paper, small bottles of sauces, a small bowl of green tea. Her own was balanced on her lap. She searched his face for approval. "My instincts warned that Kalbi Tang.... cow bone soup.... was safest for your tummy. We boil it for a whole day and night to kill off the bugs."

He smiled thanks at the girl and placed his tray on the warm bonnet, emptied the rice into his soup, poured in the sauces, then tore the paper from his chopsticks and stirred, cooling the soup, mixing the rice and sauce. She sat, chopsticks flashing, filling her small stomach at astonishing speed.

O'Brien asked casually, "Did the landlord bring out these trays?"

She laughed between mouthfuls and told him, "You're my old grandfather.... he wanted to carry you inside..... I regretted that you were eccentric and hid from strangers."

"Near enough reality." He tried the rice gruel and enjoyed its savoury bite. "Where is David?"

The chopsticks stopped half way to her open mouth. "At our home."

"On the island."

She nodded then ate more rice. "He meets the other people in their houses."

"Their parents' houses?"

She dropped the chopsticks in the bowl and her eyes smouldered. "I mean, you agree, how absolutely stupid when the police follow him everywhere!"

O'Brien wondered if her brother had a sensible reason that was not obvious. "But David isn't foolish.... rash, yes, but not daft."

"Cocky is your English word," She displayed startling fury before she calmed down. "I don't know, Mike, perhaps it's too clever for my normal brain. David regards the police and army as stupid."

His mouth burned from spiced rice broth and he sipped the stale tea. He considered this accusation an instant longer. "Diana, sometimes that ploy works. Who are his main helpers? They're the walking clues who might alert a security force."

She stared intently into her tea bowl, tilting it enough to examine how the leaves lay inside: content, she replied, "All from our island high school, yet it's odd, something is wrong."

"Are they from David's year?"

"Oh yes, that's normal." She put down the tea bowl, started on her soup, then brooded. "It's too open, Mike, they're discrete but not secretive, not enough..... this Government is horrid, but not foolish, not that way."

Mentally he applauded Paul, who pulled off a coup, mastering this girl's spirit. Next came harnessing her wild emotions. And Paul, wisely, left that daunting challenge for a barbarian foreigner who cared nothing for tortuous minuets over preserving 'face'. She talked sense. Yet from his own training and experience, he knew the brother might simply employ a proven tactic. He shrugged and said, "Nobody sane would plot so openly. Therefore, no plot exists? It's been done before." He asked her bluntly, "Sure you're not a little envious?"

She took instant offence. "In whatever way?"

"Korean sons take risks which are absolutely forbidden for Korean daughters." He gave her a sympathetic smile. "This is a frustrating time for

Korean girls your age, some freedoms, nowhere near enough."

"You men are so bloody stupid. Stop patronising, Mike, boys have no monopoly on ego." She laughed and in her melodious voice, scoffed, "David thinks that his *brilliant* master plan will force Chung to release Cha Se Dong from house arrest. I bet the police know, General Kim knows, Chung himself knows. When David moves.... they'll strike.... harvesting further proof that Cha Se Dong is behind most campus violence. They'll both be locked up for the next century."

O'Brien pursed his lips and found himself respecting her lecture. She recognised how her brother's plot rested on a flawed foundation : vanity : refusing to credit the suited general who governed South Korea with any gift for clever ideas. Park was trapped, unless a wild card entered the pack; he no longer listened to his young sister.

"Do they have any guns?"

She shrugged and with both hands lifted the big bowl to her mouth, tipping it until her face was hidden and she drained the last drop.

O'Brien silently cursed. There were guns. Paul Moon made mistakes rarely. Park sounded a clever maniac. Poor girl, poor family. He started again. "Where are these guns, Diana, have you any idea?"

"None at home."

She was right, nothing else mattered: no firearms lay hidden under her father's roof. He debated whether she knew the significance of that information. Perhaps she did, for there was a sudden tightening on her doll's face and fear lurked in those beautiful eyes while the chopsticks were ignored.

"No violence.... you wouldn't dare," she pleaded, sensing betrayal.

"Suppose we just snatch him for a few days," bargained O'Brien, keen to cool her temper, worried that the landlord would grow curious and wander outdoors, fully aware that he bore no resemblance to a Korean grandfather.

"Snatch?"

O'Brien started again. "Take him off somewhere safe."

She became a small spitfire. "You *mean* kidnap?"

"A shade safer than a mickey mouse attempt at armed rebellion."

Tears began flowing down her ivory cheeks as the bitter claws of maverick new forces dug into her troubled soul. She stared, clutching the tray, that tough facade broken, the face tormented by reproach. "I'm sorry, I'm sorry," she shook helplessly, "why must our choices always be so bloody rotten.... what have we done wrong. I need time, Mike, just a little. Everything is bleak."

O'Brien knew she was wavering and he was harsh. "I can't do the job....
without help..... we need your knowledge, girl, we need *you*."

Almost at once she became quiet, fighting back with hatred, yet defeat
slowly spreading across her fragile face. "You are a *bastard*, Mister O'Brien,
an utter *fucking bastard!*"

For once, he indulged in a moment of mute satisfaction: the little bitch
pronounced his name right. He leaned down and bared his teeth, mere inches
from her exquisite oriental nose.

"You're a bright girl. The way we keep your brother out of deep shit is
obvious.... to you... as myself. Hate me with pleasure, it helps, it's excellent
therapy, but you swear and right now, that you'll obey, because, frankly, they
can waste your brother. For me, Diana, he's just another job."

There was an ugly silence. Murder lurked in her dull eyes as she gripped
the tray with elegant marble knuckles. Suddenly she drew a long sobbing
breath, honey and pale peach returned to her cheeks, those eyes hinted at
sorrow. When the fingers relaxed, she asked meekly, "Tell me, honestly,
Mike, what did your brain call me just now?"

"I won't repeat it in front of a lady."

* * * * * * * * * * * *

When he drove into the country night, Diana fell peacefully asleep, breathing
deeply, hands open on her lap, bruised emotions no longer strong enough for
fighting with each other, her mind drifting on a hidden ocean. Within an hour
they passed through the bright streets of Onyang, where early season holiday
makers strolled under leafy ginkyos, whole families taking the cool air,
snatching a break from hot springs under cheap hotels.

Several miles beyond the little town, a distant glare revealed hundreds
of headlamps searching the darkness, buses and trucks battling on the main
highway. O'Brien ground his teeth and slowed down, paid at the toll booth,
then drove northward, blinded by the traffic streaming from Seoul. He knew
roughly where she lived. On reaching the southern suburbs, he took an exit
near the river, and, skilfully avoiding several near collisions with express
buses, found a small street leading to dim apartment blocks, each with its
number painted high on solid concrete flanks. There was a gateway in the
granite garden wall and he drove into a large car park. Few lights shone from

the rows of thickly curtained windows protected by fake balconies. A faint odour of Kim Chi fled from the nearest doorway. He was reminded of a German barracks.

She stirred, stretched, ran waking fingers through wild hair, found a comb in her skirt pocket and began stroking out tangles, pulling down each tress until they spilled over her shoulders, checking her work in the little mirror overhead. She glanced sideways, reproachfully yawned. "Already back in horrible Seoul."

"Sorry, we're late for your next supper." O'Brian clambered out, stiff from driving. He checked the car park.

A night watchman observed with disapproval from the shabby doorway of the nearest block. Over a low hedge, in a children's playground with slides and climbing frames, giant metal ladybirds gaped in a neat row. He opened her door and to his mild surprise, she reached for his hand. "You look exhausted," she apologised sleepily, "I should have done some driving."

"Better you snored," he replied with total conviction; a crash on the Pusan Highway with the girl driving would have shut down the whole operation. Her cheeks faintly flushed.

He reached inside, took her small warm hand, helped her stand in the silent car park. Diana leaned forward, her drowsy head touched his chest and she drew a deep breath, clutched his strong fingers, wanting to feel another human close in the restless night. She looked at him with wide serious eyes as her small body shuddered from spent emotion.

Meaning to release the girl, he held her gently, for it was late and he wanted no trouble from a fretting aunt. But his arms simply refused. Instead, he pulled her close, met a startled face, felt soft thick hair and a babe's cheek caress his wind-burned face, before she meekly gave a welcoming sugary mouth.

He tasted shy lips promising future pleasure, kissed her twice, gently, then kissed warm cheeks, running his fingers through wisps of long fragrant hair.

She whispered with a mocking smile, "Is this how you British recruit secret agents."

He laughed quietly and cradled her with his arms, squeezing her strong little body, amazed this creature was soft and yet supple, enjoying his tempting troubled angel, knowing he was highly irresponsible: she still might prove herself dangerous North Korean honey. Meanwhile, a falling star had landed in his path and when he reached down, grasped it tenderly, a miracle sparkled in his hands. And he reminded himself, this lost star was a breathing girl from a strange and remote culture, whose emotions were like a secret code.

He glanced over her head towards the sombre apartment block. The doorman had retreated into a mean office. O'Brien pulled himself together, gave her a last hug, deliberately kissed her forehead. He was in a dangerous mood.

She stared into his face, tempting, flattered after the mild shock. "Do British men always kiss a girl's *mouth*."

O'Brien sensed the aunt and Mason loom like a shadowy moral patrol: for a second he almost believed she might actually let him take her among the ladybirds, Diana seemed so curious, so taught to respect male whims. He controlled strong rising lust and reluctantly prepared for parting. "I wish we could escape to a cottage down on that beach."

He paused to make sure that she felt trusted but saw no suspicion, no alarm in her face. "We'll sort out your brother later this week. Is that a fair deal? You survived rather a long day."

"I've known worse. A girl could develop a taste for espionage..... Mr *O'Bean*."

She stood on tip-toes and kissed his mouth, a tender exploring press, her a smile full of mystery, then walked slowly towards the apartment block, turning only for a furtive wave, hurrying inside to catch the worn lift.

17

Jade mountains wore misty avalanches where cotton trees blossomed on their steep flanks; below, a pewter Han flowed westwards towards Seoul, following clouds torn by a strong hot wind. O'Brien stood against the skyline with his brown arms folded in resignation, stamping down red earth with old suede chukka boots, contemplating a scrape larger than two soccer fields, bull-dozed by Korean army engineers working throughout the night under emergency lights. Already wind dried the top soil, orange dust flew like a desert storm between widely spaced steel towers capped with dead flood lamps. Footsteps sounded behind in the tufty grass as Rose joined him and, testing his new fake Reeboks, kicked at the fresh soil, just missing a Korean workman furiously shovelling below.

"Losing my touch," said Rose in disgust, drawing shoulder to shoulder with O'Brien, before his stone grey eyes amiably softened and his right finger and thumb strayed to rub a black eagle nose. "Perfect day for watching others sweat."

Koreans swarmed over the vast excavation. O'Brien stamped the earth, once more, checked its strength, then reminded his companion firmly, "We need these people, Abdul, no open season: remember, there's been a truce for thirty-five years..... and we're in South Korea."

"Have to take out somebody before I fly home." Rose sucked in smooth hollow cheeks, and gave his boss a mutinous grin.

"I'll supply you a hit list, Abdul," said O'Brien with forboding, "after the Games."

"You know," said Rose, whirling long sinewy arms as though firing from the hip at the toiling Koreans, "publicity always helps."

Now O'Brien laughed and watched Rose leap over the spoil to land a full four yards below and beyond where he stood on the pit rim. Thank heavens

Mason allowed enough time for recruiting his own personal team on this Korean operation. Rose strode onto the site, knowing he was the rock on whom all depended, his face enjoying that sunken look of the super fit, bright sunlight throwing a long shadow, its every movement recording a swinging panther lope which constantly threatened a spring in the least expected direction. O'Brien permitted satisfaction in his calm eyes when the Koreans, including those on the far side, stopped and stared, waiting to see where Rose went, already wary of this swarthy giant with his wiry brush of black hair, suspecting a dangerous and possibly superior animal. And he reflected too, how fortunate for Her Majesty's Orders and Directions, that Rose instantly took a liking to Kang, ruling after a day that the boy, given time, showed enough promise to make a *sprog* trooper.

"If that letter box faced bastard, Yoon, drives this chain-gang," Rose stood forty yards off, artistic hands resting on his snake hips, while his tenor voice cut through the dust storm, "you will have lift off within thirty days."

"No sweat, Abdul?"

Rose leered over the heads of a feverish Korean work party. "Put it this way.... a lot of theirs - but, my God, they work hard."

"Try and keep a civil relationship with Yoon," shouted O'Brien in a futile attempt to delay the inevitable collision of strong wills.

"Stop nagging," shot back Rose disdainfully. "Keep Yoonie' sweet? I'll just step up his daily dose of rat poison."

"We need these buggars or our ship won't fly!"

Rose bounded back across the dusty site and took the earth bank at a sprint. He scrambled up to O'Brien's vantage point, arriving in a flurry of soil, breathing normally, before his eyes carefully measured the amount of work required and his brain swiftly calculated the number of days concreting and steel erecting until their hangar stood finished. Rose would tell him real figures, not bluff.

O'Brien felt the hot sun burn his arms, glad that the warm weather had arrived early, thankful that from now onwards their work would keep them in the open air and away from Seoul's grime. His mouth tightened when he jerked a thumb at the sleek figure of Yoon climbing out of a black car, followed by three worried civilians in shirt sleeves, whom he guessed were architects. Yoon began fussing over some drawings which flapped against the strong wind; as the architects tried to clutch the sheets, every fresh gust nearly ripped them into countless shreds.

"Abdul."

"Want me to kiss 'ass?"

O'Brien shook his head. "Let him come over here, Abdul, make him know your status."

Rose showed his fine teeth. "Now I realise why Little Orphan Annie sang that song!"

"Your kind of land, Abdul."

"How about you, Mike," hinted Rose, genuine concern blended with sly humour, "Clever corrupt people with exciting morals. Where else could we ply our retirement occupation?"

"Most of the globe," answered O'Brien, trying to look serious. Yoon was marching his little party towards their temporary lookout.

"Natives approaching B'wana."

"Seen..... are you happy with those boxes stored at Kimpo Airport?" He worried about tampering and pilfering until the airship kit was safely stored in a hangar governed by Rose.

"Not really," said Rose philosophically. "Don't worry, boss, *nobody* will go near that ship without my personal chop."

"Kim's capable of adding bits on a dark night," said O'Brien while Yoon was still out of earshot, though Rose, fully alert to the danger, watched for precisely this development. A cloud drifted overhead and O'Brien enjoyed its shadow chasing dust over the building site before once more the morning sun scorched though his thick copper hair and sweat formed on his lower back. He said quickly, "Quite a lot you should know, Abdul."

Rose took in this message with a sudden question in his grey eyes and absently reached into his jeans back pocket for a pack of small cigars. "We can take a stroll along the river when Yoon's lost himself with his artichoke team."

"Quite."

"How far away is the border?" Rose tore off the cellophane wrapping and watched it fly among foamy wavelets.

O'Brien had a map in the car which they could study later. "Just under twenty miles." He converted the distance into flying time, "Let's say ten minutes."

"No big mountains."

"A few at three grand," replied O'Brien, hooking his thumbs in a leather belt which he had brought the previous night in Itaewon when giving Rose his first taste of Seoul's bright spots.

"Clear scan all the way to Pyongyang."

"The whole DMZ from coast to coast." O'Brien turned to greet a seething Yoon leading three unhappy architects. All were dirty after struggling along the bank of fresh earth, slithering in thin office loafers, now coated with thick dust. Rose laughed softly, offered a cigar to O'Brien and reached into his shirt pocket for matches, then formed a cup with his long fingers. Their heads bent low until blue smoke joined the fierce wind.

"Good morning, Mr. Yoon," said O'Brien, smoke escaping disdainfully from his hard mouth.

"Mr. O'Brown." Yoon hissed a warning to the architects who were plainly terrified of their escort, then flatly announced. "We will have the hangar ready in eleven days." He spun round silently but none of his three victims dared challenge this snap forecast.

"Excellent," decreed O'Brien before anybody could waver.

Rose thrust out a hand which Yoon countered by an attempt at finger breaking and came off worse. Controlling his training to follow through with a knee into the testicles and an elbow into the throat, instead Rose recorded the position of Yoon's shoulder holster from the cut of the dark suit: only his sudden friendliness warned O'Brien that a fight was a real risk.

Rose tested Yoon. "So you want to fly airships."

Yoon replied as though giving evidence, "I have helicopter experience."

" Excellent," smiled Rose without taking his eyes off the bulging left pocket of the policeman's dark suit. "Smith and Wesson, point three eight, Mr. Yoon?"

Yoon's face muscles froze as he fought an urge to draw and shoot Rose. Yet both men knew, the brake was fear. Yoon was concentrating on Rose's long and dangerous forearms, not absolutely certain he could pull his gun faster than the Briton could break his neck, probably with a single blow: Rose merely returned a vague smile.

Pleased that morning was shaping well, O'Brien steered their energies towards the construction task, believing that both would work hard as a form of therapy to brush aside mutual distaste.

He beckoned the timid architects forward to display their drawings. After much slithering, Korean chatter, several threatening glances from Yoon, the plans were held steady in the blustering wind. There was definitely enough length, more than four hundred feet. Two hundred feet of width was generous, but the hangar lacked height. An airship was inflated inside the build hangar.

No other method allowed the crew gondola and the engines to be fitted underneath in still conditions. This airship involved a further complication: clearance of another foot was required for the satellite camera suspended beneath the gondola and a larger, stronger pair of wheels had been fitted on the under-carriage to cope with this modification and a special electronics suite. He checked the drawings twice with no wish to create problems - enough were arising from thin air - but the hangar door height was marked as twenty meters. That was too low.

"Sorry," he decreed facing an emotional Yoon. "You can build our ship in this easily. The roof is twenty five meters. But, when it's finished, you either make the door about twenty four meters high or dismantle the whole hangar."

Yoon looked suspiciously at the cringing architects. "What do you mean?"

"It won't come through the hangar doors," explained O'Brien, aware his cigar had gone out.

Rose put it more simply. "You need a bigger hole, mate."

Yoon stared crestfallen at his foreign tormentors and O'Brien almost felt sympathy except this was not a time for kindness: perhaps there never was in Korea. "Take the roof up to twenty eight metres," he instructed sharply, "make the doors twenty four meters high."

"Better allow twenty four meters width for the doors." Rose winced as another dust cloud rolled over the hole and work parties vanished in murk thick as the debris thrown by an artillery salvo. "We may lose your airship to the permanent gale that blows along this river valley. What cunt chose this site?"

"General Kim," scowled Yoon.

O'Brien loudly cleared his throat before Rose destroyed his painstakingly nursed kibun with Korea's most powerful man after the President himself. "*Nothing* wrong with the site."

"We'll cope, Yoonie'," Rose became biblical. "What's a few cubits between friends when we're building the modern ark!"

Yoon withdrew, tense, hostile, intent on repaying the terrible loss of face just suffered from a pair of savages, while the three pitiful architects stumbled in his wake, knowing that once beyond hearing, they would suffer all his frustration. O'Brien and Rose watched them depart. When the Korean policeman drove off, they felt looser, impressed by the tireless workers on the great dust blown stage below. From where they stood, following the progress of hundreds of boiler-suited ants, neither doubted that a hangar would rise within eleven days. Nor, judging from Yoon's slow anger, that it would provide enough space under its roof for constructing an airship which took up more room than a jumbo jet. Their problems began after first flight.

O'Brien lit his cigar, thrust his hands into the pockets of his faded jeans and faced into the refreshing wind. Two hundred yards distant, tiny waves danced over the slate river: he remembered a time when the Han was a shallow and brown eel, far out across flat sand. "Come on, Abdul," he invited, striding off the rim towards overgrown brush along the river bank, letting his calm blue eyes enjoy lush mountains rising from its far shore. "Let's take that walk."

"I can treat you with the latest news from Mum's islands," announced Rose as they set off.

"She's sending her daughter over here for a fortnight," remarked O'Brien, trailing faint smoke.

Once a week, Mason signalled the latest list of Royalty, athletes, officials, media and famous faces coming for the Olympic Games. Yesterday brought the stop press number: five hundred athletes and officials selected for Seoul. The media gave six hundred names. Around a thousand people were buying tickets in London for the thirty competitions and demonstration sports. Linebacker was largely for their personal protection. All were targets.

"Genesis - Dick Mason - assured me two days ago," Rose was still trying to regain his body clockwork," or was it a couple of days back, anyway, your fellow countrymen pose no threat."

"Thanks, Abdul."

But he agreed. On an island where blood was thicker than conscience, hiring killers from a country, where within living memory, they tortured Irishmen in prison camps - he recalled that the Chinese threatened awkward captives with North Korean guards - seemed the swiftest way to kill the green dream. Mason, for a while during winter, toyed with the idea of setting up the IRA, until O'Brien refused to soldier.

They reached the wide river, started scrambling down its grassy bank towards foamy waves blown onto a grey sand shore where soil had been bull-dozed far out from the river bank.

O'Brien led, jumping over stones and bushes, towards the lively water. "I'm meeting Music Maker this week," he called over his shoulder, "we're planning our worst case scenario."

"Is that necessary?" Rose seemed amazed.

He stopped and waited, hands on hips, while Rose scrambled down the bushy slope and caught up, their eyes level, not a yard apart. "What would you do, Abdul?"

Rose recognised defeat. "Take no chances."

"I fear Mason over-loading our circuits," continued O'Brien as he started picking a way forward among thick bushes.

Rose bore no illusions about the enormity of their approaching task. "We could justify our presence by looking after the Queen's daughter properly."

"The Princess will have her two detectives."

"Armed?" Rose left complications for his leader.

O'Brien smiled wisely over his shoulder. "Not quite as heavily as you and me, Abdul."

Rose enjoyed the smug sensations that went with superior firepower. He started life as a REME apprentice before volunteering for the paras' and finding his way into the SAS. Technology *was* his personal business. He explained, "Mason briefed the two detectives. They have three bleepers which our electronics suite can monitor from a fair old altitude."

"Good man." O'Brien reached the river shore. "Does the Princess know?"

Rose fell in behind. "Guess who has the third bleeper."

"No questions asked?" O'Brien thought this somewhat out of character for the collected lady under discussion.

"She just smiled."

"I should have guessed."

The Princess would be the least of their problems in any real danger. She had survived an attack on her car in Birdcage Walk, she probably could run a covert operation quite skilfully herself. Sometimes O'Brien felt like a fabulous beast, once upon a time praised and feared, now discarded as splendid legend, no longer wanted in a complacement and timid world. Rose came from the same rough litter, war dogs bred on lush rainy islands. History. Until narrower brains created an ugly cancer somewhere on the globe then desperately searched for the elusive surgeons of warfare. In quiet times, fear brought more suspicion, envious critics who hid behind the press and hurled spiteful accusations. No wonder Mason built a web of camouflage for five years before his first operation. Now their wild don led the sharpest weapon in the western armoury.

"Who deals with the British Ambassador?" queried Rose in a rare moment of concern for diplomacy.

"Nobody, Abdul, nobody in the Embassy is cleared by *Genesis* and thus for *Andromeda* material... We don't exist."

Rose finally kindled his cigar and breathed out smoke. His personal style as an envoy seemed to bring more lasting results than most public efforts by the Foreign Secretary.

They left no trail in worn grass and wind-beaten bushes along the river-bank. Sheltered from the gusts, cooler near the lapping water, there was a sensation of stolen calm. O'Brien remembered his own cigar and found the wind had kept it smouldering. He drew smoke. "Somebody in the Police or Kim's Olympic Security HQ is trying to put a hex on our operation."

"In what way?" Rose stood enjoying the foam flecked tide flowing between green mountains.

"Wish I knew, Abdul." O'Brien, contemplated the waves, thought he saw a fish jump, knew it was only a trick of his eyes. He worried, "Check every single item of gear before fitting anything onto our ship. The North Koreans may be trying to pirate our pictures."

"They would need a foolproof communications network for that much effort to pay off." Rose picked up a stone.

"Worth it..... if they want to know if a hit team has been spotted."

"We know what the South Koreans hope from our blimp," said Rose, hurling the stone far across the sparkling river. "Can North Korea think of something better?"

"They're more aggressive," said O'Brien, stooping, picking up a stone himself and testing its weight, before, with an effortless flick of his right hand, it flew low over the water, marking its end with a brief splash. The cigar stub clenched between his teeth became soggy and he took a last puff. "Quite often sharper."

Rose squatted on his haunches to examine the riverside plants. "How do you mean?"

"Two years ago they made Chung's Government look complete fools. Announced Kim Il Sung handed in his rice bowl.... the bugger came back to life after three days ... then last year they used the bombing beauty to kill an aircraft full of construction workers coming home from the Middle East."

"Yoon is parading his police mechanics this week."

"We can have somebody sent from Detfold."

Rose picked a wild flower and held it under his nose. "These grow in Northern Laos."

"What else did you pack, Abdul?"

Rose layed the pastel pink flower on the pale skin of his open palm and examined its delicate petals. "We have a dormant system which enables us to take over the airship by electronics. There is a closed circuit system for watching anybody in the gondola.... and it's wired for sound."

"Nothing else to declare?" When O'Brien asked this question, his gaze relaxed, settled on Rose.

"You know me, boss." Rose twisted the flower over on his palm. "Three of the new Enfield rifles, three more lightweights, plus enough rounds to fight the Alamo twice over."

"Safe?"

"Tucked into the gondola and spread among the tool kit. The whole lot was scanned in Pusan."

"You were present."

Rose dropped his flower into the thick grass. "No problems, sweet vibes'."

"And J P?" How absurd, thought O'Brien even as the words left his mouth, yet in this country your own brother was an automatic suspect.

"With me the whole time."

Paranoia was catching. O'Brien felt guilty, Kang had served loyally for months.

"Tell me the rest, Mike," demanded Rose, still squatting, listening to the river slapping its bank, watching clouds hurry west.

And O'Brien also sank onto his haunches, a habit learnt years before in the mountains of Laos and Vietnam. He owed Rose the full gloom, Rose was next in line were he taken out.

"Kim's security command is packed with badly paid and highly educated national security agents, senior policemen, military officers. Apart from normal graft, plenty earn two salaries : one from the Korean Government and another from CIA's generous budget. And a few, Abdul, make a little extra."

"Where do they get the money?" Rose lifted thick eyebrows and his leather forehead creased. "People were moved out of Pyongyang last month because of food shortages."

"Their leader's priorities are not exactly visible but I follow your drift. It bothers me." O'Brien looked over his shoulder but they were completely alone. He said calmly, "One official involved with the airship is probably a North Korean agent. Probably quite senior, which narrows the field, thank

God."

"But doesn't tell us who."

"Suspect everybody attached to the airship operation. Yoon, those architects, your ground crew, even General Kim." Shrugging his shoulders, O'Brien, at that moment, doubted whether they would survive the next four months when he could glibly list the Olympic Games Security Supremo as a potential communist mole. "Nothing is too far-fetched and one thing is certain," he told Rose, "neither side will slow your build task. They both want our magic balloon."

"I'm always lucky," declared Rose, bending forward, picking a yellow flower.

"Perhaps, you are, Abdul," said O'Brien, suddenly cheerful, spinning round on his haunches, purposefully scanning the summer mountains: low in the southern sky a flock of big white birds sailed on the wind. "I do believe your luck has arrived, more than a month late, but making good speed despite this cross-wind."

Rose admired the snowy birds. "Where're they heading?"

"Far beyond the Yalu River," exclaimed O'Brien, jumping to his feet, delighted like a schoolboy. "Manchurian cranes, Abdul, one of the world's rarest birds, on their way from Japan to Northern China."

They stared enviously. When the birds passed overhead, the wind fell, left the swishing beat of huge wings.

O'Brien stood facing the low mountains, following the living arrow on its journey northward, a slow smile spreading. "Koreans believe sighting a flock of cranes brings much fortune."

18

Fickle dusk closed, the night wind swished and garden trees became shadows waving on an apricot sky. Lamps triggered around the dong, flooding steep walled gardens with white light; the air fell pleasantly cool. Somewhere a car hooted, before angrily roaring away, leaving a golden aureole haunting the evening with its fluting call. O'Brien, clad in a pair of beach shorts, his muscles aching, stood back, admired the result from two days hard graft, cleaning the garden pool, which had been covered all winter, perhaps for several. After hours scrubbing, more hours hosing, back-breaking patience in a sweaty shed, the pump started, the filters worked. Now, deep smooth water slapped at the marble poolside, challenging him to test its icy welcome.

Too many hours spent sweating over a steering wheel, not enough burning energy, left him grumpy, restless. He flung himself into forty-eight hours of grinding toil, heartened as sweat poured down his back and legs, while his muscles lost their stiffness, and the sun steadily burnt his bare legs and shoulders. But the pool was ready; for once in Korea he savoured a finished job. He put a toe in the glacier green water.

"You look like a virgin about to endure rape." Rose strolled to the poolside and bluffed, "Cold water is excellent for the minor veins."

"Your blood has been boiled."

O'Brien flexed his muscles before launching himself into a forward somersault, watching sky and house rush backwards, then hit freezing water, plunged into a deep green world, breaking the surface with shocked energy.

Rose was soaked. "Bastard."

O'Brien taunted, "You sound just like a certain girl."

Rose threw his towel aside and ran, jumping high, curved into a sweeping dive, leaving hardly a ripple and swam several lengths under water before he surfaced with a wide smile. "All we need is steak, wine and, did you say, women."

"The first two are organised," spat O'Brien, wondering if that moment of mild flirtation already was forgotten.

Rose swung himself onto the poolside and sat, dangling his legs in the lively water; white pearls of spray shone in his wire sprung hair. "Frankly, Mike, don't suppose you had a lot of time for hobbies." He gave an approving grin at the spacious house. "Though you pulled off quite a coup with this mansion."

"You're obviously in a flattering mood," called O'Brien as he swam on his back, finding the water invigorating.

Dripping, Rose stood loose, intending to fetch some cold beer. "Started un-packing.... found some toys. Couple of infra-red sights. They double as simulators. We can play cowboys and indians after dark."

O'Brien trod water. "We're over here for an international sports festival, Abdul!"

Rose leered and strolled towards the french windows, leaving his chief to reflect on their extraordinary marksmanship which had freed several hostages from Iran's embassy in London. When he returned with two foaming cans, O'Brien stood by the pool, rubbing himself down with a thick towel, watching Kwachon mountain turn to slate and blur with coming night.

O'Brien took a swig of gassy local beer. "Talking about women, how is your better half?"

He had been best man at the Rose wedding at the parish church in Port Antonio on the spectacular north coast of Jamaica.

"Sarah sends you her love," announced Rose through a mouthful of cold beer. "She's running an art gallery in Chelsea, modern stuff, flogs it for company boardrooms.... coffee table paintings, I call it, though she goes mad."

"And the children?" For a fleeting moment, there was time to talk, catch up, enjoy civilised escape.

"Both at boarding school.... we sent Barbara.... can't quite believe it myself, time flashes past." Rose put down his beer and did a hand stand, then stood upright and needled without mercy. "She also asked me to check on the jockey."

Rose had fingered a sensitive nerve and O'Brien found himself rubbing his wavy hair until the towel became a ball. Throughout his army career there had been quite a few romances, even two broken engagements, broken because most intelligent girls would not marry somebody whose job was secret and dangerous and overseas. When Mason approached him with employment at the Olympic Games, he had seized the chance, flung himself into the intense preparation. One segment of his training was learning about all Olympic sports, the layouts for each competition, the people involved. Despite an Irish boyhood, he knew not one end of a horse from another, and one blustery Sunday, had driven west from London to study three day eventing.

For security, Mason despatched him to a private equestrian centre on the northern edge of Salisbury Plain. O'Brien found the place, eventually, lost along a wide horizon under racing clouds. He stopped his car, breathed in the cold blast, leaned on a white rail to admire some horses playing in a vast pasture. Over a brow galloped a rider with hair flying and jacket streaming. She rode like an apache, steering a huge chestnut stallion straight at the white rail fence. At the last second, she reined, boots and breeches spattered, wild strawberry blonde curls cascading down her back, reckless eyes green as a tropic sea staring down, before granting him a promiscuous smile with tempting lips, and slightly breathless, demanding if he was the *spook* sent from London.

"Aha," sniped Rose in friendly triumph, "*we're* still broody!"

"Don't torture a wounded man, Abdul."

Only self-mockery lifted the corners of his mouth. Coaching on the three day event began to occupy most weekends. Mason recruited from a discreet world. The wild girl came from a family whose pedigree matched her classic beauty. She became his bold goddess, until the day Mason invited him for lunch at the club, took him upstairs into the sunlit library with its wall of Reynold's portraits, but concentrated on the middle pages of Horse and Hound. His face was there alright, not large, nor alone, but printed for all the world, not quite hidden by the soft muzzle of a handsome chestnut stallion ridden by Susanna, third daughter of the Duke of Durham, reserve rider for the Seoul Games. Mason suggested prudence, 'a little cooling off', not permanently, just until the operation was over, the file closed. After the Olympic Games nobody would have any interest in the British Three Day Event team for several months. Mason applauded his splendid taste, thought the signs auspicious, bearing in mind that he knew both the partners rather well : O'Brien knew their friendship was doomed.

Despondent, suddenly empty, he lamented, "My Olympic highlight will be the last plane climbing away from Kimpo with the rear party of our British team."

Rose wagered without much compassion, "Twenty quid that Susie' catches the British Team's flight."

O'Brien forced a laugh. "Don't throw away your money. The chestnut went lame. She doesn't have another horse that's ready."

"Otherwise, we could have slipped Susie past Dick Mason's thought police, and into South Korea," said Rose with a far more understanding tone.

* * * * * * * * * * * * *

When Kang arrived, sweaty from cruising his taxi downtown and more than hungry, thick pungent smoke already drifted over the pool from a new barbecue on which sizzled a long fat strip of fillet steak. O'Brien waved Kang welcome, then concentrated on cooking, while Kang stood gazing at the pool, mouth slightly open when his mind grasped the thorough handwork of his surprising leader. Impressed, he accepted O'Brien's wry invitation to borrow some swimming shorts and minutes later, plunged into cool emerald water, thrashed glittering spray with his powerful legs, until his broad shoulders trailed a foamy wake and his head sported a bow wave.

Rose nodded approval at Kang's fitness and natural strength, as he placed a small round table under the lone pine tree that had captured one corner of the garden. Returning for plates and cutlery, he also brought a tray loaded with glasses, two open bottles of dark Australian burgundy, and a jug of orange juice for the disciplined tae kwon do champion who still splashed backwards and forwards in the small pool.

Kang eventually vaulted ashore; drops of water streamed down his pale olive body and he shivered from the night wind; he rubbed vigorously at his stomach muscles, tugged on a college sweatshirt, fetched a huge salad bowl from the kitchen which agima had left ready in the refrigerator.

O'Brien stood back from the barbecue recently 'bartered' from the American PX. Wielding a pair of steel tongs, he turned the huge steak one last time, before expertly flipping the smoking meat onto a large wooden platter and hurrying towards the pine tree.

"I'll give the baked potatoes a few minutes more," he warned the hungry pair already seated at the round table then cut thick slices off the long steak. Few words were exchanged while they attacked their evening meal. Stomachs filled, the first wine bottle empty, conversation returned. Kang had spent his time wisely.

"I circled around the National Assembly and KBS studios this afternoon. Picked up journalists from both places. Took them downtown."

He paused to explain for Rose how Koreans share taxis: passengers hail cabs with seats free, heading in the right direction. That afternoon, Kang stopped every few hundred yards, shuttling reporters to their city offices and learning the headline news.

"A fantastic scandal," his voice fell, "which the government can no longer hide after a suicide, today, downtown from an office window. A single death may bring down Chung's government."

Through a mouthful of hot baked potato saturated with salty butter, O'Brien asked painfully, "Who?"

"A guy named Chay..... President of Dream Shipping and Trading Company.....jumped from his twentieth floor office this afternoon." Kang shook his head in disgust: taking one's life meant an endless sentence of lost face for the surviving family.

"Was Mother in law after his balls?" Rose rapidly learned local customs.

Kang smiled broadly. "Chay owed three billion dollars."

Both his listeners stopped chewing, Rose was envious. "My bank manager writes a stiff letter for a 'tenner. A man can live well on that size overdraft. Clever sod."

O'Brien swallowed the lump of potato without choking. "God Almighty.... how the other half survives..... I thought Chay was married to one of Chung's younger sisters."

Kang laid down his fork. "The company was employed as a financial garbage can by Chung's wife."

The first lady's reputation for avarice and graft suffered no rival and O'Brien supposed that she dumped so many of her failed companies onto her brother-in-law's healthy firm that it finally crumpled.

"In Korea," resumed Kang, "everybody borrows the money for running their business from dozens of friends. Nobody small touches a bank, rarely the government." Watching the indigo night, Kang forecast, "More scandals are on the way.... and who pays.... today's youth into their middle aged years."

Rose asked quietly, "When did this firm crack, JP?"

Kang showed traditional flattery towards a teacher when he replied, "Song Seng Nim... about a week back.... our generals were most unhappy *but* very discrete. It's their party in power."

Todd's sources within the ROK Army were alert and well placed. The Americans would know whether the generals were cloistered during the afternoon and the terms drawn up for Chung's digestion: perhaps he should call over at Music Maker's later that night? Kang answered the crucial question.

"My father says the generals met this afternoon at the senior officer's country club." He rested both hands on his lap and spoke with sudden pride. "Chung may remain president until after the Olympic Games. Cha Se Dong is to be released. The Army will take orders from a special council until an election at the earliest moment.... after the Games."

Glancing across the table, Kang noticed O'Brien's blue eyes harden and swiftly volunteered, "Kim was invited but declined.... not protocol.... his duty lay with protecting the Olympics for our nation.... instead he awaits the general's thoughts with concern and respect."

Moon had done it. Since early winter, their most elusive target was General Kim. By edging him away from Chung, they drew Kim closer to the Army, perhaps those generals seeking democracy. O'Brien enjoyed a moment of smug pleasure. "Do any reporters know what the generals have decided?"

"Not so far." Kang sounded confident but emphasised wisely, "My father only found out when they approached him as a potential member of this special advisory council."

"Many others will hear soon," cautioned Rose, "word travels fast on the eastern side of 'Momasan Earth."

"Of course," said Kang, "but Chung alone knows whether he will accept their terms..... some generals remain loyal.... the others must advance with stealth and courage."

"It's their personal future at risk," said O'Brien. "This afternoon they opened a gate.... into a new maze."

Rose impaled a steak lump on his fork. "I thought your Dad was persona non grata with this present shower?"

"Was.... by the sound of things," laughed O'Brien, fascinated, an instinctive belief forming in his mind.

The confused patterns of South Korea's politics were changing like the shake of a child's kaleidoscope: yesterday, that seemed impossible. Tomorrow's men were pushing, a seed, liberty, planted in the public mind, grew stronger, fought for survival. He reflected that the elderly master gardener of this precious flower enjoyed a special brand of stubborn wisdom. At this stage, he recognised, the generals wished only to shuffle their hand of cards, nothing more : face was paramount. Small wonder they dreamed up a special council. Chung would be urged to convene its first meeting, hear its distasteful message which still he might not heed, report back on how to solve the national crisis. Even so, Chung must go... not at first... one step at a time; while the new generation of generals bought allies. Yet he doubted whether they were ready to hand over the card deck to a mistrusted face, one they regarded as a traitor, who led the rebellious south west corner, who was not a class mate from the Military Academy. Or was he wrong and Moon, once more, brilliantly right.

"My father accepts this council is intended as the old king's new seal." Kang smiled helplessly.

"Worth a risk." O'Brien stirred the salad. The sauce was perfect.

He guessed that Kang, pensive, still debated whether his father should let his name go forward as a member of the special council. There were risks. Candidates would be chosen and a final list presented to the National Assembly. Not entirely cosmetic. Failure meant shame. Chung might dismiss the whole council, brand it a junta in disguise; after all, however dishonestly, *he* had gone to the country and won an election within a system not too different from the United States. The generals dare not launch a coup before the Olympic Games.

"The ruling party are clever," he assured Kang. "Two opposition parties. One led by Cha Se Dong from his suburban prison. Another by a teacher from Taegu. And both weak. Combined they could sweep into power."

"But they never agree," objected Kang.

O'Brien smiled savagely and filled their glasses. "The generals want Chung gone.... without losing their own power. They free Cha Se Dong from house arrest which keeps his followers quiet, and splits *their* rival's vote right down the middle. Overnight a second opposition party is on the streets. Another election becomes safe *and* far cheaper.... less bribes and favours in the large cities and Seoul. The Ruling Party wins by another landslide. Masterly."

"Father rather enjoys returning to the cockpit. He says Chung will fight a delaying battle. There is much respect for a president, however ruthless, no matter how corrupt : Chung will exploit these feelings. Chung is stubborn. Don't dismiss him."

O'Brien rubbed his sunburned upper arms, debating whether he should fetch a sweater, watching only the brightest stars conquer a thick haze above the fickle city.

"Heaven tells me that we face some fast foot work."

Rose stared overhead. "How long does this good weather last, JP?"

"Around ten weeks. July brings rain."

Rose sucked a piece of meat wedged between his front teeth. He gave up and used a match as a toothpick. "We'll sweat over the airship," he remarked morbidly.

An argument existed for failing to deliver the airship on time, perhaps at all, save for a major complication : no airship, no money, which Mason would veto. Such a gambit risked a public scandal over squandered millions from the British taxpayer's pockets, threatened their cover, their operations worldwide: no.... the airship must fly.... despite a potential snag which dwarfed all others. O'Brien rubbed his hollow cheeks with rough fingers.

"Tell me, Abdul, how many hours does Yoon need before flying solo in the airship?"

Rose generated an aura of massive concentration, inwardly weighing experience, personality, the language barrier, changing weather, sweeping all factors into one vast calculation. With a stern face, he demanded in a hoarse whisper, "How long does an airship need for a flight to Andromeda?"

Kang burst into laughter while O'Brien experienced the pleasant sensation that good times might return and he asked hopefully, "Can you get away with that, Abdul? Yoon is smart."

Rose leaned back, enjoying himself. "A helicopter has powerful engines, sharp rotors chop through the air, all positive sensations. Our dumpling bird is like a kid's balloon. One breath can spin it ninety degrees and out of control. Yoonie' won't find learning easy!"

O'Brien had taken a course on airships which included five days flying. One breezy afternoon, he had lost three pounds sweating. Never did Detfold's vast grey hangar look so inviting below the downs. But then he never trained as an army pilot. The Korean was a gifted aviator. He repeated his concern. "Yoon may be a natural."

"Doesn't matter," smiled Rose. "A little contrived excitement will loosen Yoonie's tightest abdomenal muscles."

And O'Brien accepted how absurdly simple this ploy was for a real master pilot. Rose logged hundreds of hours each year on fixed wing, rotors, gliders, airships, some during combat in Her Majesty's secret wars, most deniable. Throughout thirty years of distinguished soldiering, Rose chalked up a thousand HALO jumps, several on clandestine operations. Alongside

Rose, even Yoon was a novice."

"He may fly wherever he wishes." Rose's stone eyes considered them both with mild amusement." Only Uncle Abdul will know how to land and take off, under *all* conditions, day *and* night."

O'Brien laughed. "You keep the rabbit's foot."

"Yoon may beg in any of my ten languages."

"What about our electronics?" asked O'Brien.

"I shall pretend ignorance," answered Rose calmly. "We'll have JP monitoring on the ground. I want my eyes on Yoonie and his camera crew. One of 'em is probably a North Korean."

The chill air finally won and O'Brien retreated indoors for a sweater and cigar. Rose and Kang went on talking, oblivious to the falling temperature, engrossed in the remote realm of fifth dan martial arts. When he returned, they were barely aware of his presence, which gave a moment for smoking, planning. Chung would accept or reject the generals' demands, and, if the latter, with much deliberation, countless false dawns, before the final dismissal. And even should he bend to their will, consent to quit, several weeks of bargaining would follow. Chung wanted to sit in that Royal Box at the opening ceremony of the Twenty-fourth Olympiad. The games were his personal gamble. South Korea opened its door to the World upon Chung's order. He deserved recognition. Which made it all the less probable that Cha Se Dong would enjoy freedom.... without a fight... and all the more likely that others would struggle for his swift release. He let cigar smoke escape into the night. A cool wind brought the distant traffic and a policeman's whistle from the sleepless dong. He watched the smoke disperse. That girl and her brother? He must call Paul Moon, find out what his father thought, but, judging from today, better to remove David Park from the scene without delay. The girl would hate him but peace was never cheap.

His mind moved on to the message from Sister Moon. Abdul must know the entire Olympic geography for it stretched over many miles. Wondang Ranch for the Three Day Event was north of the Han River and forty minutes drive from the Main Stadium. Susanna! Mason's harsh bargain. Did she really understand that awful night in London? God alone knew.... not Susanna.... and certainly not himself.

Kang was describing the final contests for higher dans in tae kwon do. "Those guys are not real," he complained respectfully, "they react faster than a computer."

"I hear you're pretty swift," prompted Rose.

"Quick enough," Kang smiled slowly.

O'Brien studied his glowing cigar. "You still train, Abdul?"

Rose grinned as though the question was wasteful. "Everyday.... at home in Blighty... started again this morning, while, my dear sir, you were so kindly filling our pool."

"You fit chaps make an aging spook feel safe in Olympic City." He took a pull on the cigar which he laid smouldering in a saucer, and loosely folded his arms across his chest. "Tomorrow, I'll call Kim and request a tour of the Olympic sites for you, Abdul."

Rose, instantly serious, nodded. "You want a full security sketch for our eyes only."

"Please. Mason has to brief the Prime Minister before the Queen goes to Balmoral for the summer break. I'll tell Kim that a tour will orientate you for flying training."

The telephone rang in the lounge and Kang leapt from the table and dashed through the open french windows. They heard a conversation in soft Korean. When the boy returned, he gave them a polite though bothered stare. "I don't understand," he grumbled without rancour, "but that was Paul Moon."

O'Brien could not stop himself leaning forward nor hide the catch in his otherwise steady voice. "Paul Moon?"

Kang stood mystified. "I wonder how they found your number, it's not yet in the telephone book."

"Probably asked Kim," volunteered O'Brien with an encouraging grin, "what was the call about?"

"The Buk A want to interview you about airships. Off the record. At Doctor Francis Moon's summer house among the hills south of the Han Valley."

O'Brien felt his veins flood with controlled excitement. "When?"

"Tomorrow at noon." Kang stared down. He remained troubled.

"Out with it, JP."

"He was listening to music. I could hear it in the background."

O'Brien pretended mild curiosity though his pulse quickened. "They're famous as music lovers". He felt almost dishonest, so easily drawing Kang.

"That's the weird part... it was the Olympic song." Kang towered, hands behind his back, loyal though silently demanding a seat round the campfire.

O'Brien enjoyed absurd pleasure. She was safe. The mirrors stood firm from Seoul over the mountains to Pyongyang. Brother and sister Moon held two aces, Harry Todd a third. And now he held the fourth: Kang reminded he was waiting and with misgivings.

"Paul Moon urged that it's difficult for a foreigner to find their summer home. A Korean friend must drive."

O'Brien said pleasantly, "He means you."

19

At two in the morning, O'Brien sat in the study, waiting, a whisky bottle and glass for company on his desk. Under the reading lamp lay a draft signal to Mason, which, for the reputation of its author, needed collateral, before despatch to join Her Majesty's most secret records.

A bleeper started inside a small electronic typewriter that shared the wide desk. He reached over his glass, touched a switch on its side, alerted their secure communications system. The noise stopped. He fed in a sheet of paper, typed the daily code word then his own trigger word : *DANIEL* : and waited.

A minute passed, while on the other side of the world, deep below the cloisters of Westminster Abbey, pampered by dry air in a huge Tudor wine cellar, a computer decided whether to abort or proceed. Soft whirring on the desk confirmed a *Sugar* codeword and the ink cartridge flew across the bare paper. Tired, he leaned forward, reading line by line, expecting a sentence from Hong Kong for London and repeated to Seoul, settling that, tonight, Sister Moon slept peacefully in Pyongyang.

Not at all : Mason's after lunch eloquence flowed onto the virgin page and yawning, he sat back, watching paper emerge until the machine stopped. O'Brien tapped in his personal codeword for that day and the machine switched itself off.

Through the open door, he heard Rose snoring in the spare bedroom, a soul justly at rest after assembling a pair of the latest British rifles with powerful night sights. He poured himself another whisky before reading Mason's latest Commandment.

SOLAR FROM NOAH : FOR GENESIS REPEATED DANIEL. Fragile goods delivered. No damage reported. Cancel insurance policy.

The last sentence was an oblique reference to the order for O'Brien and Rose to quit the Korean peninsular immediately and forever..... had Hodori's re-insertion gone horribly wrong. Live British witnesses were the last sore Mason needed when the Southern and Northern Koreans discovered that London had spied on both, from each other's countries, and for years.

The second signal opened with NOAH's de-briefing HODORI on board a Royal Navy nuclear submarine during the return passage for her insertion on the north-western Korean coast near the Yalu River; clusters of small islands made for a safer run inshore while the submarine ECM confused North Korean radars.

This signal followed precisely her words at the beach library, warned that a key part of South Korea's security resembled a Swiss cheese, singled out the airship operation as confirmed target. She revealed nothing of the leadership's personal enthusiasm for Operation Mole. What masterly discretion: she granted her brother and himself absolute freedom to judge the dangers for their own necks.

She also made plain the leadership's obsession with a single Korean nation, boasting the ancient name of its mountainous northern neighbour, Koroyo, otherwise known as Manchuria. Though his health stayed strong, Kim Il Sung was growing older; the dynastic faction had fought and won power over his living corpse. Sister Moon's message was stark, she tolerated no confusion : destroy the power of this new regime before all the disciplined and isolated resources of North Korea passed into gambler's hands. Now only spies and assassins obey the inner clique's wishes. Next time it might be nuclear rocket troops.

He reached for his drink while reading the next paragraph which described living conditions in North Korea, emphasising Kim Jong Il's personal grip on education for all ages through his twin roles of ideology and propaganda chief. 1984 was history. He took a sip of whisky, enjoyed the lingering bitter taste, then, feeling stronger, tackled Mason's personal analysis.

NORTH KOREA recognises its failure to bring about a boycot of the Seoul Games, rally its allies in support, force reselection of the 1988 host city. What next? We see no evidence, from any direction, that a single (determined and realistic) plan exists for international terrorists, particularly a Japanese Red Army faction, to attack the games on behalf of NORTH KOREA. Neither is there any sign of the inner ruling clique in Pyongyang relaxing their hostility towards a successful Seoul Olympics. Any spectacular display of ruthless and competent daring must strengthen the political fortress from which the son has captured power before the death of his father. Apart from at least one live terrorist cell within your operational area, RESEARCH identify a new and highly malignant threat : over some months CORONA satellite assets have monitored a site in north-west KOREA which is confirmed as a plutonium plant. HODORI reported this site, sealed off by strict security.

Could they make a bomb? And how small? America produced the Davie Crockett weapon in the early sixties and that rocket was no taller than himself. Were the North Koreans still kept at arm's length from lethal research by a failing and desperate Soviet Russia? He felt the back of his neck stiffen from concentration : who banked this lunatic though a stunning option.

Suppose there was no need for Rose, no need for himself, no reason for any foreigner involved with the airship patrols. Whoever ran this operation for Pyongyang could remove one hostile force at a stroke. Was that why the Americans - and Kim - wanted Britons in the Olympic sky? In which case, Rose was prime target, next in line himself.

He had sent men to the remotest lands on the globe, nursed their sense of balance, reminded at crucial moments, that, no matter how fearful the odds, they were pitted only against mortal man, weak and often stupid. Never dismiss a strength or weakness. Now it was his turn up front to ride those animal instincts that tell a man where to move on the smoking battlefield and which saved his neck (and others) during violent years. But Mason must defend their actions before a secret Star Chamber, and that took equal nerve and greater trust. Through this telegram Mason absolved him from any blame for failure. A noble gesture, subtle, which left no doubt in O'Brien's mind : Mason and the entire Service depended on his brains and courage; anything less than success would be despicable.

He smiled. Old tricks seldom fail. He saw a wild evening on the Brecon Beacons, one of those mournful Welsh dusks when hungry clouds swallow black mountains and icy rain strikes like shrapnel in the face, turning combat suits into wet tents. Rose perched on a stone wall, squinted into the wild storm, sometimes glancing at a truck almost hidden by the swift darkness. Slowly, across a steep field, they came. A dozen worn figures dwarfed by huge back packs, struggling forward, a loose line, spent bodies still marching after many sleepless days. One reached the wall, stopped, dragged himself over, not aware of the watching Rose. Soon the rest closed. Some peered at their watches when their wiry tormenter crooned through the gale that enough was enough. Why go on, hinted Rose kindly, there was no shame, pointing towards the truck ready for their ride back to a warm bed in Hereford. Most hesitated, three slumped, two shapes forced themselves over the slab wall, set off into blinding rain. Rose let them cover fifty yards before lifting frozen fingers to his mouth and whistling. His smile told the shocked faces what had passed. Wise Rose. Wise Mason. Why must fools always prove themselves, rush before the cannon's mouth? You're a fool, O'Brien; they hooked you again, those rare wizards of the human soul, who conceal their own spirits in cunning webs and he heard Rose's voice cut through howling wind : "Thank you, gentlemen, that's all we want to know."

He took a long sip from his drink and focussed on the message sheet.

We must cope with the immediate but watch for long term aims. Northern leadership believes in a thousand tiny, relentless advances, repeatedly offers overseas Koreans.... those victims of the 'Japanese and U.S. invasions' driven from their homeland... citizenship of Juche Korea. We should not assume that one mind is fixed on the view beneath its nose.

The leadership will not attempt open warfare against SOUTH KOREA while there are large American forces on the peninsular and a strong American fleet, armed to deliver nuclear strikes, cruising within a few minutes flying time from NORTH KOREA.

The huge dam under construction among the border mountains north east of Seoul is scare mongering while preserving domestic face through a visible assault on the Seoul Games. SOUTH KOREA gains a convenient aunt sally and jobs for its redundant construction workers returning from the Middle East.

Rule out attacks on the Seoul water system, indeed food supply, generally and within the Olympic Village. We have no evidence of increased research into germs and toxics. Widescale suffering among the workers does not tally with the leadership's pursuit of mass adoration.

O'Brien's mouth stretched with cynical amusement. Mason failed to mention the Press Village as a target : perhaps he gambled the North Koreans might poison nine thousand sports reporters. His smile faded when he read the next paragraph.

We need your military opinion on the vulnerability of Seoul City to surprise attack.

NORTH KOREA has deployed its main field army along the DMZ and threatens invasion. A bombardment of Munsan is possible before Olympic teams arrive thus scaring overseas participants into withdrawal from the Seoul Olympics.

Keep in mind that in 1970 ten frontline NORTH KOREAN Divisions were ordered to each drill a pair of tunnels under the DMZ into SOUTH KOREA. Only three tunnels have been discovered, none since 1978, but the programme remains live.

The leadership's most easily deployed assets (JUCHE) are a personal clique who include the Political Security Division of a private Cabinet, large numbers of special force troops under their direct command, student cells in SOUTH KOREA recruited by agents loyal to the leadership who themselves have sensitive positions within SOUTH KOREA.

We know from recent reports that at least one live cell is attacking the Seoul Games. We suspect their task is far wider than brief embarassment of SOUTH KOREA. Permanent political goals cannot be discounted.

The world will focus almost entirely on the Olympic Games, rather than SOUTH KOREA, even Seoul City. You must not ignore other targets. But an urgent sketch of security around the Olympic Venues is requested.

That meant within the next forty eight hours and covering everything from Kimpo Airport to the Olympic Village laundry shop. Then came absolution, those key lines, the operational cage within which they must prowl. *You have our full support to concentrate the LINEBACKER TEAM around the Olympic Games Venues, if you judge them the most under threat.*

O'Brien whistled softly. Not in Korea, my dear Chairman, where a thousand lies hide a single truth. Focus on the games venues implies enhanced value for our airship. *You may take all measures to keep the airship under our covert control.*

O'Brien read the last sentence twice. A blank license! What was Mason holding back? Tomorrow at the Moon's they must decide a line on the airship for London. O'Brien sensed danger. Sometimes Mason believed he could forecast events so accurately that *no* advance warning to the overseas team served as perfect security for his original sources. And Mason himself forecast trouble.

The protection of our team, which includes two members of the Royal Family, warrants determined and, if required, harsh action. Our personal links with the British media can sweep your trail clean. Your operation is monitored with admiration at the highest level.

O'Brien's eyebrows rose.

Koreans are notorious for a dreadful diet. Mason refered to a local taste for barbecued live dogs. *Let all Kims eat our airship when the Games are over and the British Team, some very young, safely flying home.*

He placed the message sheet on the table and drained his glass. His reply, now barely valid, reported the threat to their airship from hostile agents within South Korea though directed from Pyongyang. South Korea's latest political vortex was also recorded. He covered the Park family and the girl's recruitment. Already, she earned a code name, *STOWAWAY*. Last came an outline of his action plan, which, written an hour earlier, no longer fell within Mason's new and much tighter boundaries.

"Busy colonel?" Rose loomed in the doorway, strong face alert, body nearly awake, clad in a pair of bright red shorts.

"Sorry Abdul, did I make a noise?" He passed Rose the message from London. "Fancy a drop of the hard stuff?"

Rose speed read then handed back the flimsy sheet. "Better fetch my tooth mug."

"London wants our hearts and minds chained to the Olympic Stadium..... Stowaway and her brother, by implication, become a nuisance, a diversion at best."

"Mason can't have it both ways. I just read something about looking ahead with eyes bright and tails bushy."

O'Brien swung round in his chair as a tired smile carved deep lines on his sunken cheeks. "Abdul, guess our main conjuring trick."

Rose scratched the grey fuzz over his mahogany stomach and chest, a slightly puzzled expression giving way to growing dread, then he yawned, tilting his head to avoid the bright lamp. "You're pulling my plonker!"

"No, Abdul, right on the nail." He watched a rare display of surprise when Rose's hard mouth hung open for a mere instant and he quickly delivered the final punch. "Chairman Mason wants us to steal the crown from North Korea's next king."

"Chieftain?" haggled Rose from the doorway.

"As you wish."

Rose returned with a plastic mug which O'Brien filled with whisky.

"What's your feelings?" Rose sat on the desk top.

"I'd rather hear yours." He handed over his draft signal for London.

While Rose sat reading, O'Brien opened the middle drawer of his desk and took out a black carton full of electronic typewriter cartridges marked 'correctable' though otherwise seemingly normal. He removed one, replaced the box. After closing the drawer, he tugged a hair from his scalp, which he licked and carefully stuck across its top right corner. An intruder would have no idea how the machine worked and the tapes just typed normally when used on alien equipment. There was no real fear of robbery. Eaves dropping was the main threat: modern technology allowed a hostile intelligence service to pick up electronic signals within a typewriter from long distance.

Rose held the signal with one hand, stared at the drawn curtains, resembling a hound sniffing its bearings; absently, he scratched his right shoulder, eventually laid both pages on the desk. "No problems from my side, Mike."

Engrossed with preparing the machine for cyphering and sending his return message, O'Brien grunted, then removed the tape cartridge, slid in the waiting replacement. He snapped the cartridge home, closed the plastic flap and enquired over his shoulder, "How do you want to tackle the venues, Abdul."

"I need two bites at that cherry. Tomorrow morning, by all means ring Kim, but arrange my trip a day later." Rose reached for his tooth mug on the varnished desk. "I'm going to book myself on a tour from the Hyatt Hotel."

"Hyatt's just along the hillside from this dong."

"Drop me off on your way out in the morning. A preview will make Kim's tour a day later much more entertaining... I doubt if the hotel owns a hot line to Kim's control centre."

"Not before August."

"Are they thick?"

"Rather behind schedule."

"We could pack the Royal Box cushions with semtex between now and August."

O'Brien grinned and watched the machine start. "We shan't be idle Abdul."

"I'd better show my evening's homework," said Rose and disappeared to his bedroom. Moments later he was back, a shiny modern automatic rifle tucked under each arm, the latest Enfield 480s with their distinctive magazine forward of the pistol grip. Carefully, he laid both on the small table then closed the curtains fully, trapping the sweet smell of armourer's oil in the warm room. He lifted one, cocked it with a soft click, opened the chamber, proving the weapon empty, before releasing the short rifle into O'Brien's open hands.

Its weight felt less than a tennis racquet, though made from steel and hard wood. He cocked the rifle, smoother than butter. A long night sight sat low along the varnished stock. He took casual aim at the window, enjoying its perfect balance.

"Special Forces batch," said Rose proudly, "designed this model, myself. Couple of pounds less heavy than the standard weapon. Accurate over a thousand yards in all weathers. Sights can magnify a hundred times. Light as a feather. Drove a truck over that solid woodwork."

"How good are these sights over this city at night?"

Rose slightly parted the curtains. "Take a peek."

Cradling the rifle, O'Brien advanced on the french windows, heard Rose move across the room behind and switch off the reading lamp : darkness cloaked the soldier's black magic. O'Brien reached between the thick curtains and opened the window catch. He slid one glass door sideways, climbed onto the small balcony.

He let his eyes adjust to night, cool wind slapped tiny waves round the ice green pool. Beyond the silent dong, strings of yellow pinpricks marked the river, an endless murmur gave away traffic hurrying across Panpo's twin spans as businessman quit Yongdong's fast sex for a last cheap drink along Itaewon : Koreans feared dreams more than empty pockets.

"Try something easy," coached Rose at his side, "watch the police creep from their box on the bridge and piss into the Han."

"Won't streetlamps blind a nightscope?"

"Not this one," Rose lectured aimiably. "I designed our kit for long winter evenings on the back streets of Paddytown. That scope reads heat signatures.... a lamp resembles a lamp, a man is gathered in his own shape. Try."

Two miles distant the weak white lights of Building 63 probed the heavy night. O'Brien raised his rifle, took aim at the top floor restaurant, peered into the nightscope. The cross hairs swept a row of windows, he counted eight customers and twenty waiters. Menues were propped under lamps on each table. He searched deeper, scanning the room, astounded, spotted the headwaiter's dignified shape hovering below a hideous dazzling chandelier. Faces were obscure. But not much else. He lowered the rifle, let his eyes and mind rest; modern weapons were monuments to human wastefulness. Suppose the range was far shorter.

A lone car crossed Panpo Bridge. He trailed it over open sights, switched to the nightscope : two cheerfully drunk Koreans slumped in the backseats, one wore thick framed glasses; chauffered by a stiff faced third.

Nothing hid from the scope's hungry sensors. They cheated night.

"My God, Abdul, you're dangerous," he congratulated, finally lowering the rifle, questioning mankind's priorities while staring eastwards where a bend in the river almost hid a milky reflection low in the night sky - the Olympic Stadium.

20

A staircase of paddy fields climbed the narrow valley. Along one side, a grass track, bordered with butter marguerites and a high hedge, led towards steep mountains cloaked with stubby pines and basking under noon clouds. Small rice lakes planted with emerald seedlings reflected the pewter light. Kang's taxi slithered on the warm grass and O'Brien scorched his fingers gripping the open window. Kang dropped a gear, recovered, stopped under an old cherry tree near a gap in the tall hedge. O'Brien smelt heavy sweet air with a threat of summer rain, his ears sharpened to busy insects; beyond the hedge, swallow blue tiles shaped the perfect curves of an old Korean roof.

He swung out his legs and stretched. Water bubbled over an earth dam holding back a rice pond. Lower down the valley, fluting calls gave away a pair of golden aurioles darting through an ash copse. He waited for Kang, enjoying the humid heat, wagering that Moon had pulled off the sorely needed miracle, then walked hopefully into a simple garden. He stood for a moment, admiring dwarf cedar trees snipped over many years with loving care, until each resembled a fir poodle. There was a clever rhythm about their shapes which perfectly complemented a small traditional house.

Steps ran its length, sliding japanese doors stood wide open. Slippers for the guests waited in a row on the top step. Inside the open room stood a tiny rustic table and legless cushioned chairs. Doctor Moon appeared from the middle doorway, pleased with their prompt arrival, and Kang bowed to the old man with good natured respect.

Moon lowered his plump chin, slowly came down the steps, grasped them both by the hand, letting them feel his silent jubilation through soft warm palms while his misty eyes delighted at the prospect of future mischief.

"You are young Kang Jae-pil," he said in Korean.

"My father sends his good wishes for your health and family," replied

Kang, again bowing politely, summoning his humblest smile.

Moon then spoke in English. "It is ve...ry good that you brought this boy, my dear Michael, because we have much work for a younger pair of hands. Come.... follow."

O'Brien knew at once: Moon *had* lured their crucial guest. If nothing more, they might find some middle ground, at the least respect each other. Relief spread on his exhausted face and he pumped the old man's hand several times. "Never play cards against you, Francis."

"You have no reas....on."

"Where is he?"

Kang glanced at both hoping for an explanation.

Moon laughed until a rasping cough took over his lungs. "Fol....low."

He led them round the small open house towards a whispering though hidden spring. Beyond a tall bamboo hedge, the ground fell away into a tiny valley. They followed Moon's leisurely shuffle down a narrow path under waving bamboo, until the thicket opened and became a small clearing perfumed by banks overgrown with spring flowers that climbed among sunflecked woods. Water splashed into a clear pond from a jug poured at a determined angle by a graceful naked girl made from green bronze.

A huge Korean stood waiting, back soldier straight, razor creases on the short sleeves of his fake brand shirt. When he turned, a cigarette smouldered from heavy lips while familiar raw black eyes recorded their faces for some private list. General Kim smoothed back greying hair, threw the cigarette over a little waterfall that emptied the pond, leaving a small grey cloud above its bottle green water.

Moon shuffled to a stop and flapped a hand at a pair of rustic garden seats. "No protocol, gentlemen, we all know each other."

General Kim rewarded Moon a military tilt of his brow, next crushed O'Brien's hand, finally Kang's, before they sat, Kim and O'Brien on one bench, Moon and Kang on the other, enjoying the waking pond and late springtime woods.

Moon laboriously settled his short legs, propped his thick soled plimsoles on their heels, sneezed twice, then noisily cleared his throat. "My man is making a pic.....nic with beer and soft drinks. Let us spend time well."

Kim faced O'Brien. "Are you surprised?"

"Frankly," answered O'Brien, "bloody relieved."

Moon reached forward and gripping Kang's wrist, commenced to exploit fortune's windfall, opened the street market with his dignified charm. "This boy's father may join the special council.... I hope you will consider also, General?"

Kim passed. "Each must obey his own destiny."

"And yours, General, where lies yours?" gambled O'Brien, his voice lifted just above the splashing water, still catching faint piping from aurioles far down the valley.

"Becoming less obvious," sighed Kim.

Moon rocked silently, lifting his free hand, patting his shaking chest, though seeking kibun; he offered a snapshot of his bargaining terms, making it plain that nothing else was intended, at this stage.

"My good General, several of us have been approached to join this council, which I will, providing Cha Se Dong is released and full political freedoms restored immediately. Some of your fellow generals confidently report that I am not alone."

"Song Seng Nim, that is our national problem," Kim's voice shot over the pond and startled a finch exploring dry leaves under a young oak. The bird fluttered further into the thickly grown trees: Kim listened for its next landing, heard the rustle, dropped his guard just a little. "Nobody is alone. We are a people obsessed by factions." Kim laughed at the irony of his situation. "The President is not alone either. Which makes it hard for him to decide."

Moon leaned forward. "Chung....com...pro...mise?"

Watching the woods, perhaps hoping the tiny bird soon would return, Kim breathed out heavily. "Resign."

"Bright Korea Party won't allow resignation," protested Kang, "far too many of its members need protection."

Kim stared enviously at O'Brien. "I congratulate you, friend, my staff assemble committees to work out the obvious."

O'Brien leaned back, allowed himself a broad smile: Kang got that one right. He opened another grate. "You need a political force behind the government and the army appears no longer in that business."

"Membership of Chung's party machine is half a million." Kim examined his shiny handsewn shoes. "The Bright Korea Movement.... are our ruling party's backbone....just look at their effort into youth programmes, quite mad, seventeen hundred kindergartens... the government only run three and a half thousand. Bright Korea's rural programmes will overtake the government within a decade. Kim Jong Il could learn from our Diamond

Bright League. Two billion tax dollars were pumped into their party machine since Chung became President. My figures are right..... I deal with those people, Mr O'Brien, almost daily. They and a powerful religious sect are behind the Seoul Olympics."

Moon glanced up the path, when no sound disturbed, he confirmed Kim's forebodings. "We cannot ignore Bright Korea. The movement boasts great strength, many humble followers, who are the foundation of political dreams. It is cleverly directed and the corruption inspira...tional. Leadership trai....ning is given to country people, after which, their villages are encouraged to elect leaders! You see, dear friend, our good general speaks candidly. A hundred thousand people elect a National Assembly member in Seoul, but, only ten miles north, in Munsan, just thirty thousand voters form a country constituency. Chung owes favours to these loyal followers." Moon delivered an old man's verdict. "My good Kim Shi, I also do not think resignation an easy option for Chung, too many followed his dazz...ling star."

Allowing his American education to take over, for a moment, Kang forgot the social rules and gave a sharp reminder to the wise and strong about how things work at street level.

"They won't give-up influence, wealth, privilege! Bright Korea Movement bought their widespread support from small farmers and leading families. Some own Chaebols and they're more influential than our government. Chung ignores the National Assembly which he packed with his own party. Bright Korea is run by his wife and she's no pushover!"

Kim tolerated this outburst with a rare smile. "Not quite that strong, boy, although it took me a good five years to weed the National Security Agency of small town politicians."

O'Brien looked across at the doctor, wanting confirmation that Kim was breaking new ground: Moon lowered his hooded eyelids, only for a second, but long enough. The general implied that he purged his own senior staff of Chung's private command network, but how long ago? After the special Olympic Security Command was set up five years earlier? Or had Kim drifted from the President during months, years, perhaps since Kwangju?

Moon's eyelids briefly hovered again when the old Doctor lured Kim forward with a narcotic bribe. "My Buk A group will support *all* who welcome democracy."

Kim's brow furrowed and temptation scored. "We need time."

They understood each other perfectly. Once released, Cha Se Dong faced more danger than President Chung. Nobody relished losing either leader before the world's television cameras. That Kim worried on this pleasant weekend, meant Cha's freedom within days.

"Two high risk targets gobble a lot of skilled manpower, cars, special equipment," said O'Brien.

"We have an excellent close protection division in the National Police and I tripled its bodyguard strength for Olympic VIP protection. I don't want it any larger..... I can't risk diluting its quality." Kim folded his smooth arms across his chest. Somebody else could make the next move.

Gen...eral......... the Police have not been pur...ged," rasped Moon, barely lifting his eyelids, waiting.

"I have no fear over their loyalty."

"You have been busy," said Moon warmly.

"When are all restrictions lifted from Cha Se Dong?" asked O'Brien, who wanted no misunderstandings later.

"Buddha's Birthday."

"Only another week."

Kang grinned ominously. "Our leader's bribe to his unruly people."

Kim scowled. "The President wishes to emphasise his devout soul and human face."

Sandals flapped on the narrow path. Moon greeted a grey haired man wearing a bush shirt. The newcomer stopped a respectful distance from the garden seats.

"My man has lunch...eon ready." Moon returned a friendly wave, let his plimsoles fall flat, launched himself from the garden chair, then attacked the path, Kang keeping pace at his side, opening a gap between themselves and the other two.

Strong sunlight spilled through pale young foliage as they started up the short hill. Aurioles called further down the warm valley. Was this a last peaceful moment before the typhoon struck? Kim's stern face told almost the same story.... somebody must make the first move, but not him, not with his personal honour, his professional reputation nailed high on the Olympic stadium's flagpole. Silence was madness. It risked refusal, but there was no second chance.

"We could help."

Kim stared ahead at where Kang was listening attentively to his small companion. "You work him hard."

"He's good," claimed O'Brien.

"Among students."

Kim slowed and took a last thoughtful glance at the bronze maiden and her endless fresh water splashing into the little pond. "Alright..... let us try, but on my terms. Last week a hot agent vanished for forty eight hours. I watch him closely but suffer considerable anxiety at the present time."

"Does this young gentleman, by chance, play Santa Claus to pretty girl students?"

Kim stopped abruptly, hooked both thumbs into his eel skin belt and permitted himself a sarcastic smile." We must stop pirating each other's work, O'Brien."

"General, at this eleventh hour, nothing else makes sense."

"What about his friend?"

"Kang tails from a distance. We don't have enough pairs of feet for covering a target day and night."

Kim's smile froze. "I thought the Americans employed our counter intelligence teams on your behalf."

"We're lone wolves, General, big operations aren't our style."

Although Kim remained dubious, he did not pursue the matter. South Korea's police routinely watched all foreigners, tapped their telephones, bugged their homes, filmed hotel bedrooms. Whole floors of the downtown hotels were wired for sound and the Foreign Press Club was an electronic aquarium where Korean editors chewed steak while barbarians spoke eloquently for hidden microphones. There was no point in making their lives more difficult.

"We're under orders to protect a sports team which includes our Queen's daughter. Nothing else involved. The airship helps us *both* with the same overall job. I accept that your duty encompasses the entire country, not just these games, however, I believe the threats are few and after the same target."

Kim resumed a slow walk, listening to the busy woods.

O'Brien fell into step, silent, not ready to reveal the precise frontier of his operational task. Nor did he feel the time ripe for telling Kim that the main threat might involve their troublesome balloon. The Korean would take the logical step : drop the project, which lost their quickest path to the terror cell. Somebody involved with the North Koreans must show their hand during flying training. For a start that person must have physical access to the airship and its ground crew who numbered around a dozen policeman, not counting his own three man team.

"Personally, O'Brien, I am convinced that Cha Se Dong is our Olympic target and those two students have a key role." Kim paused, deciding how far he should include his new allies, before he eased one door a little wider. "We ran Shin as an agent until you nearly shot him downtown."

"He *was* trying to rocket President Chung."

Kim's face stiffened. "I had a tougher job.... afterwards.... explaining your tin star drama to our national President. He's not terribly understanding of human rashness."

"Then he hasn't changed since Vietman." O'Brien felt a shaft of sunlight warm his face.

"Chung believes that iron discipline solves the most complex riddles. Few dare utter the painful truth that some problems need gentle fingers. We warn him, often, but Chung scrambled up the tree by force and strength." And Kim added in his sombre baritone, "It's the only style he knows."

"Now he pays for his own economic success."

At this, Kim rested one shiny toecap on a thick root, leaned on the young ash tree, somehow looser, as though wanting to share his private burden. "The trouble with building an economic miracle, O'Brien, is that people suspect a man who pulls off one miracle can bring about another. Wealth doesn't mean much if there's nothing on the store shelves worth buying."

Somewhere amongst the brush a tiny animal scurried over a dry leaf. Kim listened until satisfied and O'Brien wondered why the general came without a pistol: did Moon make it a condition for the meeting? Later, he must ask.

"Chung designed our ruling party, created vast industries behind thick walls of import and luxury taxes to keep out you foreign barbarians and your expensive toys, your wasteful habits. Our factories are worthy of Kim Il Sung with their uniformed and disciplined workers who toil a dozen hours for six days a week on a monthly hundred American dollars. Chung even chose the union leadership as though selecting bright corporals."

He noticed how already Kim slipped into past tense when describing the presidential methods. They must know where Kim stood on politics. He tried another route. "South Korea has run a monster trade surplus for the last three years. Nobody can deny Chung that miracle."

"Chung revived our middle class.... it's his downfall."

"Your army generals must have great faith in the people's self control.

Any other country would be heading for utter chaos. There's no time for an election before the Olympic Games."

"Koreans know the Games are crucial to our country's future. Politics will wait." Kim leaned one hand on the tree, while the other strayed to smooth his silvery hair. "Chung has reserved the Royal Box."

"Did he order an extra red velvet cushion for Cha Se Dong?"

"Cha must campaign for his own seat among the gods."

Along the dry path, Moon and Kang reached the formal garden. O'Brien glanced at his companion, lengthened his stride, struck by Kim's tiger lope, that proud head searching either flank, those intelligent eyes on constant watch.

"My flying manager, Mr Rose, ought to have a tour of the Olympic venues. Would that be possible?"

"No problem, nor is your hangar. Yoon believes it will be ready next week..... without fail."

"Excellent," replied O'Brien, mightily released.

Despite heavy smoking, Kim was fit, his breathing steady and, keeping his voice low, taking advantage of O'Brien's looser mood, the general brought out his immediate problem. "There is a matter.... where you could help.... this coming week. A local difficulty, perhaps trivial, yet bearing the seeds for *civil war*, which I would prefer not to encourage until this Olympic fever has died off."

O'Brien felt the skin stretch over his scalp as his mind raced back through the previous weeks, groping for defence, wondering what Kim now knew about their operation.

Hiding alarm, he fenced. "Are you sure a foreign pair of hands won't bring trouble."

"Not at all. I need a repeat of your street drama, if the circumstances leave no choice."

"Where?"

"Tosonsa.... the Buddhist Temple on the hill above Yonsei University." Kim looked worried. "Yes, O'Brien, that's where Cha Se Dong will go first.... after his liberty."

O'Brien pictured the festive and excited crowds wandering around the old temple as thousands of paper lanterns glowed in springtime's early darkness. A nightmare.

"Even if we're careful, suicide, less if you're there and visible."

"You think Shin and Han will try and kill Cha Se Dong?"

"I don't think, O'Brien," explained Kim in a tired voice.

"Throw them off balance."

"It may work."

They reached the small lawn. "I rather fear, general, our Olympic summer just began."

PART TWO

21

Royal palms grew like fan vaulting in a cathedral, and between two, from his huge armchair, O'Brien saw right across the Hyatt Hotel's cocktail lounge. A wall of glass doors provided a ceaseless stream of black cars and taxis that delivered Seoul's chic. Ignoring a whistle blast from the old doorman, O'Brien read the Korea Times, impressed by yet another huge Korean trade surplus, watching for the hotel bus, soon expected from the Olympic sites.

Wearily, he tossed aside the paper, glanced towards the lifts as teak doors slid apart and a pair of malaysian pilots emerged, their black uniforms loaded with enough gold rings for Russian admirals. In their wake chattered a line of hostesses in lilac sarongs, pulling small luggage carts, heading for the electric glass doors. Two harrassed American businessmen stared after the pretty procession before switching their gapes to a group of young Koreans in the latest bizarre fashions from Itaewon.

Vast windows looked over the garden and swimming pool. Evening softened a landslide of tiny roofs sloping towards a wide bend in the rusty Han, crossed by Hannam and Panpo's concrete spans, now choked with rush hour traffic: beyond stretched half Seoul. Apartment blocks along the far bank resembled a sea wall holding back countless streets and leafy avenues marked spring in discrete new quarters that climbed towards the thin spires of a fake Notre Dame. Flat sun picked out thick woods surviving on suburban hills. Westward, Building 63 resembled a black needle while a new eastern twin glistened white as cranes still worked on the World Trade Centre. Past the distant main stadium, more cranes swung above another steel skeleton, and a welding lamp sparkled like a star.

"They'll finish the wiring around the feet of their first guests, Mike."

Rose stared at the embryo hotel some five miles east where a lone cloud drifted inland from the Yellow Sea.

"What's your verdict?" O'Brien waved to a young waiter who instantly sent a waitress in a grey blazer and matching long skirt slit to reveal her thigh. Sweating, thirsty, Rose sank into an armchair, glad to escape thirty American pensioners. The girl approached and they ordered two large OB beers.

Rose flung his legs alongside a low table and folding his sinewy arms, contemplated his dusty trainers. "On the surface it looks thorough, lots of policeman manning scanners at each venue, high security fences, plenty of standing patrols. But that's not good enough. Koreans obey rules by knee jerk."

"They also push and jump lines."

"Quite professional," conceded Rose exhausted after his day as a tourist. "We turned up at the gates in a posh bus with Hyatt painted on either side. Nobody made us dismount, nobody checked identities, nobody searched the luggage bay. Our girl tour guide smiled sweetly at the gate police and we parked beside the main stadium."

O'Brien glanced around the room but nobody sat close. "What happened at the Olympic Village."

"Much better. Our bus drove slowly past. No stops, no photos."

"Were you allowed to take a camera into the stadium?"

"And the venues at Olympic Park." Rose confessed his awe at the beautiful main gymnasium under its gentle dome of fibre glass sails. The swimming pool was only half built and the Olympic Bridge over the Han resembled Meccano. "Why so slack at the main stadium, Mike."

"Because they must show it off to the working people and farmers who support Chung and his ruling party, not just barbarians. Kim will take the whole place apart about a month before the opening ceremony."

"Whose sniffer dogs?"

"American Air Force Alsations.... cheap but innocent compared with our sharp nosed veterans from my native island."

"Lots of sensors, Mike, thoughtful sites. Their electronics people are on the ball."

O'Brien saw the girl approaching along a path through the fat armchairs, balancing a tray. "Can you write a report tonight?"

"Providing it doesn't cover the military threat. That requires more time and a look at the city rim."

"Our airship will cover most gaps. It's actively programmed."

"Jargon.... Mike, I could load a whole terror cell into that bus for on the job training."

O'Brien's distant smile reminded Rose that his quiet colonel had started life as an electronics prodigy in the Royal Signals.

"Our camera searches for faces..... Kim and his experts remain ignorant of our private toy.... that's why I need a covert control room on Harry Todd's base."

He paused when the beer arrived safely, nodded thanks at the girl, who stuck the bill among artificial flowers on the low table, bowed demurely and withdrew, leaving her scent like an invitation.

He described their day with Doctor Moon while Rose, steadily sinking beer, stone eyes neutral, listened in silence, until O'Brien asked, "Are we wise?"

"You're the leader," Rose dodged cheerfully.

O'Brien suffered qualms with which Moon fully sympathised. Three players meant more risk if the game plan was compromised.

Rose rubbed his strong forearms in defence against the relentless air conditioning. "Kim has a hundred thousand squaddies, yet needs our help! He *knows* which key players are bent."

"We can't prove that .... nor can Kim. Buddha's birthday is our first test."

Rose descended into a morose calm. "OK.... we save Cha Se what's it from the student killers this week. So when do we kidnap the hari kari brother?"

O'Brien smiled over the plastic orchids. "Abdul, we're in Korea, that's next week."

* * * * * * * * * *

Sunset lingered on the mountain as cool wind whispered through short pines and found a hollow in the scrub grass from where O'Brien and Rose kept watch through field glasses. The mountain fell steeply and far below, where the light already faded, a tiny human column struggled along a steep path bordered by a stream which trickled from a saddle in the main ridge: scores of pilgrim families drawn by faint, steady thudding from temple drums. Garlands of fairy lights revealed timber halls within a huge walled garden divided by the stony stream bed; but once night came, on the eighth day of the fourth lunar month, hundreds of lanterns would glow from its terraced courtyards.

Rose studied timber halls and sandy yards. Each marked one rung in the next life. The dozen restfully curved roofs merged into a hungry dusk. He lowered the field glasses. "Kim's thrown a cordon around the whole valley."

"Police, I trust, not party thugs." O'Brien swept his own powerful glasses down the mountain flank and over the opposite ridge.

Just below the skyline, every hundred yards, men in blue jeans stood in the windswept grass. He followed the stream that led the path down through the valley until it reached a tarmac road, and spotted two police buses parked by a jeep bristling with aerials. Several officers in combat suits examined a map spread over its green bonnet.

"They're pulling students off the path for frisking."

O'Brien pursed his lips. "Not sure about that... Abdul... Koreans expect searches, but it's heavy, almost too obvious."

"Tonight Kim's game is deterrence... might scare them off."

"But we slipped through that ring, Abdul, by coming over the back hump of this mountain."

"Somebody else can work out that solution.... only they won't expect a tail."

O'Brien calculated there was another twenty minutes light. "Soon need the night scope." He patted a bulge under his blue anorak.

Once more, raising his field glasses, he swept the mountain, next searching the valley beyond the path, down the tarmac lane which led to the main road and the crammed houses of Yonsei Dong. Silent traffic flowed on a distant highway raised on concrete stilts. The last sun plucked flashes like morse code from racing windscreens. Kwachon Mountain resembled two grey pyramids printed on the lemon sky.

Along the main Yonsei road, buses and cars were parked for a mile with more arriving. Somewhere among those little streets, avoiding the crowds, Kang should have dropped his passenger, parked his taxi ready for a fast escape and by now, vanished into the stream of people climbing that steep path. Letting the glasses hang from his neck, O'Brien flicked the switch on his wrist radio and spoke softly, "How do you read, Walkman, over."

Rose moved closer while they waited, staring at the tiny straggling line climbing towards darkness that crept into the deep valley.

Static heralded Kang's hoarse whisper. "Loud and clear, Uncle."

O'Brien sucked in his cheeks, regretting his rash choice of call sign, picturing sly smiles on the monitors' faces at Kim's Olympic Security HQ. He glanced sideways; Rose smirked without mercy. "I suppose something more dignified might improve my image."

Rose displayed his superb teeth. "Would you believe... Daddy?"

O'Brien returned a withering smile then enquired sharply into the wrist microphone, "All business complete?"

There was a long crackling in their earplugs before Kang's voice spluttered, "Bait in front, within sight."

O'Brien's left wrist covered his mouth. "Walkman..... *keep* within sight..... give a marker."

"Uncle... about to leave the road and take the foot path..... now passing the last dried fish and ramyon stalls, over."

"Catch all that on your headset, Abdul?"

Rose nodded and looked through his own field glasses at the last quarter mile of tarmac road where agimas served hot food from stalls under makeshift tents surrounded by hungry Koreans. "Got him," he said quietly.

"Where?"

"Pushing through a human wave attack on the last chinese soup kitchen."

O'Brien tugged the zipper on his anorak and took out the small night scope, focused on the soup stall, flicked the power switch. For an instant agitated thermal faces floated, then he spotted Kang crossing the circle of dancing umber puppets. He aimed the scope a fraction left, found his target, relaxed, switched off power, raised Kang.

"Have you both in sight. No movement up here yet. We'll wait a further five, repeat five minutes. Link at the ceremony."

"You have less than sixty minutes," replied Kang.

"Roger... out."

Where else could they evade the police cordon? Frustrated, he looked at young pines scattered over the mountainside, merging with night, then back at Rose." We're missing something."

Rose slid a hand inside his blue anorak, checking, grey eyes thoughtful, until he felt a machine pistol and its spare magazines. Content, he pulled his zipper higher against the cold wind. "Would they hide, Mike? Not in the temple because that's searched, but on the mountainside."

This thought had passed through his own mind, but there was barely a dusting of topsoil before a spade hit granite.

"Ground's precambrian rock, Abdul; one would need explosive for a worm hole."

"A hollow could serve as a hide with night for camouflage."

"We need them to move.... and soon." Far down the valley the first orange streetlamps flickered into life.

Rose stared beyond the temple where the spring cascaded from a saddle in the main ridge. "Try up there.... when the light fades just before moonrise."

Ten minutes later O'Brien settled his elbows on a rock. Night wind ruffled his copper hair. Alert for the slightest movement, he worked the nightscope leftwards, starting from the temple, climbing the stream bed, until the saddle gave way to an early star. He tried further left, where the mountain face joined darkness. A small umber shape moved within the grey circle, seconds later followed by another. His chest tightened. He breathed out slowly, releasing some tension.

"Bingo."

"Positive." Rose was on his feet, ready.

Although he could not identify features on either face, he knew, simply from the way they moved; he switched off the scope, tucked it into his anorak, checked his own pistol and magazines, lifted his wrist radio.

"Come in Walkman."

"Uncle." Kang's voice was soft though clear.

"Two bandits sighted just below the saddle. Heading down the stream bed in your direction. We'll circle round up here for a click and descend behind. They can't break past us nor slip the cordon. Questions?"

"None. Bait one hundred meters forward but keeping in sight. Bandits still concealed within shadow at valley head. Watch your own tail, Uncle, out."

He signalled Rose. They moved into the trees and listened for a few seconds. If the ghosts of generations wandered tonight seeking their earthbound children, all they heard was cold wind hurrying through young pine branches on the haunted mountain.

"Keep reporting, Walkman, out."

He nodded at Rose and they set off along the mountain flank, striding across the steep awkward slope, their ankles working though neither noticed. Years spent moving and fighting on their feet, reacting as an elusive team, locked both agile minds onto human quarry. They moved fast, silently, rarely stumbling on rocks and stones scattered over the mountain face and hidden by scrub grass, keeping among the stubby pines for cover. Once they stopped while O'Brien raised the nightscope and checked the stream bed. The hunted pair were almost half way down its sheer course. He switched off the scope.

tucked the short monocular safely in the anorak's inside pocket, smoothed the velcro tape seal and spoke softly into his wrist microphone.

"Walkman.... targets making good speed... we'll cut across the dog's leg and follow downhill."

"No contact yet." Kang's voice betrayed slight tension.

"Only when we're eyeball to eyeball, Walkman, not before."

"Eegoo!" The surprised cry hurt their eardrums.

O'Brien stared into the dusk. "Walkman... we want at least one live bandit, if possible, two.."

"Shall I pull back our bait?"

This decision could wait until they were within striking distance. "We'll play it by ear, Walkman, there's no danger yet. First let's make visual contact. They may not even react.... they're not expecting bait.... they're after Joseph."

Even as Kang acknowledged, somewhere on the main Yonsei road, a police siren nervously wailed : tonight Cha Se Dong enjoyed his first moments of an ironic freedom : house arrest swapped thirty minutes earlier for close escort by the morning's gaolers. He glanced at the green digits on his watch; General Kim had been forced to change their game plan and they had been out of direct touch for three hours. The general detailed a superintendent with his two best inspectors for guarding that turbulent cheerful prophet: Cha believed his fate strolled hand in hand with God. Less than five hundred yards ahead, two killers scrambled down the mountainside and somebody else monitored their mission, perhaps all the radio traffic around the dark valley. This third person was the one they wanted alive.

Rose closed and faced downhill. "We can rule out a sniper rifle if they go much lower. They're almost at the temple garden."

How he wished a signal from Hodori would end the worrying silence. Kim flung a superb net over dissident and Trotskyist movements throughout South Korea but relied on American technology for most penetrations into North Korea. Without that other dimension which the Moon's enjoyed; honest mouths speaking discretely from all quarters and both halves a feuding land; Kim was running with a blindfold.

Taking no chances, he pulled out the night scope, turned his back on the valley and for several seconds, watched the ridge line. Nothing moved. Still uneasy, he tucked the scope inside his anorak and declared, "No visible tail."

Rose squatted in the grass: his exceptional sight followed the pair scrambling down the streambed." Now look at that..... one of the bastards just whipped out a portafone."

He stared down at the rough slope, picked out their targets. Rose was right. He called over his shoulder. "Abdul..... they're reporting to a house or a car."

"Another person on foot?"

O'Brien instantly raised Kang. "Walkman.....one bandit has a portafone. Keep a sharp watch for company inside the temple garden."

"Closing on bait," replied Kang, trying to sound calm.

O'Brien's mind filed this new worry and revised their plan while he strode down the mountain, heading straight for the stream, now only a hundred yards below, splashing over a bed of large boulders before descending through the temple gardens.

Few stars shone through the haze of a fine spring night. Drum beats and voices came faintly from the valley. Soon they picked up a trail of flattened grass that revealed their quarries were a little clumsy at field craft. He glanced at Rose and without exchanging a word, both men moved off the fresh track, keeping the garden wall on their left, shadowing their targets from a respectful quarter mile.

Rose slid his machine pistol from its holster and tucked the weapon inside his anorak, ready, then hissed, "I've got you... Mike... any time you want."

He let Rose drop back about fifty yards before he closed on a pine copse which screened the nearest corner of the temple garden. Seconds later, they watched both figures huddle under a tree for a further message, probably a position report, then dash through the pines and slip over the low stone wall.

Still watching, O'Brien lifted his wrist. "Walkman.... bandits just landed in the northwest corner."

"OK..... Uncle.... now passing through gateway and keeping bait within twenty paces."

On a hunch that the North Korean control might watch his team's tail through night vision equipment, he decided to chance another short message. "We're figures two hundred from the wall. Taking the stream. With you in less than five..... Walkman...... pick up bandits inside the gardens and wait instructions. Out."

He hurried forward. He did not relish losing visual contact but, from now onwards, the risk of alerting their quarry increased with each footfall. Despite the din from voices and drums filling the valley, playing this lethal game, shock was the only card. He could forego line of sight providing Kang picked up both targets inside the gardens: cornering them became less difficult, taking one alive a real prospect, they might finally discover why the North Korean's wanted an airship over the Olympic Games.

Checking that Rose understood his intention, he dropped silently into the rocky streambed and keeping his trainers dry, bounded along the shallow ravine until he reached a small gap in the dry stone garden wall where the stream flowed into the temple gardens. Gurgling water smothered his leaps from one boulder onto another until he crouched between the high grassy banks. In front the stream hurried down a little stony trench through the garden. Nobody moved among the pines along its right bank.

Tall ginkyos hid the nearest timber hall from which drifted sombre drum thumps, wailing reed pipes and rising Korean chatter. Several children ran among the trees, laughing, screaming, but turned back at the stream. He debated whether to abort the mission, then began working his way further along the stream bed.

Through the rustling ginkyos, loomed the main hall, filled with white hanging lanterns, looking over a wide stairway cut into the hillside. Directly below this terrace, thousands more paper lanterns hung in neat rows like a flimsy ceiling about six feet above a wide sandy courtyard. Each white lantern bore the name of a beloved ancestor in beautiful black calligraphy. Watched by a gathering crowd, dozens of men worked feverishly preparing wax tapers, for shortly, when the Moon rose, at every temple across South Korea, glowing lanterns would greet returning souls. He admired the charming scene and let his ears separate new innocent sounds from others in the cold night.

Static came from his right front. A low voice recited the gutteral opening of any Korean telephone conversation. "Yobbasayo?"

Sprawled in the damp grass, he estimated the voice forty yards off, among the pines, probably waiting an order to cross the stream. For once, he granted himself a brief moment of silent victory, then mouth against his wrist, whispered, "Uncle is inside the magic circle and has one contact. Will let bandit cross from my right front, presently figures five zero yards downstream from hole in the wall. How's your position, Walkman?"

"No problems...... but many children."

"Understood, Walkman, but that's why they chose tonight. Our bait may draw them away from the main crowds..... where we shall need your special talent."

"Joseph walking up the track with a huge police escort. They're waiting for him before lighting all the lantern candles."

"Any idea how much longer?"

"Ten minutes."

O'Brien kept his voice just above a whisper. "OK... come over to the main hall and stay on those steps, watch all round, there's a third bandit somewhere, possibly another. I can only hear one voice over here.... but the second bandit remains close by. Report when you're in position. Uncle sits tight until his neighbour moves."

Time to bring in Rose and right behind the nocturnal telephone caller. Watching the foreground and the pine copse, with extreme caution, he ordered quietly, "Let's have you, now, Sleepwalker."

He became aware of his steady heart beat when he lay on his side and took out the nightscope. He edged forward, raised the scope and peered among the pines as the moon's silver light climbed from behind the mountain ridge. Concentrating through the scope, two umber profiles became blurred faces : one looking sideways then behind, one bent low as though listening. He slid backwards, glanced up stream, saw movement. Rose, doubled to keep his tall body hidden by the stream banks, reached his side. He jerked his thumb at the pine trees and handed Rose the nightscope.

After one squint, Rose returned it, and looking round, whispered, "When they move, you follow, Mike. I'll cover your back, block their escape."

He nodded, tucking the scope into a pocket, knowing Rose monitored his conversation with Kang. Shouting came from downhill, a police whistle shrilled. Cha Se Dong. Suddenly the crowd became noisier, swarmed across the courtyard and under its roof of waiting lanterns. At the same moment they saw two figures slide from the pine copse and scurry across the streambed like a pair of human rats.

"See you, Abdul." His right hand gripped the pistol under his anorak as he scrambled up the grassy bank. Fairy lights strung through the trees made his task confusing. From his headset came Kang's mild voice. "Ready Uncle. Bait inside praying."

No harm in that, grimaced O'Brien; well hidden yet working on divine intervention. "Walkman.... they're coming your way..... I'm thirty yards behind. We want the one with that portafone. And watch out. There may be another bandit within yards of your position on the temple steps."

"Munche Obsimnida."

"Don't get cocky," hissed O'Brien, following the two Koreans, realising both seemed taller than his memory recorded. For a moment doubt flooded his stressed mind, until they roughly shoved a child aside, something impossible for traditional Koreans. He drew closer when they plunged into the expectant crowd, old men and children, drunks and mothers, all pressing forward, welcoming the mild champion of simple people.

Sweat, beer, spirits, dry fish and strong garlic, attacked his nose. Half the noisy crowd were already drunk. Both men shouldered a path through, contemptuous of the milling throng, pushing towards the courtyard where expectant families dressed in their finest traditional robes gathered with glimmering tapers. Over excited heads, O'Brien caught the humble smile of Cha Se Dong, reluctant general thrust before this cheerful army which advanced onto the sandy courtyard, his heavy lidded eyes blinking in the sudden glow as candles flamed and lanterns spluttered into mellow light.

"Uncle," Kang was excited, "possible bandit up here.... watching from temple doors."

Distract boy, throw him off balance. He covered his mouth, "Tell bait to take a look, not too close, but enough that he knows."

"OK."

"And for God's sake don't become an incident. I want on of this pair alive." He just hoped that Kang would stay cool. He usually did. But this was Korea and the circumstances turning nasty.

"Joseph is about to light a lantern," reported Kang, as though nothing else mattered.

Still listening, he closed on the two killers, barely an arm length from their broad backs. Neither heard footfalls. Was a fourth man tailing Rose? Suddenly his quarries began pushing further right; cold night wind lifted his wavy hair as the crowd thickened, slowed and shoved, hoping for a fleeting glimpse when the great man lit his personal lantern.

The taller swerved and fumbled with something inside his ski jacket, looked round. O'Brien forgot cover. "Watch my back, team..... I'm going after both bandits."

He ignored the black tufted hair: right fingers dug into the sweaty nostrils and dry mouth, left forearm locked onto the windpipe, right trainer drove into the back of the target's knees: something solid hurled him onto his victim, both went down, glass smashed, sweet smelling petrol soaked through the Korean's ski jacket.

O'Brien kicked backwards, his trainer found a waiting groin, he heard a drunken moan. Choking his sagging captive, regaining balance, he leapt sideways.

Shaken, desperate, kicking aside a body, thin face contorted with disbelief, Shin's narrow eyes darted between Han's frantic struggling and a black giant who charged from the bewildered crowd. Brandishing a coke bottle which slopped petrol over his worn jeans, he fought with a plastic lighter and even as Rose leapt over the writhing drunk, its cloth wick flamed and the bottle curved like a small comet.

Whole families craned their necks, reverent faces, old and young, caught the expectant glow from thousands of lanterns which roofed the temple courtyard: the bottle exploded, yellow flame licked at dangling paper lights, torched the cold night. Silent wonder became horror as hundreds of shocked faces watched flames sweep overhead, attack row after row of flimsy lanterns that clung desperately on smouldering strings, before they sagged, fell onto the panicking crowd. Fear brought screams. Already Cha's escort party recoiled in utter confusion as a man wearing a business suit caught fire while fresh lanterns tumbled in flames like the death of a miniature air raid.

On the damp earth, fighting for control over the struggling Korean, O'Brien cursed, powerless to use his throat mike, and stop Rose chasing Shin through the terrified crowd. A thousand prisoners meant nothing..... if the man they protected tonight turned into kalbi steak. Where the hell was Kang? Where *was* their bloody bait, *Kim's* hordes? Rough hands fumbled at his ski jacket.

He jerked his captive onto both feet, throttling nose, mouth and throat, blocking air from desperate lungs, staggering towards growing chaos.

"Uncle.... come in.....", croaked a rattled Kang, "Cha's trapped by the fire. Must help. Bait in tow."

Commanding incredible strength, clothes stretched to breaking across his back, fingers like steel clamps, he dragged Han kicking and fighting, towards the angry flames, twisting the Korean's sweaty obstinate head until sound Irish teeth fastened on the wrist mike, moved the tiny switch. Ignoring soaked black hair and foul Kim Chi breath, O'Brien snapped, "Get over by this fucking fire, Walkman, before I burn alive."

"What about Cha?"

Ramming Han's head and neck down into his shoulders, he drove his trainer into the side of the Korean's right knee, stunned the nerves, felt leg and body collapse. Flames singed O'Brien's sweating face, thick smoke choked his lungs. Blinded, he croaked, "Give me a line, Walkman, I'll dump Han but can't see a fucking thing."

"Fifteen meters, on your left. He's trapped.... with some children."

He locked an arm round the slippery head, wiped away tears with his anorak sleeve. A plump man in grey Buddhist robes beat at flames on a little girl's long diaphanous Hanbok dress, oblivious that small flames hurried past his polished shoes and grey sharkskin trousers, devoured the hem of his own baggy grey tent.

Kang warned urgently, "Watch your back, Uncle."

Even as he swung Han between himself and the attacker, Cha's robe exploded into orange flame.

The smooth face clouded with desperation : Cha dared not stop beating at the child's dress yet suffered agony. Jerking round, O'Brien found the drunk advancing, swaying, fingers spread stiff, small weapons moving before his face, ready for vicious stunning chops.

He was short. An anorak hood and dark glasses obscured his face. He moved as though about to kick high and hard. O'Brien' flexed. His powerful arms catapulted Han straight at the open mouthed drunk, whose trainer, already flying, smashed Han's other knee. O'Brien leapt forward, spun, landed a backwards kick into the drunk's face, caught the mouth, heard the dark glasses crack. Two kicks on Han's temple were followed by a pair deep into the drunk's groin and stomach. There was no time for more.

"Walkman.... dumped two stiffs.... going for Cha."

"You looked good. We'll take over."

Thick smoke carried the stench of burning paper and attacked his eyes and throat. Wild flames shot into the night as mass cremation swallowed more lantern rows. His long stride carried him painfully over smouldering strips of blackened paper and sand oven hot. He reached the small girl, tore off her flimsy burning dress, lifted her with one arm, ripped away Cha's heavy fiery robe, wincing as his fingers blistered. Lines of lanterns fell blazing, cutting them off from the prostrate bodies only a few yards away, leaving a single chance for safety. From a gentle round face, mild watery eyes searched his own - for orders.

Steering a dazed, plump Cha, clutching the terrified and crying child, he struggled towards the temple gate. Flames scorched and smoke choked. Sweat poured down his roasted back. Suddenly they were in clearer air then hands reached for the sobbing girl.

Leaving a shaken but effusively grateful Cha with only a bleeding neck, his crestfallen and flustered police escorts busy yelling at each other, he slipped away through the chattering crowds, sprinting hard, circling the glimmering timber lodges round the blackened courtyard, dreading that his prisoners were already surrounded by puzzled, nervous Koreans.

He lifted his stinging wrist. "Walkman..... Cha's delivered safe to national police.... *where* are you?"

He tried again. "Walkman, repeat, Walkman."

Rose answered as though inside his cold brain. "We were bounced. Somebody good pulled a clever rubberdick job. I lost Shin to a student mob, repeat mob, at this moment, pursued back up the mountain by Kim's ski club."

"We cocked it."

"Steady, Uncle, we could hardly take out twenty or thirty students in front of ten thousand almond eyeballs."

He conceded this bitter truth. Cha was safe but they had fumbled a golden chance. He reached the long steps, raised his wrist to give Rose a location report and mouthed, "Bloody Hell!"

On the sand below, pungent grey smoke drifted, night wind chased scraps of flaming paper. An angry mob of students, curious on-lookers, many the worse for drinking Soju clear spirit, encircled a tall young man and a tiny defiant girl. There was no sign of Han or the mysterious drunk. Somewhere along the distant main road, sirens howled on a firetender struggling through blocked traffic. Heads turned but most concentrated on a bitter argument between three furious students and the restrained young giant. The girl hurled venom back in their shouting faces. From among the dark pines surged a squad of super fit Koreans in blue jeans and ski jackets, waving ugly batons, scattering the student mob, chasing dozens of screaming fugitives into the night, leaving two lonely figures, one dwarfing the other, standing in the foul smoke. The young man grabbed the small girl as though intending to run back through the woods towards the steep mountain.

Reminded absurdly of a greek tragedy, O'Brien ignored his wrist mike and shouted down. "Forget it, JP, by now they're probably half way back to Pyongyang."

Leaping the steps in pairs, growing aware of Korean families emerging furtively from the timber hall, that his left hand shook as its skin peeled in watery strips and the throbbing pain mounted, he asked "What were *they* complaining about?"

Kang stood crestfallen, broad shoulders almost sagging, "Why do we work for National Police instead of supporting democracy."

The girl stared at them both with hot eyes that still accused and her tight mouth ready to savage its next victim. She resembled a small furious boy with her long hair trapped inside the hooded ski jacket.

"We told them Cha Se Dong will bring democracy quicker than their petrol bombs."

She began to shiver from delayed shock. He squeezed her trembling shoulder with his right hand. "Who took my two bodies?"

Kang seemed confused, still seeking reasons, replaying the last intense minute within his numb mind, troubled frown switching from O'Brien to the scorched sand, back towards the steps and timber hall now glowing with beautiful light from thousands of hanging lanterns. "A well organised team, mature thugs, eight or ten strong, poured from the temple and down the steps, seconds after you went through the flames towards Cha. A small man followed, older, rather humble, face hidden by dark glasses and I can't even remember his clothes. The original face in a crowd. We called you, then followed."

"Sunspecs appear the terror club badge," grumbled O'Brien as his left hand tortured without mercy.

"We bluffed for a few moments, hinted we were national security, nobody was impressed."

The girl shoved small hands into her ski jacket pockets. "You know Korea! A crowd mushroomed, more students, women and men reeking of soju, everybody ordering the others around. JP can't fight ten men and a stupid crowd." She suddenly noticed his raw skin and gasped.

"My doctor's coming now." O'Brien smiled grimly, studying his weeping fingers.

A huge form emerged from the darkness, loping across the courtyard, ignoring the strong wind still hurrying scraps of ashen paper across his rapid path. A hood covered his head, barely revealing a stern black face as grey eyes scanned the night like search radars on a prowling warship. Rose lifted artist's fingers in a resigned salute.

"I'm sorry Mike, what a screw up... let's fix your wounded paw." Gently, he examined the burnt hand.

Rose steered his patient along a path under the pines until they sat on flat rocks by the burbling stream. A few muffled voices from shocked families reached their private haven. Most people were drifting homeward, down the crowded track, drained after several minutes horror.

Kang and Diana watched in shaken silence as Rose zipped open his anorak, pulled the velcrotape on an inside pocket, slid out a fat plastic pack, crammed with a lavish medical kit. Rose rolled open the pack like a miniature carpet on the huge stone that served as his operating table. He examined its plastic pockets, slid out some tools. Scissors snipping, balm cream squirting, rapidly soothing, Rose treated the suffering fingers and thumb with delicate skill.

His patient watched the bandages wound expertly, his good hand holding a hip flask, washing down two red pain killing tablets from Switzerland with fine cognac. How many times, how many places, he thought, at last freed from agonising pain : Radfan, Malaysia, Vietnam, Ireland, West Falkland, now South Korea. Every fourth man in an SAS patrol was a medic' but Abdul always found a line waiting for his surgeon's touch.

Rose starting packing his medical kit. "You won't throttle any North Koreans for roughly a fortnight. Grow some new skin first."

"Thanks a fucking million, Abdul. How's the little girl?"

"Not a mark, small neck wound on Cha - odd : I just came from them." Rose suddenly apologised, weary, almost bitter. "Should never have chased that bastard..... oughta' stuck to you like glue, Mike."

O'Brien, fingers numb, pain retreating slowly, dismissed this outburst. "You had no choice, Abdul: tell me how many other weapons Shin carried. We don't know, same goes for Han. Somebody got very close to Cha, flames don't cut. I couldn't break off wrestling; modern technology hasn't solved that one fully. Switched on the radio with my bloody teeth, but, by then, no way I could call you back."

"I never had a clear shot anyhow," said Rose, tucking the plastic bundle into his large pocket.

"We weren't there to open a shooting gallery. The crossfire might have killed and injured dozens. Our cover is toilet paper but our pensions remain safe..... besides", he admired the fat bandage, "Cha was our prime task."

"General Kim was very cautious tonight." Kang wore a respectful though questioning stare.

O'Brien jerked round as though somebody had punched him. "Where is Kim?"

"Already left in a big car taking Cha Se Dong and a couple of his best shots," answered Kang, promptly brushing a hand through his windswept hair, a sign that he still turned over events in his mind, believed there was something wrong but could not yet find the right words.

O'Brien stretched his legs then stood, concluding silently that General Kim enjoyed the most blessings on Bhudda's Birthday. Somebody else fought North Korea : Cha was safe. The President might not like that result, but, tonight, fragile though vital links stayed open between Kim and Chung. Nobody changes the world during one day and Kim held enough cards to keep public order while playing power poker. Yet Kang was groping along the right trail. Who scratched Cha's neck? Who ran that drunk? The hostile controller who stood on those temple steps? He never saw the snatch squads. They sounded more like trained soldiers than rebellious students. There was something Kim had not disclosed, or worse, did not know. At that moment, tired from his burnt hand, he felt horribly blind. Vanity never paid: his secret ambition had been the look on Harry Todd's face when he threw a live North Korean terrorist onto his office carpet. Now, he must confess the loss of one big fish and from his own bare hands.

Standing by the shallow stream, realising what probably lay behind the whole fiasco, he glanced at Rose and the girl, then Kang. "I think, JP, you're near the jackpot."

The girl's lips parted, before she changed her mind, chose silence, wide mouth locked into a firm line as her cold face watched him from the hooded jacket.

"Any ideas, Diana?" said O'Brien, staring down, meeting her troubled eyes and observing small nervous hands straying from jeans to jacket.

She shivered before answering softly, "I was so scared. None of the faces were more than a blur, except that man on the temple steps.... I knew him, knew his face, but I can't think where or when."

"In which case," he told her frankly, "we'd better bring forward our trip to your southern sunshine."

22

The sun's golden swords filtered between huge shark teeth crowning Pukhansan Mountain and furtive light crept over empty rice fields stretching from the wide road. Todd's white Mercedes comfortably ate the last miles north from Munsan towards the Imjin River. The General enjoyed dawn humour when the young soldier at the wheel shrugged camouflaged shoulders and remarked to him and a drowsy American army chaplain, "Bootiful country, Sur, Kohrya.... Only gotten one problem..... Kohryans."

O'Brien stifled a yawn and smirked obligingly. After a night spent consulting General Kim, Paul Moon, Mason in Oxfordshire then finally, Harry Todd at Yongsan, he fought heavy eyelids and the warm car. Major's oak leaves and discrete bronze crosses sat on the lapels of his green and brown combat suit which bore the name POPE over his right chest pocket. Sometimes Harry Todd's wicked side dreamed up simple though brilliant schemes. At every check point, fully armed though tired Korean MPs sprang to attention and saluted the approaching white car tailed by two green staff saloons. Nobody paid the slightest attention to the chaplain riding in the back with the UN Commander who often gave the pastors and rabbi lifts from Yongsan out to the forward troops. Four small stars on a red sheild above the front fender served better than any pass.

O'Brien looked at the racing paddies, trying to stay awake. Something large stood in deep green fields on their right; a shell punctured, rusting steam locomotive which never finished its journey north from Pusan to Peking.

Todd's driver asked, "Would the Chaplain like to stop for a few moments at the Imjingak museum, Sur."

"That's OK, Kowalski," answered Todd swiftly. The last thing they needed was a North Korean spook snapping the UN Commander in Chief and a Chaplain taking a daybreak walk at a tourist site on the river bank. Kim Il

Sung probably paid the museum and restaurant cleaners more than their salaries from National Security HQ.

Ahead they saw a collection of old tanks, guns, propeller aircraft and a sabre jet fighter, parked before a giant concrete pillbox, itself defended by a small bronze statue of President Harry S Truman. Behind the Anti Communism exhibition Hall stood a simple three storey restaurant with large windows overlooking a wide peaceful river.

Kowalski swung left through a deserted parking lot. Two American soldiers wearing german style helmets, bayonets glinting on their rifles, dragged aside a black and orange painted barrier. A small pagoda with a blue tiled roof served as a control point where a sergeant threw a brisk salute, waved the cars onto a narrow road between white railed fences. Beyond rose the grey box spans of a long bridge.

The Mercedes thumped over rough deck timbers on the old steel structure that once carried trains over the placid Imjin. A few hundred yards east the brick supports of a long bombed road bridge stood forlornly in the sluggish brown water. Every fifty yards along the worn deck an American sentry in full combat gear snapped rigid, presented arms, bayonet fixed, yelled the battalion war cry.

Todd's cold blue eyes filled with his familiar dry mirth. "I guess, Chaplain," he remarked softly, "your own regiment favours a rather more discrete style."

O'Brien's yawned, "We tend to reap the Lord's harvest a little more silently."

Kowalski assumed both officer's were slightly drunk while O'Brien recalled the previous night. They had driven back to the dong where he debriefed each one individually, taking notes, then questioned them together, pooling their memories. That produced surprising detail. Rose enjoyed superb recall, described his chase among the crowd, yard by yard, took himself right through the sequence when a masked squad came from nowhere and screened Shin. There was sudden physical contact, hard shoves and an unspoken warning, disciplined bodies blocking his path, threatening, starting to encircle before their next orders.

But the girl saw things that the others missed. Diana remained convinced : she knew the person on the temple steps. When was difficult. The name impossible. Somewhere in a troubled past that face moved through her short life, not for long, but enough to bring back instant sickening fear. She must have been far more frightened than they realised, for she blurted out detail after detail : one nagged throughout the long sleepless night. They wore different clothes but each man had strapped his watch on the right wrist.

More than ever, he suspected a military operation and after an hour of confrontation with Kim whose answers left only questions, followed by a calmer hour with Paul Moon, next seeking clearance from Mason to indoctrinate the US commander at Panmunjom, finally he warned Harry Todd that the evidence pointed towards the North Koreans.

For a second he stared at the khaki water drifting towards to the Han estuary and open sea. Tonight they would set off for a milder climate on the girl's small island. She had talked about that, too, during the small hours, those exhausted eyes growing hopeful as she chattered, trying to control fear, without much success. God, she was tempting, his groin ached with instant want though it was disaster for a tight disciplined team. He felt more like a monk than a protestant chaplain, the outfit cruelly realistic. There was an emptiness about the whole house after Kang piled her into his taxi dark and early that morning.

The car jolted off the big timbers and cruised onto smooth tarmac. A small group of American soldiers stood in the road: no Koreans civilians were allowed onto Freedom Bridge. Thirty years earlier, thousands of POWs had trudged south over its splintered planks, released at last from years of torture, starvation and captivity. Now only Korean soldiers and rare farmers lived across the muddy river. Kowalski waved regally to a captain and three NCOs and then drove through a wooded valley, passed a Korean Army camp and climbed a low ridge which hid a wide valley watched by steep bottle green mountains where sunrise explored North Korea.

The road wound into a wide gulley behind the gentle escarpment, a classic reverse slope that screened the wired and sandbagged camp of an American armoured cavalry regiment, its tracked reconnaissance vehicles parked in four neat lines. Sleepy soldiers hosed off thick red dust.

O'Brien stared, twice, before muttering, "That is a Mig pilot's prayer."

Todd glared behind as the escort cars sped past the outer wire and minefield, the main gate with a gaudy unit sign painted on a board. "I'll deal with Meyer's outfit when we reach Camp Boniface. They're supposed to be on Condition Three alert.... since last week."

Kowalski descended into the silent valley. Behind some distant trees a pair of water tanks stood on steel legs, supplying long green huts almost hidden by a copse of delicate young birches.

Three check points later Kowalski pulled up outside a low hut with a signboard over its porch that proclaimed, "Home of the Merry Mad Monks of the DMZ."

Todd noticed his companion's puzzled expression. "The maddest monk is the one with the least time left in country." He allowed a knowing pause. "At the moment, your British brigadier."

O'Brien knew the man, they were old friends. Any contact was out of the question. But that wasn't the highest price, he thought, hankering after a game on the American's one hole golf course, despite his fingers.

Todd clambered out of his Mercedes as the two staff cars arrived in front of the low building. Weary yet waking, O'Brien opened his door and breathed deeply. Cold clean wind rustled the young ash, birch and ginkyos. Birds sang from every tree and bush. A summer day slowly took over the tidy camp. Almost no industry existed for hundreds of miles northwards. He felt like a cat given its next life.

A tall colonel strode from swing doors under the hut porch. He was tanned, lined, tired and losing thin hair, though sharp grey eyes hinted at reserved charm. "General we've hot coffee and doughnuts, full breakfast, a briefing team, armed escorts or just myself, whatever you require."

Todd drew both men away from the parked cars. "Jack Kelly commands the Joint Security Area, otherwise known as the JSA, home for thirty four years of mindless talking." Todd faced north. Trees screened the low mountains.

"We'll drive into the valley. First a geography lesson. Six hundred meters downhill from here is the southern boundary of the DMZ. That's our defensive line, walled against tanks, wired and mined, right across Korea. Two clicks beyond lies the JSA where we live uneasily with our North Korean neighbours. It's our last patch in the middle of no-man's land, where the troops breath quickly, sometimes quiet, most times the nearest experience to a combat zone."

O'Brien tried hard to look like an Episcopalian Chaplain but without much conviction for it was his first time in a uniform since that night in Armagh. Memories flooded back. Standing there with Kelly, listening to Todd's clear though simple language, he could no longer forget how much he missed the Army. Suddenly the soft wind brought a distant orchestra and a woman's choir.

"Revolutionary music." Kelly jerked his eyebrows.

"How often do you suffer that?" asked O'Brien after the strange haunting sound faded when the wind died.

Kelly stared at the thin trees. "Most times it's all night. How the Swiss and the Swedes stand that racket beats the shit outa' me.... their camps are right on the MDL."

O'Brien's expression warned that he had lost the habit of US military jargon.

"Military Demar-cation Line," added Kelly.

"I guess Chaplain Pope could use some breakfast," Todd noticed O'Brien's gaunt cheekbones and troubled look. "Coffee wouldn't do me any harm.... either."

Kelly moved with the stride of a courteous wolf, pushed open swing doors leading into a cheerful bar, behind which hung a row of navy blue baseball caps, each bearing the name of a current 'monk' in gold letters. Near the doors stood a bookstall loaded with postcards, pamphlets, slides and souvenirs for the daily busloads of tourists. America's new army opened a business outlet wherever they saw a fast market.

An aroma of fresh coffee joined with thin smoke from steak, eggs, bacon and fried potato grits. O'Brien's morale soared. Hot greasy food served by a gloomy Korean cook brought his weary body some energy.

Colonel Kelly made polite conversation while they ate but a sceptical glint lingered in his resigned grey eyes that left little doubt : Kelly was not fooled for a second though his caution proved that the colonel kept secrets.

Todd began disarmingly, "This place been swept lately?"

"0400 this morning, Sur, " answered Kelly with a thoughtful smile.

"Nothing?"

"Electronically virgin, Sur."

"Chaplain Pope had an exciting night, Jack."

"I guess not with a woman," smiled Kelly who had read between the lines of a personal signal during the night and caught on fast." Buddha's Birthday?"

O'Brien nodded, sipping his third mug of strong coffee, holding the hot china handle with respect. Kelly had been up half the night as well, judging by his raw eyes; he sympathised before explaining blandly, "There were some remarkably disciplined pilgrims out last night."

The colonel leaned back in his chair and glanced at his general. They were alone. Diverse strands from intelligence reports were all converging on the person sitting opposite. Their eyes met.

"Be my guest, Harry," deferred O'Brien, who cleared the need for indoctrination with Mason at three in the morning, because he doubted whether Kelly would be satisfied with half a story, nor risk any of his troops, without knowing enough.

Todd rested his large farmer's hands on the mess table. "Chaplain Pope has a link with Heaven, Jack. He's a fellow countryman of yours who works for the British Government and is in Korea to build, test and fly an airship equipped with smart security systems, then train Korean police pilots, if humanly possible, before the Olympic Games. Pope's boss in London set fairly wide ranging tasks.... I guess you oughta' explain the rest, Mike."

Leaving aside some obvious questions, rather than insult Kelly's fast mind, he described the previous night, the sudden arrival of disciplined squads. Kelly listened intently while sipping coffee, sometimes nodding, concentration chiselled sharp lines on his forehead, before he looked directly across at Todd. "I'm not saying it isn't possible with the sandy soil in that valley.... but Jesus Christ... we drill bore holes over all the ground this side of the minefields."

Todd rested his elbows on the simple table and with both hands, rubbed his nose, trying to draw together tiny threads, scraps of intelligence which might expose a pattern, allow him inside the enemy's brain. He asked Kelly, "What if they had bored a shorter tunnel, smaller, one which came out near Taesong dong?"

"How far away is that?" interrupted O'Brien.

"The village is well forward.... five hundred yards south-east from the MDL", said Todd. "Also has the richest farmers in South Korea. Nobody else wants to farm there so some own ten or twenty acres. Most Koreans reckon they're rich with a couple."

Kelly scanned the spotless tiled floor. "Possible, Sur, possible, but bloody difficult for them to hide over along period."

"The tunnel order goes back a dozen years," Todd reminded him, "twenty front line divisions were told to dig one each. We've found three."

Kelly reached for a cigarette packet in his breast pocket but changed his mind. "All the others were drilled through solid rock. Seismographic echoes travel well through rock. Sandy soil *would* absorb sounds."

Todd nodded, hands now clasped, leaning slightly forward. "Any new houses in that village?"

"Somebody down in Taesong dong is an NK agent?" Kelly pursed thin lips, folded his arms and studied his jungle boots. This had implications. Two hundred ROK special forces served under his command alongside a slightly larger American force. He was dubious but never ignored the remotest threat in Korea and voice held low he stressed, "They're all screened by ROK Security Command.... special people... with powerful political friends."

"Bright Korea Party 'select' the villagers," explained Todd for O'Brien's benefit. "ROK Army intelligence watch them for moral deviation."

Todd reached over and took a glossy covered booklet off the stall, flicked through its pages until he found a photograph which showed a scale model of the valley, then passed O'Brien the open book. Taesong dong lay inside the DMZ, only a few hundred yards south of the small Sachon River, between two hilltop lookout posts manned by Americans, no doubt packed with the latest night vision and infra-red sensors, which according to Todd, could isolate body heat miles inside North Korea. Across the river was another village, Kijong dong, empty houses clustered around a tall steel mast flying the world's largest flag. A tunnel from the North Korean bank of the Sachon which emerged beyond the South Korean village and its barely shorter flagmast, defeated both American outposts.

"Risky.... bearing in mind the village politics," ventured O'Brien, yet every instinct warned that they drew close to the secret key.

"Or else bold," hinted Kelly.

Thoughtful, Todd sipped coffee, then asked Kelly, "Any abnormal activity across the river... work details, trucks, noise, lights?"

"Over their side." Kelly rubbed his shrewd chin. "Nuthin' special since last week, when a Swedish film crew went into Propaganda Village, Kijong dong. North Koreans brought in a lotta' people, geese, pigs, chickens, quite early in the day before the Swedes arrived. But after they filmed and left, rentacrowd went home by truck, en masse; farm animals, people, poultry, all jammed together." He shrugged blankly.

"Patrols."

"Normal, Sur, most night probes came from along the river line."

Todd drained his coffee mug and glanced towards O'Brien," We'd better show you on the ground."

Kelly scraped his chair on the floor and rose from the breakfast table. "I gotta' a jeep and three cammo' scarves to cover all stars, birds, oak leaves and crosses. No escort?"

"None," confirmed Todd.

O'Brien asked tactfully, "Do you mind copying those three monkeys, John."

"Never seen 'yer," declared Kelly with a disarming smile.

When he stood, O'Brien tried moving his sore fingers, relieved. Gone were those cruel stabs from any movement that left palm and wrist throbbing without mercy. Rose gave him more pain killers during the night but the cream was winning. Twenty four hours and he might even forget the thick bandage.

Near a cotton tree thicket, beyond sentries guarding a small bridge over the minefield, Kelly slowed from breakneck speed, drove the jeep onto scrub grass, braked hard, killed its racing engine. Over the Sachon River an operatic chorus rose towards a crescendo of strident female voices. Kelly leaned round and resting one arm across the steering wheel, pointed at the main defence line: a great concrete wall holding back red soil, a high mesh fence and lookout towers, marked its relentless journey, following rolling hills into morning haze.

Kelly dug into his side pocket and found a cigarette pack. Todd and O'Brien declined, watched as the colonel flicked open the inevitable zippo lighter, breathed out pale smoke.

"Suppose they burrowed under the Sachon River, Sur.... how do they scale that anti-tank wall? They can't fly over. Damn' sight simpler to come in low much further south along the coast in one of those Antonov bi-planes, land miles from Seoul, then travel north."

"Depends who greets this end, Jack, that's the bloody riddle." Todd pulled the net camouflage scarf loosely over his mouth and nose. "When Jack's finished his cancer ration, we go forward, but cover your face. The NKs on those mountains have new soviet kit monitoring this whole valley. I wouldn't want the Fatboy to put us on between blue movies in his private late night cinema."

As his eyes betrayed amusement under the camouflage baseball cap, O'Brien's mind pictured Sister Moon in a navy blue Mao suit, face smooth, never fully relaxed, working in some spartan office block, three hours drive north on poor roads.

Kelly tossed his cigarette onto the scrub and crushed it with his jungle boot. Soon the growling engine drowned the massed choir and orchestra from North Korea. Two small hills rose from lettuce green paddies. On both summits were sandbag emplacements, watchtowers, aerials, electronic dishes, small stars and stripes flapping in the light wind. Further west stood a huge steel tower from which lifted the mostly white South Korean Flag. Over the river, flying a vast red blanket, soared an even higher structure, resembling a slim Eiffel Tower, somehow lost in northern Asia. Nestled around its feet were odd white and pastel pink houses like boxes cut with crude empty windows that stared back across the warm valley.

"Propaganda Village," explained Todd, glancing sideways at Kelly, deciding their next move. "Skirt round the back of Taesong dong, Jack. I don't want the ROK army spooks stumbling on our morning tour."

Kelly drove west on a dirt road that wandered among thickets encircling flooded paddies. Several times brown speckled pheasants crashed through bushes, took off, wings beating, flying low for the young trees. O'Brien, sitting in the back, yelled with excitement. "Ringpheasants?"

"Right on," Todd shouted cheerfully, "We even spotted a four hundred pound cat out here last winter. A native tiger. The DMZ is Korea's finest wild life sanctuary. Only man is open season."

"Let's hope it doesn't sink to that," laughed O'Brien as morning sun warmed his back and the cool slipstream refreshed his drained mind. Only the shallow river split the hostile paddy fields. He shouted at the pair in front. "Why a tunnel?"

"Because my troops patrol all along our bank," Kelly yelled over his shoulder, "there are people sniffers all over this side of the Sachon."

"My orders are shoot first," explained Todd frankly, "I'd rather field nasty press questions than recover from a tactical blunder. This is the most heavily armed frontier in the world. One and a half million troops are on alert both sides of the DMZ with another five million reserves *each* in both Koreas. Chung is in deep shit south of here in Seoul and Fatboy plots in Pyong-yang...... I don't rule out anything, terrorism, massive ground attack, special operations."

O'Brien shouted through his net scarf. "Our money then is on the Bureau of Reconnaissance Special Forces."

"Eighty thousand are forward, hyped to the bloody eyeballs, ready and waiting to sabotage the Olympics, yet without any march orders. Last night they may have let off some steam. Perhaps they were watching the barracks TV in Kaesong City over the border... nowhere near Seoul. We don't know. But I can't ignore the possibility that it was a risk taken for something bigger in September."

Through thick trees they saw the low roofs of the Military Armistice Commission where American, British Commonwealth and South Korean officers met the Chinese and North Koreans for endless barren words. He picked out the North Korean's fake white building, no wider that a stage set, waiting for the other side's tourists later that morning. The Swiss camp nestled beneath a little wooded hill on which stood a North Korean watchtower overlooked by another.

"They can scan the whole JSA from that hillock," said Todd, swivelling round in his seat, pointing out landmarks. "Those roofs are the MAC complex."

O'Brien asked, "How often do the villagers leave the DMZ?

"Everyday."

Kelly slowed for some ruts then volunteered, "It's a steady trickle. Shopping in Munsan, Uijongbu or Seoul. Gotta' be back in the 'ville before dark. We check 'em out but my Koreans provide the Civic Action Group. They check 'em back into the houses."

"How many gates?"

"To the DMZ? You came through it," Kelly added with a wise smile, "and there's only one bridge."

The colonel dropped into second gear, charged a mound overgrown with scrub oak and young birches. Once among the brush and trees, he slammed the brakes, switched off the engine and swung his long legs onto rutted orange mud overgrown with wild grass. The hill was no more than a hump lying forward of the main escarpment with its minefield and concrete wall to stop infantry and tanks, but, when O'Brien stared through leafy branches, he could watch the whole valley.

"Pretty good," confided Todd smugly.

"Fantastic."

Todd looked towards village houses tucked among ginkyo saplings. "OK, Mike, you're the expert. How would you sneak upwards of twenty North Korean spetznaz into the South Korea?"

He took his time answering. It was a question which they must answer, without fail, without error, without facts. All three knew what a mistake brought in its wake. Todd did not press; he was only glad that fate delivered an old friend, that one of the world's most experienced captains of special warfare stood at his elbow, perhaps the only man on the peninsular who could invert his mind and think like a North Korean commander, relying not on technology or fire-power, but skill, daring, and bare hands.

Surveying the gentle valley, O'Brien felt more strongly than ever a nagging hunch. Six hundred thousand troops defended the south but along the whole front line, perhaps Kelly's four hundred Americans and Koreans faced the sternest test. The reason lay a mere few hundred yards east : two villages existed inside the DMZ but in the southern one, two hundred people lived *behind* the UN forward patrols.

Kelly reached under the dash and found a map wrapped in tough clear plastic and spread it over the jeep bonnet, stood back, loosened his camouflage scarf, lit another soothing cigarette. The map showed a kilometre square of countryside with the Sachon River curving towards its bottom left corner.

Leaning on the warm jeep bonnet, checking the map before measuring distances with his eyes, O'Brien began working out how much time a man would need at night to ford the river from starting points around a wide arc and slip into the silent village.

Thick copses grew along the river banks. A small rise screened the MAC complex roofs among bushy foliage that also hid the abandoned Bridge of No Return. Somewhere along its deserted approach road stood an old poplar stump which cost two American lives, murdered by axe wielding North Koreans a dozen years past : now maturing poplars gave lavish cover.

O'Brien considered alternatives: coming round the back of the MAC compound looked promising, where the JSA bulged into the North Korean lines. It was the shortest distance. Less time for electronics to feel body heat. Taesong dong stood inside this salient.

He studied the US Corps of Engineers' map. A shallow lake formed an obstacle west of the tarmac road which led from the MAC compound through open country between the two watching hills, past the winding track to Taesong dong, through the minefield and up the steep slope into Camp Boniface.

Looking across the gentle valley with its copses and thickets basking in the sharp early morning, he saw no obvious reason for a tunnel. Feeding small numbers into the southern DMZ was a realistic if daunting option. But how did they cross a minefield and tank wall? Moles in Taesong dong? Suppose they managed, the Imjin River was a far more effective barrier; unless the same moles also defeated that obstacle. Why cross here at all? Why not buy a plane ticket in Japan, insert at Pusan, even Kimpo International. Through fear of tight security? It was tightest where they stood. Lack of a proper support network amongst the million Koreans living in Japan? This seemed a more plausible reason. But there could be others. And, if smuggling twenty men was safer over the shortest though most alert and lethal distance, what else travelled that covert trail.

He lifted his gaze from the large scale map. "Jack, would it be very difficult for your Americans to watch that village without their Korean counterparts knowing?"

Kelly removed the cigarette from his hard mouth and exhaled a pensive smoke cloud. "We're too stretched," he objected in a polite reminder that his experienced American *and* Korean troops faced another three months of dangerous games : he glanced at Todd, obviously hoping that his commander would refuse any fresh burdens.

O'Brien sympathised but also was under growing pressure and strict orders. He must win Kelly as a close comrade and tackled him gently with selective facts. "Are they probing much more since the last weeks?"

"Every bloody night." Smoke escaped from Kelly's mouth and nose. "They're pushin' for an incident... a UN Command reaction.... provoking a burst of fire to scare the shit outa' America's media. No team, no tourists." He added with deep feeling, "Restraint gets tedious."

Todd had been watching both men closely while exploring his own thought line. Perhaps convinced that they closed on the heels of a major North Korean spoiling operation, he lowered the temperature before Kelly, rightly suspecting a hold up, formally protested, thereby killing any chance for secret teamwork: Todd also wanted a live North Korean hostage kept warm for the TV cameras.

Glancing at both, he tackled O'Brien first, "Don't keep spookin' my JSA Commander, Mike, tell us your bloody hunch."

O'Brien smiled helpfully at the cornered colonel. "Was there much pressure this week?"

"Three nights back, there was so much shit, we thought they were coming across in division strength. I think you're right," Kelly conceded without rancour, "there's bin' almost nothin' since."

"Why keep on alerting your patrols." O'Brien paused, worried about preaching, before he went further. "Suppose they wanted to bring in a team with special equipment. They would need you looking the wrong way."

A thump announced Todd's jungle boot resting on the front fender. "One man or bit missing and the rest becomes worthless. I buy that. Hit us with your grocery list, Mike."

"No real proof."

Todd brushed aside the constant fear of chasing false trails. "We don't have the luxury of endless time. Your hunches often turn self fulfilling. Uncle Sam bought technology worth billions of dollars for checking our worst nightmares. None of which can crack this problem."

Todd's irony restored Kelly's good nature and, wasting no time, O'Brien rested an arm along the windshield's metal frame, began guessing.

"OK.... for a start, take their new industrial plant up north on the Yalu River. A bomb doesn't worry me, Harry; but some kind of lunatic bearing a container loaded with radio active material does.... every Olympic team would scatter to the four fucking winds in utter panic. I can't put my finger on what, but they intend something specific, aimed at somebody, perhaps only at Cha Se Dong, but employing a trick that still eludes our intelligence gathering networks."

O'Brien stood back from the jeep, arms folded, staring through the rustling leaves, weary from thinking always in riddles.

Todd asked casually, "When will your blimp fly?"

He foresaw Todd's purpose and described the airship role in Olympic security. For source protection, neither hinted at a direct threat to the British airship. Though he left out the link into Todd's HQ, the Colonel's blank face proved that Kelly reached home base. O'Brien finished innocently, "The Koreans will need our help throughout the Games. My pilot is also chief engineer. He starts building our airship next week."

Todd's ice blue eyes challenged. "Certain?"

"Abdul's seen the hangar and Kim's contractors are busy this week putting on its roof sheets. Certain."

"Christ, they cut it fine." Todd suddenly made up his mind and confronted Kelly across the jeep bonnet. "Put an extra watch on that 'ville', Jack. Those bastards could porter SAMs through the JSA like bits of Leggo. If that village is playing for both sides at the same time... anythin's possible."

Kelly nodded, silent, while he absorbed the paralysing news : among those tidy farmhouses in Taesong dong someone ran a North Korean command post, well inside his Joint Security Area.

"It's another manpower burden, Jack, when you're stretched thin," conceded Todd firmly, "but this job demands micro local knowledge. No Green Berets.... at least, not yet, so delay leave, rotations, courses, hide it from your ROKs, because this watch is for American eyes only."

Ash lengthened on Kelly's forgotten cigarette.

23

Violet dusk, mirrored on the wide Han, already faded before the first summer night when they drove onto Panpo Bridge. Lights blinked in discrete yellow rows from apartment blocks along the southern bank while headlamps constantly flowed on the Olympic Highway. Fighting a path through city buses and stinking trucks, Kang joined nose to tail traffic crawling from the bridge ramp onto the Pusan Expressway. An hour later, bumper to bumper, Kang drove south at suicidal speed, braking smoothly when a red lights serpent flickered ahead, returning his foot hard on the gas pedal as though a magnet towed his taxi behind the silver train of buses that forever raced in front. O'Brien copied Rose and wisely fell asleep. He did not wake for two hours and found Kang speeding along a wide road where few headlamps searched the night sky.

"Want a break?" yawned O'Brien, drowsy from pain killers.

"Munche obsimnida, Mike. We're west of Taejon on the Honnam Expressway . . . Route Three for Americans . . . only a couple of hours from Kwangju City."

"How far after Kwangju?"

Kang silently calculated then answered confidently, "Maybe another hour, but we will reach the farmhouse before midnight."

Moonrise flooded onto a wide coastal plain and eastwards, found distant mountains. Rose slept soundlessly. Wise man, thought O'Brien, letting his heavy lids fall. Yet sleep eluded him, slumped in the back seat, trying not to kick Rose, whose legs took more room than his own in the droning saloon.

Before leaving Seoul, they sent Mason a signal offering their own gamble on the military risk from North Korea. Anything was possible, but eighty thousand special forces camped over the DMZ and supported by several score Russian bi-planes made some things more possible than others.

Small groups, determined experts, commandos flown beneath the American and South Korean radar, threatened the Games with night landings: Antonovs could set down and take off from new parks around the Olympic Village and along the southern bank of the Han River. They discarded this threat as a lavish diversion. Sister Moon's information pointed away from a mass attack towards a clever strike pulled off by a select few and Buddha's Birthday seemed further proof.

Their journey south was a dice throw: North Koreans would not tamper with those boxes stored at the hangar site, now almost ready; both sides wanted an airship flying over Seoul during the Olympic Games. Dear God, O'Brien prayed silently, make us right: whoever survived a disaster must explain a smoke pillar worth seven million dollars.

Sleep conquered doubt for another hour. Tunnels through a mountain inflicted orange light on his sore eyes before night once more swallowed the countryside. For the first time since putting a foot on Korea, he sensed standing on firmer ground. Only his emotions still drifted. A cold white glare climbed in the southern sky: suddenly blinded by the headlamps of over laden trucks, he realised they raced on a freeway around Kwangju City, drowsily aware that half a million people slept under the watch of Shinyang Mountain, and all but a handful stood behind Cha Se Dong.

Another hour passed. Kang drove south west through low mountains and crossed wide valleys where flooded paddy flashed silver under a fat moon. Rare weak lamps blinked from villages tucked among tall bamboo thickets. Windhowl from the racing car soothed O'Brien's troubled mind. He just hoped father and mother Park really were in Seoul, otherwise, they could have a heart attack patient on their grimy hands. Friendships seemed doomed in South Korea. At least, Cholla Nam Do was gentle country, fertile, old, a southern province which the last Korean war never found.

* * *

Rusting concertina wire cleverly hid a steep path winding down into a narrow cove between low cliffs; night waves hissed and sucked, washing the sandy beach with milky surf from a glittering ocean.

Tasting fresh salt wind, O'Brien stared behind at a small hill which sheltered an old farmhouse and the barn that concealed Kang's taxi and a sturdy nylon boat. "No soldiers yet."

Kang assured quietly, "Munche obsayo . . . problem no longer exists! This is Cha Se Dong country."

O'Brien followed the barbed wire a short way along the cliff top. Orange paint peeled from rusty metal signs which bore the skull and cross bones. He beckoned Kang.

"Cha Se Dong never laid those mines, JP. How often are they checked?"

"Each month. Last time was five days past."

"The ROK Army patrols once a night . . . when and how many soldiers?"

"A six man patrol moves along the cliffs between a pair of outposts on nearby headlands." Kang swept his arm round a wide arc from south to north, pointed at a hill further along the rugged coast.

"When does the patrol reach here?"

"Around three in the morning."

"They go back the following night, according to Paul, they're slack . . . this is also holiday country."

Kang nodded with a patient face. "His farmer has watched this coastline every night for thirty years."

"Just playing safe, JP!" O'Brien smiled through the bright moonlight. "Are they ever late?"

"Rarely. Most are fresh from recruit school. We are along way south." Kang stared at the earth track but no tyre marks showed.

"Where's the island?"

"We should see the house at daybreak." Kang looked past a rocky shoulder which fell into the lonely cove, at where the moon caught black shapes on the shimmering pearl sea.

O'Brien was pleased. "Chowayo, JP, aju chowayo."

Back at the farmhouse, they found Rose working like a demon quartermaster in a patch of moonlight that slanted through the barn door, checking the nylon boat and its equipment. They set to work for the next hour before closing the heavy timber doors, crossing the dirt chicken yard where a sow snorted inside its hut and huge kim chi pots stood in rows, silently walking towards the farmhouse with its curved tiled roof.

The old house was cool inside. They began rolling out sleeping mats on the clean wooden floor in the family bedroom. Small Korean chests stood against the old lathe walls and a wooden crucifix hung over the low doorbeam. That morning, Paul Moon sent the farmer and his wife away for a few days with relatives, no questions asked, simply a message which implied that somebody wanted to borrow their farm. South Cholla province people understood these surprises. They had fought Seoul governments for centuries.

O'Brien kept watch first, back hunched, gazing through a small window with open shutters. Bright stars still pricked the moon's glowing trail. Wind rustled through short apple trees in an orchard beyond the vegetable garden where rows of lumpy shadows marked tomato and pepper plants. He glanced out to sea at the dark humps where strange islands floated on a million mirrors. How many times as a boy had he looked west at islands, wondering what secrets they kept, what lay beyond the western ocean. Faint lights winked on the nearest island as he listened to the restless summer sea. Down in the cove high tide crept forward, throwing small frothy waves from China onto pale Korean sand.

Three o'clock passed. He thought about waking Rose who would take the remaining darkness. Voices chattered in the seawind. Moonset caught six soldiers coming over the cliff shoulder, picking a way down the rough slope.

O'Brien nudged Rose then Kang: silently, resembling robots, they jerked upright, threw off the thin quilts, knelt and rolled their beds hard against the seaward wall. Squatting, fully awake, they watched him peer through the small window.

Marching along the cliff top, ignoring waves murmuring into the cove below, the patrol closed on the silent farm. A cross grunt exploded from the drowsing sow. Instantly, the line halted, each man listening, before one realised from where the sound came from. The leading solder tittered like a girl and aimed his M16 rifle at the animal pen, mimed spraying the wood hut with automatic shots, then ambled past the farmhouse followed by the others until the tail man shouted excitedly. O'Brien silently cursed.

Huddled against the plaster wall, Kang and Rose searched his face for a clear message.

O'Brien's hand ordered patience. The patrol stood in the earth yard only a few feet from his tiny window. None wore ammunition bandoliers; he suspected their rifles were empty. Yet he was powerless: they could not kidnap six South Korean privates and keep the operation covert. He pleaded under his breath, "You silly little cocksuckers . . . shove off."

Rose tucked a hand inside his windjacket, closing his fingers round the butt of a large automatic pistol, which fired big drugged darts that could knock out a race horse.

The boy wandered among the tomato plants, stopped, legs wide apart, leaning back at an amazing angle, gently swaying, gaping at the barn doors. Monotonous splattering disturbed the cool night.

O'Brien slowly breathed out while Rose bared ivory teeth and displayed two fingers which he closed like hungry scissors.

* * *

Dawn crept over coastal hills and the last stars faded. Sleeping islands lay anchored on an oyster sea. Morning calm left wet sand in the silent cove. Refreshed, O'Brien stood in the farmyard, watching the sensitive early light slide overhead.

Contented grunts came from the sow, chickens fussed near the vegetable garden. Fat red tomatoes already hung on short bushy plants supported by wigwams of strong sticks, and peppers grew waist high bordering the apple orchard where thick foliage hung in the windless morning.

He smelt strong coffee and passing the files of huge dark brown pots for storing winter pickled cabbage, which seemed the farmer's real livelihood, he strolled across to the lathe and timber farmhouse. Its bottle green tiles shone as morning sun spread over the low hills. He found Rose in the tidy kitchen, wearing swimming shorts, a bath towel draped over his wide ebony shoulders, sitting cross legged, frying eggs in a pan that smoked on the low wood stove. Hunger ruled his stern face as the pan sizzled and pale smoke layers floated past shelves of tins, boxes and jars, all marked with hangul writing strokes.

"You look like a mad African wizard, Abdul."

"Morning, Colonel," said Rose, lapsing into their past lives, concentrating hard on the wood stove. "Won a dozen eggs in the yard at dawn."

Judging from his scant clothing, Rose also had taken a bath, and somewhere nearby. O'Brien's brows lifted sharply, "Where did you shower this morning?"

"King Neptune's tub."

"I'm serious, Abdul."

Rose looked up without blinking, "I did hand stands all over that beach this morning."

"No mines!"

"Not a 'fing . . . Paul Moon is pretty keen on tidy beaches or bloody clever."

"What about our smoke, Abdul?" O'Brien tapped the hot flue with his knuckles as he realised who else might have landed in the quiet cove.

Rose calmed his leader. "No sweat, Mike, country Koreans never go a day without a fire under these old houses.

Fucking incredible," he added brightly, "this iron pot cooks all day and heats pipes under the house through winter. Central heating, older than Rome, and still going strong."

Rose cracked more eggs into the spitting pan. "Anyway, we've a clear morning. That means cloud by early afternoon."

"Rain tonight," forecast O'Brien, reaching for a steaming tin jug that wobbled and rattled on the stove, and poured himself a mug of treacle thick coffee which he laced with grey sugar from a dented tin.

"Jamaica's best, Blue Mountain, picked 'em myself last year near Swift River," said Rose proudly, who never left home without the tar dark beans. He took a sip from his own mug. "Funny thing about those buggers the last night round that temple. . . how come nobody sniffed some fall out. JP swears nothing leaked through any student group."

"I wasn't wholly convinced by Kim last night," admitted O'Brien, over taking Rose's next question, "but my gut reaction lingers: Kim didn't expect those squads. Our general tripped over his pants almost worse than we stumbled in ours."

"When's low tide?"

"Around noon." They heard Kang noisily clear his throat in the sleeping room.

"No water?"

"Almost none. Ebb tide leaves a narrow sand spit between the mainland and Moon Island. Happens twice each spring. Around here its called the Moses miracle."

Rose swung the frying pan off the hot stove and started piling eggs and bacon into three big porcelain bowls. Without looking round, he asked, "How far is this walk over the exposed sand?"

"Under three clicks."

"Blimey!" Rose handed a bowl to O'Brien." That's an invitation."

"More or less." O'Brien tested a hot egg yolk; unable to resist, he swallowed quickly then stressed, "There are no lookouts or guards on many of these small southern islands. Chung's Korea begins when the ferry nudges Ho Po quayside and the Police scramble aboard. I reckon the North Koreans took out an insurance policy."

"And it happened last month."

"Every April and May, it's a local feast; there's a legend about a granny left behind on the mainland by her family when hurrying from the tigers that once prowled these coastal hills. That's why the local town is called Tiger Port, Ho Po."

Around noon, O'Brien climbed the headland, walked along the cliff top until he found a sandbagged emplacement. No cigarette ends or sweetpapers lay around. The lookout was rarely manned. Steep rocky cliffs curved southwards to where distant muddled roofs hugged a waterfront in a small town roughly three miles along the coastline. Far across the sound, a strong wind dried sand islands while tiny breakers raced over clear water as the tide fled from the mile wide channel. He stared at dwarf mountains rising from the open sea. Shorebirds screamed above the rugged cliffs. There was a touch of Troy, men and ships, legends. Through powerful glasses he followed a thin file of black specks in the sluggish grey water: a human chain linked both shores. Adults were barely in to their ankles by half way. Last month the water fell even shallower. How easy, he thought, watching small children paddling through wavelets. He spotted Kang, not obviously hurrying, just another keen tourist relishing sea air and a day off.

Thin flat clouds stole over the sea's western rim when Rose climbed through long grass rippled by waves of light and shadow from a blasting wind. Sandpipers whistled, diving over lazy foam, soaring towards clifftops. The sharp islands lurked against gathering clouds and far over busy waves a small warship kicked white spray.

He passed the glasses, and Rose looked for some moments, then let O'Brien study the island and Kang clambering over a rock strewn shore before climbing a path between fields walled with lumps of dark volcanic stone. Fruit trees sheilded a modern house with wide verandas and long open french windows. Turtle green tiles on a traditional roof shone in the windy afternoon. He swept the glasses around the garden, searching among the taller trees, found them sitting beneath an old lofty ginkyo. A tea-set stood on a white garden table, forgotten, while a man and a girl were locked in mute argument.

O'Brien rested his elbows on the sandbags and steadied his field glasses. Even at that range her face was tense when she brushed back her loose hair snatched by the afternoon breeze. The brother appeared tall, his hand movements languid, perhaps a thinker. Frameless spectacles glinted beneath his black mop. She opened her mouth and the brother smiled, listened, never protesting, though O'Brien could guess about what.

"She sticking with the game plane?" muttered Rose as he settled in the lookout.

"Or else playing us along."

He made room for Rose, and squatted behind the sandbag wall, admiring the sound, watching the coast. There was a military post about a half mile distant though plainly deserted.

After a while, he stretched his legs across the emplacement, glancing from Rose to the ebbing tide. "She has no choice," he resumed, uneasy that already he justified her motives. "The plain truth is that she can obey Paul Moon or General Kim. Korea won't stop after the Olympic Games. We're just beachcombers."

"The Moons run better cells," grinned Rose, intrigued by his companion's despondent mood.

For a while they watched, hoping for a glimpse of Kang; but loading Diana with an electronic eaves dropping pack, however tempting, invited discovery and failure. A fugitive David Park would force the girl into a hopeless corner.

"This is frustrating," declared Rose, "I should have fitted JP with a long range set."

He sympathised but did not relent. "What if somebody picked up their voices . . . what we hear, so can Chung's security net or a North Korean trawler."

"I haven't your patience, Mike." Rose slid over the sandbag wall. "I need therapy, I'll check the equipment for tonight."

Once more, O'Brien found himself alone. Seabirds hooked on the steady wind floated sharp white below drifting clouds. He aimed his glasses on the garden conversation. Diana flicked her hands anxiously, but the man's head jerked back, laughing. Neither seemed ready for compromise, they just sat and talked. At one point she rose, spoke angrily, moved from the table. She wore extremely brief shorts which showed off surprisingly slender thighs for a small Korean girl. Around five, the sun burned through a gap in the thick clouds and reflections danced like silver arrows on the pigeon sea. Across the sound, wavelets still chased between the sandbanks, making a thousand tiny rivers, hurrying inshore as ebb became flood. Through the glasses, he observed crowds heading towards Moon Island while more strolled and waded back to Ho Po. The rising water flashed and sparkled but nobody hurried. Though he searched the line, all ages, some children on parent's backs, most splashing along wearily, there was no sign of Kang. He took a last squint at the house; both garden table and chairs stood abandoned beneath the magnificent tree. Reluctantly, watched by seabirds, he hurried back down the cliff path.

* * *

Black clouds raced before a moaning wind, grey seas boomed into the cove, hurling spray over the low cliffs. No sandpipers cried. Only screaming gulls dared glide on strong gusts that spat cold rain. Kang returned without lights in a sudden dusk. He drove the taxi safely inside the dry barn and closed the bleached wood doors. Not a lamp shone from the farmhouse when they sat on the warm kitchen floor, drinking ginseng tea, Rose listening intently to the walkman tape.

"How close were you?" Rose asked, fingers tips buried in his wire hair, pressing the headphones tight.

"I found a clump of nutmeg trees about five hundred yards from the house that gave me a hide with direct line of sight."

"Not bad, not bad, for a new gadget." Rose gave Kang a hard stare. "Barely a crackle. You did well, JP. Frankly, nothing's yet invented that overcomes a strong wind. Try out your Korean lessons, skipper."

O'Brien took the padded headphones. Wind bluster sometimes distorted the girl's soft demands which the man dodged, warm, smooth, a born politician. Their conversation rambled, silences lasted many seconds; still his smattering of Korean words and crude grammar soon stumbled, trailed behind. He consoled himself that Japanese found this remote tongue hard work as chin lowered, he strained for their next words, engrossed, tiring steadily; he reached for the tea pot from which earthy steam escaped. Rose was a mastermind: one tiny walkman bought from a Strand shop, mated with a sophisticated microphone for televising outdoor sports, picked up conversation perfectly from a distance at which faces become blurred. Absently, he filled their mugs and slid the pot back onto a cool corner of the shiny stove. He could tell from the girl's hurt tone when her brother rebuffed each question, kindly though steadily building an emotional wall.

Kang sipped his bitter ginseng. "She went right through our shopping list."

Lifting one headphone, while Kang repeated his words, O'Brien debated why Park withheld so much from his worried young sister. She asked whether he could trust all his former classmates; no names were offered, which implicated fifty young men, or a handful whose lives earned files in Kim's records, National Police Headquarters and, perhaps more alarming in this rebellious southern province, military security in Kwangju City. Park's family would not be asked questions about mere names. Something was missing. He took off the headphones, dropped them in his lap, reached up and scratched his windswept hair, then asked Kang, "Does David Park sound cool and confident, a man about to lead an armed rebellion?"

"He kept repeating that he would never take a foolish risk!"

O'Brien's bandaged fingers reflectively curled round a picture of Hodori on his tea mug, which he clutched at chest height, enjoying ginseng's alert sensations exploring his nervous system before a long night. He glanced towards Rose, who firmly shook his head.

"Don't unscramble this mission now, Mike, we'd court a cock up. Let's take first bite of the cherry ourselves. Stick with your plan and let Paul's people collect Ho Chi Minh tomorrow morning."

And Rose urged that returning in darkness made more sense than staying on the island for several hours. Where would they hide the boat for a start? Besides, on the mainland, Paul could send faster support if something went wrong. Though reluctant to abandon a chance of learning who else worked for North Korea on Moon Island, O'Brien recognised his partner's wisdom, and conceded with humour. "We'll rely on my script and your stage tricks, Abdul."

"With a little simultaneous translation by JP." Rose tilted his head slightly to better observe Kang's reaction while outside, night fell. "Reckon you could have the tape ready for when we come back?"

"Munche obsimnida," Kang offered modestly. The task of wiping out the brother's voice would take hours. Surprised, aware that Paul thought the job required several days, he asked, "We're going to question him?"

"Only about guns," decided O'Brien.

Rain struck like grapeshot, a wild gust punched the farmhouse roof. All three stared at the rattling kitchen shutters. O'Brien grimaced: time to move. Worsening weather promised a soaking ride across the choppy sound but perfect cover: no squad would tarry along their patrol, nobody on the cliffs could squint for more than a second into this foul night.

Breakers exploded on the rocks, foaming into the cove arms, rushing the dark sands. Rain lashed their faces and squalls snatched at the thin nylon tube which they portered, scrambling down the winding path, narrow and often steep, towards the sheltered beach. Both men wore hooded wet suits, tough camouflage material that stretched easily when they bent forward, both loaded with heavy back packs, belts armed with dangling flippers, night vision goggles hung loosely around their necks, zipped pockets across their chests packed with gadgets a thief would envy.

Short waves licked the sand at the cliff foot, when, back toward the rising storm, O'Brien laid the rubber tube away from hungry surf. He slipped off his big pack and silently squatted, took out a metal bottle and one-handed, plugged it into a valve on the stern, tugged a safety clip. High pressure helium blasted through, finding every last space, making the nylon live, fatter, longer, swelling until a black streamlined boat lay on the rain washed sand. He checked the valve, stowed the empty bottle in his pack.

Rose carried the motor and swiftly fitted a steel brace across the stern; he hooked on a tiny turbine, reached for its long shaft and fan blade while O'Brien held the craft steady. They clipped a fuel bottle inside the boat and joined thin leads from a battery pack built into the turbine casing. Last, they sat on the sand, pulled on their flippers, then lowered both packs inside the hull, lashing them aft with thick rubber bungies.

"Gear on board," he rasped into the howling wind.

"Shall we go," mouthed Rose, standing, facing the gale and thundering waves. He jerked a thumb rigid, grabbed one side of the lightweight craft and they started wading, pushed the small boat over boiling surf towards tumbling breakers. Rose leapt aboard.

Keeping her nose straight, O'Brien felt the craft lift, despite Rose an instant balloon. Soon he struggled thigh deep, strong currents sucking his legs, needing all his power, strained face shiny from salt spray, as a soft whine began and astern bubbles fountained.

"Come on you fucking lunatic," grinned Rose as a rain squall drummed over swirling waves.

O'Brien swung his legs, grabbed the waiting hand, rolled into the boat as Rose pressed a tiny red light. They shot forwards, charging huge wave crests, bucking and flying, surged from the cove mouth, trailing frothy wake soon lost among huge snowy explosions smothering the headland. Fighting giant force, he hauled himself alongside Rose, now wedged between the motor and stern, rubber fingers locked onto the propeller shaft and its steel rudder. The craft flew at waves curling over the black sea.

"We took enough fuel?"

Rose patted the metal bottle. "We could dine in Hong Kong. Our charger high on JP Four!" He launched into a hoarse sea chanty stolen instantly by stinging wind.

O'Brien screamed into ice fresh spray. "You 'blody nutcase! Mason recruited experts at mad thrills."

A wide turn at more than a dozen knots took them far across huge sparkling combers charging the sound. No wake showed. Blinding rain spattered white seas heading for a lost coast. Four hundred yards from the island, through another squall, they heard waves beating its northern shore. Soon they rounded the eastern point and found themselves in a choppy bay where the boat wallowed. O'Brien slid on his night goggles. Across broken water and through sweeping rain, beneath pine trees along the shore, he saw a beach just as Kang described. Lamps burned weakly from a large house. Nothing moved on leaf strewn lawns under whipped trees.

"Looks clean," he eventually declared.

"No little Chindo doggie ayo?"

"Can't see one... she must have fed the little sod one of your canine candies."

Rose's fingers stretched the corners of his frozen mouth. "Snake boy vellee clevar. Make doggee go sleep alnye. Koh lean no 'tick. No harm done other than hung-over hound."

"If she obeyed . . . we should break into that mansion like a knife through butter."

Small waves slapped a narrow beach bordered by huge round stones, shining wet when the rain lifted briefly, leaving a sodden Japanese sand garden: sturdy pines guarded the shoreline and on the sloping lawn two palms thrashed. The house stood on its rise protected by more pines and an old ginkyo copse. Rose let the craft drift shorewards, turbine idling, then cut the motor and both men rolled into waist high cool water. They lifted the propeller clear, slipped a cover over its fan and the plastic rudder. O'Brien held down the boat in the blustering rain squalls . A slope climbed behind the house towards the point and sheltered the garden from wilder weather howling beyond the headland.

Carrying their boat ashore, over the soaking lawn strewn with twigs and foliage seemed effortless after the breakneck crossing. The house loomed through waving ginkyo branches. A chair lay on its back and the garden table stood forlornly under the huge old tree which creaked when gusts tugged its highest branches snatching fresh leaves for the stormy night.

They slipped off their flippers and climbed the last mushy slope, brought the boat right under the carved and painted eaves of a wide roof. Rose fastened two nylon ropes round thick timber pillars either side of the varnished front door. O'Brien towered like a giant rubber frog dripping water onto marble flagstones.

Rose whispered at his grotesque twin, "Who gets the first kiss?"

"Had mine already, fat lot of good it did, Abdul."

"Don't be bashful, Mike, 'dong the bell."

"No need - I brought the rabbit's foot."

O'Brien tugged a pocket zipper, found a key which he slid into the brass lock.

The latch clicked. Slowly, he eased the door open, determined not to send wind blasting into an ornate hall. They slipped inside, closed the door without a sound.

Careful not to squelch, nor slip on the smooth marble while their eyes settled in the dark house, he made sure that Rose shadowed, before he advanced from the hall, found himself in a spacious lounge; low antique tables and small sofas faced a magnificent embroidered Chinese carpet beneath a huge crystal chandelier. Night almost hid beautiful silk tapestries covering the pale walls: grey deer drank from a waterfall, white cranes flew over a pine forest, green turtles crawled from a summer sea, fabled creatures born with the secret of long youth, that oriental craze. He imagined the room full of light and people, while wind and rain beat at tall french windows which faced south. Avoiding the carpet, leaving no puddles on the shiny floor, he reached an archway that led into a small sitting room. Piled on a chaise-longue, roughly folded newspapers kept open a book which lay abandoned for the night. Cigarette fug hung in the warm room. He listened.

Somebody breathed steadily behind a varnished door. He beckoned: Rose came swiftly - night vision goggles perched on his forehead resembling giant eyes as liquid strides brought him silently across the cosy room.

Warning Rose to keep right behind, lungs empty, pulse faster, he closed rubber fingers round the brass door knob and slowly twisted. Covered by the door, gripping the knob tight, shoulder hard into the smooth wood, he pushed gently, stared inside the small room. A monk's cell. Opposite stood a small Korean chest with countless tiny drawers above which hung a wooden crucifix. Net curtains lifted from the the french windows; a young man stretched peacefully on his ondol, breathing heavily though sound asleep, body long with strong shoulders and a mop of straight hair framed by the thin pillow. O'Brien moved forward.

Rain pelted like gravel on the windows and the body shifted in its humble bed. Silently, Rose knelt at the bedside in his shining rubber skin, deftly pushed a small steel tube on the bare neck. A hiss violated the innocent room. Startled dark eyes opened on a boyish yet wise face, strong though gentle fingers searched groggily above the pillow, a mouth gasped, shock followed, the body fought and twisted, slumped half over the polished floor. Rose checked the pulse and held a hand vertical. For a second, O'Brien gazed down at a mild intelligent face and wondered if they were all mad, tricked by time, prisoners in a secret clinic where both patients and doctors suffered from a rare though incurable sickness.

Both men crouched in the shadowy room, waited silently as the storm beat harder on the french windows. The girl slept beyond a thick wall which blanketed sound, and should not have heard them opening the front door, though perhaps she lay half awake tonight. Nobody else was in the house apart from a drugged dog, providing Diana followed all his other instructions: after a telephone call from Kang, the agima snored on the west coast of Moon Island, relieved that her sister was not in hospital, doubtless confused because the urgent message that afternoon proved a false alarm.

"Doctor Rose," breathed O'Brien, "let's get out of here before we trip over a Ming vase."

"Look at that, Mike, sleeping like a baby . . . 'wot amazing stuff."

Rose smiled approval, content after a job done properly, that at his molecular gun left no marks. They flicked back the quilt, searched the shorts pockets then placed the wiry arms across the young man's stomach. A black bag drawn from O'Brien's pack unfolded into a weatherproof suit.

Starting at the warm feet, they worked the bag over Park's limp body, leaving his face showing from a weather hood: O'Brien tightened its string, then tied a slip knot while Rose delved in his own pack and brought out a black life jacket which he fitted as they lifted Park's heavy shoulders clear of the polished floor. He was hard work. Their bodies thawed from the rough voyage, and O'Brien's fingers soon burned with adrenaline. He squinted through the gloom and whispered, "I'll bring the boat."

Fists tight round the nylon rope, he towed the sleek black Zeppelin through the front door, struggled until he shut out the hungry wind, paused in the hall, glanced along corridors in both directions, heard a tiny sound. The girl waking? Somebody else was in the house. Better hurry. He felt like a fool floating his new and incredible toy at waist height through the ornate lounge, relieved when he guided the craft into the small bedroom.

They lowered Park into the boat which at once sank onto the floor, yet, when they lifted, their cargo on its helium raft weighed less than a child.

Rose went first, wary of priceless fragile ornaments, skirting the magnificent Chinese carpet, dreading an ambush from behind the archway. They portered their strange craft across the hall, stopped at the front door: O'Brien grasped the brass knob, pictured a horrific gale explode through the lounge, smashing glass and porcelain, ruining the family home, besides stealing its future owner.

"Treat him kindly," pleaded a small voice from the dark corridor.

A slight figure timidly approached. She wore a blue raincoat over her nightdress, bright yellow rubber boots, and a matching rainhat; O'Brien started to smile until he saw her defiant eyes flood with misery, and holding the boat steady with his good hand, rested the other on her shoulder. No words could heal this deep wound. In Diana's mind, she had betrayed a brother, not saved one from his own reckless dreams. Rose coughed softly: smooth talking was not his job.

O'Brien felt squeezed by time and chance. It was some while since he lied, under orders, to somebody close. "Paul will take good care of him, don't worry, we're just a taxi service."

She gaped at her brother's sleeping face in the black hood, turned away and volunteered flatly, "I tried again this evening . . . tonight he was less confident . . . I know where David hid those guns."

"Is it far?"

"No."

"What do you reckon, Abdul?"

Rose smiled kindly. "He won't float off."

They left David Park beached in the hall resembling a large oriental Moses wrapped on a nylon raft, another miracle for the remote island. Still wondering whether they were all mad, he followed Diana through slanting rain towards tall ginkyos which bent slightly whenever the impatient wind rushed through their leaves. She moved fast, raincoat flapping wildly, damp hair streaming, one hand clinging to her yellow hat. Beyond the garden, huge waves roared sullenly onto the headland. She climbed down a steep bank, slithering on wet grass, waited at the bottom under an old pine tree which sheltered a rocky outcrop about fifty yards from the narrow beach.

She pointed at a wide crack almost concealed by huge ferns, recovered her breath, spoke clearly above the storm. "Three heavy boxes . . . inside the cave. . . padlocked."

Taking Diana by the arm, he moved her under a drooping pine branch and shielded them from wind and storm. He pulled a pencil torch from his biceps pocket and shot a white beam into a small seacave, left beached when the land rose thousands of years past. Three boxes: hangul scrawled over their grubby sides. He called Rose, who picked the nearest padlock, eased open a heavy lid. The torch beam found black metal and varnished wood. Brand new Kalishnikov 47 automatic rifles, sweet smelling from weapon oil, a Chinese version made in North Korea.

"Try the others."

After a few seconds, Rose picked the second padlock, more rifles. The third box was tricky but eventually opened, larger, though not completely full. Rose began counting the carefully packed automatic rifles.

"How long is that box, Abdul?"

Rose straightened, his right fingers measured quickly. "Shade over four foot."

"Room enough for a Sam Seven."

Rose pushed the lid further back and almost put his nose inside before committing himself. "Looks a bit tight . . . but . . . sure, I could fit one in here . . .just!"

Then where, pondered O'Brien, did that leave the loyalties of the young Korean doped on the hall floor? He shone the torch on a varnished rifle stock. Not a mark. The beam flickered over others. "Nobody else has opened these boxes."

Rose closely examined several rifles with his own torch. "There's dust on each weapon. How was the silly cunt gonna train a strike force? Take a while to remove the firing pins. Quickest is dump the magazines . . . which are empty . . . nick the gas springs. We can ditch them in the sound." Rose began lifting out rifles, snapping free the distinctive curved magazines. He remarked, "The ammo's stacked on the bottom in canvass pouches, but, without magazines and springs, these are no shot weapons."

O'Brien remembered the girl shivering under the pine tree and called,

"Anybody visit David over the last few days?"

She stared at him with less composure, fighting tears, half frozen from the constant wet wind. " I asked Agima, I'm sure . . . nobody for days."

"Would he bluff."

"I don't understand."

"Pretend nothing was wrong after somebody cheated him, cover a mistake, save face?"

She defended obstinately. "David stands on his own feet."

O'Brien's patient eyes returned a withering smile. "Is that why we're out here in the pissing rain, Diana."

Leaving her to sulk under the pine tree, he climbed the grassy bank, trying to think it through. The girl's replies would not solve the questions forming in his tired brain. He stared westwards into the cleverly wooded garden where old ginkyos reminded him of the park before a country house. Firs and palms, cherry and magnolias screened the shore line. A month earlier the blossom must have been spectacular. Further from the house, beyond some young trees, a paddock fence stood white in the rainy night. A huge beehive shape rose among some neighbouring firs.

"What's that?" He pointed wondering if the girl heard above a sudden squall but she scrambled up the bank, yellow boots sometimes slipping, clutching her hat.

Rain drowned any tears on her sunken cheeks. "We keep Ramyon there . . . our old pony. My sister Maria and I still ride him sometimes."

He let the wind carry his voice. "Abdul."

"Yeah . . . Mon."

"We're taking a walk over to that barn by the little paddock."

"No problem . . . g'wan der, mon. Fee work near done. Soon come." Rose's cheerful tenor escaped from the cave though no torch light. O'Brien sighed gratefully: there was a rare charm about Rose once he dropped back into Jamaican when working under stress. He called Diana.

Walking slowly into the strong wind, cleansing rain bathed their faces. He rested an arm around the girl, hugged her shoulders, felt soaking tangled hair plastered down the shiny raincoat and tried to warm her body, doubtful that her soul would respond fast, reeling from another betrayal. He decided against telling her the full meaning of the weapons cash. Park was naive, not a terrorist, at least, not yet. She rested her head against him, one hand clinging to the yellow hat, let fat tears roll lazily down her lily cheeks.

When they neared the paddock, snuffling whinnies came from beneath a huge ginkyo which groaned and swished, casting leaves into the stronger gusts. From under its foliage plodded an old mongol pony, resembling a huge bay dog whose straw tail brushed the wet grass. She called and the animal came, peered over the low rail with large grumpy eyes while she kissed its damp nose, fondled its soft ears standing from a main thick as hemp. The old pony followed inside the rail as they walked among small trees with green oranges and pale lemons clinging to lovingly pruned branches: fallen fruit and twigs carpeted beaten grass. The pony watched from its paddock when they headed towards the low barn built from coal blue lava stones large as cannon balls, its rice thatch roof held with thick ropes against endless wind.

Diana blew the pony a kiss, lifted the wooden latch on a low door and murmured, "Sorry," before she ducked in the warm barn.

O'Brien felt his rubber hood brush smooth rock then shone his torch round rough walls. Sound, safe, warm, dry. No better hideout. Spades and rakes leaned on the wall, a plastic hose hung coiled from a steel spike hammered between blue stones. He moved the ring of white light over earth and straw until it found some flattened spoil, knelt, brushed loose straw, poked with his fingers, touched cigarette stubs buried under loose earth.

"Does your gardener work every day?"

She squatted by his side, tears forgotten, quiet and resolved. "Sometimes he takes Wednesday for his own vegetable garden."

"In the village."

"Near the mountain."

O'Brien still knelt, thinking.

"The hill behind our house and the village." In the torchlight, her eyes lost their sorrow.

"What about holidays?"

Her lips parted as she grasped what took place. "My God, last month, the Moses miracle, our village festival. The crowds would have been larger than yesterday."

"I believe its's why David brushed off your questions all afternoon."

She touched the loose soil with her finger tips, "Perhaps I never asked him the right one."

"That's my fault," said O'Brien firmly. Rain pelted the thatch but the wind seemed quieter.

"No, Mike, I could have used my brain, instead I rattled through your list like a parrot. Sorry - nerves - and emotions."

O'Brien shook his head. "Don't worry; keep an open mind. Despite that space in the third box, those cigarette ends, without David's help, we can't prove that a party of North Koreans crossed to the mainland last month with a SAM."

She frowned, bewildered. "Sam who?"

O'Brien sat on his haunches, suddenly drained. In Korea the most surprising things demanded explanation. He described simply." Surface to air missile. A rocket may have been hidden in that box, one which a man can carry over his shoulder yet shoot down most aircraft flying lower than a few thousand feet."

Slowly she stood, hands thrust deep into the raincoat's big pockets, mouth bowed with disbelief, until her mind found a trusted landmark, and she faced the next horror. She began marching round the barn in a tiny circle, hat pulled low, yellow boots squelching on the earthen floor, voice urgent at first, gradually lower, ignoring the bemused giant frog squatting in his rubber suit, chattering to herself, almost comic.

"Hardly a soul knows there's a cave at our beach. David tells... invites ... North Koreans for an overnight stay...who pay with guns! Our lives mean nothing. He's intelligent and stupid - I always feared. Father wants David to run the factory! He'd lose everything. Then what? Poor Mama, poor sisters, poor workers?"

The marching faltered, she stopped, faced him, begging," Please, please Mike, take away all those guns and throw the lot in the sea. I don't feel safe ... what if somebody wants them tonight."

O'Brien rubbed his lean face. There was no danger but perceptions rule the human mind. He shone the torch on his watch. Allowing for bad weather, by now that patrol must have passed the farm: they should leave. Noah could send a covert team for the guns within the following twenty four hours but how did he convince an alarmed Diana.

"Agima comes back around seven this morning?"

She nodded warily. "Won't they see you from the coast?"

"Its nearly three. We can wait another hour."

"No longer?"

"Not even in this weather. Could you survive three hours alone if we give you a little microphone? You won't hear us but we'll hear you all the time. We didn't give you one before, in case you were searched at the Ho Po ferry."

One yellow boot kicked at the earth and straw while she pouted like a suspicious child.

"Why bother with this ... Sam ... David's rebellion will keep Chung in power for years."

He waited till her stubborn mouth relaxed. "My guess .... and....it's nothing stronger ... is this: come September, North Korea wants Chung sitting in the Royal Box at the Olympic Games."

"But that's absurd." She blinked into the torch beam. "Everybody knows North Korea demands half the Games in Pyongyang. We're bombarded with pamphlets at Ewha University."

O'Brien reasoned quietly. "Their Azalea Stadium will look magnificent ... by next spring. Kim Il Sung is a chess master. He knows the Seoul Games will take place. Kim, however, grows old. Orders are given behind his back. Some people intend to spoil the Olympics with a spectacle on the billion TV screens that count."

"David hates Chung but detests Communists, he wouldn't become involved." She watched his face closely as though not completely sure herself.

"They tricked him." O'Brien brushed back some dry straws and hid the loose earth. "David would have dealt with one member of a cell and there are hundreds in South Korea. I hope David will help, reveal the front man, their shopwidow."

"He kept swearing nothing was wrong!" Her face brightened. "I only guessed because David became so agitated when I suggested a walk along the beach for a look at the cave!"

O'Brien kept her talking, watching confidence return, glad that her observant mind was once more taking control. He smiled wisely, "Our headache is why they need a SAM."

"Who on earth would they shoot at?"

O'Brien picked up a straw and drew a small airship on the earth floor then wiped it away and sprinkled more straws. "Only one aircraft may patrol over Seoul ... one that no trigger happy soldier can mistake ... loaded with a large chunk of the Olympic Games' security screen."

Concerned brandy eyes peered from under the wide yellow brim. "Why didn't you tell me before?"

"There was no pattern. We wanted David's answers raw. Besides, we are not complete bastards, we wouldn't risk you for a hunch!"

Soft footfalls sounded on the barn threshold. Rose loomed from the stormy night.

"Mike, rather than cart those mag's shall I give Noah a bell?"

"Better than a toyshop in Ocean Terminal," grinned O'Brien knowing Rose wanted to present thirty shiny AKs to the communist weapons range at Hereford. Why not. He showed Rose the cigarette graveyard.

"We're starting to trip over a trail, Mike," declared Rose, sitting on the patch of straw.

"I don't think they were planted," said O'Brien, glancing at Rose for any change in his opinion.

"Too clumsy, not their style, so far." Rose slid a small radio from his chest pocket and pulled out a long aerial. A switch lit up a tiny computer screen and he began typing. After a minute O'Brien leaned over his shoulder and read the glowing umber message.

'NOAH from DANIEL. Repeat SOLAR for GENESIS. LINEBACKER REPORT. STOWAWAY found toxic waste in a cave on the moon. Request disposal within 24 hours. Firework stolen by sales team. Taking legal action. PRODIGAL found and swotting before he enrols in summer school. Chewing gum stuck. Ends.

He complemented Rose. "When you retire Abdul, you should write cross words."

There was laughter in Rose's slate eyes when he glanced from the miniature keyboard. "All from the code school manual. Never confuse but always demand current knowledge of a case. One piece must not show an alien reader the whole jigsaw. Last not least, make sure Dick Mason doesn't nod off in an arm chair after lunch at the club."

O'Brien felt Diana's shy hand rest on his shoulder when she bent forward trying to read the tiny screen. "What is funny?"

Rose held the message closer to her serious face. "Stowaway . . . that's your codename and there's's no money for guessing Prodigal . . . the rest is a flippant riddle."

Fascinated, she disapproved. "Do British people always make jokes about danger? Other people may read your coded messages."

A smile creased O'Brien's damp face. He decided this conversation was better not started. Half a dozen American and Russian satellites in low space orbit plucked signals through the rain clouds now passing overhead. One American bird taped thousands of telephone calls, coded telex and fax messages from South Korea. Another snatched conversations and digital codes from North Korea. Computers chose numbers, attacked codes, broke some for Harry Todd's breakfast reading or the small hours watch keepers in Virginia and Scotland. Some cyphers kept their secrets, others not. Leaving aside photograpic snooping by American, Russian and Chinese orbiters, radio locating nets criss-crossed South Korea, could isolate short bursts among the tapestry, separate portaphones from military messages, though rarely long enough for fixing a grid. From beneath the yellow hat a perplexed face depended on future decisions which she must not understand: where did one begin to describe this fairy land at their finger tips that allowed a single person to bring down governments.

"Diana, look." Rose came to the rescue by pressing a command button. The screen cleared. He typed a telephone number on Hong Kong Island, waited about five seconds, let her watch until a red blip glowed.

"Is it broken?"

"No, sweetheart, talking." Rose allowed the tiny red light to fade before folding the aerial and tucking the radio back inside his rubber suit. "We don't want Kim and his NSP or Chung's military security finding us here through our radio traffic. So we type messages onto a tape which the computer sends in a split second. They're called burst signals. We file our story then run like foxes."

"Am I safe?" she asked doubtfully.

O'Brien tried an encouraging smile. "Don't fret. We keep some of our business private from General Kim . . . not a word about the missile, Diana, I want to see if his spies can protect our operation."

She nodded with more confidence. Rain no longer drummed on the thatch roof. Only a sad wind pulled at the garden trees and tiring sea.

Through a gap between shadowy rhododendron bushes grown as a wind break on the headland, far over an indigo sea, climbed a white halo. Diana stood facing northwards rain hat jammed tight, hair lifting slightly with the strong wind. Her blank face could not decide which emotion hurt most.

She faced the floating lights. "There's our fishing fleet."

Darkness soon must scurry over the western horizon. He tried to occupy her mind with last instructions. "You have about three hours before Agima returns. Lock yourself in the house and don't open the door to anybody."

She recited bleakly, "Moon Island, known for wind, women, sailors and rocks . . . no gates, steeples or beggars . . . no longer innocent. I'm an island girl. We're famous for enduring loneliness on windswept shores."

Down on the beach, muddy breakers threw spray onto dark sand. The boat bobbed on choppy waves beyond the shore surf, impatiently squirting foam, strong wind drowning the turbine's whine. David Park lay hidden below its nylon sides, warmly sealed in a plastic wrapper, sleeping through a dramatic night. Only the lythe shape of Rose gave away human cargo.

"Somebody will move those guns about this time tomorrow."

Across the windy sound pale lights flickered distantly from where shadows revealed coastal hills. She opened her mouth though found no words.

Rose waved him to hurry. His throat tightened, time ruled harshly. He made her switch on a bleeper which resembled a tiny watch battery. "Pop it in your underwear, even your belly button, because it sticks hard yet easily pulls off."

She gasped primly, brows raised with indignation. "You will hear everything?"

He took her by the shoulder while she examined the bleeper in her cool palm. "Forget modesty. We'll know your exact whereabouts, day and night. That's a very smart little toy. We'll look after David. You concentrate on fooling Agima. Catch the ferry in the morning, calm your parents." His blue eyes flooded with sudden warmth. "You're a fine girl, Diana: loyalty forces lousy choices. This one wasn't easy but now sleep sound. Your instincts were absolutely right." He bent forward.

She drew back and held a little strict finger over her curling rose lips. "I won't kiss a frog before breakfast."

24

White crests chased their nylon cockleshell over an ink sea. Huddled in its stern, they shielded Park from cold spray bullets. Night kidnapped Moon Island and the white glow sank below broken waves as the fishing fleet roved further north. Straight on the bow, a dark smudge marked where the coast merged with a dismal sky. Another time, he thought, always another time. Strangers escaping through false dawn, who never saw the tropical island flowers nor those famed yellow rape fields on a spring day; instead they stole a human souvenir. At that instant his mind dwelt on another brother and sister from a wiser generation, who searched for each other and now walked hand in hand, rarely together though never alone, seeking fate.

For he feared the young man stretched in the boat bottom lacked the sharp intellect which led the Moon's onto their rough, tandem roads. And he reminded himself that Doctor Moon and Paul held this deceptively mild young man in great worth. Only age solved those riddles: meantime, barely a brace of hours remained for discovering first hand what clever blackmail made David Park allow several North Koreans a bed under the family roof and help smuggle a guided missile into South Korea.

Waves smashed at low cliffs ahead. Rose steered slightly north, lined himself on the hidden cove, dropped speed, let the boat run with angry seas. Spray burst over rocks awash with foam where the swell boomed into the cove mouth.

O'Brien slid a small radio from his rubber suit and pressed its transmit switch, twice, listened until a single burst of static answered.

"That patrol's late."

Rose wiped salt spray from his mouth. "J P's on the headland with a night sight. We'd have warning."

O'Brien stared at the gloom overhead, they must reach the farmhouse before first light. He pressed the switch one more time, hooked the radio inside his rubber suit. "Abdul... we've only minutes.... hit the beach."

Rose nodded. Salt smudged his black cheeks, he braced on the transom, pushed the throttle button onto full power; the boat surged forward. Breakers curved and exploded onto the glass sand. O'Brien jumped into freezing waist high waves as Rose shut the motor, lifted the fan and rudder clear of cream surf that threw the boat sideways and snatched their legs. Desperately hanging onto its gunnels, they fought the craft through sandy breakers, staggered onto the windswept beach. With frozen fingers, Rose spun loose the fan shaft which he secured through the cargo bungies. Off came their flippers and were quickly hooked on the packs inside the nylon craft. Ignoring their drowsy passenger, both men reached inside the boat, released nylon harnesses at bow and stern, threw padded loops over their shoulders and began climbing the narrow path.

O'Brien at the bow, hand feeling no pain, moved steadily, glancing behind after a few yards, concerned their burden was lashed tight enough, that Rose kept pace up the slippery grey track. He strained forward in case the whole weight of David Park, turbine, packs, fuel, defeated Rose's willing shoulders and stole his balance. Soon his stomach squeezed into a ball as sweat filled the rubber suit. Breath came faster and the boat seemed more awkward, his thighs burned and he swallowed often. Huge waves swelled and burst into the cove, drowning rocks and sand. Clouds raced on a wind that snatched at their frogman hoods. At last barbed wire coiled against the fugitive night.

Beyond the wire, tufty grass bent before the strong wind; nobody was on the cliff path. Their farmhouse nestled like a squat shadow in its small valley. On the southern skyline the headland seemed deserted : several seconds search failed to reveal anybody near the sandbag emplacement. Where was Kang.

Shy grey light found grass and bushes along the cliffs. Stepping over the wire, he felt the boat nudge his lower back, stood as Rose followed silently, then led off, jogging towards the empty farmyard, swearing when the sow released a hostile scream as two giant green frogs portering a black monster scattered chickens among the tomato plants.

"You fat bacon bitch," growled O'Brien at the angry animal when he slithered across the muddy farmyard.

"Bloody hell," moaned Rose from behind as he stumbled and a green rubber knee sank into foul mud. "We shoulda' kept wearing our fuckin' flippers."

"Over here!"

Kang stood in waving grass behind the farmhouse, pointing at the low stone wall enclosing the yard which the huge and bellowing black sow trampled into a swamp.

"Jump on the wall," called Kang.

Somehow they scrambled on top of the rough stones without tipping David Park into ankle deep slime and struggled round to where Kang laughed helplessly.

"I am sorry," he declared without remorse when they jumped down and reached the farmhouse threshold.

"We're knackered, JP," panted O'Brien, glad when Kang pushed open the door.

They squeezed the boat into the small kitchen and lowered it hard against the windward wall, shed their green rubber skins. Sweat ran off their faces, shoulders and backs. Two shivering humans stood in shorts and vests, wet untidy hair brushing the low beams, rubbing themselves down with local hotel towels. Rose sneezed twice.

"Gesundheit," congratulated O'Brien, who smelt coffee and saw the dented tin pot bubbling on the wood stove. He glanced at it hopefully before asking Kang, "What happened to the ROK Army this morning?"

"Rained off..... they won't move before evening."

Dull light advanced through the shutter slats. Kang poured black coffee into three mugs while the other two pulled on tracksuits. Carefully O'Brien slid the bleeper monitor into a trouser pocket. David Park slept in his nylon ark taking up most of the kitchen floor. They moved him into the family room where Kang had the tape recorder set up on a low cupboard.

O'Brien approved this forethought with a question. "Wiped him off?"

"Every last word," said Kang and started to loosen the hood string on Park's rubber cocoon.

Coffee laced with soju spirit pumped warmth and energy back into O'Brien's cold body. His face became less haggard though mental effort stayed hard after a third night robbed of proper sleep. Absently his fingers strayed to the tiny metal cylinder in his pocket which he held against an ear while it faithfully broadcast soft heart beats. He relaxed. Five in the morning. Roughly four hours before Paul Moon's parcel service called for David Park.

The medical kit lay open on the wood floor. Sipping hot coffee, Rose wound a strap around Park's left arm, pumped hard, read his blood pressure, released the linen strap : heart and pulse nrmal. Rose prepared his molecular gun.

Holding his coffee mug, O'Brien crouched beside the sleeping body. "For God's sake, Abdul, don't kill the shithead"

"Merely a strong hallucinant," retorted Rose, shocked by the very idea of questioning his craftsmanship. Only his sombre face gave any hint of gradual weariness. The molecular gun descended on the smooth pale skin and once more Rose triggered its ruthless kiss.

His face tensed until the pulse became steady. "I dunno' about anybody else," he finally sighed, "but I'm starving."

Park began shifting in his amphibious bed while they sat on the floor eating bacon and fried eggs. Listening intently, Rose helped himself to another fork load of bacon, but eventually disregarded shuffling noises in the next room. Only after pouring his third mug of coffee did he stretch and scramble onto his feet for a quick inspection; Park lay still though his writhing had moved the nylon boat half across the wooden floor. Rose called Kang.

"Bring your pencils and a thick pad."

Obediently, Kang settled on the floor, legs folded so his knees formed a writing table, fat shorthand pad ready and a row of freshly sharpened pencils close on the swept boards. At first Park did not respond, stretched almost rigid, occasionally flicking back his lids, squinting with disturbed eyes while slowly absorbing the simple room that within his tangled mind, already became somewhere else. O'Brien tried the walkman headphones. Seawind blustered and birds piped while the girl's low voice pleaded, fell silent, drifted in melancholy Korean, then allowed the wind and birds their stage. Dubious if the charade would work, he discarded the headphones into Rose's waiting hands.

"I'll rewind the tape," Rose warned Kang, "just be ready."

"He actually believes it's yesterday!" said Kang with amazed respect.

"Not yet." Rose fitted the headphones over Park's tousled hair. "Right now he's floating on cloud number nine..... dreaming.... but in his mind, any second, he's about to wake, thinking that he dozed off in that garden chair. Our memories record much more than we know. Recall is our problem, both for short and long memory. This drug enhances the short memory.... total recall sometimes. I don't want anymore than simple facts. When his sister's voice asks a question, he sees the whole scene all over again, starts answering her, truthfully, supplying every detail that, yesterday, he kept back."

"That's the theory," shrugged O'Brien and made himself comfortable.

Sullen daybreak filled the narrow room. Stretching his legs for a moment, O'Brien moved to the window, rested his forearms on its ledge, debated whether he should open the shutter slats, peered through a gap between the varnished frames. Grey waves mounted by white spumes attacked the rocky coast, scudding clouds barely cleared the island's dark green humps below which the house stood white among sturdy trees. He was tempted to fetch his field glasses though it looked quiet. Instead, he reached into his pocket for the monitor and the movement altered his vision field : six specks walked southwards on the cliff path.

Suddenly, Park mumbled in Korean and Kang, tufty hair almost touching the writing pad, scribbled in hangul, pencil flying across the paper, trailing neat characters.

"Abdul," said O'Brien sharply, "we've got company."

"Not the Mickey Mouse patrol." Rose leapt onto his feet. He did not take kindly to idle pestering or pointless interruptions at any time. "I think the little sods deserve a lie in this morning." He searched his back pack and pulled out the huge dope pistol.

"All six?" O'Brien grinned yet his brows lifted.

"We can't stop now," said Rose bluntly. A thick vein swelled on his strong neck. Furious with cruel luck, fighting his temper, Rose snarled, "We dare not risk psychiatric damage."

Rose could shoot all six because they disturbed his important moment. O'Brien pulled on his trainers. "Did you bring any booze?"

"Of course.... a bottle of that ghastly blended stuff."

"Perfect. If they don't slide past, knock 'em out, we'll dump them full of VIP on the headland. It means extra humping but spare a thought for the poor bastard farmer."

Ten minutes later the patrol straggled past. None took the slightest notice of Park babbling from the hard floor. Either they could not hear because the wind strengthened with daylight, or, judging from their chalk faces and scruffy combat greens, they had spent a night without sleep though ample doses of soju liquor for keeping warm. He saw them slowly climb the headland.

"One problem obsayo?" remarked O'Brien tersely.

"Isoyo," answered Rose pointing towards the sandbag lookout. There was no doubt. The patrol leader moved along the path towards the emplacement and the others definitely followed.

"Nothing we can do right now," said O'Brien, watching the patrol clamber over the sandbag walls.

Park shifted on the floor and Rose gazed down briefly. "He'll take more than a couple of hours to become a drained canary. They might piss off."

Korean mumbling soon daunted O'Brien, nor could he read Kang's hasty script. Sand, salt and sweat tormented his scalp and he craved a hot shower. Near the barn stood a wash house but within full view of the headland. Soon daylight discovered the quiet farmyard. Temptation postponed, he settled down for a long wait, careful not to disturb Kang whose pencil raced over another clean page.

Around eight o'clock Park ceased talking and fell asleep though Kang sat a further half hour. But the syrup voice no longer rambled. Stiffly, Kang eased his legs, stretched his fingers. Every pencil was blunt, the pad full. Through the loose shutters, O'Brien saw thick clouds break apart, sunlit patches slide over the sea and cross the grassy headland.

"Cracked it, JP?" Rose asked from the kitchen where he brewed more bitter mountain coffee.

"He talks riddles."

Rose leaned round the doorway and mildly scolded Kang. "Remember..... when we scripted her questions, we suspected that only rifles came ashore. We didn't bargain on a Sam Seven."

Kang good naturedly flicked through his note pad and found the crucial pages. Before he could speak, Rose stepped into the room and urged they should let Park sleep, led them back into the kitchen where he rolled out his sleeping bag. Within a few minutes he too snored, leaving the others on watch.

O'Brien found a better gap between the sun warped slats of the kitchen shutters, propped himself against the rough plaster wall and observed the headland through field glasses, keeping himself awake, while Kang ploughed sombrely through his notes. Now and then, O'Brien glanced enviously at the slumped Rose, listened to a steady wind sighing among the apple trees.

"She asks if there are guns on Moon Island."

Reading aloud, checking his memory against the jottings, Kang flicked over a page, found a particular line.

"Many owned by Chung's police..... does it make sense?"

Lowering the field glasses, O'Brien scratched his wavy copper hair which felt scruffy around his neck, briefly astounded by the strong will buried below the mild face. "He answered that sharply during a deep coma!"

"Pretty smart dreamer," admitted Kang with a resolute smile. It could be his turn one day. He read further. "She next asked if he kept a gun in the house, then, how many guns he kept on the family grounds. Reply : I didn't count."

Hot sunshine streamed into the warm kitchen. David Park had not lifted the box lids. A remote chance suddenly grew real. O'Brien prompted, "We assumed that reaction and tried another slant.... if I recall.... without success."

"I have the original tape. Yes, he was bland, gave away nothing, which is why we followed with a tangent : how many of his friends keep guns on the family grounds."

"Answer."

"This morning... he remains consistent... none."

"Which may prove those three boxes were the whole lot."

O'Brien rubbed his prickly chin, determined to shave once that wretched patrol departed.

Staring pensively at his notes, Kang turned a page and read the next one carefully, before remarking, "I found this next segment curious. We wanted him to reveal who else knew his secret plans. She provokes him by hoping that only a few people are privy. Now, at that moment, Diana, faithfully following your instructions, did not wait for his reply. She repeated.... who, who?"

Though his face seemed relaxed, O'Brien's temples throbbed, "Did he bite?"

Kang shut his note pad with a soft thump. "Nam, he repeated, Nam."

A smile softened lines on O'Brien's bristled face though his raw blue eyes became sharper. "I think we're closing the net at last....... but we want a lot more."

"That's Han's alias."

"No assumptions, JP. When we get back to Seoul, check all coastal shipping movements between Japan and North Korea. I'm looking for a cargo vessel which sailed from a smaller port on one of the southern Japanese islands and passed close inshore on its way to Haeju or Nampo in North Korea."

"Han managed that!"

"Somebody did, JP."

His mind vividly recalled painstaking hours of detective work when nights in Seoul still fell cold. North Korea worked through tiny cells.

Attacking their rival during an Olympic Games presented only gambler's choices. Cells spread throughout South Korean society, particularly around Seoul, daily gathered intelligence and ran clandestine messages. Scores of students toiled, ignorant of each other, supporting a political strike force which delivered turmoil on campus or city streets. This was a traditional communist approach, effective for widespread unrest, though fraught with risk for any more complex task : one leak might show Kim's security forces where they should probe next. And that was the frustrating riddle; despite CIA, US and ROK Military Security, General Kim's agents prowling throughout North East Asia, there was no patchwork, no leaks from other sources, all trails came back to a team of disciplined thugs. Suppose North Korea adopted a surgical option : attacked the Games with one elite cell, just large enough to support itself, a single mind in control, its backing and logistic base inside South Korea? Wasn't that philosophy wrapped inside Sister Moon's warning? Han seemed their first step alongside a cell which ran an entire operation with somebody experienced and brilliantly camouflaged, calling shots from its core, yet moving with total freedom.

"Any other names?"

"Only his friends but they were never indoctrinated about these weapons."

"What was the price, I wonder?" In his mind Sister Moon's calm face urged him to persist and follow the arguments right through. These were clever people. Some form of blackmail? He doubted if David Park *found* the North Koreans.

Kang thought the question aimed at him and misunderstood, shook his head in apology. "Our script was not designed for that purpose. She followed orders. None of his answers bring us any closer. Would all the North Koreans have crossed this way last month?"

"Don't worry, JP; perhaps she should have asked David how they wear watches in Pyongyang."

* * * * * * *

Strong wind refreshed O'Brien when he sauntered towards the headland, clutching a thick cherry walking stick, frequently grabbing for the greasy trilby hat borrowed with an old coat from the kitchen store. Leaning forward, he tried to pass as a dignified old man, stooping to hide his six feet, cautiously yet steadily closing on the sandbag lookout. Fat white gulls and dainty sandpipers hovered over low cliffs, screaming and diving for the shallows, gliding above waves that hurried across the wide sound. Pausing, fingers gripping the dope pistol hidden in a coat pocket, he listened when odd sounds escaped from the sandbag outpost. He went another few paces, stopped, peered over the fat green canvass sacks.

An empty bottle flashed in the hard morning sun. Slumped bodies lay on damp earth, muddy boots rested on stacked American rifles. He leaned forward, made quite certain : all dozen eyelids were firmly closed, all six mouths hung open, snoring alone proved life among a breathing heap of faded denom lumps. Rice grains stuck on dirty bowls filled with loose chopsticks and piled in one corner with their belts and tin water bottles. Petrol fumes hung in the seawind; without question the pervading vapour from three empty soju bottles. God help them mused O'Brien, if one dirty night, North Korea sent its spetsnaz forces with more violent orders and counted he four seconds worth of throat cutting.

Shaking his head, smiling vaguely, he quietly withdrew, and found a hollow from where he watched both farm and coast. Tiny waves rippled between flat sands for the tide flowed past Moon Island's spinach hills to join a lively celadon sea. Far across the water, a car ferry chugged like a blue and white raft, its wake slowly spreading over the calmer sound. He took out the monitor, held it in his palm, watched its electronic compass find the distant ship, closed his hand and pressed the disc to one ear, heard firm heart beats. Then he waited, reflective eyes following the little ferry, while another ten minutes passed, and his brain searched for the reason behind David Park's strange voyage into treachery that put his own family in mortal danger. Dollars seemed an unlikely cause in a clan which owned so much discrete wealth. Perhaps David Park kept back a few last secrets from his shrewd young sister. Raking his memory for clues, finding none, convinced the answer must draw the noose tighter, he watched the ferry creep into the small harbour.

A new sound broke his thoughts. An old blue truck rumbled on the coast road. Nobody in the emplacement stirred when, gears crashing, it rolled into the empty farmyard. Two spidery Koreans clambered from the cab and dropped the tailboard. Without wasting time, though never hurried, they began loading huge brown kimchi pots from the tidy rows, stacking them upright like a terra cotta army, until the truck was crammed full. One seemed particularly awkward but went on board without harm. They slammed the tailboard, but from that distance, seawind snatched the rattling crash, before the truck drove off, rounded a bend and vanished along the Ho Po road, worn engine fading among the coastal hills.

25

From the roof beams of a steel cathedral, floodlamps glared onto numbered squares chalked over the concrete floor like a vast hopscotch game. On each square stood piles of parts, some small, others huge. O'Brien recognised only the crew gondola and consoled himself that he was an electronics man, not an aerospace engineer. His bandaged hand deftly took the mill board and packing list offered by Rose: pencil ready, he waited in the morning silence, not daunted, though conscious of how much faster he must learn than Yoon and his Korean policemen.

"We'll start by checking if it's still here!" said Rose, waving a wooden pointer at the first stack of mysterious boxes. More than a hundred chalk squares held scores of parts which, together, became an airship larger than a jumbo jet.

Sweeping the pointer along an entire line, Rose shot whole phrases from his mouth like bursts of automatic fire, forced his listener to concentrate. "We have the whole kit dumped on this floor; hull which includes the envelope, load curtain and ballonets, gondola, tail surfaces, power controls and power plants, propulsors, undercart, navcoms, electrical system and mission avionics, mechanical controls. Tucked away in this little lot is my personal gift to aviation science.... finger tip control.... through a fly by light system."

"Not too fast, Abdul, you'll lose me. Run through that about fibre optics?"

It was six o'clock and a whole early June morning lay in front for making certain he understood exactly how the complete skyship worked. They would not enjoy a second chance for screening the stores without others peering over their shoulders. Any day, monsoon rains would fall; if they built the airship in record time, test flew before the weather changed, serious training would become impossible until August brought the first hints of crisp northern autumn.

Rose read his thoughts, smiled a genial apology, pulled a torch from his pocket, checked that its beam shone strongly, then took it slower.

"All airships currently flying use straight forward mechanical controls, worked through lots of wires, bloody sweat and toil, but they'll keep Yoonie' busy while learning. He won't have time for any diversions. *We* shall hide a fibre optic system... as we build.... tucked inside the envelope, the airship hull, ready in a real emergency."

"Won't they realise?"

Rose seemed to grow a pair of wings as he described the simple geometry of a perfect ruse. "No way.... we'll have computerised flying controls for mission take over... they'll think its part of the electronics suite."

"But what's the purpose, Abdul, other than reducing the physical demands on our pilot?"

"What we gain? Star wars flying. She performs like a big stunt plane, almost loops and rolls."

A bat fluttered in a frantic circle high among the maddening lights. O'Brien stared, engrossed, amazed how it flew overhead, navigating faultlessly among the steel latticework by sonic waves. No wonder Rose asked so many questions about electronics during the winter months.

"How do we check for North Korean tampering?" he asked with growing approval.

"While we build."

Ignoring the bat, Rose surveyed his boxes and parts, started down the left hand row, counting the bits of his complicated toy, vigilant for the smallest sign of tampering or theft.

"Nose battens.... fifteen," he called.

O'Brien ticked off his list which matched the chalked numbers and stacks on the hangar floor. They arrived at the next square, drawn round an enormous folded silver polyester lump, the size of a small house.

"Envelope."

Two neighbouring squares enclosed more bundled material which Rose listed aloud, "Load curtain, ballonets, pronounced ballonaze... fore and aft."

O'Brien wandered towards the huge squat white balls of plastic coated material.

As they checked the silver folds for damage, he pictured the inflated ballonets, two spheres, fitting inside the envelope skin, which was not rigid, but held its shape from a quarter million cubic feet of helium at a pressure so low that it suffered almost no gas loss. During rushed training at Detfold, he flew once, but that week no airship was under construction, a gap in his education that worried him; now these fears came home. "Remind me, Abdul, exactly how we inflate the ballonaze?"

"Air.... they're open to the atmosphere through four valves, which we fit onto the envelope. Inside we link the balloneze together by coated nylon trunking and a flapper valve system.... called a T chest." Rose paused to make sure the class kept pace before describing how the ballonets worked during flight. "When we climb, our helium expands in the lower atmospheric pressure, so we release air from the ballonaze to make room. When we descend, atmospheric pressure rises, our helium contracts, therefore we drive air into the ballonaze...... helped by our propellers.... otherwise the envelope would collapse. Simple as a lung breathing."

"Provided *you're* on board to work the valves right."

Shaking his head, Rose carried on down the line, marking packages and small boxes full of nuts, bolts, clips, tools, calling them out for O'Brien's blunt pencil. Despite painstaking inspection, it was impossible to tell whether a few people or dozens had examined the stacked parts. Each day a chattering squad of burly agimas swept the hangar floor to hospital standards and such blatent Korean zeal often served more purposes than a single result pushed under the victim's nose. Kim was nobody's fool, nor Yoon, nor any third party. Instinctively, glancing from a carton, they exchanged mutual foreboding and examined the next square.

All four tail surfaces had been shipped ready to fit onto the envelope once inflated. Doped fabric sheets covered a honeycomb of metal ribs that strengthened and shaped their lightweight steel frames. An angle on the root spacers showed that the horizontal surfaces, once fitted, sloped slightly downwards.

They approached the last squares; bulky wooden coffins housed a pair of two hundred and fifty five horsepower Porsche turbos. Rose lifted the lids on both crates and shone his torch inside, repeated the search at a further pair of tough wooden boxes packed with a bevel gearing system adapted from that fitted on Lynx helicopters used by the Royal Navy. He lowered the last lid, hammered it down with his fist. "Looks OK.... munche obsayo?"

"You're the judge."

Both knew that checking all those parts on the floor, spotting damage, loss, tampering, demanded an intricate knowledge. Only Rose enjoyed that gift which he gained solely by taking over the design shop at Detfold in the spring, putting an airship together, taking it apart, twice, before packing hundreds of bits for their voyage to South Korea.

"Nuffink's been nicked," declared Rose without much surprise, then rubbed his nose with finger and thumb, a sign that he suspected more subtle tricks.

Despite sixteen thousand miles at sea from Tilbury to Pusan, white paint still smelt fresh on the gleaming cabin. Large glass vizors, tinted blue against Asia's sun, gave the pilots almost three hundred degrees vision below the flight compartment. A single door on the port side served both flight deck and passengers. O'Brien propped a trainer toe on its aluminium sill, looked inside the surprisingly spacious cabin: three large windows down either side allowed those on board superb lateral observation and almost directly beneath the airship flightpath. One window next to the door doubled as an escape hatch. Sealed off by the rear bulkhead, the engine compartment also held a thousand pounds capacity fuel tank and their water ballast. This compartment had its own door at the gondola tail, a full forty feet back from the glass bow.

Paired ducted propulsars resembled stubby fan jets. Inside each was a five bladed wooden propeller nearly six feet in diameter which pushed the airship forwards. Twin alternators, powered by the engines, gave about thirty volts for the mission system and flight avionics. A special piston motor provided a further twenty four volts for mission avionics. The last square enclosed a pile of kevlar cables and carefully folded material.

"What's this?" O'Brien turned for help.

"Load curtain with fourteen gondola suspension cables." Rose laid down his pointer, knelt and working himself sideways, ran his fingers underneath the gondola hull, though found nothing. He retrieved the pointer, stood, scratched his African hair before reaching a wise conclusion.

"This can't last."

Perched half inside the gondola, O'Brien felt the door frame, disquieted by the hull's thin skin. He had forgotten how fragile the gondola seemed on that first flight months past over a cloudy London. "Is this thing tough enough to withstand groundfire?"

"Made of Kevlar," assured Rose with ominous confidence. "Weight for weight, six times the strength of steel with an infinite life and near zero maintenance." His pointer tapped the narrow stern. "Engine compartment....

stressed deck and enclosed by titanium faced nomex panels which can withstand twelve hundred Celsius for a half hour. Those engines can catch fire and melt but not the passengers."

Face drawn from concentration, Rose checked through the packing list, but they had missed nothing. Each item bore a pencil tick. Still reading, he remarked, "My fibre optics are packed with the electrical power systems. We'll have to slip them inside when your private mission avionics and the spy camera arrive from Detfold."

"The Koreans will recognise fibre optic wire."

"Only an idiot wouldn't." Then Rose permitted himself a distant smile and continued, "They're quick but not Einsteins.... I shall heartily congratulate the first guy who spots the spy camera picture feed."

It was clever. Face would take care of deception. No Korean could make an obvious mistake. Therefore no Korean would admit one before his watchful peers: it was a gamble but shere gall often worked better than the most devious cover inspired by more disciplined brains.

Stepping down, he measured the gondola roof, imagined it suspended beneath a full envelope, a huge flying radome which would hide easily all his covert communication links with Harry Todd's headquarters.

Mirth prowled briefly at the corners of his mouth, he enjoyed risks; and he brushed back his untidy copper hair, irritated by new grey tufts covering his ears in a Korean summer. The land of morning calm gave a sense of contented purpose after two hours without stress.

He stood back and watched Rose fuss over the airship parts like a nervous mother confronted by a clever though moody child. Deep within, O'Brien doubted their chances of total success without penetrating the North Korean cell. Each minute of the Games would peel off another layer from their worn nerves. While they worked in the hangar, Kang would spend the morning sweating in the Buk A newspaper library, delving into the finances of Diana Park's family. Even with hard intelligence, real relaxation must wait until the Princess and Olympic team took off from Seoul early in October.

Tension fell away as he reflected on the rare pleasures of running this small lunatic crew, despatching Kang and now Diana, on obtuse quests, listening daily to earthy wisdom as Rose bubbled fresh ideas: money could never buy a holiday that rivalled this mad crusade. He saw other dawns, hangars where sweat drops splashed onto the warm concrete while swinging a parachute on his back, hitching an eighty pound kitbag underneath the green nylon pack, lashing an automatic rifle from shoulder to thigh, before vaulting into cool air three miles above endless Borneo hills smothered by glittering cabbage. How many years more? He could still feel blood freeze inside his veins when he launched a kayak from a submarine under the brilliant aloof stars of southern winter, still cursed the cold fear and eternal damp on his own bitter island. Each place, each time, mission and equipment changed, often faces, while their maturing bodies stayed strong and only their brains grew no wiser, because the human spirits trapped within defied time, believed their own stars never would fade. And his oaken fingers strayed to his trouser pocket where a small disc guarded its secret pulse and waited for the gods to cast their dice.

* * * * *

A hundred feet overhead steel girders threw a roof around the main stadium's giant cradle. Thick ropes fell. Jet black figures plunged, sliding headfirst, monster bats suspended from hooks, faces masked by goggles, rigid arms thrusting Beretta automatics at the empty crimson seats below in the Royal Box. Hooks snapped open, each man somersaulted from his rope, six steady pistol mouths covered O'Brien.

Throbbing closed from the south; helicopters threw echoes into the main stadium, spending sound along rows of blue and orange seats sheltered by the graceful curves of its lofty canopy. Rotor beats deafened as huge shadows passed across the thick girders and two dark green Hueys flirted with the stadium roof. Ropes swirled from the helicopters, down slid more black clad commandos. Within seconds the Royal Box was ringed by a team of masked Koreans. A whistle blew. O'Brien watched with approval as the hooded troops swiftly holstered their pistols, slack ropes shot skywards, both helicopters boomed into the stadium, loitered near a huge scoreboard lit with hangul characters.

He hurried down wide steps towards a maroon running track which ringed the vast emerald lawn, reading the electronic numbers. A significant improvement: this exercise lasted under five seconds. A thin plastic pass hanging from a metal chain round his neck ensured that rifle armed police kept their alsation dogs on shorter leads, stared curiously, though stood aside when he leapt the barricade and strode towards a tall figure in a blue blazer who paced the manicured turf, lecturing a squad of young Korean generals.

Kim looked round, finished his conversation, paused for the generals' curt bows, sauntered over the smooth grass. Embroidered in beautiful gold thread on his breast pocket was Seoul's scrolled Olympic symbol. Drawing closer, O'Brien discerned that Kim was ready for the human festival: beneath the cleverly cut blazer of a senior official from SLOOC was the gentle bulge from an automatic pistol.

Kim shouted over the helicopters' racket, "What is your verdict, O'Brien? Give me your candid opinion."

"Impressive!"

Kim absorbed this compliment with a faint scowl, "Leave that game for American Senators. My black berets look intimidating. But are they fast enough? We can improve.... always.... but is something else better, faster, more lethal."

O'Brien shouted back, "Stick with it, General, otherwise the troops become confused!" He dreaded the Korean urge to suddenly abandon lengthy preparations on a high level whim. "Just make sure they know every VIP face...... including bodyguards and personal aides.... below in the Royal Box."

Slashing blades drowned their voices and they watched the helicopters hover above rippling grass. Twin files of black figures ran forward, ducked into the rotor wash, leapt aboard the deafening Hueys. Kim looked at his watch then complained acidly, "I put on this show for American TV news reporters last week and was told to lay off. My men scare the teams, many tourists cancel. In Pyongyang perhaps they better understand the months of sweat and toil required before troops perform like human machines."

Both helicopters slid forward, noses dipping, then lifted, banked above the scoreboard, clattered over cheap apartment blocks and leafy streets in Chamsil dong. O'Brien followed their flight before settling his gaze on the brooding general as the huge stadium fell quiet. "You'd stop a snatch squad leaving the Royal Box... you might not save a hostage.... you would kill the terror squad."

"At what odds?"

"Even."

A cold smile flickered over Kim's harsh face. "Last week they were a half second slower. Next week they will perform a second faster." Kim inspected his polished shoes and hissed an order in polite Korean at a wiry Ranger general, who returned a salute then murmured his own orders to the little group wearing camouflage and stars.

"O'Brien, let's walk."

Leaving the rest earnestly chattering, they fell into step and strolled over the cropped grass, heading for the athletes' tunnel, tailed by Kim's personal aide and a bodyguard. The young major and sergeant also wore blazers which hid machine pistols and long range radios. Already O'Brien grew used to his own burgundy blazer and grey flannels but still tried hard to convince himself that their task was a sports event. The general glanced sideways with cynical approval while his stern mouth released words like spaced shots.

"You left Seoul."

"Business." O'Brien answered as though the matter were closed.

"Important?"

"Not any longer."

Kim sucked breath through clenched teeth but never slowed pace until he growled softly, "Our President holds me responsible for Olympic Games security. Not foreign bandits. We can't afford dirt less than three months before the first team arrives."

"Trust me a little longer."

Kim strode faster, hands clasped behind his back. Cool wind from the mountains took away a lingering sweetness from burnt aviation gas and blew strands of grey hair over the general's iron brow, behind which a sober and brilliant brain plotted without cease.

The general's silence made O'Brien uneasy : how long could Chung last? That morning the Korea Times carried a headline that Cha's followers would rally in thousands on Yoido Plaza next Sunday morning. Less than a month earlier such a call sounded absurd. Sammy Song still recovered from that awful spring morning.

"What becomes of the Bright Korea Movement if Chung resigns?" The question bothered O'Brien more than several others.

This time Kim faltered, stopped before the red clay track marked with immaculate white tram lines, faced the vast empty stadium. "I cross that bridge when we reach it."

"The first lady?"

Kim drew in his heavy cheeks and strode purposefully onto the running track, stepped over starting blocks, solemnly counted police snipers perched like birds on the splendid roof.

"Is she an impossible complication?"

Kim sighed. "Our steel butterfly is famed for charity works such as taking good care of close friends. Last year she selected her younger brother as president of the Bright Korea Party Institute. That rivals owning a bank with two million customers who make deposits every year and never cash cheques. She is much loved by the Ruling Party."

"Will she fight?"

Kim nodded gravely. They entered the short tunnel. Armed police sprang to attention. Even the sniffer dogs sat respectfully panting, their morning search for explosives done, facing a long afternoon. Beyond the tunnel a road ran under the stands and a black limousine waited, engine whispering, water leaking from its air conditioner, doors slightly open, driver and security man sitting patiently in front. Escort cars waited at discrete distances. Mindful of confucian manners, O'Brien took the left hand seat.

Thirty minutes later they wound up a steep mountain road and after salutes from heavily armed black berets in full combat gear, passed through a fortress gate in a high granite wall that wandered over the mountain top. Kim told his driver to stop, their escorts to wait, then started up a steep path which hugged massive stonework that resembled the chinese great wall. They reached a crescent battlement. Kim rested his folded arms on the smooth sparkling masonry of a firing slot and faced north where mountains hid among heavy clouds that wept summer showers in slanted shadows. A rain grey Han slid between deserts of apartment blocks towards thin woods in the Olympic Park, and the main stadium loomed from sudden mist like a great castle watching over wet southern streets. Across the river, almost lost in drifting squalls, Namsan's wooden shoulder brandished its white needle and much closer, westwards, hugging low mountains, Songnam's concrete runway lay black in the stormy afternoon. Tiny transport aircraft stood in a row before camouflaged hangars. Fine rain blew coldly over their own fortress.

"I take your point," said O'Brien, wiping his damp face. It was a clear shot and although for a Stinger or Sam Seven, the runway was beyond range, somebody could hide among these hills and take out VIP aircraft on their approach to Songnam Airbase. A big Soviet rocket could easily hit the main stadium from these ringside mountains.

Ignoring the drizzle, Kim admired the panorama from his mountain top fortress; thickly wooded flanks fell steeply towards shiny streets in a toy suburb. The general became mellow and indulged some simple pride. "A mongol army once retreated rather than scale those forest slopes."

Letting his eyes measure the distance from where they stood to the mountains behind Songnam, O'Brien told himself that the elusive key was something obvious, reliable, which would not change throughout the Olympic Games. He dared not openly tackle Kim, not on North Korean smuggling, at least, not yet. Kim's steady probing in the car, coupled with his own vague replies, merely fed the general's latent suspicion that he deliberately withheld fresh information. Driving up the mountain road, Sister Moon's placid face kept floating before his mind, that gentle voice warning, a double agent controls part of the Olympic Games security. Whichever path his thoughts took, he returned to an airship floating alone over the Olympic sites. Was he obsessed? Thousands of American and Korean specialists stood on alert since early summer. He scanned grey mountains to south, west, north, saw bunkers and watchtowers, radio masts and dishes, defended by sandbags and wire on rocky peaks.

He asked flatly, "Do your chaps have radar and electronics on every site?"

Kim's deep voice sounded bored. "All mountain lookouts were strengthened last year.... radar, infrared, both passive and active, plus more powerful nitesun."

"Generators?"

"Each site has its own capacity." Kim leaned over the ancient stonework. At the mountain foot lay a clearing where a pair of Hueys rose from a landing zone and flew like fat humming birds over lime paddies. Silently, Kim watched, a hint of pleasure on his rugged face as men and machines performed their warlord's clockwork, showed off his effortless power. Brushing fine rain from his sleeve, Kim delivered a blunt message. "Tell your airship pilot to forget a missile threat."

O'Brien felt his stomach retreat into a tight knot. It was absurd, mind blowing, but not impossible.... and more than clever.

26

Naked lightbulbs swung in time with the humid draft from fans humming under a huge attic ceiling. Sweat trickled down O'Brien's temples and the golf shirt clung to his lower back. Doctor Moon shuffled in front, exploring the twilight between rank after rank of spotless metal shelves that bent under the massive weight of stacked musty newspapers in a maze built from paper. For ten floors below and four more underground, telephones rang, typewriters chattered, coffee spilt and cigarettes were crushed as a thousand frantic Koreans strived to close the late afternoon edition, and print more than a million copies of the Buk A Ilbo then deliver them onto the Seoul streets. Moon commanded his personal hive through old fashioned brass tubes which sucked glass cylinders loaded with scraps of paper, thumped them into padded post boxes all over the old office tower: some bore rare short messages from Paul in a suite on the floor immediately beneath their feet, but most an editor's question. Moon paused by a shelf of supplements in fading chinese characters on the opening Korea's first railway; grey photographs featured bearded engineers, firemen looking like stage magicians in baggy trousers, robes and pill box hats. But when no hiss alerted, no scribbled message thumped from the tube that ran under the ceiling, Moon ignored the present, dawdled thoughtfully through forty years Japanese rule until beneath a central skylight, Truman spent a whole shelf sacking MacArthur in big chinese print. Following his gnomish friend, it occurred to O'Brien that Moon lived through most of the history filed in this sultry loft. Swept each dawn, there was hardly any dust on the packed shelves, most papers looked almost fresh. Moon stopped, listened: sudden rain thrashed the window, drilled on the roof, almost threatened to burst through the pale ceiling. The small shoulders heaved, a sneeze exploded among the full shelves.

    "Song Seng Nimun?" Kang's muffled voice came from somewhere to the right among twenty years rule by a previous general, Park Chung Hee.

"Nae," coughed Moon and his thick soled slippers squeaked on the polished boards as he increased speed. They found Kang barricaded by newspapers, sitting at a steel table jammed under a window fiercely attacked by the monsoon storm.

The Doctor asked in Korean whether Kang found an article which the old man, that morning, draining his memory with his breakfast tea bowl, recalled structuring with his editorial pencil around eight years back. Neither Kang nor O'Brien doubted his memory for an instant. Sixty years in publishing and broadcasting, owning a quarter of the nation's presses, including its most read quality newspaper, left Francis Moon a vast walking archive.

Kang rose behind his table, bowed; there was no room to come round and Moon, declining the empty chair, bent forward, held onto his glasses, lowered his head until those small inquisitive eyes stopped within a nose length of a crisp page spread over the table. Slipped into the business section, a long article strayed across several columns: Kang revolved the whole paper and the small grey head bent even lower.

Concentration made Moon's chest sound like a worn bellows. "Ve....ry good. Written by Chay.... ex..cellent report...ter. Alas, promoted him to City Editor, great success, wide contacts: killed himself, car crash, two years ago, Friday night drinking of course. Chay was tho...rough."

They stood respectfully while the old man read further in melancholy silence. Finally he peered at the two younger men, perhaps assembling his memories of the mangled city editor, resting small pudgy fists on the table, contemplating the chinese characters which served as a half forgotten memorial, clearing his throat.

"This time was most difficult for anybody from South Cholla Province. Chung and his military clique first gained control of national intelligence, next army headquarters, then gathered enough troops to snatch government. But they were by no means con...fident." Moon loudly expelled more dust from his old lungs and swallowed hard with touching frankness. "Once Cha spoke out they knew a large and also distant province stood firm against the coup leader."

O'Brien wiped sweat from his forehead. "Chung only ruled Seoul."

"Little else.... during those first tense days." Moon emphasised these words by another throat clearing explosion. "So... like thieves, Chung and his generals decided to strike quickly, take Cha's capital."

Watching rain indifferently strike the window panes, O'Brien fingered the damp paper, trying to understand better the vanity and greed behind tragedy in the quiet rural city. Koreans followed a brutal logic when dealing with each other and he suggested softly, "Chung showed his power, Francis, before any other province wavered."

Moon puffed his wax cheeks, "Dug his grave."

"Song Seng Nimun," began Kang, looking at the open newspaper, objecting with traditional humbleness by avoiding eye contact, "Chung sent a shock wave through our country and *still* he rules."

Moon explained further. "Business confidence in South Cholla evap...orated. Orders waned, factories shut, thousands lost work. We campaigned over our radio stations, warned this government how their approach would split our nation, long after their own downfall."

"I can guess, Francis: nobody listened?"

"On the con...trary." After a rasping grunt, the ghost of a smile flickered across Moon's dignified face. "Chung and his soldiers 'nationalised' our radio stations." And his small chest heaved up soft merciless laughter, another coughing fit, more throat clearing.

Rain drummed harder on the flat roof. Kang glanced through the steamy window then leaned over the newspaper. In the afternoon gloom he appeared doubtful. "Song Seng Nimun, Diana Park swears that her father was always politically neutral, that as the situation worsened, he dared not act otherwise, because many families relied on his good standing. But, in those days, as a prominent local Catholic with a revolutionary son, Chung would not favour Park's house."

"Lynched with a tightrope.... poor sod." O'Brien guessed the rest, appalled and sobered by its cynical thrift. Every riddle solved in this remote country, led into another.

"You took a big risk, Francis, they could have run a repeat of the reformation."

The old man's hooded eyes shone from stubborn pride. His voice became hoarse with roguish humour. "There was more! After we lost the stations, Chay still followed this story. To our astonishment... it was so sensitive... that Chung forbade anybody but Yonhap Press, our government wire service, from keeping reporters outside Seoul. Still today all provincial reports are filed to the Central News Service by government officials. Chay found out that like everybody else, Cholla's senior businessmen were screened, only a few selected for economic growth.... bank loans... and only supporters of the coup qualified, save one special case. Desperate, Park came to Seoul, ignorant of this conspiracy, went to a friend whose brother ran the Chosun private bank, a kind fellow who held out no hope but would try. Imagine their amazement when the Enterprise Planning Board gave its blessing... because by then the board was managed through remote control from Defence Security Command. The soldier's wanted our Chaibol's, big industries, to feel grateful *and* insecure. But, also, they wanted a hold over David Park, nature's understudy for Cha Se Dong. Father obtained his loan."

"By selling his family's entire future," despaired O'Brien.

Moon folded his thin arms and shook his head with a brisk wobble. "I don't think he even sold his own life."

"He still doesn't know?"

"A wasp guards its stings," remarked Moon.

"But the silk factory prospers, Francis."

"There is no com...petition... in South Cholla! He hires at low rates because there *anybody* will take clean manual work. Park brings hope to Moon Island and makes much profit... which... as a good man... he ploughs back into the family silk business. Wealth is not yet a crime in South Korea... Park's family lived happily un.....til somebody decided to call in his son's politi....cal debts."

"Clever bastards." He realised they must have been torturing David Park in Kwangju military compound while presenting his father with a huge cheque dressed as an apology. "But who is in control?"

Kang, looked across the newspaper at the old man. "Paul believes that Shin made the first burn judging from David Park's description."

"He is only a small fish. We search for a whale," replied Moon gruffly.

O'Brien raised what alarmed him almost as much. "How has David kept all this secret from Diana?"

Moon's eyes half closed under those heavy lids. "She may guess.. Diana is bright... she found the hidden guns, and she suspects worse."

O'Brien thought back. "She swallowed his tale about a southern rebellion for several weeks... then didn't we all."

Perhaps they should wait a little longer. If somebody else told her the harsh facts, intending blackmail, where else could Diana turn, other than the Moons, Kang, even himself. Face was paramount: family, friends, none relished challenging the Bright Korea Party and plenty of people wished

David Park stretched on a rack. She might go to Kim but that meant a further debt, this time on her own future.

"We can't stop her seeing David. We can't keep him under lock and key much longer. Kim's people must start snooping." And O'Brien added with frustration, "I would almost bet that Kim knows."

"We have no evi.....dence, Michael, nor dare we ask. He is too strategical.....ly placed."

"Absolutely, Francis, absolutely," sighed O'Brien, wondering for a horrible second how the North Koreans laundered the ready cash. But Moon was right, no gambles, no risks. Kim ran a vast operation, relied on loyal barons cleverly placed in committees on each tier of the secret wedding cake which decided most things in South Korea. Delegation and communication were vertical for survival. Anything they told Kim would either go everywhere or nowhere at all: it was the second case which bothered O'Brien as he glanced past Kang at the wild afternoon.

Rain drowned huge cranes that swung over the cream flanks of the Lotte Hotel's rising second tower. Staring at the storm, he remembered that spring squall and street violence a few hundred yards from where they stood, and began working out the risk of tackling Kim head first.

Moon guessed. "When the World comes to Seoul, Korea needs Kim, and for.....tunately, Michael, the general now needs *my* tacit support."

"I'm not dismissing an approach.... Francis.... just can't find a plausible reason for David swimming that sound at night when there's a perfectly good ferry service every morning."

That evening, standing before the study windows, O'Brien sipped green tea, watching ragged clouds hide Kwachon mountain and mist washing the dong roofs. This foul weather must break soon. All over Seoul half-finished roads led to half an Olympic bridge, hotels still were nursed by giant cranes while plumbers sweated in a half-finished Olympic swimming pool coated with builders' dust; his own contribution, a half-finished airship, wallowed on a hangar floor a mile along the river bank from a half-finished rowing course. Though suddenly cooler, breathless humidity still sucked him down into gloom; he faced a loathesome duty within minutes. The buzzer sounded and he heard agima open the front gate followed by women talking quiet Korean. Soon stockinged feet padded on the stairs; he poured a second cup of tea and wished it was single malt.

She peeped round the door, offering half a worried smile with that wide willing mouth and he wondered if a whole city was locked in rigid mindless harmony. Her face shone from the rain and the ankles of her jeans were soaked but not her thick white socks.

"You look grumpy."

"Blame the weather."

He placed the tea bowl in her cool palms and after she sank into the armchair, let her take a first polite sip, and lower her bowl safely onto the fawn carpet, then began opening wounds, knowing the surgery must be hurried and with no time for pain killers.

"Have you talked much with David since last week?"

"Paul only let me see him once.... yesterday... but he's well."

O'Brien threw himself into the chair by his desk and marvelled at her grave face, smelt her fear rise more than heard it in her low voice, noticed her fingers restlessly part her long hair straight down either shoulder over a boy's blue shirt. She tilted her head to examine him better, vulnerable, though she smiled bravely. "Why wouldn't Paul let me see him before."

"Paul thought you both needed time. I fully agreed. Whatever made him stop fighting?"

"Money."

"Much?"

"He won't say."

"For what reason?"

"Personal debts..... he's evasive.... told me it's his own problem."

"Are you convinced?" It's always money, thought O'Brien, more depressed.

"He's lied once."

That startled him. It was quite a confession from a Korean girl about her elder brother. Cultured English changed her soul no more than wearing a foreign fashion label. She bore fresh scars since the beach library in only a few weeks, small wonder the Korean kings once executed missionaries; gone was that bold defence of her own blood. Might she have known for years why her brother suffered less than the girl students after Kwangju?

He tried innocently, "Can you think why our friend Shin could squeeze David so hard that he smuggled rifles and rockets into South Korea? Would money talk? We never really know each other, it's not impossible, these days revolutions don't come cheap."

She stiffened, and her eyes became sad black jewels, one small hand froze to the chair arm and elegant fingers gripped the china bowl. She murmured, "I've told you before... perhaps I wasn't clear enough... we won't take bribes."

"Your brother was in no position to be squeamish, Diana; before you judge David, remind yourself what they were doing to the girls held in that military compound... you told me... ask whether they promised to stop the tortures... if he talked. You were all pawns in a war with Cha Se Dong. David had no choice... his friends suffered... overnight his family wealth mortgaged to his captors. He gambled that he was younger than General Chung. That took nerve but you admit he's cocky." He knew it was cruel, but he must rake until there was no refuge and no lies before he played the marked card and watched her eyes mist from shock. "David owed the coup leaders a fairly un-scarred body, dozens of released girl children, plus about six billion won."

"Six billion!"

"Remember when your father put up new buildings and bought Swiss silk looms. That was the general's deal with David after Kwangju. It's all perceptions my love. David took their promise, not to block your father's expansion plans in exchange for the girl students release; not a fat loan for calling in later."

Her mouth froze into a pink oval. When she found a mind, words, they blurted from a smoker's husky voice. "Chung owns our family business."

"Not Chung, Diana; all such deals were soon buried in the investment portfolio of the Bright Korea Party, mostly bank loans secured with worthless equity, pay-offs for silent support from religious groups, big business, industry. Others were hooks. Eight years later a North Korean hitman, Shin, also on the payroll of our good General Kim, starts cultivating your girl student group. All those questions, family, money, Shin knew every answer. He was interested only in you as a key to your brother. The clock ticks. Urgency made Shin grab you that evening in Myong Dong. We were a surprise twist. David is modest, a loyal Korean. Paul believed we would find Shin's master through David. We haven't - yet."

Someday, decided O'Brien, somewhere, he would draw a second pension from the Queen and try the sweet taste of normal life. Diana didn't ask a question, she didn't cry, she just sat, mute, tiny fingers clasped in her lap, body less stiff, legs thrust limply forward, black hair screening camelia cheeks, brows pensive while devasted eyes concentrated on her wool socks. She spoke without malice though alarming resignation. "I hate life."

He felt those invisible bonds of fear which ruled everything in Korea slowly but firmly claim her spirit, taking her from him, without protest and no courage left. He could not fully reconcile all his reasons when he fought back on her behalf.

"It's not entirely gloom. The good news is that Kim will accredit our whole squad as Olympic Security. Our passes take us anywhere during the Games. But he wants to 'vet' and train you : covers him over rules about recruiting and personal favours."

She seemed almost in shock. At least he knew one answer. She hadn't a clue who tightened the strings both north and south.

27

Night mist hung along the riverbank; the taxi headlamps caught a military road sign emblazoned with five Olympic rings, then another and another until the expressway followed a bend of the Han and briefly lost the efficient reflectors. Kang reduced speed for a concrete bob run that led onto a bridge over tar black water explored by feeble reflections from apartment blocks. More arrows waited across the long bridge. Shreds of fog lay in ambush along the road near the huge fish and vegetable market and the new Olympic Family Town as they drove south towards Songnam. Traffic was scarce. Kang relaxed at the wheel once the beams caught more arrows that pointed left.

"Somebody on your arse, JP," growled Rose from the backseat. "Three in fact."

Kang watched the mirror as a huge black limousine flying the stars and stripes on one wing and a blue flag ringed with stars on the other, drifted past, chased by two crowded cars. Further ahead, traffic lights changed.

"Overtake the 'yanks, JP", said O'Brien calmly, intent that the gate security should focus on diplomats, not contractors. Kang swept his taxi through the lights in a skidding turn, ignoring whistles, furiously flashing headlamps, then foot hard, soon passed the Cadillac and its racing convoy.

"Thank God for inheriting my Mum's nerves," sighed Rose when armed policemen waving red torches directed them through gates in a high steel fence and into a car park alongside the domed gymnastics hall. From the darkness surged more armed police who checked their car sticker but only Kang's personal ID card.

"I hope our country's Olympic Games is organised as well as SLOOC's food tasting party," said Kang, tolerantly sliding the plastic card back in his wallet.

They set off for the gymnasium and O'Brien called an apology. "Did I tell you JP, that Diana passed her interpreter's test and is on duty tonight."

Kang locked the car and caught up the others. "That's ridiculous, she speaks English better than most.... she made Cambridge."

"English was marginal. Kim checks patriotism and moral fibre. Diana reckons the Rangers have an easier time on selection for Special Forces." He followed a stream of Koreans wearing dark suits, silver hair polished onto perfumed scalps, converging on glass doors which led inside the low dome.

Sapphire spotlamps flooded a carpeted arena and he felt that subtle magic before a great event. It was the discrete size which impressed as he craned his neck to admire the roof of fibre glass sails resembling a vast tent. Five hundred people chattered on the gymnasium floor. Koreans bowed to each other, gave foreigners slack hands, hurried off, searching out those with power over this stern ambitious land, concerned that their faces were recorded amongst the chosen handful from forty million mouths who would taste the cuisine for the Athlete's Village : no complaints were expected and none invited. Girls in green blazers, grey skirts and sensible heels, black manes glossy under the blue lights, hovered around the crowd fringe, still in awe of their countries' elders, not yet convinced their surroundings and duties at last were real, looking lost because they could not interpret between elderly Koreans.

Trumpets sounded a dramatic fanfare. From a tunnel on the far side of the gymnasium emerged a column of white hatted chefs with the bearing of guardsmen, followed by waiters in four serious files. They took post behind dozens of flower decorated and perfectly laid dinner tables placed in ranks around a large roped off podium. Watching, O'Brien spotted a tiny figure wave away a tray of gin and whisky, dismiss an entourage several strong, let the crowd part respectfully, where-upon Moon shuffled forward wearing his favourite suit and shoes from London.

Rose rested a hand on Kang's broad shoulder and confided, "Tonight we'll leave Mike in peace to deal with business. Those young birds look desperate for some live practice.... so remember.... I can't speak Korean and you can't speak English."

O'Brien watched wistfully as Rose and Kang chose their prey, weaved through the throng, presented themselves helpless, towering over a constellation of shy giggling girls.

Somebody touched his sleeve: Paul Moon pretended to introduce himself while a waiter offered a drinks tray.

"Korean pantomime, Michael, highly respected for great artistry and more commonly known as dramatic story telling."

He grasped Paul's waiting hand, felt that same dry skin that marked his father. "How much is this loan in British pounds?" he said with a broad smile, remembering to behave as a strained export director from a small company recently awarded a flagship contract for security, and thus saviour of his chairman's skin through a big cheque drawn on a bank in New York City. They each took drinks and the waiter bowed.

"Six billion won... a shade under five million sterling yesterday in Hong Kong."

"I'm tempted... and would love to pick up the tab and shake the bastards till one of them rattles.... though we're probably paying for the Chung family pensions."

"They might cost rather more."

"Paul, I wouldn't blink if Shin walked in here serving a tray of soft drinks."

Paul Moon admired the roof sails with sad sympathy. "Kim is our finest Olympic athlete and runs in the toughest contest. There are no rules and the judges, let's be frank, all Koreans."

"We have a great need for the wisdom of those elderly Koreans in your family."

Paul acknowledged this compliment with a faint smile but he quietly insisted, "We can't prove Kim's playing on four sides, we know that he plays on three... Chung, the generals and his own. That adds up. Kim used the North Koreans at the Asian Games for that airport bomb. One of their girl operatives for the airliner bombing sits in Kim's special prison. He's shrewd and thorough and daring. Kim plays his cards in the shadows..... as we ourselves.... never underestimate him."

"That's my fear. He's formidable but if you burn the North Koreans twice, they must learn something: become too confident, next time, they'll let you walk deep into a trap before showing their own hand."

Since that awful afternoon, when she fled into the rain under his golf umbrella, he debated whether Mason would consent to another route; slip past the North Koreans, deal direct with David Park, earmark the airship price for a dollar fund in Hong Kong, employ the money as a reserve loan and *play* the Parks as wild cards. The whole mess existed because when the generals tried to destroy Cha Se Dong, the Park family were perfect tools. Years afterwards the North Koreans milked this deal with such frightening leisure that only somebody senior inside South Korea could have blindfolded the most watchful counter intelligence force in the Far East. Mason's Finance Controller, sitting before his computers in a tower office looking onto the Thames and Lambeth Palace, distracted by millions of secret man-hours invested in crumbling the Warsaw Pact from which returns were flowing, might not balk at another five million risked in Korea - until the airship costs flowed homewards and within the next corrupt month. Though he remembered Mason's lecture: nowadays Olympic Games made profits and he expected no less from his own team.

Frustrated, he smiled cautiously for the roof cameras, pumped Paul's suffering hand. "I'd love to cover the lot, but it'll double our stakes and Dick Mason can't lose his shirt on the secret vote."

"Let me talk with father, perhaps we can help," said Paul, parting with his mild smile. "Can't you sell Kim another airship!"

The old man approached obliquely over the fawn carpet. Perhaps Paul already knew his father would gamble without qualms providing the bank deals were hidden deep enough. Payment was due with the first flight, which fulfilled their commercial contract. The training package was separate. Why not hold onto that money in Hong Kong, anyhow, as an operational reserve? It could work. The Queen was making a huge profit, as was Kim's private advertising syndicate. Nobody was in a hurry: finance built three months payment delay into the overall price.

Conversation faltered all round the gymnastic hall as another fanfare heralded burly Koreans in royal blue blazers who surged among the crowd followed by Kim himself escorting a small elderly man with a suntan and receding silver hair. Two more Koreans in blue blazers covered from behind. Watching this procession, O'Brien guessed the IOC President's bodyguards packed more fire-power than an infantry platoon and hoped that none of the waiters dropped a glass.

Perhaps Kim feared the same disaster, for that massive head revolved in his direction, scanning young and older faces which suddenly lost their oriental paper skins as simple pride ruled. Under the beautiful roof, for the first time, O'Brien found Korean confidence infectious.

Kim ushered his guest onto the podium and withdrew into the shadow of a huge bronze discuss thrower while the IOC President and the Korean President of SLOOC exchanged flattery, and the bronze athlete, before a writhing mob of television cameramen. More blue blazers surrounded the press corps, barged forward, knocking aside equipment, leaving no question that the show was over for this particular evening. Shafts of white light fell upon a string and piano quartet : four young women in wedding dresses began to play faultless Beethoven with robot fingers. If only, wished O'Brien, they would sing without instruments, bare those searching hearts, rather than anxiously parade disciplined brains copying perfectly. Through the romantic lighting, Moon closed with stealth, followed by a tall greying American in a banker's suit, himself shadowed by two fit young men with short hair cuts and wearing identical grey flannels and blue blazers. Once more they performed a human charade for the video cameras ringing the roof, for hostile eyes nearer at hand among the cocktail guests.

Moon, directing the little scene, stopped in front of O'Brien, gasping boyishly, "How plea....sant a surp...rise to find you in this nightclub. May I present General Todd who commands the U...nited Na...tions Forces."

Farewell sanity, despaired O'Brien and solemnly introduced himself to Harry Todd while Moon closed his eyes until the lie was done: only an impish flicker of his lids revealed lasting delight at schoolboy pranks.

Todd looked down at the old man. "I am told diplomats get paid for eatin' and drinkin' because it's a way governments share the bill and hide their spies."

Moon replied with a mischievous glint, flapping a hand at the sparkling tables. "Our magic carpet is thick with plotters and thieves tonight! General, in this splendid gymnasium are many Ko.....reans who may eat some words during this lavish feast. Earlier today my paper denounced Chung because his term as president expired after seven years and we are still without any sign of another election. None of his lackies made a squeak when he signed our Consti....tution. Chung was not bold enough. He could have written ten, twenty, one hundred years, rather than only seven - a personal time bomb."

"What's the latest split?" asked O'Brien searching the crowd for Rose and Kang.

Moon puffed his smooth cheeks until they resembled tennis balls. "We gave crude choices and took street polls. No election, not now: Games much too close. Support for Cha grows in Seoul which is new and signifi....cant because Chung's Ruling Party look upon the capital as their private booty. This coming Sunday Cha intends shaking that complacency on Yoido Plaza. His slogan is one million faces, forty million hearts."

Todd bent forward. New lines around his eyes revealed tiredness and strain. "Kim told me just before lunch that the generals gave Cha the green light." He straightened while Moon considered this news further.

After throat clearing loud enough to wake the most drowsy monitor, the old man pronounced. "Chung is finished though not his party. They will keep a corpse on the throne while secretly crowning a new king. Cha has less grand ambitions: all he wants now is a seat at the Olympic Games, not from vanity, but because his face may heal wounds, particularly in his native Cholla, bandage our people together for a great national moment. All other questions.... strikes, riots, the North.... can wait for November. The world watches us closely from tonight onwards for the next fifty days."

Todd lingered a moment though alert for his waiting escorts. "Doctor Moon, my country has assembled an army of television newsmen and that expected from our British friends may outnumber their team. If I may speak candidly, sir, around five hundred political reporters are flying towards Seoul. Employ them well."

"Just keep moving your head, Harry, in case somebody lip reads. This whole evening is on tape!" O'Brien gave a warning smile.

"I've already booked your copy," replied Todd smoothly and his cold blue eyes signalled mutual suffering.

"My troops are long on the streets, General," said Moon.

Todd grinned down at the old newspaper mogul and gave his honest reply. "I'm not expecting any other invasion although we're ready for anything." And glancing at them both, he added deliberately, "I read each report from our patrols along the DMZ with utmost care."

"That's most kind, General," cut in O'Brien. A small Korean suddenly appeared, bowing to Moon, offering his card with both hands, and wearily he recognised the squirrel body language of Mr Park from Magnolia Trading, frontman and fixer, television marketing specialist, plumber for Kim's personal graft.

The mouth opened and buck teeth released a garlic cloud. "Song Seng Nim, General and Mr O'Brien. How fortunate find everybody under one house. I bring greetings from Kim Dul Chi. Most concern that we meet soon on board your Britishee 'stealth' airshipee... and.... genelmen... flying over this Olympickee Park." He stood back and peered at them through thick lenses which cleverly destroyed any clear view of the eyes lurking behind.

O'Brien recoiled from the pungent breath. He replied lightly, "Doctor Moon and General Todd were just asking that same question," shrugging off his imaginary burdens with a frozen smile, before insisting with a wave of his full glass, "My company waited weeks for a hangar, Mr Park, but let's not start muddying the waters. We'll be ready. Olympic security is in safe hands."

O'Brien stressed that line, he wanted no direct involvement with Park and the vast amounts of money destined for overseas banks, however much he wished to nail the exact frontiers of Park's role as paymaster for Shin and any others. He took a sip of whisky and let Park absorb this message. Taking no chances, he put it another way. "General Kim has moved mountains on our behalf and the airship nears first flight. You'll have your advertising revenue."

"Sure, sure," allowed Park, growing agitated, leaning closer, slightly offended when O'Brien stepped back. "You solve problems. I got clients stamping all over my spine."

"But how splendid, Mr Park; my chairman and no doubt the Korean government, must be delighted by your success."

He hoped the mention of his own cheque would remove Park, since Todd and Moon still waited, patient though conspicuously silent.

"Every man and his brother jump on my back," whined Park in his abrupt mid-Pacific speak, a thief masquerading as a clown." Hyundae, Samsung, Goldstar, Daewoo, Korean Air and OB Beer. All very interest. Everybody knows we suffer hold ups... my job complicated.... everybody screaming for my shit.... where's your bloody airshipee, Park.... we sick of snapshots."

"She'll fly within a week," promised O'Brien, staring down at the wretched little man, noticing he wore a thin wig, before rashly throwing away caution. "Possibly sooner."

Park wiped spittle from his lips and became more nervous. Had Kim breathed fire over his personal business team, told Park to start rounding up the cash because a milestone bill was coming fast and, probably, Kim wanted his own share safely banked in Geneva before the Games started. An airship flying within a week, under those circumstances, became the last news wanted by Park who had five days to round-up sixteen million dollars.

"Less than week!" despaired Park as drink remorselessly heated his ruby cheeks.

"We'll give you a ride, Mr Park," offered O'Brien.

"Korea's guests don't want to suffer your problems, Park." A baritone voice spoke silky Korean that threatened trouble.

Kim towered over Park, smiling dangerously, forcing the little man from the circle, sparing him no embarrassment before the group and Paul returned brimming with curiosity. It was impossible to tell Park's exact age. Not a grey hair showed yet his skin wore the coarseness brought by middle years. Perhaps Kim assumed that neither Westerner understood a word and spoke so slowly and menacingly that, despite a struggle, to his amazement, O'Brien could follow. Kim was blunt.

"Mr O'Brien's contract is with the Korean Government.... I am its representative. You were chosen by me to find sponsors and report to me as the Korean government's official in charge of Olympic security operations. There is no panic. Our sponsors will pay during the next three days. Our banker understands why there is some pressure this week and that no advertising is allowed before the opening ceremony on the seventeenth September. Don't confuse things. And don't try and delay our first flight. My pilots will fly during the Games.... with the foreigners advising.... but a Korean at the controls. Secure command links demand that we speak in our own language. Anything less would bring great loss of face, a national disgrace: understood, Park." Kim switched into fluent English. "Good evening Song Seng Nim, General and my friend O'Brien." Kim half turned but already Park bowed deeply, muttering, "Yeh...yeh...nae," while withdrawing backwards, thick glasses like milk bottles reflecting the spotlamps, hiding pain.

Kim shook hands as though checking pulses and the gracious host took over, brushed aside the incident, deftly blocking questions. "Park sometimes exceeds his instructions," said Kim expansively, "although he makes things happen. I regret that his one serious failing is a habit of passing messages through third parties. He will tell you something which is important to me... and vice versa.... dragging us both into a muddle, which is precisely why I kept him out of your feet all these weeks."

"That was very considerate, General." The relief on O'Brien's face proved that he meant each word.

There was no further reaction from Kim who invited Todd to sit at the SLOOC President's table with the Sport Minister, IOC President and America's ambassador. Next he bent at the waist in respect for Doctor Moon, gave a cordial flicker of his raw eyes towards Paul, before directing both. "Song Seng Nim Moon Shi, you are with SLOOC Vice President for International Relations and fellow members of the Seoul Olympic Committee." Next Paul was despatched to the National Assembly Members' table. Finally he reached O'Brien. "I took a liberty and placed you with my Ranger Force Commander, a young general, more than good and on whom we rely greatly. Your table is hosted by one of SLOOC's most competent officials who directs the Opening and Closing ceremonies. There you will also meet a senior National Security Liaison official, my public face at SLOOC Headquarters. Ask them anything, O'Brien, all speak in my name."

He hoped that Rose and Kang were not placed among the lower ranking tables. Although neither would complain, he was concerned about face, that they gained credibility. He need not have worried. Kim pointed through the crowd and he saw them led away from another group of green blazered girls, by Yoon. "You've forgotten nothing, General.... I'm envious."

Kim's broad shoulders lifted with sudden laughter, and, straightening his blue blazer, he aimed a hand at a suited security man who dashed off looking for somebody among a crowd chattering under the podium and its forgotten statue. For a second, O'Brien imagined the video camera controller with his feet up and smoking, bored with the simplicity of trailing two curly heads around the gymnasium floor, one copper, the other black, leaping to the controls because a new quarry caught the warlord's fancy. Nor could he resist a dig at Kim and enquired with a far off smile, "On which table did you banish, Mr Park?"

"He talks too much," said Kim curtly, "he's with the foreign press."

Undaunted, he tried another shot at the general's armoured skin. "I suppose Cha Se Dong was excluded for reasons of security?"

"He was never a member of the Seoul Organising Committee," returned Kim pleasantly while he stared over the throng towards a group of interpreting girls. One was under escort by two security men and heading their way, a small girl, rather fetching in a new green blazer, whose eyes flashed hesitantly and lustrous hair shone almost midnight blue when caught under the spotlights.

O'Brien swore softly : Kim scored high marks for his trick.

Todd overhead. "Your boy rioter?"

"She's Peter Pan; one moment so open that you can touch her soul, next vanished beyond reach to a remote galaxy."

Todd blinked then delivered a final wound. "Christ alone knows how you mistook her for a Goddam' boy."

At once Kim became gallant in a most paternal way; introductions, cautious flattery, those little touches which Korean men tend to ration for their daughters, showing a charm which conquered easily though never rattled its victim in front of others. It was all rather quaint and definitely calculated. He wants to provoke, realised O'Brien, he wants to know the exact line up, those undercurrents which are essential homework in a Korean deal, and also prove a point: nothing happens in Korea without his personal thumb print. Or does it? She came shyly, straight to him, clearly released from a burden, happier, as though glad a hard test now was over, modest yet proud of the green blazer which labelled her a trustworthy Korean.

"I detect a bounce in your step, Diana."

Before the girl could reply, Kim, who, dwarfed her slight figure, heaped more praise. "An excellent student, O'Brien. This young woman gained such high marks that I have decided to attach Miss Park to your airship project. You need a person with brains and rare language skills; its technical terms can baffle those less alert. I'm sure Miss Park will find it a rewarding assignment."

"Tell us about the test?" said O'Brien partly for defence, but also because the girl very obviously wanted to share her personal adventure.

"We climbed a mountain at night with lanterns. I had to lead the way and find a village on the other side. We were more than a hundred girls." She stopped in horror when she realised the American Commander-in-Chief stood listening to her simple story.

Todd looked straight at Kim. "Was that village near one of my emergency airfields on Route One?"

"They're all good but she was the best," purred Kim with a surprising pride. "We could march the entire Olympic family over those mountains guided by these young people. No problem."

"In that case," said Todd, smiling down at the girl, "I can go to church tomorrow morning with less worries."

28

Silver lightning forks hunted each other through a wild morning sky, rain
swept across an empty parade ground plastered with fresh leaves then attacked
rows of red brick offices in the Eighth Army Headquarters. A fifteen mile an
hour limit ruled on the base and O'Brien was in no hurry. At a cross roads, he
turned right and parked among a row of station wagons filled with family litter,
sheltered by thrashing maple trees that grew on a grassy bank. Steps between
more trees led to the colonnaded porch of a brick colonial style church topped
by a short white steeple. Apart from the glimpse of another white needle on
the wooded mountain behind the chapel, he could have been in any small town
in the Carolinas. The storm slackened and wasting no time, leaving the car
unlocked, he dashed through puddles and leapt the steps four at once. Rain
caught his face, damp patches spread over his sports jacket. Muffled singing
came from varnished double doors as thunder wandered among clouds piled
over the spent city.

Nobody looked round when he let himself into the dark packed church.
The chaplain, green satin sash draped over white vestments, book held open,
prayed in a southern drawl. O'Brien picked up an American version of the
English Common Prayer, and slid into the last empty pew. He searched the
congregation while the storm rumbled overhead, surprised how many
Episcopalians served on the US Eighth Army staff, then saw Todd, sitting in
the front row beside a pepper blonde, his back straight, head bowed. American
children entered in silent file, hand in hand, following the Sunday school
teacher, a stocky serious American with cropped brown hair. A hymn came.
The plate spilt green dollar bills and lay blessed on the altar: Todd pecked the
woman on her right cheek, nodded thanks at the priest, rose from his pew and
started down the aisle. Half way along the Sunday school teacher stood quietly
and followed. O'Brien took the hint and slid sideways.

Outside the rain already was less wild. "Leave your car, Mike, we're only crossin' the road. This is Colonel Baker . . . Marvin commands my signals regiment." Todd set a fast pace as a squall advanced onto the parade ground. "Colonel O'Brien used to ply your trade, Marvin; he speaks fluent electronics."

Baker went ahead and dashed under dripping maples planted alongside a dull red brick building that reminded O'Brien of a British barracks. They entered though a side door and hurried down a short corridor. The far end was blocked by a solid steel sheet protected with an electronic lock. Baker placed his thumb over the sensor pad, the lock clicked open. When they were all inside the dim room, he closed the door tight as an airlock, switched on strip lights.

"What you think?" asked Todd.

O'Brien took in three rows of television screens and complex control panels, an illuminated map of the city and surrounding countryside from the DMZ south to Osan airbase. The Americans had even installed a finger print search and photobank.

"Someone's been busy."

Baker flicked on the main power and stood willing life into three dozen screens. "Warm up takes a few minutes," he apologised needlessly.

"You can stay on line all during the Games?" asked O'Brien, who suffered nightmares about self-defeating technology.

So did Todd and his blue eyes glittered beneath a tanned brow from a summer soldiering and rare golf. "There won't be any point in switching off. They're not gonna' find time for sleeping, Mike."

It must have taken hours to install and implied watch keepers and constant monitoring of circuit boards, because the whole room was useless should a fault happen. One person could not keep pace. O'Brien worried. "Who else worked on this job?"

Baker moved towards a waiting chair. "Six . . . counting the general and four sergeants who will man and maintain this station plus myself. They know about everything concerned with the airship operation . . . . except your own identity."

O'Brien showed his relief. "You work miracles, Marvin . . . perhaps my young Korean can be presented as an interpreter."

"Which one?" Todd invited deceptively, hoping to ambush O'Brien on troublesome ground, before his quarry once more slipped away. When O'Brien didn't rise, he pointed at the far wall. Another steel door was decorated with a fire exit sticker. "My personal staff colonel sits on the other side but only my thumb print gives access. He has a sealed envelope in his safe which, if I become disabled, straight away he hands to my Chief of Staff. Inside is a description of this operation and instructions to speak only with Marvin or yourself. His thumb print is stored in the lock memory by a system we use for such emergencies. He doesn't know. I can't do it any other way, Mike . . . we might both be out of reach . . . Marvin must leave his sergeants running your blimp . . . he's gonna' be busy."

Baker took off his jacket and sat before the main monitor, typing in his personal codewords. Soon most screens flickered and steadied with colour pictures of tiny umbrellas in vivid shades of pink and blue, human confetti thickly sprinkled over Yoido Island Plaza. He typed further instructions and more blank screens came to life with a beautiful child Elizabeth Taylor riding a huge racehorse. Baker sat back and viewed the whole battery for several seconds.

"My kids rioted before Sunday School . . . miss National Velvet? OK, let's see . . . both Korean TV networks are running Cha's rally . . . quite a crowd given this stormy morning . . . while our American Forces Network keeps off ROK politics: zero audience rating. During the Games this control room will become more versatile because we can take all feeds from the International Broadcast Centre. We'll enjoy a selection from many different camera positions in the main stadium. General Kim has his own secure TV system monitoring key sites. . . the Royal Boxes at every venue, to name one example . . . and we'll take constant feed from your airship."

O'Brien pulled a folded paper from his pocket and spread it over a spotless steel table. "You *should* pick up our telephoto shots clearly."

"We'll see what you see . . . no worse . . . no better. A lot is riding on the skill of your airborne cameraman." Baker turned down the sound as a flat Korean voice competed with horses leaping a hedge in the Grand National.

In the cold room O'Brien studied his complex chart of circuit boards and optic fibre wires hidden in the airship gondola's roof.

"Sound . . . I want to plug you into the airship flight deck and give you everything that happens up there . . . the simplest way is a hidden broadcast mike' but Kim's people might pick that up fairly quickly. We could scramble. We could broadcast on constantly changing frequencies."

Baker preferred the second method. "Makes jamming *almost* impossible," he urged.

Todd intervened. "In America, when you buy a car, it's the extras which count: we need a direct link from this room into your own headset."

Bent over his complicated drawing, O'Brien nodded, for this opened wider opportunities. Put a friendly voice into the system which he could trust and they would exploit data instantly. He asked Baker, "What other assets can we feed into the communications sytem?"

"Where do I stop?" laughed Baker though his grey eyes were serious.

"Could we pull in AWACs?"

"Depends what you mean." Baker plainly thought he was paranoid.

"Not radar pictures, data, over direct voice link."

Todd stared distastefully at mudspots on his loafers and then at the shining stone floor. "By the way . . . who cleans this place?"

"My sergeants, Sur."

"Sorry, Marvin, I shoulda' guessed. It's immaculate and nothin's broken."

O'Brien smiled wisely. "Suppose you had a radio link with the AWACs patrol aircraft, two way, which enabled its crew to brief you direct . . . that same information could be passed by your watch keeper to me in the airship."

"We understand what you want," Todd rested his behind on a table and arms folded tight, contemplated the screens, "but is it the most effective solution?"

"We could make that enhancement, without much work, Sur," offered Baker distracted by almost a million bright umbrellas.

Todd stared blankly at the busy screens. "North Korea isn't going to fly fighters over Seoul. Antonov biplanes are only a possibility. You're worried in case they nail you with a SAM but, frankly, Mike, AWACs won't help . . . you're talking short range, flight measured in seconds."

"AWACs can pick up a missile."

"Not always easy over Korea," Baker was unconvinced. "There's a lotta' ground clutter and radar can't see through mountains. Even flying six miles above the peninsular our AWACs might just be in the wrong place and therefore sweeping at too shallow an angle. But we can sort out somethin' if you want that stuff." Baker waited for his commander's decision.

"How about sticking a missile warning system on your plump gas turkey," suggested Todd, distracted when Elizabeth Taylor fainted on six screens. Once more that glitter strayed into his friendly eyes when the jockey cap fell off and revealed glamorous black curls and the winner as a teenage girl. He glanced quizzically at the final scene. "Charmin' movie . . . we really oughta' give you somethin' smart that'll watch your tail up there, Mike."

O'Brien grinned a wry surrender. "AWACs might make all the difference, Harry."

Todd nodded consent with a distant smile.

Baker was lost though knew better than to pry into his commander's private joke. He said efficiently. "We'll work out frequencies."

"Switch it off, if you wish, Marvin."

Todd walked across the room and placed his thumb over the sensor pad, opened the door into his own offices, listened for a second then invited both to follow. Baker shut down his equipment, then the lights, and firmly closed the door behind. Todd ambled through into his own large office. Rain splashed lazily onto soundproof panes screened by net curtains which looked onto a gravel parade ground bordered by windswept maples. A large cherrywood desk was defended by a line of family photographs, a beautifully varnished table, flanked with several chairs, filled a corner away from the long windows. Beyond some armchairs, stood the American and Korean Flags, their short poles capped with polished brass, flank guards for the pale blue banner of the United Nations. Todd moved behind his desk and pulled a string which drew back floor length green curtains to reveal a map of the DMZ that stretched right across the large room. Military symbols in red and blue marked the locations of North Korean and UN forces. The upper half was thick with red symbols.

"This is confidential and my office door locked behind a combination until after Kim's great human festival closes and the World flown home from Seoul."

Todd picked up a pointer and tapped the Imjin River. "Look at that fuckin' concentration; armour, mechanised infantry, artillery: forget the whole lot. It's all bullshit. Those little rectangles holding parachutes are the ones we watch. Special Forces . . . eighty thousand . . . along the entire DMZ but with concentrations near traditional invasion routes: North Han Valley, Imjin Valley, Inchon coastal plain. Now take a look south of Seoul City." Todd crossed his office and drew back another green curtain.

O'Brien stood closer. It was the best map he had seen in Korea, large enough to show every street in the capital and its surrounding cities, and each tiny path over the encircling mountains.

"Let's take the worst case." Todd sat on the varnished table and stabbed his pointer into the restful green carpet. "Your northern colleagues are rated about equivalent to well trained VC. They're busy rehearsing hard for one of your theories, Mike, a hop over the border . . . or round it . . . in those old biplanes. Kimpo Airport is no sweat, right on the coast, almost in North Korea, just a frisby ride along the surface of the Han Estuary. It's not even ten clicks. Roughly two minutes flying time. They risk it. Kimpo is closed: I have a quarter of a million shit scared people on my hands. That's only the start. They land on each road south from Seoul and block my exits for civilians. They hit Songnam and close my secondary supply airfield and my primary field for extracting VIPs."

"I begin to see the logic in Kim's selection methods."

"Frankly, I don't think it'll happen, but nobody in this town is willing to stand by their own judgement. So we all plan for a nightmare. Kim swears his Koreans will bring out the VIPs by chopper and the rest on foot."

"Why not, they're mostly athletes, young people, the press could probably use a workout."

Todd smiled cynically at this surprise bonus. "Kim has nearly all the Rangers in R O K Army for several crucial tasks. Rangers will sweep the exit routes and hold them open . . .while young kids like your personal interpreter . . . lead the Olympic family, some twelve thousand people, through the mountains to Osan and our emergency strips on Routes One and Ten which are both about fifteen clicks south from the Han bank. The VIPs go straight out from Osan. Everybody else is extracted by the airlift which inserts our first wave of troops and stores from Japan and Stateside."

"You'd activate Team Spirit."

"Absolutely."

"We can stay airborne for fifteen hours at a pinch by cutting back our speed and cruising at thirty knots . . . so long as there's only light winds."

"Outstanding. With your TV cameras, you could monitor all groups headed south."

"We can scout ahead as well, Harry. We might pick up low flying aircraft with a mark one eyeball. What about all the tourists, military families, foreign residents? There's four or five hundred 'Brits in Seoul without an Olympic Games and they're a drop in the ocean compared with US Service families."

"Leave aside tourists. The others would attempt implementation of their normal evacuation plan. That's what it's for. We might keep the roads open long enough for them to drive and get further south, take some pressure off Osan and the emergency strips. That airship would be a Godsend for avoiding traffic snarlups."

"OK. I make that about seventy thousand bodies, counting the media down at the broadcast centre on Yoido."

"If the North Koreans don't grab the island and hit KBC."

"You wouldn't fight, at least, not hard; be honest, Harry."

"I'd defend Madame Chung's virtue, if my President so ordered."

"Who takes them?"

"Kim."

"It'll be a brave man who drives that hearse."

"Probably a retired Kamikazi," remarked Todd and closed the green curtains.

They went out through the back door of the headquarters and stood under a colonnaded porch, watching the rain fall, for they were a good hundred yards from the Base Chapel. Baker glanced at his watch, shook hands and ran through the downpour, taking the grass bank at full stride, and went into the church hall where his wife served doughnuts, juice and coffee, a comfortable ritual which followed the morning service with military clockwork.

"I'd invite you along, Mike, but I suppose spooks must stay cold, wet and hungry."

"Might be a trifle public, Harry . . . never mind, another day, another doughnut."

Both men stayed under the dry porch because its sturdy wood columns hid them from a tall white office block which housed the Korean Armed Forces headquarters and discretely mounted video cameras that monitored their American commander's backyard. Somewhere behind Namsan they heard thunder grumble then fade.

"Anything else I should know?" asked Todd, and listened without interrupting while O'Brien described the journey south and its result: another cleverly marked trail leading deeper into Seoul's lost alleys where each landmark bore no meaning.

"I'm not lost," he finished eventually, "I simply can't trust a single bearing. It's too straightforward for my peace, almost as though we were meant to find the stuff, rush straight back to Seoul, problem obsayo."

"Did she lead you to those cigarette butts?"

O'Brien shook his head. "The barn stood out from anywhere in that huge garden. There was no missing it. She found the boxes, led us right to the cavemouth, took us to the guns."

"Hand in hand?"

"Something like that, she was crying."

"Your girl may work for the North Koreans. Besides Kim."

"Everybody works for Kim in this country, Harry. The questions are when, whether they know and for how much? You and I are working for Kim unless we're extremely careful. In her case, it may be just for that green blazer, a little safety for the family Park. North Korean? Its all too obvious and my best agent swears by her family, indeed recruited her, often reminds who runs the biggest risk."

"Brother aside."

"Not him, not yet. If David Park grows forty years in the next decade then he might become President. Meantime I lean heavily on the judgement of my Korean agents and they rely on bold and bright young people from old families . . . trusting that good wood usually lasts longer."

"Where's he hiding?"

"Buried deep in a family private library, happy to be alive, researching for an old man, a scholar and bookworm with countless crusades."

"That's a mark in your lady's favour."

"She'd be his worst threat. She knows where to find her brother . And that's why I can't believe she's a communist plant. If I'm wrong . . . well . . . they're making fools of us all with nerve and skill . . . "

"We'll write Kim Il Sung that the kid deserves an Oscar. Flush him out with cunning praise. Fucked her yet?"

"I should have weeks ago."

"Sleep on it."

"Sleep on what?"

"You're worse than my forward troops. A month outpost duty, you'd think they'd been castrated."

"How is Kelly?"

"A little stretched. For the past week those bastards in Taesong Dong have been trucking in building materials and taking out junk."

"Big or small."

"Sofas, old TVs, radios, stereos, mattresses, cookers, armchairs, it's as though an entire village launched a mass car trunk sale . . . except it's nearly August, not spring. The stuff is bloody awkward to search." Todd stared morosely at ceaseless rain. "Kelly's troops could take over searches from their Katusa's, Korean troops, which is not fair on both. Shit, we can ride the storm, but we may simply alert whoever runs this underground train."

"Set up a bleeper system, Harry. I'll have Kang follow the next shipment. A Korean won't attract the same attention as a car loaded with American MPs. We must tail all runs, they'll keep their heads down shortly, wait for September."

The rain slackened and a fresh clean wind found the damp porch. Todd suddenly became distracted.

"Smile, Harry, in another few weeks everybody will fly home."

"My main problem this morning will outlive early October." There was foreboding in Todd's eyes when he glanced towards the church hall. "A wives posse waits across the road and they're in a lynching mood. It's all about that new PX store going up at Gate Five."

"A PX ... aren't the Koreans after this base ... I nearly asked to borrow that huge shed for building our airship."

"The ladies demand why we need the largest PX in the whole World." Todd sighed stubbornly. "And I keep telling 'em that it's not excessive for a city of ten millions."

29

A white whale floated beneath twin rows of skylights, captured by a huge string net held onto the hangar floor by fat turquoise shotbags. Red canvas sheets spread over the concrete were stained by chalky powder. Low ropes warned off the curious and light fingered. Near the nose, stood a white gondola, propulsars fitted either side, its roof conveniently protected by a dust sheet held tight with steel clamps. Alone, roped off, forbidden to unclean hands, a workbench waited, altar for the next communion by a fraying though confident Rose.

"What the hell possessed you to make a bet with that little prick, Park. We're almost knackered."

O'Brien ignored the grouse which was Rose's way of coping with over work. "Abdul... look at your airship."

"She's not fully inflated. I'll do that once she's outside. Some cunt might scrape off the polyurethane skin going through the hangar doors."

"Will she float out with the cameras on board?"

They had arrived at Kimpo the previous night and at that moment were on a container truck under armed police escort from customs with Kang riding diplomatic shotgun.

Rose stood back and admired his second night's work. Near his feet lay a huge white diaphragm, the nose cone ready for fitting on the gleaming envelope. He rubbed both eyes with tired fingers. His complexion had lost its normal healthy shine after forty hours on coffee and bacon sandwiches. Rose gripped his belt buckle, tugged it twice, discovered why his jeans felt looser, then answered testily, "Of course, Mike, of course, all planned on the drawing board at Detfold."

O'Brien respected the warning signs, yawned and employing a theatrical touch, stretched. "We need some sleep.... soon... otherwise we'll cock up something vital.

"All Leggo, apart from the control wires: bit of bolting, fitting the under carriage. The worst job was sorting out the inside of that envelope, which is complicated enough without becoming a nightmare when your leader starts adding modifications. For God's sake don't lend *anyone* your headset."

"I hope it receives as clearly when we're flying.

Two nights earlier they ran a test with O'Brien driving around Songbuk Dong, a wealthy new suburb on a mountain over looking downtown Seoul and almost level with Namsan's needle. At the appointed time Baker drawled a few garbled words and O'Brien mimicked an American provo' patrol. The broadcast system worked perfectly. Whether microphones newly concealed in the gondola ceiling would relay every sound on board direct to Baker's control room at Yongsan, must wait for proof, when the airship flew its first test.

"They can't do it to me," snapped Rose as a small shadow crept through a narrow gap between the hangar doors.

"Come in, Mr Park," called O'Brien pulling a face at Rose. "You *are* an early bird."

"Catch da' worms," giggled Park, stamping a smouldering cigarette into the concrete just beyond the threshold. "She looking fancy. How long before finish?"

"Why?" asked Rose protectively.

"Ceremony.... gotta have ceremony.... Kohrean fuckin' way." Park flung his hands outwards like a bird testing its wings, almost disappointed when they failed to lift his body.

"Is this for the media?" fenced O'Brien, beginning to feel tiredness and temper burn on his cheek bones.

Perplexed by their stony hostility to a small though important detail, Park lifted his thick glasses, revealed sad eyes below hooded lids while he vigorously polished with a handkerchief starched stiff as cardboard. He smiled regret. His grey business suit shone in places from constant pressing. A Swiss watch and its solid gold wristband seemed out of place.

"Private, private, official photographer, only. Just a lillel' word from the General, your goodself and yours a truly. Taka' ten minute," he enthused hopefully,

"What do you reckon, Abdul, shall we say in two days?"

"They'll have to rise fucking early to watch this chick hatch." Rose scowled consent.

"Number one! Sponsors make short speech. That take another twenty minute. Followed by 'runchee for all participant and major sponsor. Thanks one million." Before either could protest, Park bowed a farewell, scurried to his waiting chauffeur and black car.

O'Brien moved swiftly before there was blood on the hangar floor when the next Korean walked through the doors and distracted from the main task. "Better resign ourselves, Abdul. Korean business consists of endless meetings arguing over a tiny detail followed by far more over protocol before the deal goes through at the last second. Nobody respects contracts. Promises die as they leave your partner's lips. The golden rule is don't be drawn into deciding who stands where and who speaks and in what order... that's strictly Korean business or we'll still sweat inside this shed a year from next September."

"We're just a pair of barbarian mechanics."

"Providing Park doesn't become a hourly pest, yes, that's how we play it. Don't forget; JP and I spent days and nights, winter and spring, while this dinosaur gathered dust in a Pusan Customs shed. We couldn't take a second screening." And he shuddered inwardly, drained by vivid memories.

* * * * *

Not a ripple sounded on a river still held by darkness. Cool, breathless air greeted a shaft of white light that escaped, broadened, spread, groping for the last indigo night as the hangar doors rolled apart, shoved by two teams of Korean policemen in navy coveralls. Yoon stood by Rose, a silver whistle dangling from his thin lips, ready to blast each order. The huge doors ground on their steel rollers until one, then another, refused to slide further.

Yoon blew one sharp blast. The Koreans sprinted across the tarmac and formed two lines, standing loosely, hands clasped behind their backs, a physical training class more than an airship ground crew. O'Brien worried about all this mindless energy and blinkered discipline. Presently it served a single obvious purpose: bringing the airship from its steel womb without damage: but afterwards, he might risk a rare foray into Rose's kingdom. Rose tolerated this folklore on which Koreans plainly thrived, felt secure and wanted more. If they ripped open an airship, wiping out months, all could swear it was the team's fault, not the crass incompetence or brute strength of one mindless fool.

Near the hangar doors, Kang and the girl lingered, both shivering despite raincoats for there was a bite to the dawn calm. She still solemnly clutched a tiny dictionary that served no purpose since a whistle was the only language trusted for this delicate task.

"Mike.... I need you now," shouted Rose.

"Where?"

"Can you go inside the hangar and watch the tail as she comes out. I don't want her to drift sideways."

"On my way".

Rose faced Yoon. "Right, two teams, guide ropes either side, tow driver in his cab.... ready.... for my signal. Remember... she's jelly.... a slight movement and she'll throw a wobbler and buckle her stabilizers on the hangar walls."

Yoon sucked in his cheeks with a hiss so intense that it reached O'Brien near the hangar doors.

She looked impressive, shining white, reflecting cold floodlight: huge blue letters fixed on her chubby sides spelled 'Welcome'. Kim came near murdering Park when the IOC reminded about their rules on advertising within range of an Olympic Games and only the personal intervention of Francis Moon stayed the execution... with a whole page gratis for the sponsors in the weekend Buk A Ilbo.

Walking from under the bulging envelope, Rose checked the yellow tow truck : securely hitched, its driver sitting with hands off both ignition and wheel. Ducking beneath the gondola, he paused, examined a white torpedo with a large glass lens on its slim nose that swung well clear of the concrete floor and cost more than the airship. Rose checked shot bags tied onto the under-carriage. They looked alright. Twin files of Koreans shuffled along either side and took up their guide ropes. Rose reached the tail fins, muttered a prayer, then shouted.

The truck burst into life and Rose screamed at its driver until the engine surge died to a gentle throb.

Little by little, she slid forward, a monster suddenly shown its real environment, timidly leaving a warm metal womb for the dawn chill. Five minutes later Rose shook Yoon's hand and they both clambered over the gondola door sill. O'Brien and Kang stood back on either side, reserve linesmen for the rope crews while the girl watched sleepily, collar pulled round her long thick hair, hands thrust into raincoat pockets, the dictionary forgotten.

Still there was no wind though blood streaked the eastern sky. Floating, the airship resembled a ghostly monster, docile and stable, deceptive, almost friendly.

Rose leaned from the gondola door. "Mike, we're about to run the engines, nobody pulls a rope, nobody wets his pants. Can JP and Diana convey the two crews this message.... hold your rope and don't even scratch your balls."

Shocked, the girl protested furiously, "Abdul, I can't tell Korean men to stop that dreadful habit! They'd lose face."

"Pass the word, JP," ordered O'Brien and watched with a disbelieving smile as Kang made certain in Korean that each serious face understood fully.

Loud buzzing shattered the stillness. Rose ran the motors for ten minutes while checking all control wires, wagging the stabilizers, testing air valve controls, studying the instrument panel with an almost diabolical intensity which was matched only by Yoon's waspish face peering over his shoulder.

An hour later the airship hung in the cool morning, a massive silver bubble eager to fly among violet mountains painted on a copper sky. The Koreans chattered holding their taught ropes and the tow truck driver dozed. Over by the river bank a windsock hung limp from its short pole yet the river already whispered as its first ripples danced. O'Brien sat with Kang and Diana on a pile of shot bags, talking about whatever both wished. If she was living another life, it did not show. She seemed in a placid mood, deeply thankful that her brother browsed safely among the Moon's private archives far from Seoul, fretting about the financial sword which hung over her family though wearing her concern with less guilt. Soon she reverted to questions about flying terms, perhaps comforted by the distraction until her mood switched as it did so often.

Kang finally laughed into her earnest face, "Use English, there's no Korean words: anyhow, we always copy."

Rose's voice cut the morning. "We're going to launch."

Kang yelled at the Koreans, whose cheer woke the truck driver.

She climbed at a steep angle, towards the mountains, brushing aside tranquil air, driven by her fans, nose aimed at daybreak. Soon she droned southwards over Namhansan and vaulted its tiny fortress wall. For a few seconds they watched, enthralled, silently willing Rose to turn and cruise directly overhead. When the bubble reached the first sunrays and glinted, quite spontaneously, O'Brien grabbed Kang and Diana, whirled them round in a mad polka while the ground crews laughed from bewilderment. He took his time releasing that small warm body and once more enjoyed her soft scented hair before discipline and sense returned.

"When Abdul comes back, JP, stand with the starboard rope crew. I'll take the port side. You stay with me, Diana, I may need some rapid Korean."

"Can we fly," she asked excitedly.

"Up to Abdul." O'Brien saw disappointment sweep over her anxious face and relented. "Everybody will have a flight this morning, you two, all the ground crews, before Kim and Park and half Seoul turn up for their free trips and lavish lunch. But Abdul's the boss... it's his decision."

Faint droning warned that the airship returned, a silver tennis ball, low over the paddy fields that spread westwards among scattered woods. Landing was the first harsh lesson for the Korean crews and it scarred their pride... Rose went round four times before they managed to halt the floating balloon and he deliberately kept the speed far lower than his normal slick approach. The unspoken truth was that he didn't need a groundcrew, a message the Koreans understood and which a furious Yoon determined to prove hasty within the coming hours. O'Brien left the policeman snarling at his teams and ran forward; hurried consultation took place at the gondola door while the fans idled noisily. Rose beamed down with weary elation.

"She handles like a fuckin' milk float!"

"Can I put Diana and JP on board?"

"Let's have 'em.... we'll do the lot if the wind behaves," shouted Rose and waved at his two passengers forward.

They lifted Diana into Rose's waiting hands and he plucked the girl, hair blown wild, into the large cabin. Kang tried another way, jumped backwards, sat on the doorsill before sliding on board.

"We need steps."

"With greased wheels," shot back Rose with a sadistic glance at the empty pilot seats.

"I'll take one man from each rope team and have them waiting to board," yelled O'Brien and shut the cabin door.

After two hours everybody had flown except O'Brien and when the airship approached, this time the ground crews stopped the monster without a word of coaching. Its door swung open and Yoon stood ready to jump down. For a second he even smiled. "I take over. Your turn.... OB!" Was it friendship?

Slipstream tugged at O'Brien's golf jacket and tousled hair. Reaching inside the doorframe, wedging a trainer toe over the carpeted sill, he heaved with both shoulders, pulled himself on board and shut the door.

"Alone at last," he smirked and felt his unruly hair brush the ceiling panels.

Rose passed him the special headset but the soundproof cabin made talking easy despite the fans' steady buzz.

"I'll wear it once we're airborne."

"Take the right hand seat. Forget the valves. Start your checks."

"You're going to trust me with her? Abdul, I'm touched."

Rose grinned cruelly. "I've trusted Yoonie since dawn."

A nonchalant wave told O'Brien that he was in command and should angle the fan ducts for take off, increase power, then haul back the steering yoke. He obeyed faultlessly.

Nothing happened. He remembered fast. Pulling with full strength, he felt the cabin slide forward. Suddenly invisible force tilted the deck steeper, from somewhere behind a giant flung the craft at a mountain ridge filling the immediate horizon. Hangar and concrete apron fell away. The bottle green river slid beneath his trainers and along its banks, leafy copses flowed backwards.

"Sweating yet, Colonel?"

"On the brink."

"Watch the birdie'." Rose reached up and flicked a switch marked auxiliary fog lamp. "Now try a steeper climb."

Effortless. A baby could fly with fibre optic controls. He forced his lips into a grateful smile. Rose deserved a gold medal. With a gentle twist, he turned the airship starboard, felt it follow its nose, towards Songnam's concrete runway that shone white as sunlight woke the valley floor.

After a few moments, he handed over, went aft, found the television screen and its controls, settled in the empty blue linen seat. It took less than half a minute to ensure that nothing had been damaged, nobody had tampered with the monitor, nor its control board. He switched on the main power, slipped on his headset and as though inside his brain, heard Baker repeating, "Please would Specialist Four Valentine report urgently to the USO club by twelve hundred hours today otherwise he may forfeit two tickets for the Olympic Opening Ceremony rehearsal on September Fifteenth."

A microphone hung before his mouth. O'Brien spoke crisply. "Please remember to bring coffee and doughnuts for your family when attending meditation and prayer at the Religious Retreat Centre on this coming Thursday night during which a collection will be made on behalf of the Church in Uganda. A children's movie and crèche have been arranged."

Baker's calm voice continued a few more minutes with other announcements before either he, or one of his sergeants, switched off the tape recorder. Contact.

O'Brien's eyes strayed back to the television screen which showed a mountain covered with young ash trees. Glancing down, he twisted the dial for zoom control, watched a tree rush towards the screen, black and white flutters when four magpies broke from thick foliage.

"Give me a range on the mountain bearing three three zero, Abdul?"

"Sort of timbered?"

"Over its summit."

"Seven point four nautical miles?"

"I've just seen enough national birds for a birth."

"Try a shower window at sparrowfart in Songnam. Much more exciting."

"Won't they realise the camera angle changed, Abdul, from the ground?" For a moment, they spoke at cross purposes, laughing away stress, before Rose answered.

"We're south of Songnam.... Uncle Sam owns everything for the next hundred miles.... Kim's Special Forces and Rangers might pick that up, but not without high power glasses."

As though proof, Baker's dry voice once more invaded the headphones.

"Volunteers for the DOD High School Chamber of Horrors on Halloween Night should report to Specialist four Grace Pittatacci at the Yongsan Youth Activities Centre no later than thirty September." The frequencies gymnastics worked perfectly. Baker, closeted in a spare office on Yongsan Base in downtown Seoul, heard every word they spoke.

"Five minutes and you can play pilots," said Rose from the flight deck.

"One more test," replied O'Brien, pushing an illuminated green button which revolved the camera torpedo. While it swung, he reduced its magnification, slowed its search, slid the riverside hangar onto the television screen: no larger than a matchbox, two tiny smudges in front, the rope crews standing on the concrete apron. He started the zoom lens, not surprised that hand and eye co-ordination was quite difficult, all the time keeping his fingers and wrist safely away from a glowing red button marked 'relay'. One brush of a sleeve would switch on screens all over Seoul. Soon he sharpened the picture and open hangar doors rushed towards the screen; he altered the camera slant, read easily a hangul number plate on the yellow tow truck.

"Range from airship base, please, Abdul."

"Seven point one nautical miles."

"Amazing!"

"I confess a certain satisfaction," said Rose, giving the yoke a contented pat.

Slight deflection starboard brought Kang's taxi into view with two young Koreans, coats now discarded, leaning over the bonnet, a tall boy and a lovely girl, sunning themselves while chatting happily. Diana laughed at something, yawned, flicked her hair straight, a perfect snapshot and he remembered this camera could run countless such innocent pictures through a vast computer bank.

"I'll come forward whenever you're ready and try and fly her back, Abdul!" But it took him about three minutes to shut down the system.

On the return flight, they first cruised further south as Rose made him carry out a series of turns, climbs, descents; gradually O'Brien learned to think faster, confidently request opening or closing the ballonets' valves which resembled four taps above Rose's left shoulder. Hardly any sounds guided these decisions, which at first, he found disconcerting. Soft hissing from ram air scoops under the tail, pushing up the 'ballonaze' pressure during each descent, quickly became a comfort. After thirty minutes circling, at least he understood how the airship pilot altered the trim, pumped air into the forward ballonets, deflated the aft ballonets, pushed helium backwards inside the envelope and made the airship nose heavy. He also understood that Yoon would never fly solo missions over the Olympic Games. When Rose switched off his fibre optic system and they went back on manual, wrestling the heavy yoke, bright morning sun flooding through large portholes behind the flightdeck, sweat streamed down his face and back.

O'Brien took off his jacket, threw it over his shoulder. Rose merely laughed. The vision was superb. Pale blue mountain ranges were missing only to the east where fine mist stole a late summer sea. From three thousand feet, peering north over straw paddies, he recognised the ridge behind Panmunjom, wondered what they might find this beautiful morning, if they flew over the

Han River and Seoul's barren sprawl.

Rose broke into his thoughts when he warned Yoon to have the ground crew ready.

"Take her down, Colonel."

"OK... ballonaze.... please, Abdul."

"Steer for the field. Don't worry about the descent rate. It's fine."

"Angle looks terrifying." Without warning, the airship took over, swung earthward, gondola chasing the nose.

"No two landings are ever the same.... your line's perfect."

"I'll take your word!" Ginkyos, dark green water, steep wooded mountainside fled beneath his white trainers.

"No wind. Go in straight." Rose pointed at the slack sock. A tiny Yoon had the groundcrew standing in a large V and the yellow truck parked a safe distance back, near the taxi, where Kang and Diana shielded their faces from the dazzling sun, riveted though prepared to run fast.

"Steer, Mike, don't alter course! I'm dropping the speed to twenty knots."

The airship seemed to hang, then gently sank towards blurred asian faces. A moment later the Koreans clasped fat hands on the ropes and grabrails under the gondola, walked a tame dinosaur across the ramp and before O'Brien realised, hitched it onto the sturdy tow truck : Rose slapped his shoulder hard then shut off the fuel supply, killing the fans, rapidly checked his flight deck. Even as they clambered from their seats, without warning, the yellow sock stood from its pole and flapped wildly.

Rose grounded them all until the wind fell. Later that morning, champagne and warm sun, hazy mountains, clean air from the paddies and adrenaline burning in her veins, Diana, overwhelmed, fell asleep on a raincoat bed in the sweet grass under the shade of Kang's taxi. She slept deeply giving hardly a sound, through Mr Park's lunch speeches, though Yoon's and O'Brien's, several sponsors, and lay there so peacefully that Kim refused to have her woken for his own stirring words.

*   *   *   *   *

Clouds became rare and spent of rain, the sky climbed higher each warm day.

Faint motors somewhere over the mountains, distant glimpses of a fat silver cigar became daily rewards for those few Koreans with a moment spare for gazing at the southern sky. Ringed by green mountains, trapped in the hot city, tensions rose among the lawmakers and often tempers flared, yet social order held while - after sending the students on extended holidays - Korea's generals in suits squabbled among each other, the national cancer rarely bursting through the national thick skin and then only with small riots and the odd teargas whiff. By late August, General Kim ruled in all but name, holding apart three rival factions : one was the ROK Army, another led by Cha owned the peaceful Seoul streets, while a third glowered over the sparkling granite walls of the President's Blue House, no longer King though without a Dauphin. Invasion came: foreign media by the thousand, team advance parties by the hundred, threatening the prices in the discos at the few luxury hotels fully booked for the tourists pouring through Kimpo's new terminal, splendid yet deserted by ten at night. Flags and bunting fluttered along the main streets, famous faces became commonplace in certain parts downtown, a holiday mood infected the most stubborn Korean.

And there was no fresh raw intelligence. Nothing happened at Panmunjom: until one Saturday morning. A small plump man with odd thin glasses, wearing a golf jacket and clutching a bulky shopping bag, stood at their gate: Mister Rhee, gentleman's tailor, sent by General Todd, who proposed in an old man's soprano, that, "Mr O'Been consider purch' a few shirt an' mebbe' noo' soot'."

O'Brien stood in his shorts about to enjoy a morning swim. It was all rather sudden and he needed reflection. Did his suits look that old? Surely conservative styles never date.

The tiny visitor persevered and declared without the slightest pity, "He say you need bad, Sur, bad."

"When did he tell you this?" asked O'Brien, taking the offered fat sample book, suddenly interested, flicking through pin stripe cloths.

"Dis' morning. You like blew?"

O'Brien selected a lightweight navy wool, stood still while his small visitor sat cross legged on the lounge carpet, chewing a pencil, chattering to himself while he measured.

"OK... come 'gain Tersday.... two maw' fitting." Mister Rhee slowly stood, carefully wrote out the order in a crumpled notepad, held it sideways near the glass doors. Satisfied, he enquired, "You 'lone?"

O'Brien nodded: Agima was shopping down the hill at the local market buying vegetables and ginseng roots.

"Packagee' come last night but post office no deliver."

"I'll order some shirts after that news, Mr Rhee."

A short telephone call sent Kang, armed with a small tool box, the make, colour and licence number of the truck, north towards Panmunjom. Several hours passed before the telephone rang. He had found a roadside payphone by a hiker's restaurant beneath Pukhansan Mountain.

"Must be short, they left a paid line and everybody here wants a turn before the money runs out."

"Talk sense, JP."

"They 'phoned somewhere, long distance. We're using up their change."

"Who?"

"Six of us standing by this machine."

"Start again, JP."

"Vehicle belongs to a scrap company..... driver and another guy..... number plate from Chung'ju..... blue Bongo truck. They just phoned someplace, then went into the restaurant."

"Chung'ju? That's quite a distance south."

"More than one hundred kilometres from Seoul. Near edge of the Woraksan Mountains.... hang on, sorry, they just finished eating ramyon.... I'll call later." And the line clicked as a young Korean mountaineer began calling a friend for a lift home, using the change still left in a payphone by two North Koreans and Kang.

Reliable as ever, Kang called, several times: from a bathhouse in southern Seoul, from a garage outside Ichon City, next a country Yogwan inn, then a brothel in a lost town along the South Han River as he headed nearer its source in the Taebek Mountains and for an hour O'Brien wondered if the truck aimed for the east coast. But then Kang's quarry turned south towards Woraksan where the landscape climbed and rivers tumbled off steep wooded peaks. O'Brien dozed on the sofa with the telephone perched on his chest when the final call rang softly.

He reached forward. "Delivered?"

"A scrap yard in Tamyang."

Lying Comfortable, O'Brien groped for his map on the carpet, held it at arm's length, balancing the telephone with his chin. He found the place, a small town west of Woraksan, known for its caves. "They're certainly consistent."

"I thought that also." Kang laughed from a phone booth; this time in a noisy bar, perhaps another brothel, God knew where but he was not done.

"I went over the wall."

"Good man.... now come home."

"Just big old freezers."

"How many, exactly."

"No more than twenty.... I fixed three trucks but not a car." There was a questioning silence. "You want me to go back."

It was tempting. "No... you've done more than enough for one night. Shouldn't you sleep somewhere.... rather than risk landing in a ditch."

"Munche...."

"Don't say it, just drive carefully, and, if you're weary, sack out by the road side."

Darkness still owned the streets when Kang returned, though not for long. While roofs and trees slowly resumed their shapes, over an hour of eggs, bacon, toast and coffee, they relived Kang's busy night.

"What do they want with freezers?"

"Nothing, JP. It's packing. Where better to rip apart freezers than a scrapyard. Sketch a map. Paul's bound to have somebody who covers that little town. After all, from next week, the media's liberalised."

"You gave me only three bleepers... the car isn't tagged."

"Munche obsayo... they won't use their own vehicle for moving the package next time. We might learn a little about their habits, perhaps their friends."

"How long can those bleepers last?"

"Roughly six weeks."

"Won't many trucks and cars visit that scrapyard," pointed out Kang reasonably.

"In a normal world, of course, we'd tell Kim and he'd put a hundred policemen on the job." He allowed a moment for Kang to absorb the reverse logic.

Accepting fate, Kang smiled back. "I have to watch who goes in and who goes out."

"Enjoy the country life for a week and not a word to anybody about your busy night. I'll tell Paul."

Kang frowned hesitantly across the breakfast table. "Diana could help me keep watch."

O'Brien shook his head firmly. "We're dealing with dangerous people and probably all highly trained. Tiger's work, not lamb's. For her own protection, JP, nothing else." He hoped it sounded convincing.

Kang proved right. Two dozen cars and trucks called on the first morning. Desperate for hard facts, O'Brien risked a training flight to Pusan by a scenic route and personally requested clearance from Kim, in case those huge eyebrows jerked, a facial muscle twitched: not even a doubtful flicker passed across the general's busy face. Their flight plan was cleared in seconds.

Rose let Yoon pilot while he 'played' with the camera and noisily praised the beauties of Korea's inner mountain ranges, at one point suggested they should beam pictures back to headquarters, whereupon Yoon became conspiratorial, swore that Kim would disapprove, which left a question mark over Yoon and added frustration. From twenty miles slant range at five thousand feet, Rose filmed the scrapyard for a full twenty seconds, spotted a brand new workshop tucked in a corner behind piled rusting freezers probably thrown out by a local meat plant. It was enough to target American satellite passes. Kang came home.

* * * * * *

Orange roof lights glowed through rush hour fumes that hung in Namsan tunnel. Half a mile further, rejoining the night, Kang sped towards the line of toll gates and slowed for his usual overarm flick. A silver coin clattered into the metal scoop. Along Sogongno's gentle hill, fairy lights decorated the Shinsaegae department store. Floodlit fountains sprayed in front of the Bank of Korea's new granite tower and across the street, from behind the Central Post Office, happy crowds surged from Myongdong. More fairy lights climbed the Plaza Hotel and lanterns glowed over the Dynasty Hotel's rustic gate, welcoming the whore's limousines.

"Is the Mayor throwing a party?"

Kang spoke over his shoulder as he gunned the taxi for amber lights. "All Korea is throwing a party! Look at the main square.... on your left, now."

A floral cone rose from the middle of the square between the Plaza Hotel and the electric clock on City Hall. Beyond, safe behind a low rope, guarded by two policeman, burned a lively orange flame. Reflected in its friendly fire was a small ring of curious Korean faces. Now and then a flashlight blinked.

When they reached Moon's office block and stepped from the lift onto the executive floor, a sharper atmosphere prevailed : this time Hodori broadcast the Olympic Song.

Moon shuffled across his son's huge office for the tenth time, head bowed, hands clasped behind his small round back, quietly fuming. "Chung has made a con....cession! Still insists that he will open the Games and still refuses seats for the leaders of any...any....other party. It would lack dignity, he claims."

The old man reached a magnificent Louis Seize bookcase crammed with red leather volumes, turned slowly, surveyed the far wall and a photograph of his father in traditional robes. "Instead... Cha Se Dong and the other two party leaders may occupy the Royal Box at the Closing Ceremony."

"With the President and his popular first lady?" O'Brien waited.

Moon drew another breath and reached where Paul and Kang sat silently in armchairs placed at either wing of the vast editorial desk.

"To be decided!"

O'Brien moved towards a window. The massive Sejong cultural centre stood in almost total darkness. Cold lights shone in ranks on National Police Headquarters and the upper floors of the Foreign Ministry. A white glow hid the North Gate. He stared down at ten lanes searched by long fingers of light from cars and buses speeding past Sejong's empty pavements and bushy trees; offices, shops and restaurants were closing after another long day and the Olympic City hurried home.

"Francis, I begin to fear that we shall watch the Olympic Games on television while our nerves fray. Nobody will make a martyr out of Chung .... at least the Opening's safe."

"But not so the Closing Ceremony." Moon joined him at the windows, hands still loosely clasped behind his stooped back. "Surely our poli....ticians cannot be this naive but it seems they are actu.....ally stupid."

"Vanity is kinder. I understand right? For once in their lives, they all compromised, accepted."

"Gladly!" Moon shook his head in bafflement.

Neither moved. Below on Sejong, the silent cars and buses rushed past dwindling lights, past hanging streamers, past electric pinprick letters on road signs praising Chung's moribund Bright Society: a real flame burned up the street and all the world watched South Korea. Still wearing his London suit from the Mayor's reception though now comfortable in worn sandals, Moon gazed wistfully at the city, perhaps searching for something within himself, perhaps thinking about his sister in the northern twin's capital, brooding over his divided country: his son close, his empire forgotten, Moon broke the silence with a lover's breathless whisper.

"Behind us hangs my father's picture. Never signed his own name, dared not, Japanese ruled... called himself Kyongju, capital of Shilla Kingdom in our south east when your King Alfred burned his cakes. I look out from this window and marvel at a city grown a hundred fold in twenty years. I see fine buildings where once lay only rubble and corpses. Seoul changed hands three times in fifteen months. When I returned for the last liberation in 1951 only three buildings still stood in this entire city. Thirty years ago Kim Il Sung fed and clothed his people twice as well - before he squandered half a nation in a mad pursuit of guns, guns, guns, and a second Vietnam. Park changed our Southern future. But what became of our youthful dreams. Strong leaders rule by consent alone and I heed my beloved sister: what shall we gain with all this van....ity for a few, if we pay for it with people's hearts."

"The view depends on how far you've climbed the ant heap, Francis."

Over Seoul Station floated a slim crescent moon and across the Han River its silver touch fell upon Kwachon Mountain. O'Brien compromised. "The fault lies not in ourselves, dear Brutus, but in our stars."

Moon became jovial. "Ceasar was a dry general. Shakespeare filled his mouth with poetry. I wager they quote those lines tonight in Pyongyang.... Paul.... I have a whisky bottle in the bookcase, single malt..... unless dear Michael objects."

"We should drink to our *family's* health," said Paul sharply, fearing his father would say more than intended.

Moon stared northwards across the watchful city. "Taum pun pepshida," he sighed, the Korean farewell for until we meet another time.

"Mullayo.... who knows?" smiled O'Brien. He leaned towards Moon and comforted, "Francis, she might lead your next Olympic Team."

"Michael, some two thousand years past, Korean astronomers were highly advanced. Seven years ago, our new breed of astronomers built an artificial moon. They thought of everything with endless calculation. But when they launched their Olympic moon, they discovered it possessed a gravitational force so strong that it tows all behind and steers its own course through Heaven. All these astronomers can hope is that their moon lands gently at Chusok, our early October harvest festival. Until that day, we all remain its prisoners."

And he stayed at the window for some time as the old thin moon climbed for its last few nights before another slowly fattened for the Olympic Closing Ceremony.

30

From behind lavender mountains, a molten sun climbed the shining sky, planted velvet woods on small hills, woke empty streets, made the Han a wide tin sheet. Not a cloud deflowered a morning given by the Gods. Riverside gardens basked in perfume, white bunting rippled along the city streets, freshly painted lines shone white and yellow on all roads. Factories and baths shut down for over a fortnight lost themselves among spruced apartment blocks. Half a city's traffic stood in garages and car parks, banned from the central streets, odd numbers one day, even numbers the next, for the coming two weeks and already a black market thrived in number plates. But on the Olympic Highway, caught by the early morning sun, fleets of big black cars streamed towards Chamsil Stadium, chauffeuring Prime Ministers, Generals, Ambassadors, willing converts to sporting diplomacy, free tickets for a fortnight exchanged for tacit promises to keep their mouths shut about any blemish behind the scenes that might spoil modern excellence. Among this racing metal tide, close behind a new Mercedes still bearing German number plates, Kang proudly drove the black car with O'Brien cramped in the back seat, self-conscious in his new navy suit, running through mental check lists, amazed how Mr Rhee's cutting perfectly hid the machine pistol and its spare magazines and two powerful radios filling his inside pockets : one was for Kim's security network, another linked with Rose in the 'Korean' airship. From a thin chain round his neck, hung a plastic identity card which doubled as a photograph and with an electronic rim more sensitive than any bankcard.

O'Brien self-consciously flicked a new blue cuff. "Uncle calling Groundhog, how do you read?"

"Loud and clear," answered Rose's cheerful voice from somewhere east of Songnam airfield.

"We're five minutes from Tiger Pit. Any news?"

"Munche what's it. No news and what a fantastic morning for skydiving. I'll loiter south during the flying show."

"I wish that was our job this glorious morning. You could free fall off the sun, not a cloud in sight. Keep sharp watch, Abdul, somebody still might take a shot at your blimp."

"Mine hawk eyes shall seek grey smoke trails rising from the concrete wilderness even unto Dumbo at three grand."

"Stay sober, Groundhog, no drinking Park's champagne, out." He rested his forearms on the front passenger seat and watched a forest of national flags and the great Olympic ark drift into view as the highway obeyed a river bend.

"Now comes the moment where I put my reputation on the line, JP; I have not a clue what lies hidden in that wretched scrapyard, yet am forced into a ritual holiday."

"Stop worrying, Mike."

"Don't ask how I know, don't ask what, but I looked past something blindingly obvious and probably in front of my nose."

"You'll be right in front of General Kim's nose this morning; since he's invited you to watch from the Royal Box!"

"That's another mystery: I suppose there's nothing else I can do this morning, other than hide behind dark glasses and loiter with the general in the Royal Box looking for terrorists. The Princess very decently is in Hong Kong opening a tramway and our sports minister is so short, he needn't duck. I can't fly in the airship. Mr Park and his many children took the spare seats after Kim refused to hand over several free tickets to the Opening Ceremony... at five hundred US each: airship rides restored peace and harmony. Our friend Park is a nuisance but no threat; he makes money while the airship flies, gains not the slightest from the airships's destruction, moreover his future smells of violets providing he makes Kim richer. Besides... Koreans don't normally kill their own children."

"Unless they're unborn girls," said Kang, hinting at an article by a British reporter who found dead babies dumped in the garbage behind an abortion clinic.

"Diana swears it's widespread.....says women must rule this country for a hundred years before it becomes civilised."

Kang laughed. "She has a brow beaten father who wanted more sons."

"In his case the girl's cost much less : I haven't come to terms with Diana and her brother. If I take the evidence on face value.... as Paul does... I'm left with the feeling that somebody who knows all the players is pulling the strings and following a rigid time table. It's as though the whole business resulted from hours of wrangling and now everybody sticks to the agreed plan. Let us presume Pyongyang is their ultimate control, and, frankly, that's our strongest candidate; I can't believe that our General Kim deals with North Korea. The other Generals would throw him to the ROK Army."

"Somebody else. Possible? Why were those photographs in Park's office?" Kang began slowing for a steel barricade where two imposing policemen split the traffic into streams for several huge car parks along the riverbank.

"Park's duties are more than strictly commercial and he understands hard bargaining. Despite many hours, JP, we've never managed to watch anybody's pay day. How is Shin paid? Does Shin slip those North Korean squads some kind of per diem? Who finances that? No payment records exist in Magnolia Trading, yet last week Park handed me a perfectly good cheque for seven million dollars. I think Park fulfils a duel role; pays us and Shin, just as he deals with payments from the airship sponsors. I see his role as the fixer and money launderer, not banker. Park hides money for Kim in a secret operational account and somewhere overseas. That's his skill."

Kang overtook the Mercedes and reached the far right hand lane. "Are hunches good enough?"

"Our whole business is made up of hunches: did you recruit the right agent, do you understand their deeper motives, whether the information is worth risks, your collateral reliable. It's no more a science than journalism, politics, war; only a lethal art."

Even their windshield sticker supplied by the efficient Miss Secretary Kim caused whistle blasts. It also left a wake of salutes from more policemen lining the route and raised the barrier to a national security car park directly underneath the terraced seats of the main stadium. Koreans wearing blue blazers with wide padded shoulders tailored to hide pistols, hustled O'Brien and Kang through an electronic door into a spacious room where restful lighting bathed rows of televisions, computers and telephones, manned by men and women in royal blue blazers. Most screens showed an aerial shot of traffic flowing along the riverbank expressways towards the main stadium. Across the control room, surrounded by more blazered toughs, Kim held court, one hand crushing a radio-phone while the other stressed abrupt orders. Where was Diana? SLOOC shuttle buses ran past her apartment every few minutes.

Kim passed the radio phone to a giant Korean.

"O'Brien, Kang, my congratulations, excellent pictures. We employ your airship as a traffic cop' at present. The blow ups are fantastic. I had to stop my men searching the crowd for the prettiest girls."

Kim ushered them outside on to a wide balcony which looked across a vast garlanded roman circus packed with eighty thousand murmuring faces. Beneath the elegantly curved canopy, still deep in shadow, flags of all hundred and sixty nations lifted gently as hard sunlight slowly found the grass field below. Directly under Kim's balcony empty crimson rows in the Royal Box looked over the crowded press seats that sloped towards the running track.

Kim said brusquely, "Miss Park wanted to see the crowd from the field. She is walking round now." Dozens of green blazered Koreans wandered about the perimeter, mostly security, judging from the number of times hands covered mouths for short reports. He looked for Diana without success and Kim excused himself as several grey haired Americans wearing dark blue blazers came through the door, squinting into the hot sun. After considerable fuss and ritual laughter, Kim returned.

"Apologies. Deputy Director from Langley with his Asian Bureau Chief and the American Embassy. I won't introduce you." He smiled ironically. "I know your chief believes in a low profile."

In contrast, plainly, Kim did not when playing host to the intelligence superpowers : O'Brien half expected the Mossad Chief to enter next.

"Silence is golden," he smiled back.

"Wise man," said Kim with a hint of wistful envy then strode to greet a party of Japanese in suits who bowed deeply, followed by two huge Russians in plum blazers.

A seductive and familiar voice made O'Brien turn, find a girl wearing a figure hugging blazer which invited second glances, whose face sheltered under an elegant straw sunhat tied with a long black ribbon that matched her shoulder length hair.

"Good morning, Mr O'Bine, I am very happy that you come today."

He lifted the wide brim a fraction and found himself welcomed by bedroom eyes and moist lips. She smiled to reveal a pink tongue and perfect teeth. He made a mental note to ring the general's office in the near future and staged surprise.

"Why Miss Kim! How delightful you look in your outfit; ready for a fortnight's sport? Our thanks for the stickers. We owe you a special treat."

"The '*pressure* is mine always," she smiled eagerly as her surprisingly large almond eyes hinted invitation.

"Over here please, Miss Kim," snapped the General whose face stiffened with disapproval and perhaps a question. "Keep your radio switched on at all times in case I need something.... Kang may stay here if he wishes or join Miss Park down in the arena.....O'Brien, we have work."

Leaving Kang in Miss Kim's charming talons, he followed the general. At the bottom of a small staircase, the Royal Box resembled a comfortable lounge. Some seats were already occupied by gossiping western men whom Kim dismissed as ambassadors. Sitting near the front were small Korean children in Sunday suits and pretty national dresses.

"Once the President arrives, we leave, because no firearms are permitted within the same room as our head of state. That applies to mine also." Kim gave O'Brien a searching stare.

"Look upon me as your personal gunman."

Kim returned the ghost of a smile and began sharply questioning two tall dark suited security men hovering along the back wall. Finally satisfied, he said, "My men leave when the Blue House security arrive. From then onwards, its their job. The President will sit in the front row." He pointed at arm chairs before the thick glass which looked over the rows of crimson seats.

O'Brien nodded that he understood. "We should watch the show together, General, but right now, I'd like to move around, if that's possible, work out a few things in my head."

Kim studied the scoreboard clock. "We have a few minutes before I must return to my command post. Let's not dawdle."

Only for an instant, Kim seemed on the brink of saying more, but then withdrew behind that carved brass face, though leaving O'Brien convinced that the unspoken matter concerned Chung directly. If only he could trust Kim and his senior staff, but he dared not; what if Kim's headquarters was pierced somewhere near its brain, the most dangerous wound of all, for the brain gave orders. They reached a gap in the barricade and stepped onto the bright maroon track. Thousands of Korean faces, sprinkled with foreigners, watched curiously from the stands. Sometimes small flags waved above an ocean of white sunhats. A huge television screen suspended alongside the scoreboard showed the excited crowd a picture of the spectacular stadium. Admiring this was a slight figure in a green blazer who flicked tidy long silky hair.

O'Brien grinned at Kim, "At least we're something to watch after an hour: I see Miss Park standing under the scoreboard."

"She should trim that hair, it's longer than permitted," replied Kim sternly, glancing at the pure sky.

"You run a tight ship, General."

Whereupon Kim elaborated with the sourness of a man raising teenage daughters in his few spare hours. "Our modern girls spend hours bathing and shampooing when their noses should not lift from school books."

A silver whale cruised silently about a mile east of the stadium. Deciding to enjoy himself, O'Brien craned skywards. "She looks alright."

Kim only became more restless. "Any moment, the windsurfers will start their display on the river, after which the teams start marching."

"Walk round just a little further, General...... let's make certain our rivals spot us together..... there won't come a better moment."

"You're too smart, O'Brien. Which rivals? That's my problem. And I don't believe you know either."

As he walked briskly along the running track, Kim swung his arms like a tae kwon do fighter, always loose, hands free to chop and kill, harsh face consumed by brooding, doubt and power. "Where did you send Kang two weeks back?"

"I shall have to lecture JP. Your men picked him up? Where!"

"I could close down your whole operation: it's not legal, we've no liaison deal with Britain, you could be on a plane from Kimpo within the hour. Don't tempt me, O'Brien."

"But I won't," risked O'Brien knowing that Kim had both the power and the wish. Although should Kim call his bluff, the threat to Hodori remained without any counter attack: time for remorse.

"I'm not my own master, General..... I have sound reasons for caution, I'm also under orders. We both have pilots in that silver balloon.... where did your men *lose* Kang?"

It must have been in southern Seoul. They couldn't have fumbled on empty country roads during the small hours. He kept walking, studying the crowds, pictured his own Olympic beauty whose horse went lame in training, the only snippet that Mason allowed through his tight security rules. Shrugging off disappointment he waved at Diana, who frowned shyly and hurried towards the two tall men, worried, for she always expected them both in total personal control and now they seemed locked in bitter conflict.

Reluctantly, Kim divulged, "They lost him near the Express Bus

Terminal."

"Who's watching us, General, which one of these eighty thousand faces should we fear night and day? Which ones shall we run through your massive computer in the Olympic Park."

"If I knew that O'Brien, I could send a hundred thousand police and rangers home instead of living in apartment blocks all round Chamsil Stadium. We could watch the games on television.

"I'm told you see more anyhow."

Kim shortened his stride and, finally, remonstrated with cool fury. "We're not fools. I know you're running some operation against the North and I wish you'd share its secrets with South Koreans.... not just Americans. World War Two is long finished, O'Brien. America has new friends."

He resisted asking Kim, then why not approach the Americans on his private balcony. "I can't share data unless so ordered, General, which is exactly how you work. We run agents all over the Far East for a British requirement and a British purpose. I'll seek clearance to brief you as a matter of urgency." The mysterious factory near the Yalu River, however, remained taboo; its latest product might be hidden in a scrapyard below the Woraksan Mountains. Mason would have to invent a juicy bone.

"Is anything wrong?" Diana asked breathlessly.

"We're just competing," said O'Brien.

She laughed, respectful, coy, not fully understanding, nor covering her fear of causing further disharmony. How very Korean, thought O'Brien as the bickering instantly ceased and they all three hurried back towards Kim's special box. Eighty eight toy trumpeters rose behind massed choirs in bridal gowns and began a fanfare while dancers in snowy slips surged into the brilliant sunshine.

A phalanx of majorettes in white miniskirts, shakos and boots, clasping sign boards for each country, entered the stadium. Greece came next, followed by the world, each country greeted by a few bars of their national hymn. Cheers rolled like summer thunder around the great bowl. The Americans marched in a huge column of blue and grey, exuberant, after twelve years keen to prove themselves against the Eastern Bloc. Russia wore red and white, a cheerful, dignified, confident army. The Canadians numbered hundreds and hurled white frisbees into the crowd : Kim spat an order over his radio before gunfire replied. Britain marched in windsor blue, wearing white sun hats with modest pride which Kim approved while O'Brien wished Susanna owned a tougher horse. More teams entered. Mongols dressed in skins, Spaniards led by a slender blonde princess with a sparkling smile, who reminded him painfully of his lost English beauty, denied any word by a chief who matched Kim for discipline. Teams of hundreds, teams of a dozen wheeling onto the grass field. South Korea entered last, place of honour, clad in blue that rivalled the delicate sky, greeted with a deafening roar which lasted several minutes.

An old man ran a lap with the Olympic flame, trailing smoke, handed his torch to a young girl who fought a path through photographers all along the running track.

"He won the marathon in Berlin for the Japanese Emperor." Kim suddenly smiled as hundreds of flapping doves rose towards freedom in a white cloud. "We Koreans claim his medal in our hearts."

Three young people in grecian tunics soared on a lift up a hundred foot tower and at its top, plunged their torches into a wide bowl. Doves strutting round its rim fled smoke and orange flame. More fanfares sounded. The IOC President and SLOOC President turned towards the Royal Box and faced a small bald Korean with rimless glasses and a dark sober suit.

O'Brien leaned over the balcony and studied Chung. The President spoke a few words in Korean which were translated by the electronic scoreboard. After a tough summer, the little colonel from Vietnam bore no visible scars and stood below, fulfilling his ambition, bringing off a vast gamble which had cost three billion dollars in a country lacking proper medical care for its poorest, yet already the strategic gains waited before the hushed crowd : America and Russia and China stood on the crowded grass, a chance of lasting peace overwhelmed money. Would these people thank him with another seven years as their chosen ruler? Chung himself seemed without emotion.... but he always did... only, when, barely for a second, their eyes met, did O'Brien gain a flicker of recognition from that plastic face, saw in those narrow eyes the barest glint of temper, before the leader retreated behind bomb proof glass while two athletes and a judge, all Koreans, climbed onto a podium and barked the Olympic oath of sportsmanship and impartiality.

"Providing Korea wins the boxing and ping pong," growled Kim ominously as the judge finished reciting, hand raised like a roman soldier.

Diana glanced at Kim with disapproval. "I hope you don't actually mean that, General."

"This is global war," retorted Kim, not sparing the ruthless charm. "Each medal winner receives a pension of half a million won a month for life. Korea's status depends on our medal total. We must beat Japan. Don't mistake that, Miss Park, our national goal is crystal clear."

When the teams began marching out, Kim became almost lighthearted, shaded his eyes as jet fighters trailed rainbow smoke overhead, while others left five smoky rings. He even joked. "Chung saw you up here, O'Brien."

"Did I detect a certain liverishness?"

"Mike.... you know our President?"

The girl spoke less timidly though careful of Kim's new relationship with the Blue House, a problem, suspected O'Brien, which troubled Kim more than Diana Park. Perhaps regretting her boldness, when she became aware of Kang talking with a mysterious female shaded by a chic straw hat, she recklessly assumed this was safer ground and, watching the seated crowd across the field make huge flags and slogans by drill with their programmes, asked innocently, "Who's is JP talking with? Is that his girlfriend?"

"My secretary," answered Kim and moodily peered down at the Royal Box, declaring with impatience, "I want our first crisis passed."

"Chung's leaving after he opened the Games?"

"In six minutes." Kim resisted separating Kang and his secretary whose heads were bent close together. Soft laughter escaped from under the hat brim. "Why do you bother him, O'Brien."

"Mullayo.... I don't know.... possibly his past, it might spoil that austere image. We weren't friends! Maybe he believes that you're now in London's pocket. It's a wicked world."

"Perhaps, perhaps. We've penetrated Bright Korea Party for years at hideous cost and I can't find out what Chung wants. Ridiculous." Kim placed a large hand across his forehead and craned skywards. "Here comes our first team."

The aircraft lost by the glare, high in the warm morning, bright specks formed five human rings, broke apart, scattered. Parachutes cracked, blossomed, gliders in Olympic colours. A Chinook helicopter throbbed overhead and more human dust tumbled earthwards. Scores of parachutes exploded open and soon the sky became crowded with flexible wings, five stacked together, trailing vivid streamers.

"We're both fielding ladies, General; mine's a policewoman."

"Mine's a soldier." Kim glanced sternly at the girl and challenged her opinions. "Do you still say we're a breed of rigid chauvinists."

"No.... improving slowly," Diana smiled up demurely into Kim's exasperated face.

The first jumpers glided into the stadium, swooping alongside its canopy, waving to awed children, then landed, running over the smooth turf, gathering their parachutes to resemble Korean sunshades, a rather quaint duty for half the teams were Kim's rangers. Something happened to Kim at that moment: perhaps the parachutists served as a compass, showed how far Korea had journeyed, overwhelmed his hunt for the clouded future, because his haughty face wore a softer mood. Diana noticed and looked searchingly at O'Brien as though worried by the general's sudden change. When a small boy ran over the grass, completely alone, driving a hoop with a stick, Kim seemed moved.

The General clapped without restraint as a thousand children and rangers in white pyjamas performed tae kwon do. Human lines stretched right across the grass, charged each other, leapt, with perfect timing kicked small boards, not a miss, not a foot wrong, wood splinters flying. Korean dancers, village tug of war mounted on giant dragons built from knotted ropes, nothing distracted Kim from avuncular pleasure: sparse radio messages were resolved in few staccato words. Once only did he ask about the airship and then as routine operational caution.

"How's it look from your seat, Groundhog?" said O'Brien to his left lapel.

"No news, beautiful day, no news."

"Thanks Groundhog.... out." He leaned in Kim's direction. "They're running a permanent scan on the crowd from about three thousand feet while they circle. No traces picked up all morning. But it takes hours to sift eighty thousand faces properly. Fortunately most discard!"

Children and dancers rushed into the stadium and converged round a small stage where a Korean band flown in from Switzerland performed the Seoul Olympic Song. O'Brien smiled at Diana's brittle eyes and thought, why not - on this diamond morning. Let her shed a few tears in a land where emotion was ritually crushed.

He reached down and discretely squeezed her small warm fingers. Around the world, before one billion televisions, people were glued to this stadium. The Koreans had made a good start, brought back some of the dignity to the Opening Ceremony but kept its fun. No wonder she felt proud. His thumb felt an urgent pulse as charmed, he watched a fat tear slide down her solemn cheek.

He turned to congratulate Kim and was stunned to observe a similar shameless trickle on the general's rugged face.

31

Yoon hunched over the yoke, steered a wide circle a thousand feet above a small apartment town for the Olympic athletes. They passed over woods and a lake in the Olympic Park, then sparkling streets, slowly leaving astern the pewter river. Above the Lotte World Hotel's fawn tower they turned back and cruised towards the main stadium. It was hot in the gondola. Behind the television monitors, two Korean policemen dozed. Mr Park jabbered numbers in Chinese, flapping excited hands, spectacles glinting when his head swayed in emphasis, those rubber lips pouring astronomical profit forecasts into the bruised ears of yet another bewildered Korean sponsor. O'Brien and Rose stood in the gondola's stern, not exactly avoiding the others, but quietly sipping ginseng tea, watching the great Olympic bowl slide under the starboard side. It was the eighth day. The ground stayed trouble free: O'Brien hoped to steal an hour or two that afternoon, and watch a few athletics finals.

"Johnson will zap' Lewis," scoffed Rose with utter conviction.

"I thought you'd be rooting for Lynford Christie!" taunted O'Brien, making a futile attempt at breaking that Jamaican ego, failing once more; he added a last dig, "No money on Ray Stewart from the Queen's other island?"

"We're talking gold, mon," beamed Rose, unshaken, before he winked across his tea bowl, "but he might make bronze."

"With Lewis running there's bound to be a drugs test."

Rose answered with a caveat. "It's like Lewis himself keeps telling the whole world . . . an athlete on steroids has a fifty per cent chance of discovery and thus an even chance of winning gold, better odds than a person who doesn't take 'em . . .some of the Eastern Europeans haven't competed for the whole summer!"

Admiring hazy mountains, O'Brien tried to connect this wisdom with a vague theory struggling for life and form while his memory raked through almost forgotten facts. Blatant risks were the privilege of a few front runners and if the prize hypnotised, perhaps even the most worthy athlete might gamble. Supposing it was not a race, instead a contest where sportsmanship and honesty were mutually recognised as severe handicaps, a duel in which only the most nerveless cheat stood any chance of victory, and after buying every umpire possible before the fight started.

Rose noticed his sudden silence. "Nothing on the screens, Mike, just kim chi smoke climbing from several million suburban shithouses. We could have taken a lie-in today. The equipment is switched on and the police switched off."

"I think you might have found the key of this whole bloody riddle, Abdul, only I still can't quite put my fingers round it."

"See the hundred metres final this afternoon, clear you head, Mike."

He followed this wise counsel and borrowed Kim's balcony for an afternoon watching the world's finest athletes perform to a half empty stadium. Korean interest lay at the feet of Kwachon Mountain in Seoul National University Gymnasium where the men's doubles in table tennis began in thirty minutes. Kang and Diana had enquired persuasively if they could watch: absurdly, there was no work for either young person and, besides, they could observe Kim; for no doubt the general would attend with the trim and adhesive Miss Kim.

Bright sunlight bathed the huge stadium when the finalists emerged from the tunnel wearing tracksuits, shepherded by several Korean judges, some with remarkably well cut blazers: no wonder Kim had time for watching ping pong; probably half the crowd were on plain clothes duty this afternoon. Tracksuits were stripped off and handed to the coaches. Christie in his blue bermudas stood out from a line of Americans and Canadians with a Jamaican and a Brazilian.

O'Brien couldn't help leaning forward in his seat as the runners practised starts, scorching away, human motorbikes, dropping into a trot, repeating twice more before saving strength for a single dazzling explosion: four years training gambled on less than ten seconds. Christie looked promising. Johnson's muscles seemed almost too massive for a sprinter compared with the effortless strength in the thoughtful Lewis, but, charitably, O'Brien conceded that his own youth's horizons were falling light years behind modern athletics.

As the start drew close, he noticed the stadium fill considerably and soon, gone were orange deserts of empty seats. The runners settled, a blue puff. The pistol cracked. Eight men turned half way down the straight track.

This time it was a longer wait before the pistol aimed skyward and they rose, poised on their blocks. Blue smoke. Bodies catapulted forward, black and red, flying above the maroon track. Christie's blue shorts, white vest and black limbs, hounding Lewis. Johnson throwing his arms high, fingers stabbing skywards, white tape floating. A roar thundered from the stands. Along the track Canadians began dancing. Lewis and Christie shook the winner's hand. Television crews swarmed onto the dark red track as the scoreboard flashed nine point eight four seconds alongside an instant replay on the giant screen. O'Brien found himself standing, cheering Christie, when girls in snowy hanboks and others in miniskirts, chosen for their height and long legs, showing the world that Koreans were not bandy legged peasants, brought out the medals. National flags climbed the three masts and lifted in a cold breeze that disturbed the Olympic flame on its steel tower, while a full orchestra played 'O Canada.'

The stadium's shadow fell half way over the grass when it became time for the women's heats in the one hundred meters. At breathless speed, America's showgirl, 'Flo Jo', rocketed past with a wide smile and a cloud of wild afro' hair, a winner to her last flamboyant ounce of lythe black charm and American willpower. The Koreans sat in friendly awe at the mere proximity of this track goddess. Reluctantly, O'Brien glanced at his watch, formally congratulated himself on forgetting thugs and missiles for over three hours. Only one picture never faded from his mind and though some green blazers demanded more than a single glance, none cast a spell, not one girl tidied long hair with a defiant flick. To hell with regulations.

Walking back among streams of happy fans, many western, crossing the garden plaza, towards his car, once more, from beyond the Olympic Park, chill wind carried a faint purr and he saw a silver cigar patrolling the magnolia sky. How would they blow that airship from its perch over Seoul? Filled with helium which doesn't burn? There seemed less sense than ever.

Park would cry. So would Kim. That unlikely friendship. But Kim's two Olympic objectives were mutually supporting: a safe games allowed him to print money by the truck load. Whatever Park requested, Kim granted . . . almost. Somewhere Park kept a file on Kim thicker than Kim's on Park. All the delays in Pusan Customs, those insurmountable snags over finding a hangar site, every single difficulty had been a chess game between Park and Kim, while they fought each other toward a final profit split, if such a figure existed in this land of business brinkmanship. Another eight days.

Driving back along a near empty Olympic expressway, he decided to enjoy phony war a little longer. A flat orange sun slid towards Kwachon Mountain and across the golden river, car windscreens flashed on the northern road; Hannam dong clustered on its low hill and the Hyatt gleamed on a wooded neighbour that sloped towards the Mosque stranded among Itaewon's shops and bars. Namsam television tower still captured the last bold sun though already its woods wore evening's gentler green. Another eight days. Shadow the Princess. Watch the stadium when the British athletics team were competing in strength. Rowing and equestrian events presented problems because they were far from the main stadium and the Olympic Park which occupied Kim. Fortunately for everybody, Chung watched the Games on television from the safety of the Blue house where the Princess and entire Olympic Committee and Harry Todd were invited within the next hours: it wasn't considered safe for the president to venture a mere five miles from home to spend half an evening at the Shilla Hotel where his government lodged the International Olympic Committee.

The carphone rang. He reached for it while switching to the lefthand lane and the exit onto the upper deck of Panpo Bridge.

"A wonderful evening." It was Paul.

"How's the researcher?"

"Wiser from hindsight. How about you?"

O'Brien described his afternoon. "My regards to your father."

"Papa is listening to music. Much too loud. He's probably growing deaf, hear for yourself." The words were sung in Korean, but there was no mistake, a nursery rhyme told the violent end of three blind mice.

"It's more than clear, thanks."

"By the way, we had foreign visitors today, asking a lot of questions, which they'd pondered for some weeks." That was a warning, their conversation was taped by somebody other than Kim's national security. The Defence Security Command? Bright Korea Party? Nobody else had the power.

"I'll bear it in mind."

"Father sends regards."

"Please return mine." The line clicked. O'Brien turned onto the bridge and put his foot down hard.

Agima was away. She went to her sister in Chunchon most weekends. He methodically worked his way through the silent house. He didn't look for very long. An old briefcase which he left in the study, covering a faint coffee stain, had been moved. Not much, but agima possessed some useful shortcomings, dust on its sides was smudged though not around either lock. It had been opened. Nothing taken.

Back in the car, he delved in a hidden pocket under the dash, removed a small hand radiophone identical to one Rose carried on Moon Island. The garden lay still and cool when he sat under the tall pine tree near the lapping pool, and punched in Hong Kong's code number. Three seconds later the radiophone found the telephone number in Hong Kong employed for that evening and the call scrambled automatically. He heard a ringing tone.

"Hello." Penny's voice. She was slightly annoyed but then it was Saturday night.

"I've had visitors. They're rather persistent people. I'll be busy for two hours."

"Not family squabbles?" Her voice caught. The whole service lived in fear of betrayal by its closest friends.

"And wait so many months?"

Almost a year had passed with Kang deeply involved in all his work bar that precious final secret. Kang had the run of the house, knew the operation from start to finish: no, it wasn't Kang, not by the remotest chance, and the last headache he wanted now was an order to restrict Kang's knowledge. It wasn't practical, it wasn't right. In Korea lost face ended trust and friendship. Destroy kibun and you destroyed a tight team. The Moons risked their own blood in the Northern Capital. Diana roved the house for hours that night before Taechon Beach. Was she planted? Did Kim have wind of something and wanted a person on the beach that afternoon? Penny was a patient girl.

"Give me two hours," he apologised, "I'll ring when I'm done."

"No other problems?"

"Peace and harmony, Penny, lasted a whole four hours."

"Shall I call home?" It wasn't a question.

"Ask them if anybody has found a plum for my big friend."

He switched off the radiophone and sat beneath the pine tree watching the rose light fade behind shadow trees and roofs. Kim? The man was highly agitated about North Korea. But a poorly opened brief case which wasn't locked in the first place. Kim would punish such clumsiness. Which left the North Koreans, Bright Korea Party or Defence Security Command fresh from an inspection of the Buk A Ilbo office. For want of any other company, he spoke to the dark fir.

"We're getting warm."

He stood up, strolled alongside the placid pool, let his imagination take charge. One attack on Chung in broad daylight which was known about in Pyongyang because that's how Mason received his personal warning. Disciplined teams at the temple nearly burn Cha Se Dong. A small SAM smuggled into South Korea from Moon Island. Something else, size unknown, possibly larger, smuggled through the DMZ at Taesong dong and ferried, probably in parts, to a scrapyard in Tamyang. The SAM was meant for themselves - blinding the clever airship? But what was the second mysterious cargo? And for whom? Three opposition leaders all sitting together for the first time since the military coup seven years past? Hodori's warning matched. In which case, once he'd swept the place, Mason had better alert Buckingham Palace.

He went back into the dark house, sweeping each room, walls, carpets, furniture, cupboards, wardrobes. No warning squelched from the small electronic scanner. A map took shape in his mind. Suppose that original attack on Chung was stage managed? Dangerous, bold, disaster if discovered, yet that might explain the surprise turn up a side alley, and even Shin and Han's slick escape. Were they covered all the time by a select few of Chung's personal thugs from the Bright Korea Party? Sammy remarked how many were on the streets that rainy afternoon. What better cloak for a personal and cynical pact . It was monstrous, and in Korea, that talked.

Downstairs was clean. So was the cellar where their signal pack was better hidden than he realised: he stumbled on the steep staircase then worked carefully and steadily.

How exactly was Kim involved? Did he approach the Moon's because all else failed to flush out their counter attack on Chung's shaky regime. The squads on Bhudda's Birthday and a second easy escape, Kim's own evasiveness, Cha willingly accepting a seat in Kim's limousine and Cha was not a fool. Cha kept himself constantly informed all those years when prisoner in his own house and recognised Kims' security agency as his best protection from Chung for seven years. Then Kims' behaviour would fit its surface pattern. With no political backing, no party, mostly he feared a shove from behind, falling from the mountain top. Obfuscation hid ignorance: Kim was stumped. A desperate need for somebody to monitor London's team might explain some of Diana's actions but not everything - she was Paul's recruit. Wisely, the Moons still held her brother in their own hands, an old man' ace which Chung dare not challenge, providing all three opposition leaders stayed alive. He finished the landing and entered the first bedroom.

There was no question in his mind that Kim must run the girl, perhaps appealing to her patriotism, holding out a shield against Chung, his own thugs, a future owed to 'Uncle' Kim. That's how Korea works: favours, nuances, always finish by leaving from the front door. After all, it was conceivable that in ten years her brother might become President. Kim would make a tough Prime Minister and nothing beat a grateful first family.

Kang's taxi arrived in the street and he heard talking before it growled away. He stood on the landing from where he could see the glass doors and Rose take one look at the car and a house in gloom, reach for his gun and examine the lock before turning his key.

"Abdul . . . I'm up here . . . nearly done."

"Want some help," whispered Rose.

"Nurse this place for a half hour."

"Can I switch on some light down here . . . fix the steaks."

"Sure . . . just cleaning our rooms . . . but I must go over Yongsan for a short while."

* * *

Baker, God Bless America, stooped in the dusk, blowing at small brick barbecue which smoked too much. His wife was in the kitchen, busy washing salad, more than fetching in a pink bathing suit, wild chestnut hair tied loosely. She heard a sound in the garden, bold hazel eyes searched from the kitchen window.

O'Brien stepped back into the shadow of a bushy fir. "Marvin . . . it's Mike . . . keep puffing . . . don't look round. I might be tailed."

"You gave me heartburn!"

"Apologies . . . I have an urgent message for your boss . . . tell him that I deeply suspect our little colonel from Vietnam."

"Who." Baker suppressed a smile.

"I know; it beats theatre. I also have a question."

Baker's wife called, "Are you swearing, Honey?"

"Sorry. . . just sick of blowing . . . no problem." Baker moved round so he stood closer to the fir branches. "Shoot."

"Who keeps photographs of those talks last year at Panmunjom when North and South played poker over sharing the Games."

"Kelly at JSA."

"Thank Christ for that . . . Marvin, please ask your boss if he can obtain snaps of *everybody* who attended those meetings, particularly any photographs of fraternising outside the conference hut that sits astride the border."

"He'll ask how soon you want 'em."

"Last February. That number I gave you, ring anytime. And Marvin."

"Yes?"

"Blow from upwind."

"Thanks a fuckin' million."

O'Brien moved back through a thin wood. Nobody followed, he started the car.

At eight next morning the doorbell rang. Rose answered, then called up the stairs. "Mike, there's a little bloke here with some suit you ordered."

Mr Rhee sat crossed legged on the hall carpet, mouth sprouting pins, while he smoothed expensive grey material for another suit. "He your fren'?"

"Like a brother."

"OK," Rhee accepted in his thin soprano. "Genel' say no pichers. Somebody steal from office. They askee all 'sojers who gone home statesy. Mebbe' hab' sometin' nex' weeken'. Keep try har'."

He should have guessed. "Where are you going now, Mr Rhee?'

"Go back hows'. Why? You want go back Genel' Tott."

"You don't mind? He should be at home for another half hour: if he's not, don't worry. I wouldn't ask Mrs Todd nor any other sane woman to keep pace with our methods."

"He dare?"

"If he's there, give him my thanks. Say that I'm looking for somebody we both know."

One day, resolved O'Brien, when Mr Rhee hurried off, carrying his shopping bag down the narrow street, they really must find a slightly less absurd way to communicate.

Meanwhile, Mr Rhee was an inspired recruit as messenger between the UN Commander and himself, moreover, foolproof against most electronic listening devices. Few understood that sing song English when standing in the same room.

32

Last light searched a lilac sky. Ten thousand youngsters in tracksuits stood chattering on the cropped lawn where they had warmed limbs before crossing the parking road underneath the stands, walking into the main stadium, and the greatest moments of their lives. Those who were bored tonight, ran short races among the others, while another thousand middle aged men and women, managers and trainers, stale from fast living, badgered every Korean official in sight to find out when their personal flock marched through the athletes' tunnel and into the floodlit stadium. Confusion ruled. A Korean voice blared over the loudspeaker system with orders in English for a phalanx of placard carrying white majorettes, teenagers picked for beauty rather than the gift of tongues. Orders for the foreign athletes followed in Korean; the announcer was drowned by a spontaneous cheer.

Shoving dark glasses into his breast pocket, volcanic with disbelief, Kim snapped, "Let's not become drawn into this mess, O'Brien. We can go in before the teams. Idiots! Instructing westerners how to mingle and play like children."

"Some might need a little help. Several hundred on that field are Chinese and Japanese and...."

Kim demanded acidly, "*Who?*"

Korea stood fourth on the medal ladder, beaten only by the USA, Russia and East Germany. Britain came home at number twelve though with young talent on stream for Barcelona. Japan won so few medals that neither could recall its place. On the warm up field, a western trainer passed out from emotion, woke, found himself surrounded by worried Russian coaches. This evening's silent law was harmless mischief. Most athletes spent three weeks locked in the Olympic Village, guarded by Rangers, following rigid training and stiff rules, often ate cold food and rarely tasted beer. O'Brien moved widely during the second week, looking for traces left by the two terrorists, talking with young competitors : one British long-jumper starved herself all day and prayed for enough hunger to face the nightly cuisine. Now their spirits bubbled over, their competitions run, young bodies still charged. Wasn't this just the moment, when Korean officials threw up their hands in dismay, when everybody's focus lay in the elegant circus as thousands of Koreans witnessed pranks they could never dare copy, shocked into passing envy and utter concentration, when a single blow might kill three men who obligingly sat together.

Kim and O'Brien entered the stadium, white majorettes on their heels, children in toy uniforms, marching perfectly as a roar louder than summer thunder rolled and echoed around the great human cradle. Garlic breath hit like an invisible wall. Eighty thousand mouths had waited two hours and few Koreans lasted that long on an empty stomach.

Waving flags marked lonely foreign islands in a vast Korean sea. O'Brien spotted a single golden head in the Royal Box. "Why don't we stick around here, General, it suits us both."

The three opposition leaders were in their seats : Cha, squat and modest, boyish smile, waving chubby hands. The other two were more reserved; dignified enough for public face, not too starched - risking popular appeal. There were vacant seats in the Royal Box.

"Television again tonight for the first family?"

No faces peered from behind the bullet proof glass. Normally a personal appearance required weeks of mass meetings with all agencies and the party technocrats.

Kim scowled at the glass window and an empty room. "We're not using it tonight, confined space is a trap. Our three Kims can run for their lives and lose themselves among the crowd."

Another huge roar signalled tracksuits like confetti and the boisterous teams strayed all over the arena grass. Along the running track, a pair of blonde heads wearing five lens sunglasses rode piggyback on two men, Britain's Three Day Event Team going home with silver medals : poor Susanna, it wasn't her summer and he doubted if she still waited alone for his return after six silent months. Other faces were missing. There was no Ben Johnson. No Bulgarian weightlifters, nor one British wrestler, and, while he felt sympathy for their betrayed coaches, he stood for a moment and let the charming lunacy take over.

Nothing quite matched this carefree riot. The Koreans had another two hours picturesque dancing lined up for the world's television screens. He glanced at Kim. "I don't envy the ringmaster! What happens when the floorshow starts."

"Munche opsimnida."

Kim heaved powerful shoulders and his proud face risked a stiff smile. "Sitting on bleachers flanking that orchestra and women's choir in funeral white, I have a Ranger Batallion wearing white suits and cotton gloves. They'll clear a space for a silver lover's bridge that snakes the length of this stadium.... in three minutes..... or tomorrow their commander will explain in person why he failed at a simple task."

Night closed. Oblivious of secret terror, the world's fittest youngsters linked hands for giant games of ring' o roses, living daisy chains cantered over the grass field : one group dashed among the spectators, racing up an aisle between the seat rows, before Kim's white suited Rangers gently herded them back within seconds onto the running track. A Union Jack rushed up and down the long jump pit, chased by its own devoted band. Dusk became magic. O'Brien wished he could relax but his senses sharpened remorselessly, tension gnawed inside his stomach, painful stabs tested his leg as nervous messengers chased round his body, warned that a supreme effort drew close. Nothing had come in that afternoon from the United States, no photographs, no traces; they still ran blind towards violent night. Trucks visited the scrapyard each day but none raised the suspicions of a shrewd retired reporter from the Buk A who kept watch from a tabang... teahouse.... further along the busy street. It must happen after nightfall. Casually, his fingers slipped round the machine pistol and touched the radio, snug inside his plum blazer : masquerading as an Olympic judge, thanks to Kim, gave the most water tight cover for a foreigner over six feet tall. In the Royal Box, the blonde head climbed towards the curtained exit, followed by two grey haired men, whose pin stripe suits told their story.

O'Brien warned Kim, "I'd better move, time to follow the Princess and watch her plane take off from Songnam."

"She's perfectly safe, O'Brien, top priority, I gave you two of my best men. Only Samaranch has a more experienced bodyguard and that's not to say he's better. Several thousand Rangers have that road and airfield a hundred per cent secured."

"General, you know how it works, I'm responsible if the car hits a stray dog."

Indulgent lines curiously enhanced Kim's strong features. "By all means do your duty.... but the dogs were all eaten before western journalists arrived in town. Don't worry. Our base commander will ensure smooth departure from *our* hands."

"The airship will pick me up at Songnam. Say a prayer, General."

He watched the packed Royal Box for a moment, then saw the golden hair no more. The three Korean leaders gossiped, differences set aside, middle aged men sharing a magic moment for their country. "It's the first time all three are sitting together since nearly eight years?"

"My nightmare now, O'Brien, surely not yours?" Kim stood his ground, massive, forcing him to walk round, or else react. The moment passed. Both men reached out and shook hands. But, after they parted, O'Brien wished that one had turned back.

Some officials stood talking at the tunnel mouth. A hurrying girl in a green blazer, long glamorous hair falling untidily over her shoulders, collided with one; she bowed a confused apology, turned, her haunted face searching the crowded grass.

"Diana!"

She stumbled past the irate Korean official and dashed onwards as though pursued. She blurted something at him.

Fear sliced her breath into shuddering sobs. She had run to the stadium from the car park. Kang had picked up the girl, dropped her at the stadium and should now wait under the grandstand ready for their drive to Songnam: they ought to leave at once. Was Kang waiting in the car? She nodded... and gripping her arm, O'Brien led her away from the tunnel mouth, leaving the pompous official still glowering, propped her against the barricade. Over their heads, the crowd roared as Korea's team marched past them like a sky blue army, straight backed, stiff arms swinging, disciplined files advancing onto the running track to circle the stadium. Nobody paid the slightest attention when a tall foreign judge in a plum blazer pressed a girl interpreter against the rose garlands. She brushed hair from her face and with trembling lips, tried desperately to form words.

"Airship.... man brought my brother home from the military camp... Kwangju, never forget, horrid face."

O'Brien steadied her by the shoulders before he insisted tersely, "Name....girl...name?"

"Chay."

"Describe."

She sucked in a deep breath, shuddering, though mustered a husky whisper.

"Certain?"

Her lips parted, more bewildered, then she nodded.

O'Brien spoke into his lapel. "Groundhog.....leaving Tiger Pit in one minute....meet at K 16 airfield. Over."

Sharp and clear, down came a cheerful, bored Rose. "See you there mate and don't be late, the view's spectacular."

"Is there room?"

"We're running light: sponsor no show!"

"My visitor takes off at 19.50.... we'll stay on the VIP apron for pick up at 20.05. Out." He looked down at her exhausted face while his stomach muscles tightened into a hard fist. Could she have found the final key? Anything was possible in this mirror land.... but a North Korean hidden by deep cover. No wonder the girl was terrified. She was a walking target, almost in more danger than the three politician Kims waving to an ecstatic crowd.

She became composed, breathed steadier, less shaken. He shook her gently and stared into brittle wounded eyes making certain that she listened hard.

"Paul is in the press seats next to the Royal Box, about half way up main aisle. Find him, describe what you've just told me and do whatever he says?"

She nodded, more confident. "What about General.....?"

"Leave Kim for Paul..... and keep your eyes open.... stay away from Han and Shin. They're here somewhere and highly dangerous. They'll kill *you* Diana, on sight." He grabbed her thick soft hair, loosened her green collar, tucked the whole mane down inside her blazer. "Maybe General Kim's regulations make sense. One last question.....why didn't you speak up before?"

"I never saw him until tonight. I've only been to that airstrip once and he wasn't there."

"We hosted a damn great banquet....Dear God....you slept through the entire tedious affair, food, speeches....even.....never mind, for Christ's sake, child, watch yourself."

"How do I find you?"

He pointed above the stadium where the first stars pricked. Then he felt in his pocket, and offered silent thanks when his fingers touched a small disc.

He placed it on his palm.

"Where's that?"

"Where you left it," she mumbled glancing at her black, sensible heeled shoes.

He was shaken. "All the time."

"Not when I bath." Flustered peach made her cheeks like a village child's but her mouth bowed in horror when he reached past her silk scarf, plunged his hand inside her white blouse, searched until his fingers brushed a firm nipple and warm satin skin, found the tiny sister disc.

"That battery will last until Christmas."

He smoothed back strands of hair from her prim face, grasped both small shoulders and kissed surprised open lips.

For an instant her sad eyes wanted to read his own, before she blurted, "Eighty thousand people are watching!"

"Nonsense..... a billion. Hurry and no risks, stick to Paul like glue. You're an angel. We may owe you our necks." He watched her flee into the stadium where spotlights circling the roof canopy shone much brighter.

His left ear almost burst when Rose intervened. "Dirty bastard, Uncle, I saw you having a quick grope."

"Where are you, Groundhog?"

"Right over your boiled Irish head."

Tiny lights, red, green, flashing yellow, moved across the dusk as the crowd drowned all other sound. He grinned skywards, "See you at K16 in thirty minutes."

Namhansan's twin humps blurred with night when a small white jet with a red fin whispered from Songnam's huge runway and climbed southwards until its winking ruby light became lost among early stars. Autumn night crept across a plain of fresh mown grass. The air grew beautifully clear as a fat orange moon rose from behind low mountains, bringing Chusok, Korean harvest festival, and an ideal night for flying. Not a shred of mist, not a breath of wind moved over the huge airfield. The second hand on O'Brien's watch hit five minutes before eight : what else did he expect from an aircraft flown by a former leader of the Red Arrows. Standing on a concrete ramp larger than several soccer fields, ignoring the floodlit VIP lounge which resembled a chinese pleasure palace, for a moment, even with Kang at his side, he felt completely alone.

"Can we relax?" asked Kang, quietly vain about wearing his blue blazer for this final Olympic evening. "In another twenty minutes, they leave Korean airspace."

"Four more minutes and they'll pass over the Woraksan Mountains and leave Tamyang far behind. Then we'll know! If nothing happens.... which I forecast.... whatever waited in that scrapyard is now within comfortable range of Seoul."

White flickers on the northern sky marked the Olympic Stadium. He admired them with growing forboding. "Come on, Abdul," he muttered, "let's get this over."

They began walking along the airfield perimeter track, alert for jumpy sentries though enjoying the sweetness of newly cut grass that hung in the still night. O'Brien thrust his hands into his trouser pockets. The blazer was filled with spare battery packs. Kang loyally fell into step at his side. Patience, that was the trick, yet he loathed waiting : three minutes past eight and not one squelch from his earphone. Fifty miles south: he pictured the small jet which still climbed towards Pusan as four American F 16 fighters armed with radar and heat seeking missiles, just about then, peeled away and dived westwards, formed into line astern for landing at Kumsan airbase a hundred miles south. Blackhawk helicopter crews from Kumsan would have flown an airforce search and rescue team and two special forces teams into the Woraksan Mountains. Now all could carry on watching the closing ceremony on American Forces television. Another batch of helicopters still stood silent much closer to the heart of Seoul, waiting on Yongsan Base, where the hospital commander sat watching television with the leader of his emergency surgical team and Harry Todd now paced in front of a television in his own office - hoping that his thumb would open no doors this festive evening. O'Brien stopped, listened, but heard nothing.

Kang waited for him. "You really think he's North Korean?"

"He may be the world's first triple agent, JP. She was too shocked this evening, but, I think Diana saw him on those temple steps."

"What's our plan? Take him alive."

"We behave as though it's been a wonderful games and that nothing can go wrong now. We don't alert him.....I've no evidence. I can't shoot him, I could throw him off, although that risks a fight, plus damage, and there's a small matter of five hundred million dollars worth of television rights since we're feeding the aerial views of this evening's fireworks. Also, while he's on board, we have our own hostage. They'll move within the next hour........they must before the twenty fourth Olympiad ends soon after nine o'clock."

Kang grinned through the moonglow. "Suppose nothing happens?"

"We find a bar and drink, keep ourselves high."

A faint buzz came from somewhere beyond the chinese palace. "There's the airship. How the hell Abdul's going to stop that whale long enough for us to board."

"He told me to grasp the handrail," said Kang uncertainly, "we don't pull, we move with the airship."

A shadow sank through darkness, then a plump silver torpedo floated over the moonlit ramp. The airship drifted straight at them, its wheel playing with the swept concrete. Dim red lights inside the gondola revealed Rose in the starboard seat, mahogany fingers on the yoke, those stony eyes in total command as Yoon, respectful, hands away from the controls, watched his teacher make a landing smoother than a lover's kiss. Nobody else flew with such delicate control in their finger tips. Pale hands reached out for O'Brien and Kang, hauled them on board, the door closed. Sawing fans propelled the airship on a climbing turn over the chinese palace, long shed roofs, painted oil drums, barricades festooned with barbed wire. Military Policeman stared upwards, then the airship chased pale yellow beams along the Songnam highway, lifted faster, steered for a white corona on the northern sky.

The two policeman wore navy sweaters over pale blue shirts for with height the temperature rapidly fell. Both resumed their seats at the monitor screens, watching the Closing Ceremony on a feed from KBS, the national broadcaster, whose cameras ringed the stadium with the dual tasks of entertainment and security. Nearer the stadium, Yoon would switch on the airship camera system, beam pictures to the International Broadcast Centre on Yoido Island for world television while the computers in Olympic Park screened faces in the crowd seated along either flank of the Royal Box. The irony was that Yoon didn't know the same pictures and the same faces reached far more powerful computers in London and Hong Kong, nor that Mason sat in a busy control room under Westminster ready to disturb the Prime Minister's Sunday lunch. Nor did any Korean know that Harry Todd's widespread safety net formed part of the whole Linebacker operation. But their *man* must realise, at this late stage, less than ten miles from the Olympic Stadium, that only O'Brien's team of three in the airship could block his final move.

Rubber lips stretched from recognition into welcome, a narrow hand flicked at his face.

"Wunnerful' night.... whole 'whirl learnin' the Kohrean love story abow' Ochak Bridge. Princess leave OK? Take my seat, O'Brien, watch show, you finished.... now enjoy!"

Park's thick glasses reflected claret lights along the gondola ceiling. He sat near the door, close enough to observe Yoon and Rose, though within sight of the television screens.

"I wouldn't dream of stealing your place," resisted O'Brien and slipped past into the seat behind Park, reached across the narrow gangway and patted another opposite. "Come along, JP, plenty of room, windows for everybody."

As Kang started aft, Rose leaned round and passed him a two headsets. "Wear these, chaps, you'll hear everything that's going on....and you can move about, they plug into every seat." He finished with a toothpaste smile for the jovial Mr Park followed by a frown at O'Brien.

Now that he sat behind everybody else on board, O'Brien plugged the headset into a battery pack ready in his pocket, keeping an eye on the tinted hair in front, though Park seemed occupied with the television screens. He checked the radio and slightly raised its volume : America was linked.

Across the gangway both policemen concentrated on their keyboards and television screens, rarely speaking. KBS understood they would receive aerial shots of the stadium but nothing more specific which gave Kim freedom to employ the zoom lens on the whole Olympic Centre. He recognised the policemen, neither took much notice of him. One screen filled with women in long white and purple hanboks, waving banners like sails tied on long poles as they swayed and glided over a silver painted causeway which snaked among puzzled Olympic athletes, the more curious of whom, Kim's rangers tactfully invited to jump down from the lover's bridge. Strange wailing music accompanied the dancers and sudden long chords from a harp brought drama. Hundreds of men wearing Korean tassled hats and baggy trousers, clashing huge brass cymbals, swarmed along the running track and swept onto the bridge, portraying the lover's meeting for sad farewell.

"Delishus'....delishus'.....this boost our revenues many times next twelve month," cried Park, more excited, clapping elastic hands that otherwise fretted without a habitual cigarette.

In front, Rose handed over and came aft, smiling an apology about no smoking when he reached Park, who swivelled in his seat and let him pass, obviously intent on following any conversation. Nosiness, perhaps more. O'Brien wasn't certain. Astern a huge Moon carved the earth into soft black mountains. Somebody down there masterminded sixty million people. Chung....sitting patiently in the Blue House waiting for news of his opponents mass murder, playing the misunderstood leader ready to serve his nation, take command and buy out the northern bandits, make himself master. A North Korean crown prince who eagerly waited for the same news. And Kim.....what would he decide in that shattering moment. Wars start from such wild dice throws: nobody had warned the army generals. In his pocket nestled the tiny disc, he felt carefully and hiding it within his palm, covered his ear and listened to a strong beat from its twin, still near the Olympic Stadium.

"No fly.... O'Brien?" asked Park.

"Not often enough."

"Look easy but so do whore with der clap," sniggered Park.

"Mr Yoon never let you handle the controls.....take Mr Rose's seat for a moment," offered O'Brien, sounding remiss, distracted by Park and trying to somehow warn Rose.

The red lenses seemed to grow and the mouth opened like a balloon neck. "Too tricky, ver' difficul'," declined Park effusively. "Smash seven million dollar airship! Forfait twenty five million revenoo'. What General Kim say 'den, O'Brien? I tell you.......Kim say Park you stoopid shit.....you fuck up big this time. Screw my skyship, you fuckin' fired."

"Piece of cake," challenged Rose, telepathic powers on full alert. He shouted forward, "Release some air."

Yoon reached up and turned the ballonet's taps, reduced power, altered the fan's angles. Angry buzzing fell to a soft drone and the cabin floor became level as they cruised five thousand feet over Kangnam, a wooded suburb flanking a large hill on the city outskirts. Rare white and orange lamps mapped new streets. Technicolour flashes rippled round the stadium canopy and its elegant curves took shape beneath a huge white glare dispersing into the night sky.

O'Brien pretended to ignore Park and gave Rose an elliptical message. "Abdul, our aviation insurance wrote that some hefty payments are likely for short term cover."

Rose's thumb strayed over his eagle nose and began rubbing hard, "No other quotes?"

Kang obviously thought they both suffered a brief madness. Park removed his glasses, polishing vigorously, observing them from watery eyes that looked perplexed.

"Not certain yet." Then O'Brien risked, "Our insurance company haven't replied. We might face insider trading with management involved."

Rose had difficulty with his face muscles despite the bleak news. "Can't we protest".

"We have to do it in person, Abdul, they're not far from closing a final deal."

Rose visibly cringed. Few people could be that slow, despite a foreign tongue. He glanced at Yoon, as though checking his pilot skills. However, there was no reaction. He suggested, "Make an appointment."

"Difficult people to pin down, Abdul."

"At least somebody piped up after all this time."

"I don't think the person knew, just a fluke, but we can't cancel the policy without a fight."

Suspiscious lines crept over Park's temples and cheeks, the glasses dropped back over his face like pilot's goggles; without turning, he called to Yoon in Korean, who replied curtly.

Kang's brows almost met. "He's telling Yoon that we must loiter over the Han River for TV pictures, " whispered Kang, listening hard. "Kim strictly ordered him to circle at high altitude and ensure the camera pulled in the whole crowd."

Yoon swung the airship's nose away from the dazzling lights. Television pictures from above the Han River? On face value, there might be nothing odd about the course change, except, that unless they turned south after a short while, this direction put the Royal Box neatly within their vision field and at a perfect angle for their camera for the longest possible time. Chamsil's sparce streetlamps and dark apartment blocks slid underneath the banking gondola. Park relaxed though his hands strayed from cuffs to necktie and he kept glancing at the television screen which showed a woman clad in a white gossamer hanbok, singing tragic contralto, portraying a shahman priestess, paying homage to the spirits in woods and fields. The neighbouring screen suddenly filled with an aerial shot of the stadium and one Korean policeman began feeding pictures to KBS for America's living rooms. Beyond their tense cabin, floating a mile above the stadium, darkness concealed Seoul's northern mountain wall, not yet caught by the rising Moon.

Slowly, deliberately, Yoon aimed the nose until perfectly in line with a black oil river given away only by headlamps racing along its banks and tiny red lights blinking on the ramps of a skeleton Olympic Bridge. Other strings of lights revealed more bridges downstream.

O'Brien crossed the gangway, knelt on a seat and pressed his face against a window, grateful for a parachutist's sight. A mile below, human specks, stagehands or rangers, dragged off the lover's bridge. Soon rich grass and ten thousand modern tracksuits reflecting batteries of spotlamps, transformed the stadium into a huge furnace of diamonds through which a giant torch shone skywards. Perhaps the future wandered somewhere down on that spectacular field: he implored, leashed to Paul with a ball and chain. The window showed Park watching his back then aiming his glasses at the television monitors while fidgeting with something under his jacket. Almost time for Harry Todd's situation report.

He spoke into his plum lapel. "Stadium right under our port side as we loiter at five grand. Probably not visible above the stadium glare. Olympic flame fades in another three minutes."

Park called across, "Why you don't bring Miss Park tonight. Bootiful' ride.....she's a very pretty.....should bring her tonight with Kang here.....maybe she refuse join mile high club!"

O'Brien was about to reply prudently when somebody spoke inside his headphones. "Uncle....we have news....stand by one."

His blood quickened its journey around his body. Harry Todd himself, making sure there were no mistakes, complete trust, not a second squandered.

"Standing by Merlin."

"Our screens have gone wild...... chasing half a dozen traces at once..... somebody's ringed that stadium with a wolf pack."

O'Brien urged in a terse whisper. "Look for our regular pair."

"We're onto that right now."

If a missile guidance locked on the motor's exhaust fumes, the warning system should commence a nerve wracking bleep. Were two groups down there and ignorant of each other. Nothing made sense. The airship floated almost silently, fans slowing. The daisy chain of spotlights faded. In the blackness a lone orange pinprick struggled as the Olympic flame died in one corner of the vanished stadium while moonlight touched a river bend.

Todd sounded calmer than a talk show host. "Uncle....AWACs reports a trace, *very* small, heading north at about sixty knots into the Songnam VIP air corridor. We're checking with the Korean's, probably one of their choppers, but will confirm."

"Make it fast, Merlin."

Without showing hurry, he moved from the window, sat and faced Park. The odd little man seemed absorbed by television shots of the shrinking Olympic flame. Kang and Rose watched over the shoulders of the policemen, noticed O'Brien's sudden icy calm. He forced himself, make the bastard sweat, let him move, risk a mistake. Don't play first card. On the flightdeck, Yoon cut the motors, let them idle, the airship drift.

Todd's words came faster this time. "Trace holding speed at sixty knots. No choppers in that location...... still trying for an identification..... keep listening."

"Would you mind sitting with Mr Rose and Mr. Kang."

It was an order, polite, though expecting compliance, from directly across the gangway. And the voice, oddly familiar, almost comfortable, spoke in cultured English. Park's glasses enhanced the mild smile on his stone face. He threatened with surprising charm, "You're not a suicidal man, Mr O'Brien, nor is Mr Rose. What about you Kang?"

One hand stopped its journey inside O'Brien's blazer, the other hovered across his chest. Roulette had begun. Yoon jerked his head round in blank disbelief. The two police stared, mouths slightly open, neither was armed.

"Thank you for common sense." Park didn't bother with hostility. "I'm going to open my jacket and show you a ballpoint pen." He was more watchful now. "This one is filled with radio-active gas at extreme pressure..... a new weapon, a neutron grenade. Please obey my instructions." Park slid a small cylinder from a pen and held it under a cabin light. "The tube gains strength from gas pressure. But you all understand that principle. Just a tap will break it.... and our tiny gondola becomes a nuclear bomb."

O'Brien's gaze passed swiftly over Rose and Kang, warning, bide your time, don't rush, if we move together, he can't stop three people without killing himself. Or was stale mate his real aim? Floodlights flickered then dimmed round the stadium roof. Night took over. He wondered what else Park carried.... a gun.... some kind of homing beacon. Why up here? The targets sat a smile below, watching a flame die.

"Keep quiet and sit still," Park told the police in sharp Korean.

O'Brien, fingers moist, remarked for Yoon. "Not from Bright Korea, Mr Park? You must run offices in both Seoul and Pyongyang."

"That wasn't science but guesswork," replied Park smoothly, holding out a hand for his gun.

At that moment Todd spoke crisply into his headphones. "Uncle.... we hear good, we have scrambled a chopper armed with air-to-air missiles... AWACS report the drone still approaching southern Seoul at low altitude, less than five hundred feet, airspeed steady at sixty knots. Five miles out at this time. Drone heading for Kangnam and Chamsil Districts. Elint indicates your airship may piggyback some form of navigation aid."

Park snapped his fingers.

"Frankly.... I don't believe you would, Park."

"Some of us don't need guns," threatened Kang, burning for a fight.

Park seemed to reach a decision, and he ordered Yoon, "Raise your hands. Leave your seat. Walk slowly."

In the right-hand seat, Rose cleared his throat. "I wouldn't let an airship fly itself."

"When Mr Yoon has kindly given his pistol, followed by you, O'Brien, yes," declared Park languidly, "you may take over."

Behind cold eyes and a wood face, Yoon wasn't foolish and slid an automatic from inside his blazer, laid it on a seat, then, watched by Park, moved past with a scathing glance at O'Brien and joined his fellow policemen. Rose wore a white polo neck which proved he flew without firearms. O'Brien was next. He noticed an odd expression spreading on Rose's gaunt face. It was a chance and they would have not only the controls, but the rip-panel which deflated the airship in seconds, all back in Rose's skilled hands. Making a show of reluctance, he pulled the long gun from its holster, placed it with Yoon's, though not entirely beyond reach.

Park smiled sarcastically. "You have rather a primitive work style."

He's wasting time, ensuring nobody stops that flying drone from reaching the Olympic Stadium.

"You stay here, Kang. Mr Rose.... go forward..... *you* also, O'Brien." Now it began to look ugly, more an execution. Five thousand feet below huge rose bombursts explored the night while the cameras automatically watched for the world's entertainment.

Once more seated on the flight deck, Rose checked every dial with confusing speed, gambling that Park lost track of his flying black fingers.

Following closely over his radio feed, Todd warned, "Uncle.... no choppers airborne..... assume it's pilotless... roughly six feet long... seems like a large model plane... present bearing takes it straight to the Olympic Stadium. Veering east, wide turn, possibly target acquisition. Your blimp is virtually standing still in the sky.... we think drone is picking up a signal from something on board."

"What if we moved position or rapidly changed altitude?" murmured O'Brien when fabulous colours glittered over the stadium.

"Might just blow its fuzes."

"We'll try now," breathed O'Brien and hoped Kang clung to a strong seat as Rose's finger reached under the console and he mouthed a last silent prayer before electronics took charge.

Relentless force sucked the gondola towards faint stars, flung its deck verticle as the after section dropped earthwards. The nose bored towards faint stars. Muffled shouts came from behind. Iron weight crushed O'Brien into his seat. The whole cabin rolled violently. Glass smashed. His stomach stayed somewhere behind when the gondola visciously swung back, its windshield framing streetlights, long lines of yellow headlamps, huge fireworks bursting into a million pink shards, the Han reflecting brilliant colours and silver moonglow. Rose's concentrating face ignored the spectacular night. He pushed the fans onto full power. The nose chased the tail at alarming speed in a violent corkscrew, steeper, tighter.

Lids heavy, blood draining from his frozen head, he heard Todd's urgent voice though fainter. "Christ Almighty..... that thing's better than an F 14..... drone confused..... zig zagging.... keep on spinning."

He forced a reply from his stretched mouth. "Park's wearing something.... a reflector... beacon."

Todd repeated firmly, "Maintain corkscrew.... losing its way.... now crossed the river, still searching for the mother signal."

Shots crashed, thudding through flesh, shattering glass. He fought from the seat, legs rubbery, leaden arms pushing, mind numb. Cordite smoke stank. A body lay crumpled on the rear bulkhead : two more slumped over the television monitors; reflected pictures still flickered on torn sweaters. Something moved in the crimson darkness. Without thick glasses, Park groped for a gun sliding away from his desperate fingers.

The airship banked steeper. He saw Kang clawing over torn seats. *"Hit the bastard's chest."*

Fighting towards the flight deck, Kang summoned incredible strength, willed himself over smashed seats, braced on the roof: both legs lashed, caught Park on chest and face : something splintered under his ripped jacket but still he struggled forward. Loud bleeps filled the headphones and cabin speakers. Kang brushed back the shock of hair, his narrow eyes confident though puzzled, before fending off Park's counter attack, chopping with both hands, fingers like boards.

Todd's voice snapped, "Missile airborne from Han north bank."

O'Brien screamed, "J P .... *TAKE COVER!*"

A blinding fireball slammed the airship sideways. Heat turned his lungs into empty ovens, blast hurled him backwards over the control panel. Smoke choked, the cabin filled with bright yellow flames.

"*J P !*" screamed O'Brien, staggering into scorching fog, hand closing over the fire extinguisher, ripping off the cap, bracing, frantically spraying foam.

Flames spread faster. "Cut the fans, Abdul, cut the fans!"

Rose, groggy, reacted.

The airship still banked, tightly circling, while moaning wind lured swirling black smoke through a gaping hole in the cabin floor. Seats, monitor screens, bodies, all were gone. The camera's giant egg still aimed on the Olympic Stadium. Fireworks exploded in beautiful strawberry fountains and their playful crump, crump followed from the cool night.

"God Almighty.... J Ps gone!"

"Come in Uncle." Todd was impatient.

"Merlin.... we took a SAM... there's severe damage and five crew missing." His hands shook as he put out the last flames.

"Launch site was on the river bank. Take a look, the chopper's chasing that drone. You've gotten' the only airborne platform over this city."

"If anything works."

Rose leaned over the yoke, rubbing ashen eyebrows, then began checking. When finished, he reported, "OK...... Colonel...... you got helium, power, fly-by-light. Cameras but no screens. I'm not lucky yet with Nite Sun and your eyebrows are blacker than mine."

Gathering himself together, O'Brien stared through the enormous hole: a thin grey smoke trail still climbed like an uncoiled rope from the north bank. Car lights flowed slowly along the embankment road, Korean families enjoying the fireworks across the Han River.

33

Cream foam plastered the wrecked cabin, seats smouldered and charred carpet stank, from behind the fireproof rear bulkhead came loud splutters. But the engines started, the fans whined. Rose tested the controls with a shallow snaking dive followed by a nerve-wracking recovery climb.

"Thank God for that bulkhead.... we're not ship shape and I'll watch our speed." Rose leaned round and took in the damage. "We were almost horizontal when that firework bounced off the kevlar.... otherwise the envelope would look like a torn sack and our motors would have just hit the river."

O'Brien ceased bothering with codenames, no hostile ears listened now. "We're down to the mark one eyeball, Harry. Monitors.... blown away.... is the camera still feeding you pictures."

"It blacked out.... but came back. Now we have a beautiful shot of Monte Carlo bomb bursts. Where're your monitors?"

"Probably in the Han along with poor Kang, plus Yoon, two other Korean fuzz and Park. Somebody should search."

"In progress now, a patrol boat saw splashes. You never know. Let's pray." Todd went off the air for a few seconds. When he came back, it was a question. "Can you repair the Nitesun?"

"We're trying now."

Rose gave a confident thumbs up sign then held one hand open, fingers spread wide.

"Five minutes," answered O'Brien, "possibly less."

"The drone hit a mountain, we think it carries radioactive material or poison gas, its impact explosion was not a bomb. An NCB team is on the spot. Cha Se Dong had a bleeper lodged in his neck. One of your men overboard carried a signal booster that picked up Cha's bleeper - bounced it back down for the drone to home onto a strong navigation guide. There's no longer any signals. Clever, a radio controlled victim. Only a bunker would have saved him."

"Does Kim know?"

"Kim's put all military and police checkpoints on red alert. The next hour is gonna' deliver the most bloody awful traffic jam ever suffered by Seoul City. We reckon they'll head out west towards the Han estuary, then cut north, try and cross Freedom Bridge over the Imjin River."

"Why not east? More open spaces."

"My two senior guys are here with Marvin and working out scenarios.... consulting Kim's people .... we fear a hostage looks the most likely passport. This is a well run mission that screwed up thanks to your box of magic tricks. Their logistic base at Panmunjom must straddle both sides of the DMZ. Where else can they find friends?"

"O K, Harry, we can make around fifty knots."

"This TV den becomes redundant without zoom pictures, however, my chief of staff and chief of intelligence will remain here with Marvin. I'm headin' outside for my C and C chopper. RV over Wondang Ranch at three grand and let's start hunting. I don't need a bloody incident in the J.S.A.. We've gotta' trap 'em inside South Korean territory..... well before the bridge. Work on that Nitesun, Mike. Let's keep this problem low-key!"

"You'll have it, Harry. Sorry about the shambles. You could have watched from the Royal Box!"

"And risk radiation sickness... no way.... shit, besides, I'm fuckin' Cinderella, a soldier until midnight."

The airship flew with surprising smoothness once Rose drove air into the ballonets, compensated for lost weight: five human crew, several televisions and two computers. Chusok's full moon shamed the city lights but Namsan loomed, dark and huge, topped by a floodlit white pencil. Below the mountain's forest flank, faint headlamps roamed the narrow streets of Myong Dong. The railway sidings glowed pale orange and a long empty shadow gave away Yongsan. Across the river, weak lights climbed the golden mast of Building Sixtythree.

They flew west, leaving behind twin strands of feeble lanterns when the last bridge passed below, following the Han's black snake. After a few more tries, Rose flicked a switch and a green glow rewarded his tired face. Nitesun was warming and might give nearly its full beam.

O'Brien pulled out the two rifles from a ceiling panel. The North

Koreans specialised in poison and suicide pills for their most loyal agents. Heavy stakes rode on the roulette wheel tonight. Park might have been on some form of Kami Kazi mission. Of one aspect, however, O'Brien felt convinced : success or failure, the entire cast were slated for death. What other reason lay behind firing a SAM. His mind went back through the last minutes as his fingers searched for a tiny disc. Three Koreans still lived who knew nearly all the covert facts : Shin, Han and Diana. A chance car ride with Kang scared her off flying, terrified her into running away from the airship... a trip intended as a reward for loyal hard work. Kang paid her bill tonight.

He found the disc and crouched, listening against cold air that whistled through the jagged hole. A fast pulse beat faintly.

"Abdul."

"I'm OK, Mike, bit bloody shattered, but nuffin' wrong with my reactions."

"Never doubted them," O'Brien grinned, recovering from shock himself.

"How far is Wondang?"

"Right under the nose."

Three thousand feet below rare yellow lamps punctuated wooded countryside bathed in silver moonlight. Further north, red and green flashes moved along at their own altitude. Rose steered towards Todd's helicopter and its escort bird.

"Why are you so fucking twitched, Mike?" Rose gently banked the airship, slowly brought her round.

"For a start I fear Diana's with them." He listened to the pulse, its signal was stronger.

"North Korean." Rose shook his head, preparing himself for yet another mental hall of mirrors.

"Definitely a South Korean, Abdul, if this thing is any guide. Her heart's beating faster than a canary's."

Rose stared seriously at his leader. "Don't you think we should bring Dick Mason up to speed before the PM spills gravy over her table cloth at Chequers during Sunday lunch."

"He might refuse."

Rose reached under his seat and passed him a radio telephone. "He owes you."

Mason came through clearly, that resonant voice like a classics tutor, and in surprising good humour after losing two million pounds worth of equipment to battle damage above an Olympic Games. He didn't stop O'Brien's flow other than to express sadness and make certain that Kang's family received more than comforting words. They waited for Mason's verdict.

The donnish tone lifted their spirits. Show business perhaps. But they no longer felt isolated.

"I have four orders. One delicate source must remain protected. No hostile witnesses. Destroy the gondola's wiring, its fibre optics and over ride controls. And no further friendly deaths. Other than those four shackles, its your airship, and your operation : I owe you clearance in this realm. God speed and Michael, do report more frequently."

"Open season," said Rose, relieved at Mason's orders.

Distant red lights blinked along Kimpo's runways. Beyond, the Han flowed between the two Koreas and reached a ghostly sea. Rose glanced up from dials and electronic readouts glowing soft port red : not since two years had he heard that quiet brogue in O'Brien's voice: a country milkman had been shot in front of his own small children and they had waited seven weeks in pouring rain to spring the ambush, kill three men crossing the Fermanagh border, fade back into autumn night. Below them spread another divided land, ripe paddies like grey barley fields tucked into valleys among black firs, distant strange mountains, beautiful in bright moonlight.

"Play it cool, Mike, don't let this fucking country screw you in the last lap. Korea's a bit like a whore's knickers, promises Heaven, delivers the clap."

Rose found words which opened his innermost thoughts. "Can't help it...... Abdul..... part of my life is in those mountains further north. My father was killed at the Imjin River Battle. I know a million other ghosts are down there: Brits, Americans, Korean, Chinese, but that doesn't help. Tonight I lost our best man because this time somebody made a secret deal with the North Korean Leaders."

"Mike, let's keep our little wits sharp for a couple more hours, and take their fuckin' scalps."

"We've got to snatch that girl... but I suspect there's a whole education in a talk with Han and Shin." And he recognised all too clearly, both jobs would be the hardest they ever pulled.

Rose decided to occupy his leader. "Those rifles have brand new batteries, Mike, they ought to work over three thousand yards. More than enough if it's Panmunjom. Like to check both."

He tested both nightsights, picking out individual headlamps, peering at trucks, jeeps, civilian cars on lonely roads between Wondang and a small river winding through the moonlight from Pukhansan. They were somewhere down on those roads, providing combined guesswork had drawn out the right answer. Beneath the tail, directly south, a galaxy of lights fell further astern.

"We're on open 'coms," warned Rose.

He nodded thanks, feeling colder as adrenaline quit his veins and earlier sweat left his shirt damp. He called the American helicopters. "We have you in sight, Merlin."

"Likewise Groundhog."

"We have a trace on their vehicle. It's moving somewhere within about three miles radius."

"Clever boy, Groundhog. Is that big torch of yours working yet?"

"Almost warm.... probably they're driving without lights."

"I think you're right. I asked the Air Force to scramble an A 10 fighter from Uijongbu. He may pick them up with infrared. He's makin' a low level run back down Route One from Munsan."

About five miles east, bold orange lamps burned among long rows of sheds in the Combined Army Headquarters. They turned north, droned over empty woods and the Olympic cross country course for horse riders, then a poorly lit barracks and a river, before they found a shiny tarmac strip leading north eastwards over a moonlit grey plain.

"Route One below, Abdul; if they want to cross that bridge, somewhere between here and Munsan City, they must join that road."

"Burn baby," said Rose and pressed the green button. A dazzling white shaft stabbed earthwards and its small white tip swept along an empty road.

"Stay patient..... we'll loiter for two minutes." Todd was eliminating alternatives as they flew north. "A 10 reports nothing without lights on Route One. He's gonna' sweep along this side of the road, working south east. Maintain this altitude."

"Merlin, willco', but never rule out street wise deals : Chung may give a green light right through to your back door."

"You really believe that inscrutable oriental turkey's capable of anything."

"Watch him, Merlin.......I'll put money on a blue bongo truck."

"An insider deal?"

"Between Chung and Kim Jong Il, that both keep their jobs."

Todd spoke urgently with one of his command team in the Blackhawk.

He came back on the radio. "I've got Kim hooked up but you can't hear. Bright Korea have thugs all over northern Seoul intimidating the National Police."

Red and green navigation lights rushed across the luminous plain, closing fast, before the fighter banked, climbed and rolled, stubby wings gleaming under the harvest moon, then dashed north once more, this time leaving the black strip further east. Todd's helicopters slid away and circled a thousand feet below, nearer the road, monstrous nocturnal insects hunting for human prey, rotor blades caught by soft moonglow.

Todd's voice spoke sharply in his command Blackhawk, "Tell the President's Chief of Staff, diplomatically, to go fuck himself. If the Koreans weren't so busy screwin' each other, none of us would be out here, including a fuckin' truck driven by a pair of North Korean Special Forces Officers. What does Kim mean . . . . roadblocks . . . . don't the National Police follow orders any more?"

On board the airship, they shared a moment of earned pleasure while Todd voiced collective western frustration, inching his way towards the toughest and most dangerous choice dumped before any American commander in Korea since forty years. They could hear only half the conversation, but, judging from Todd's half, the argument worsened.

"OK. Pass this formally. Begins.... Personal for Chief of Staff, Blue House. I am engaged in a covert military operation which requires surgical handling with the safety of a Korean citizen as its prime objective. I am in constant touch with General Kim Dung Chi about hostile elements, possibly KPA special forces, believed on Republic of Korea territory. General Kim concurs that any air or ground forces not under my direct command for this operation will be treated as hostile and dealt with accordingly. This includes private civilian security, from any political party, some of whom are manning road blocks around the northern edge of Seoul City. With respect, suggest the National President consults General Kim Dung Chi and without further delay. My intention is that United States Forces should not become involved by defending Korean National Police from organised muggers. Henry R Todd. Commander UN Forces. Ends"

"Those sods laid on a red carpet right to the bloody bridge," declared Rose angrily and O'Brien calmed him instead.

"I never claimed Chung would give up easily; he's a tenacious little sod."

"How thick is that eel skin?"

"I think the little colonel just played his last high value card. Now

-343-

perhaps he'll switch off the telly and start penning a resignation letter."

Todd heard O'Brien. "You should write a thesis, Groundhog. Our A 10 picked up a trace: you'll never guess, a bloody blue bongo, creeping along the Imjin bank from the west, obviously allowed right through to the Imjin gak restaurant. Let's make amends for Kwangju when we held our cocks and watched. Please follow Merlin."

Rose turned north west and the wind rush increased. He started losing height, blowing air into the ballonets, keeping the flashes about a mile ahead. Dark patches scarred the rice plain as it became a chess board where harvest left small muddy fields. A tin river and the lights of a small town slid closer. Beneath mountain walls in North Korea, twinkling lights beckoned from Camp Boniface.

"How do you wanna' play it, Groundhog."

"Better ditch the Bongo first. Prefer all three in the open and use our torch. Depends on their small passenger."

"Forget what I said earlier, Groundhog; Chung sold me a ration of shit and maybe the fuckin' pass. Kim's whole problem was oriental face. He dared not piss off the final fuckin' winner. Otherwise, no pay cheque. If she's still alive, my inclination is let 'em cross, where it's my backyard and all under our control."

"Could the JSA hang onto our blimp while we're on the ground?"

After a half minute Todd confirmed that Kelly would have a party ready for a fast lesson on catching airships, then he suggested, "Groundhog, forget your torch: according to a Mr Paul Moon who claims some authority, she was grabbed at the stadium. It's still possible they assume you're all dead. I'd better call Washington."

O'Brien listened to the disc once more, fast beats came very faintly. "She sounds weaker..... sedation, violence. We don't want to risk a second ration. How do we check the truck cab?"

"No problem, Groundhog, my troops have that under control. Follow me down. We'll swing inland and cross further east. Kelly will hold the Bongo at Freedom Bridge. Let's hope that Chung is given that message in plain language and backs off."

"Otherwise, Harry, we've just started a civil war."

Todd relayed each report on the truck as the strange flying convoy crossed a narrow Imjin that mirrored full moon and slid between woods on low hills. They sank to a few hundred feet over a last ridge. Ahead an orange flare revealed a large hollow near floodlit buildings surrounded by leafy trees and the flashes circled for landing at Camp Boniface. As the airship approached Rose became calmer, soldiers stood in two long lines with a crashtruck parked ready. Soon the airship swung peacefully from its small crane.

Kelly came forward and saluted. He yelled over rotor clatter from the two Blackhawks. "They're jumpy, Sur, threatened to kill the girl unless they crossed immediately. Who is she?"

"She's their passport...... they won't....... not yet," said Todd acidly. "And we mustn't let them apart from the obvious reason. Eight years ago, her brother led the students in the Kwangju rising."

Kelly studied the well oiled rifles with fat night sights. O'Brien's plum blazer and Rose's white poloneck seemed absurd. Kelly said as much. "One target each in the Olympic killing finals?"

"That's the plan, Jack, but at the moment we're trailing one to nil with a strong possibility of losing another player." O'Brien remembered Kang's face before the missile struck. They must lure the two North Koreans out of the truck cab for any clear shots. At that moment, he envied Kelly his combat fatigues.

Kelly spoke the same thought. "We've gotten' suitable clothing waitin' at the monastery."

The Blackhawks whined into silence while Todd grilled Kelly about his deployments. "Truck checked for explosives and escorted the whole way?"

"Right to the MDL, Sur, providing that's how it's played. The North Koreans are jumpy as hoss' fleas. Somebody's rigged lights on the far end of the Bridge of No Return but nobody switched on a single fuckin' bulb over in Propaganda Village and Taesong dong seems suspiciously bloody sleepy. There's loudspeakers too." Kelly looked at his watch then pulled a radio from his thigh pocket. He spoke with the Imjin Bridge and looked concerned.

Todd shook his head. "Make 'em sweat. I want these two gentlemen settled at Checkpoint Three."

"Which one's that?" asked O'Brien quickly.

"Our end of the bridge. We abandoned it after the axe murders, too exposed," replied Todd. "Take 'em alive if you can, otherwise, kill both as they cross over, though you'll lose the girl. Sorry, Mike, it's the best deal on offer."

"By the way, Sur," intervened Kelly urgently, "there's a secure fax waiting for you in my office. Pictures of a little guy with glasses during those sports talks last year, a Korean, letting our friend Colonel Hwang light his cigarette."

"Hwang?" said O'Brien with a sudden sensation of false calm. What an obvious post box. A cigarette, cupped hands, and secret orders cross the world's most closed frontier.

"He's Baby Kim's fixer on the intelligence front."

"We'll swap you," said O'Brien morosely." I can give you some snapshots of Hwang wined and dined by business and political fatcats in Japan. Some people there don't want sixty million Koreans as a single rival country within eyeshot across Tsushima Strait. They keep the Koreans apart by paying for both sides. But somebody may want North Korea as a branch plant for making nuclear weapons."

"Christ Almighty. This gets worse by the fuckin' mile as we near those palace gates in Pyongyang." Todd set off towards the floodlit trees, glaring at the few soldiers on the field, making it clear that what was happening, never took place.

Bushy trees rustled and beyond the grey bridge over the hidden Sachon River, two poplars grew in North Korea, their leaves still green enough to glitter in the moonlight. O'Brien and Rose crouched in long grass and thick weeds, screened by worn concrete ballustrades, one man on each side, clad in American combat fatigues, stocking masks showing only their eyes and mouths, cradling short rifles, long knives rammed into their trainers. Tiny radios linked them with Harry Todd who watched from a pavilion on the small hill that looked onto the crossing point. Across the bridge somebody murmured in Korean, perhaps last moment orders betrayed by the cool wind. A pheasant crashed through the undergrowth along the river bank. Silence fell once more, broken only by a whispered radio message from Todd.

"Bongo now entering the JSA. No explosive traces. We'll insist they dismount by the poplar stump."

Behind their hiding place stood a dead tree that resembled a man falling with raised arms. It had cost the lives of two American officers and the camp now bore the name of one..... after a huge military operation to finish the felling job.

"What if they refuse?" asked O'Brien and waited.

"They don't cross," Todd answered flatly.

"OK. We'll take them walking across from the tree onto the bridge. Abdul."

Rose whispered doubtfully. "They won't stroll onto a shooting gallery.

Not without cover. She'll be wired."

O'Brien pressed Todd, "What's the joker?"

"I thought you'd prefer the bad news last. Grenades. They're both clutching grenades, keeping close to the girl, both grenades armed, not sure about the pins, suspect they don't have them handy. Kill one and all three die. Sorry. I have marksmen with thermal sights covering from this checkpoint. There's a yellow sign on a pole by the bridge ramp. That's the MDL. Beyond it, once on the bridge, you're in North Korea, where I can't help..... nor stop you."

"Let me think." He called over the narrow road. "Knives?"

"Have to be fucking schnell, but we'll have more physical control." Rose sounded resigned.

Todd brought more alarming details. "We think she's been doped as well. Don't rely on her reacting."

From somewhere south came a faint gargle, a small Korean truck. On the hillock Todd's men took up shooting positions behind piled sandbags. After a few moments, the truck backfired, slowly approached down the short road, no lights, driven by moonglow until it stopped at the little grass island before the bridge threshold. A door opened. Shin dropped onto the ground though kept an arm inside the cab. He wore dark goggles and snapped an order in Korean. She struggled down, still wearing her blazer and skirt, barefoot, face swollen from vicious blows. Han followed, also with dark goggles, which bothered O'Brien and he realised that each man had a hand thrust into a sidepocket of her blazer. Grenades without pins. Kill one and Diana would explode into a thousand bloody lumps sprayed over the road and among the scrub trees. Kill both instantly and she stood a slim chance of living another four seconds. And even that solution left only two seconds to find and throw the grenades. Behind the other ballustrade, Rose silently laid down his rifle and drew a long knife his trainer.

In the moonglow, O'Brien saw them walk forward, half dragging the girl, though without struggle and he prayed to God that she didn't understand. For a harrowing second her bruised face and puffed eyes reproached the moonlight, a small captured animal stumbling towards the final numbing second.

He slid out his own long knife, both edges razor sharp, careful it didn't glint. He let them shuffle past then slipped from the thick grass : Rose followed from the undergrowth, moved alongside, keeping pace, ready to close his left hand round Han's in the blazer pocket while driving the knife deep into the man's stomach then ripping sideways. O'Brien drew right behind Shin, palms cold, heart pounding, aware that his right hand had the easier task. The left was crucial but he couldn't miss a man three yards in front. Something stirred at the far end of the worn bridge. Both North Koreans hesitated, the girl swaying on her feet. Shin stared forward. Behind him, O'Brien swung the knife wide for an instant kill.

Silver swallowed night. Orders came from the northern side. The girl whimpered. Footsteps hurried forward. O'Brien stumbled, right hand groping. White hot sound ripped the air apart. Stunned, blinded, thrown sideways, he smashed onto rough concrete. Rose grunted, fell. Suddenly blackness returned. Music started, a wistful song by a children's choir, about a woman deserted by her lover. After images floated then night vision returned: KPA soldiers were on the bridge, efficient shadows in peaked caps lifting bodies from its surface. Rose moved. A truck drove off towards the North Korean camp. The knife still was locked in his icy fingers when his heart stopped. A few yards further onto the bridge lay a small cloth bundle.

34

They stood in the garden of the Moon's traditional timber house. The roof sloped like several tents of blue tiles over open rooms facing onto a labyrinth of tiny courtyards where the last roses spent their perfume in the warm afternoon. They might have been in the country, save that distant traffic rumbled.

Moon clasped O'Brien's wrist with paper hands. "My respects for the great Richard Mason; you may report that he chose well. He must per....mit you to return, enjoy the harvest you sowed."

"One day Francis." O'Brien fell silent. After losing precious lives, his own judgement seemed less than sound.

"Chong-go....ma-bee," rasped Moon, ignoring his mood, squinting overhead at the cloudless autumn sky. "Heaven high.... horse fat... and from eating the new hay."

"Well, Francis, now that Chung's retired to a monastery in the mountains, an election coming, there ought to be plenty for everyone still alive.... and lots for Kim."

"I am sad that we did not find a Korean Prin....cess to make you return often." Moon squeezed tighter and his shrewd eyes became vague. "Time heals and bruised souls mend stronger...... she was allowed home a few days ago. Our women are reputed obedient, they are walking rid.....dles. She feels great sadness which Koreans find difficult to express, therefore she cannot tell you..... and her parents hope she will forget the ordeal, that awful beating, therefore she is not encouraged to speak.... barely with old men."

"You can't blame them, Francis, I put her through a meat-grinder."

But Moon merely laughed until he coughed, shuffling towards the garden gate, thick soled sandals squeaking on each little stepping stone across the tidy lawn.

"She doesn't blame you for anything, Michael."

He wandered along a narrow street finding that without tension life felt empty. A cheerful woman emerged from a small shop and began setting out fresh vegetables on a stall, letting the sun warm her wrinkled bronze face; she held out a fat cabbage and cackled with pleasure, revealing a mouthful of gold teeth, when he declined a close sniff. Strolling between more tiny shops, he found a little cross-roads where another alley joined from Sejong, realised that he neared Mr Park's shabby office block. Over small steep roofs of grimy tiles, the Sejong Art Centre basked in bright sunlight and beyond, cloaked in burgundy leaves, Turtle Mountain beckoned towards the arching sky.

O'Brien wondered which lane to follow when a girl with long flowing hair came from the next alley, the first withered leaves scurrying past the heels of her tall suede boots. Vaguely aware somebody was staring, she glanced severely in his direction; a slender girl in a check riding jacket, silk scarf and cream cord pants, standing at the tiny cross-roads, intelligent eyes smiling hesitantly, still pale from hospital, faint bruise marks showing on her porcelain cheeks.

Neither spoke at first, they were both too surprised and, he realised with horror, that for once in his life, shyness took charge. He didn't know where to start except with the obvious. "I'm glad you're feeling better, Diana - compared with the last time I saw you......you look wonderful."

Suddenly her brandy eyes filled with laughter, then avoiding his worried stare, she watched dry leaves hurrying on their way. "My mother says I shouldn't go out while I can be mistaken for a cheating hooker."

"I doubt that anybody would!"

Perhaps it was modesty, perhaps she preferred not to understand, perhaps she just wanted to forget. Then her face clouded. "Doctor Moon says you must leave Korea."

Now surprise and relief showed on his hard face, sudden pleasure filled his resigned blue eyes as he stared down at a different girl. Gone was the restless tension, that feeling of trying to peer through a constantly moving screen, catching only fleeting glimpses, none long enough for any understanding, never allowed close and learn what went on inside that lovely head. She was dressed for a day in a designer saddle or more shopping in Itaewon. Somebody, perhaps her escape, made this girl forget her militant female crusade, its drab compulsory jeans and long sweaters. A white silk poloneck showed off her honey skin and her cheeks warmed with a hint of delicate peach.

She still waited for his reply. "Is it true?"

"Sorry", he stood, rooted, admiring her new outfit. "Yes..... we must leave in a few days."

She frowned though faint lines marked her smooth brow for hardly a moment. "Will you go home?"

"No..... England."

"The mad Irishman who sold...... balloons and clever...... blarney?"

He didn't want her upset in a Seoul street with the inevitable curious crowd and noisy scene. "Are you in a hurry?"

"These days I am supposed to rest mostly."

"Where could we talk?" Already passers by were staring.

"Oh dear..... a tabang.... teahouse?"

When she sounded doubtful, he remembered a perfect place, looked at Turtle Mountain climbing into the warm sky. "Let's copy the Korean Kings... I never saw the Piwon... Secret Garden." She didn't resist when his fingers closed round her arm, merely laughed when the cabbage woman shouted good luck and many sons.

Far away from afternoon traffic, beyond high granite walls and sprawling timber halls where green pillars carved from mighty trees supported the great tiled roofs, beyond a low hill, they strolled deep into a crimson and saffron forest. Sometimes they discovered smooth lawns around which grew huge and crooked chinese juniper trees planted when Robin Hood ruled Sherwood, and upon springs trickling into small ponds lost among mists of golden leaves.

She told him about her family, how her grandmother, a minor princess, suffered an arranged marriage to a Japanese noble which resulted two generations later in David, Diana and her sisters with their paler skins and silk hair, their eyes much rounder than a thoroughbred Korean. Her mother vowed to the old lady that she would never seek a favour from any mortal. And Diana apologised for that same stubborn refusal to share burdens with anybody until it was near hopeless.

"You can stop worrying about the silk factory," said O'Brien as they found another tiny lake with a spring splashing from a rock face at the foot of

Turtle Mountain.

"Chung's really finished, isn't he Mike."

O'Brien sensed that she wanted to confess something, remove an awkward barrier, though Heaven knew why : she was owed far more. He said kindly, "Chung won't be calling in anymore old debts. But he knew precisely where the North Koreans should land their SAM. David was the inevitable villain had they been discovered. Panmunjom was used for the pilot-less aircraft . . . and for you. Anyway, Francis sorted out the bank through Kim breathing down its President's neck."

"Kim ordered me to spy on you.......offered to deal with my father's nightmare, providing I found out what you were doing with the Americans. He was very angry, said it was our country, not a foreigner's."

"Did you?" he smiled.

"Have you forgotten me so soon....."

She moved towards the lake and stood watching the sparkling spring: sunlight slipped between autumn's lemon ginkyos, threw dappled shadows over her jacket, caught strands of hair teased by a mild breeze.

"I can't begin to thank you for my brother, my family......myself....I shall miss dear Jaepil though we cannot bring back those who reach Heaven first.......and I shall always remember kind Abdul........"

A host of thoughts flashed through his mind as his throat grew dry and the truth hit like a charging tiger. She stood gazing down through the clear water, fascinated by small fish darting among tangled weeds. Almost without realising, she began to sing in her soft musical voice, wistful Korean drifting over the little lake. Sometimes her thoughts were so sharp that he almost touched them - was her love not enough, what more did he want? She risked her life for her family, saved her brother, their future. She had soldiered loyally, bearing the pain of distrust, never spoken a word in complaint; she was brave yet somehow fragile, a beautiful child who survived death by a miracle : thank God for the ruthless cunning of that other brave Korean woman who let his falling star live to sing in the autumn sunshine.

At that instant, he felt stupid, knew that his heart pounded and his voice struggled for words, but he couldn't let the afternoon slip past with her standing there, say nothing, leave her innocent for the rest of life of her sweet power. Yet he dreaded that panther's temper : she would probably stalk back down the path, a flustered fury. And, placing his courage in his palms, he tried to tell her, if only once.

"Diana, my sweet girl........ after the last six months, I wouldn't feel hurt if you made Kim strap me into my plane seat at Kimpo."

She didn't look round when her laughter bubbled crisp as champagne while she watched the spring gurgling for her pleasure. Diana's soft voice mocked, "I might order another punishment. You shall be tied to the strongest tree in this lovely garden."

"Why..... would you like me as your prisoner?"

She stared down at her reflection in the smooth water. "I might share my last secret."

He couldn't quite believe her words but he walked forward, all the same, closed anxious fingers on her slight shoulders, felt a graceful yet strong body stir beneath the smooth check wool, slid his hands lower, enjoying her discrete figure gently shaping the stylish jacket, clasped his hands tightly over her firm, tense stomach before kissing scented hair.

"What a fool. Why did I wait so long? I must have fallen in love that night when I dragged a scruffy boy home from a riot, who turned into a lovely though frightened girl."

She still watched the hurrying fish. "Fall in love? What does that mean? How can we know, Mike? It's so elusive."

"Its a skydive,.....looks terrifying ..... next second you're floating on air."

He wrapped his arms around this shy creature but she didn't want to escape when he kissed her neck and ears, buried his face in her thick silk hair. Soon she forgot caution, slowly turned and nestled, soft and adorable, snug within his tight cradle. From beneath thick lashes, her tender eyes promised witchcraft, before those sugar lips opened like a rose and melted his own. Should he slow down in case she faltered? This exotic angel was born within an old Korean family, she was gambling with her future, giving her trust. Child's fingers reached and tousled his copper hair, perhaps making sure it was real, the afternoon no dream, when their eyes met in candid decision.

Sacking conscience, feeling the power rise in his loins, his hands stroked her lissom flanks. When the chains wrapped around her soul broke, her emotions flooded towards freedom: nature rubbed her pelvis into his groin, made her breath quicken as his astonished fingers strayed under the jacket, found a live and warm body frantic with desire. Neither could wait much longer: he led Diana among gold and scarlet trees, found a sunlit glade, lowered her onto a leafy bed, jacket now flung open, smoky eyes inviting, yard long hair strewn like a black pillow over the warm dry leaves.

They fumbled with each other's clothes; her cheeks bloomed at the moment of discovery, then the cord pants slid down her amber thighs to reveal a small cushion of sable down. Pushing his way deep within her, feeling himself thicken from her wet heat, for a sweet and shameless moment, he rested on throbbing forearms. The autumn sun fell warm on his back, a stream burbled through the forest, playful light danced over her face before fervent eyes gave consent, dismissed a thousand questions with a startled smile as delicious waves broke through their bodies and the thrill of love rushed home, locked them together like a single beating heart.

Afterwards, spellbound by her sleepy beauty, still wondering why Heaven sprang this enchanted ambush, he guessed a secret and catching breath, he whispered, "My lovely trickster, I worship your every ounce, my Korean *prin....cess.*"

Drowsy and spent, her mocking eyes gave her away, when her mouth opened in playful horror. "My mother will kill me for this . . . but at least yours won't make me live in her house like a slave for our first year."